UNCHOSEN

Also by Katharyn Blair
The Beckoning Shadow

KATHARYN BLAIR

UNCHOSEN

 KATHERINE TEGEN BOOKS

An Imprint of HarperCollins Publishers

Katherine Tegen Books is an imprint of HarperCollins Publishers.

Library of Congress Control Number: 2020938949
ISBN 978-0-06-265764-0

Typography by Molly Fehr
20 21 22 23 24   PC/LSCH   10 9 8 7 6 5 4 3 2 1
❖
First Edition

To my sisters—Hannah, Rachel, and Becca:
This story is for you. May your small rectory
always abut my estate.

Chapter 1

FOR ME, THE WORLD ENDED MORE THAN ONCE.

The first was when I was thirteen and the yellow eviction notice appeared on our door in Delaware County, Ohio. That ending tasted like the cherry Popsicle I was eating on the stairwell and sounded like hushed, frantic whispers. A different end had already started, spooking researchers off the ocean and causing a round of layoffs at my father's university. But I didn't know it then.

We were moving to live in the back house on my grandmother's property in the Pacific Palisades. My sisters had roots that would take anywhere—Harlow, the guitarist, and Vanessa, the gymnast. I didn't really worry about me—I didn't have a *thing*. I tinkered on the piano and sang when the sanctuary was empty in church. I drew waves on my wrist with glittery blue gel pens. I was just Charlotte, and at the time, in Ohio, that felt like enough.

I didn't know then that this was the second of my endings, and one that happened slowly: when we arrived in Southern California and I realized it wasn't enough anymore.

We'd seen Dean around the neighborhood before when we'd visit my grandma, but that day was the first time we really talked. It wasn't some earth-shattering moment or anything. It was just a floppy-haired boy helping me when my *Beauty and the Beast* jewelry box clattered against the ground outside my grandmother's tree-covered front yard.

He kneeled, grabbing the movie ticket stubs and braided friendship bracelets and other scraps of the life I had left behind, and handed them back to me. I watched his hand (big knuckles, scar on the back of his thumb) touch mine (small fingers and chipped Blackberry Crush nail polish).

Hey, he said, and his voice rumbled against my ribs.

Maybe meeting Dean wasn't an ending, but I can tell you this: it was the promise of one.

When the real end of the world finally came, it was a long time coming. Two years of watching him sneak through the window next door, lopsided smile curling up as he climbed the tree that bridged our bedroom windows so we could play Mario Kart. His boyish grin now had the scruff of a seventeen-year-old, and he had to tilt his shoulders to fit inside. In two years' time, Harlow played more gigs and was featured in a local arts magazine, her chin tilted up as she leaned against a brick wall. She hated how my parents put the article on the refrigerator. I think that's why they did it.

Vanessa rose up the ranks in gymnastics—level ten. She placed second overall in regionals and took top five at countless other competitions.

In those same two years, my greatest accomplishments were the three journals I'd filled and tucked away in my desk.

But I forgot about that when Dean came over.

Harlow would pull sour straws from under her bed, and we'd play video games until we knew we would pay for it the next morning with tired eyes and blistered tongues.

Somehow, even with my gaze half fixed on the dip of his collarbone, I would always win.

That's the ending that snuck up on me, and it felt like the grease of sunscreen and smelled like chlorine. That ending was purple, cast in the evening glow of one of the last nights of summer at the public pool. It sounded like the low rumble of Dean's laughter mixed with my older sister's voice—the one Harlow usually used on crowds before her band played. It looked like his muscled back, tensing against her as they intertwined and leaned on the brick of the shadowed part of the snack bar, his mouth on hers.

That was the first ending that really, truly felt like one. The kind that filled more journals and left tear tracks on my cheeks.

Smaller endings happened all the time, but they were the kind I couldn't really see until later.

The footage from a research boat that disappeared after finding a shipwreck—footage that kept my dad up at his makeshift desk all night.

Then, about a week later, the news confirmed the spread of a strange sickness.

That night, Vanessa's nightmares started.

That's the ending that started everything, really. When the Crimson slipped across the planet like spilled wine and stained history forever. When the stories weren't whispers, but screams.

When we couldn't ignore it anymore.

When that ending—the Real Ending—reached my shore, it smelled like chalk and tasted like blood.

Chapter 2

"THIS IS THE DUMBEST THING WE'VE EVER DONE,"
Dean says, his voice somewhere between a whisper and a hiss.
My fingers grip the edges of the roof, the ceramic tiles burning the edges of my fingertips. I chance a look down, blinking against the reflection of the sunlight in the mirrors I keep tied on my wrists and the tops of my boots. Dean's dark hair is brushed back into a low bun, his brow furrowed with worry. He has a grip on my left foot, holding me up.

"You're forgetting that time we tried to give ourselves hickeys with the vacuum hose," I counter as my right foot finds the window ledge. I hoist myself up, onto the edge of the museum's veranda. I tighten the straps of my backpack as I look back down at the amphitheater, pausing for a moment to sweep the area. Overturned tables and chairs lie still on the black tile, but other than the slight flutter of napkins and old brochures covered with Ramses II's face on them, there's no movement. We'd raided this place several times in the past two years and never had any problems. Turns out that people don't really have a lot of uses for history museums in the face of the actual apocalypse. Normally, we'd just walk right into the open front doors and go from there. But what we're looking for is in a locked room. So the window it is. A cool breeze gusts over from the ocean to my right, which toils just past the western edge of PCH—Pacific Coast Highway.

Dean eyes me. "Right. You're so right. This closely follows the vacuum hickey experiment. Which should tell you something, Charlotte, since that happened when I was fourteen."

I twist a rope around the railing that circles the veranda, testing once to make sure it's secure before I throw it over the edge to Dean. Within seconds, he has hoisted himself up next to me.

"Harlow will absolutely kill us both if she finds out I helped you with this," he says as we walk over to the sealed double doors. I slide my fingers over the edge, finding nothing.

"Nah. I'm blood. You're just her boyfriend. She'll just maim me. But yeah. You'll for sure be dead." I wipe the grime off the glass of the window and peer inside. I can't see much, but there are no obvious threats, and that's as much reassurance as I'm going to get. Dean adjusts the mirrored bands on his forearms.

"Sounds about right," he says, pulling the glass necklace from under his shirt and wiping it on his sleeve.

I wind a scarf around my elbow and then take a deep breath

6

as I turn around. With one quick movement, I shove my elbow back and the glass pane shatters.

We both pause as the sound echoes off the hills around us. I grip the iron blade that rests in a sheath tied to my belt. I've only ever used it for cutting rope and the limbs of stubborn trees on food raids, but I know that any time we step out past the perimeter of the fortress, I might have to use it for something much darker.

Dean pulls a mirror from his back pocket. "Mirror" is kind of a loose term—it's a shard of reflective glass, but he's wrapped the edges in black electrical tape. He holds it inside, tilting it to get a full sweep of the room.

"We're good," he says, stepping inside. I follow.

Wings flutter above us, and Dean and I duck. Birds leave their hiding place in the rafters, swooping over us before they take to the skies.

"Shit," he mutters, looking around at the chaos.

I turn, surveying the marble room and swallowing the weird burn of emotion building at the back of my throat.

Leaves and dirt line the floor, and vines that cover the far side of the building have since slunk in through a crack in a high window.

The Getty Villa used to be a sanctuary for me. Vanessa always had gymnastics practice and Harlow was usually getting ready for one gig or another, so I'd go alone. It was like a seaside palace—perched above the waves on a cliffside in Malibu, full of gardens and fountains and marble staircases. I would spend hours getting lost here, sipping my coffee and looking at the statues of men long since dead.

I felt at home here then.

Now I look around, at the cracked plaster of the walls, the nostalgia souring in my gut.

"You okay?" Dean asks. I feel his eyes on me. I used to love the sound of his soft voice checking in on me. I bristle at the kindness—it just shows that he doesn't think I'm strong enough.

I pull the blade out from the sheath and step over the crumbling remnants of an upturned limestone statue before giving Dean a nod. He walks to the locked door and throws the bolt. We freeze, waiting to hear any telltale scuffles on the other side of the door. When it's silent, he pulls it open. The hinges let out a low moan, and he sticks his head out into the hallway. Satisfied that it's clear, he looks down at his watch and holds up a hand, flashing an open palm twice. We have ten minutes.

He pulls two knives from a holster strapped across his chest and walks stealthily down the hallway. I let myself watch him for a couple of seconds. Only a couple of seconds, admiring his broad shoulders and the slight sunburn on the back of his neck.

A familiar tinge—something like guilt and sadness—rolls over in my chest, and I force myself to turn and scan the room. It is much bigger than the other ones we've broken into, and filled with stands topped with ancient busts. The rays of sunlight streaming through the dirty glass ceiling throw the room into a dusty haze. The far wall is made of all windows, overlooking a great hall below. I peer over the edge, eyeing the fountain at the entryway. It used to be a shallow pool surrounded by a red velvet rope—something children would throw coins into, giggles bouncing off the marble as their parents whispered softly to make a wish.

Now the ground below it has collapsed, deepening the once-turquoise fountain into a deep pit of murky brown water. I can't even see the bottom.

I creep through the room, pausing at a bust to my right. It had always been one of my favorites. A woman's face stares ahead, her mouth puckered slightly. *A Woman in Pompeii*, the plaque beneath it reads.

Not an emperor. Not a soldier. Just a woman, carved into stone.

Pompeii. The city that disappeared into ash and fire in 79 AD. All that was left of them were things like this. I bite my lip and lift a hand, half expecting to hear a security guard hiss at me to not touch the statues. After hesitating for a second, I let myself run my finger over her lip, wondering what she'd say about all of this now, if she knew that the world survived once only to fall differently. Our sky didn't darken when the Crimson came, and our ground didn't tremble when it spread from the Pacific Northwest to Portugal and then Cape Town within a week. We lived in a world that predicted our doom at least twice a week. We had shows about it; people stood on street corners, screeching about the end. We were so ready for the fall of mankind. But when it actually came—we didn't see it coming.

I wonder if this woman would tell me that we will survive this, too.

I don't know if I'd believe her.

I step around the bust and tiptoe over to the display case, wiping my hand over the dirty glass.

The velvet lining inside is blank. To the untrained eye, this display looks empty.

And if it is? I'm going to feel like a total idiot. But I'm staking a lot—a lot—on the hope that it's not. That all the hours I spent here, idly tracing in my sketchbook and avoiding texts from my friends, will pay off.

I break the glass with my elbow again. It sounds more like a violation than the window, and I feel bad as I use a cloth to hit pieces of glass aside and reach in to touch the velvet. I peel the bottom of the display up, revealing the lip of a drawer.

Usually, the artifacts would be safe in the curators' building behind the museum—on the upper back slope of the hill. But I doubt, when everything fell apart, that they'd had time to do that. The next best thing, then, would be for the curators to put the artifacts in the temperature-controlled drawer beneath. I often stayed until closing, and watched the curators move artifacts more than once. I'm sure they thought they were shutting the doors of this place for a couple of weeks. I'm sure they thought they'd come right back.

I pry at the edge, lifting it slightly. It sticks, but then slides open. My breath catches in my throat.

A gold headdress with drop-like rubies sits at the bottom of the drawer, haphazardly wrapped in a cloth. The light inside is dead—there hasn't been electricity here in years. That, I'm used to. There hasn't been electricity anywhere except in settlements like the Palisade, which has one working generator—and even that, they use sparingly. I don't even hesitate to grab the giant piece of jewelry. The gold is heavy and almost soft beneath my hands. I'd seen this so many times under the lights of the display. Even though I should be used to unlikely things happening—it feels strange to be holding it.

"You were right. It was there." Dean's voice sounds behind me. I jump, spinning around and backing up against the case. My hand hits the edge, and glass digs into my palm. I curse under my breath, and Dean rushes to me, swearing loudly as he pulls a bandanna out of his back pocket.

"You scared the shit out of me," I grumble as he inspects the wound. I stop breathing, trying to stop the wood-spice smell of him from filling my senses. He's close. He's too close.

"I'm sorry! I thought you could hear me. This whole place has amazing acoustics."

The cut is shallow, but it stings like a bitch. I whimper slightly as he tightens the bandanna across the wound and ties it around the back of my hand, just above the cuff of yet another mirrored band.

I look up at him, and he smiles down at me. A familiar twist in my gut coils around my spine as I meet his ice-blue eyes.

Dean is beautiful.

He was beautiful when I first saw him moving boxes into

the house next to my grandmother's when he was eight and I was six. He was beautiful when I was thirteen and he was fifteen, and he let me teach him how to braid hair so that he could help me with Vanessa in the mornings and we all wouldn't be late for the bus.

He was beautiful when I found him kissing Harlow behind the snack bar at the pool two years ago. I'd never told Harlow how I felt, so I couldn't blame her. Dean couldn't have known, so I didn't blame him, either. It's almost worst, I think, when there is no blame. Maybe that would have been like a cauterizer on the wound or something. If I could be pissed at someone, then my feelings for him would have been singed up in my anger. But instead, they just curled up in my chest. Never dying, never leaving—just stirring at the worst possible moments.

Moments like this, when he's standing close enough for me to see the cracks in his chapped lips, the ones he has because he always gives away any lip balm we happen to find. I wonder if they'd feel rough if I touched them. If he'd wince.

I pull my hands away from his, coughing as I adjust the straps of my backpack. I hold the headdress up between us, just so I have a reason to step back.

"You think we would have learned our lesson about treasure by now," he breathes, looking down at the exquisite piece of gold. It contrasts strangely with the dirt smudged on my fingers, and I turn it over in my hands, staring at the red stones.

To think, it was a stone like this that started the whole thing.

Dean holds his hand out, and I look up. His face carries a

hint of mischief, a smile that tugs on the corners of his mouth. The whole world has gone to shit, but I can count on that smile. The one that talked me into throwing a water balloon through the school bus window at Michael Precocci after he made fun of Vanessa for not shaving her legs yet.

That smile could get me to do almost anything. I hand the headdress over, and he lifts it to my head, setting it gently on my unwashed hair. The space between us is open again, and feels like it crackles with a dangerous promise. I ignore it, focusing on the ruby droplets as they skim the skin on my forehead. Dean raises his hands, his smile deepening as I turn to look at my reflection in the broken glass.

I think I look ridiculous. The headdress leans to the left, awkwardly balancing on my greasy ponytail. My eyes flit to Dean's reflection. His brow is furrowed, his eyes narrowed like he's thinking about something.

"What?" I press.

"I just wonder what she looked like, you know? Anne."

The sound of her name on his lips is odd, like it will always be too loud, no matter how quietly he says it.

Anne de Graaf.

She upended the world. She unwound everything. I can never tell if I hate or envy her power. Maybe both.

Dean gently touches the gold with a hesitant finger. "I always imagine her as this terrifying thing. This force. But she was just a girl once. And she had people that loved her. She probably had inside jokes and a favorite food and stuff. It's just . . ." He takes a deep breath, and his eyes get this faraway look, like he's lost in his thoughts. "It's just weird to think."

I lift the headdress off my head, wincing as it takes a couple of hairs with it. I don't want to be compared to Anne. It doesn't matter what she looked like, or who she was.

The thought brushes against the one secret I have from him, and I don't trust myself to meet his eyes. I kneel down, wrapping the headdress carefully in a towel I'd brought from the fortress.

"It suits you," Dean jokes.

I crane my neck to look up at him as I tuck it into my backpack. "Yeah? Just casually wear an ancient headpiece around the fortress while hanging laundry and picking tomatoes?" I tease.

He thinks about it. "Save it for Halloween. Go as Anne de Graaf's Chosen One."

My fingers freeze on the zipper. Chosen One. He can say it casually. He can joke about it, since he has no idea. Still, I have to fight the shudder that works its way down my spine as I stand.

"Yeah, because I'm sure everyone is still dressing up this year," I shoot back. It's small moments like these, the ones I don't expect, where I realize how much we've lost. Where I feel how different the world is now. I yank the zipper closed. "And Harlow will kill you if she hears you joking about that. You know how she feels about all that Chosen One shit."

"According to you, Harlow will have killed me twice before this little mission is over," he muses.

14

I stand, tightening the straps on my shoulders. "You, of all people, know that Harlow would find a way to bring you back just to kill you again."

Dean laughs, the sound vibrating off my ribs as he nods. "True." He looks down at his watch. "Speaking of the merry murderess—"

"Hey. *Theoretical* murderess. That's my sister you're talkin' about," I interject.

"She should be heading back soon. If we're going to beat her home, we'd better move," he finishes.

We walk down the hallway, past abandoned exhibits about the Mycenaeans and an old gallery devoted to the Bronze Age.

Wind whips up the staircase, careening in from open double doors that lead into the middle courtyard. Overgrown trees lean over a cracked, empty fountain, and weeds spring up between the stones that used to make up the walkway. Dean and I pass through, barely warranting notice from the sparrows that have taken up residence in the rafters of the covered walkways criss-crossing around the edge of the courtyard.

We are cutting through the foyer when we hear it.

Footsteps.

Dean and I freeze. I reach for my blade while he turns his head slowly, locking eyes with me. We both hold our breath, hoping that it is just an echo. Or a trick of the wind.

Anything but them.

Thunk. It sounds again, closer this time.

Dean and I move at the same moment, darting to the exhibit

room to our right, hiding in the shadows. He is pressed against me, holding me closer.

"Is it—" I whisper, unable to conjure the word as I keep eyes on the cracked floor at my feet.

"I can't tell," he breathes, his voice barely audible over the crashing of my heart in my ears.

I wrap my right hand tight around the mirror in my back pocket as I turn my face up and look into Dean's eyes, his blue irises glinting in the low light, soft and safe. Not in a poetic sense. Not just because I'm in love with him.

But because the world is different now. And looking in the wrong eyes is a death sentence.

Dean sticks his toe past the doorjamb, tilting his ankle to angle the mirror that's fastened to his shoestrings into the hallway, as the footsteps sound again.

If it was Harlow and her crew, they would have used the identifying whistle. Even a rival fortress in the area would have used some unique sound. We aren't friends with other settlements—it is kill or be killed, out here—but we know there is a special kind of alliance between free humans now. There are bigger things to worry about than who has better supplies.

I hold a hand up as the footsteps sound again. Closer this time.

Dean grips my arm, and I shut my eyes. Maybe they will just pass. Maybe they won't know we are here.

But I know, deep in my gut, that if it's *them*, the hope that they'll pass is wishful thinking, because they have a weapon we don't—a heightened sense of smell.

He lowers the mirrors, and I know what he's thinking. I feel Dean shift next to me, leaning toward the door. I grab him, pulling him back.

"Don't even think about it," I hiss. He pulls my hand from his arm.

"We're dead if we don't know what we're dealing with," he whispers back.

He stills as the footsteps sound again, but there's something else—the sound of hissing—a breath that could be going in or out, I can't tell. There is more than one, though. A symphony of breath racing past saliva-soaked teeth.

Dean leans forward, tilting the mirror on the back of his hand past the door. I can't see the glass, but I know the moment he sees them. His jaw tightens and he turns, yanking me closer as he pivots, shielding me. I can feel his heart beating through my back.

"Vessels," he whispers. One word, and my world feels like it is spinning. I shut my eyes tight, willing the panic in my gut to calm down, but the word is a current in my veins. I focus on the feel of Dean's heartbeat as I force myself to breathe.

Think.

We need our wits if we're going to survive this.

It takes a moment, a practiced, steady breath, and I open my eyes, shoving the churning terror down to a manageable corner of my mind.

From the shadows dancing through the doorway on the

floor, I know there are at least three.

And from their whispers, I know they're still aware, still—conscious. The Crimson hasn't reached the final stages for them yet. They move closer. Two shadows merge, and a wicked snarl rips through the room—one had gotten too close to the other. They are hunting together, but that does not mean that they are friends.

"You said you smelled them," one snaps. It's a woman; her tinny voice bounces off the walls like a pebble.

"The wind was from the east. I told you that before we walked up here. That breeze could carry a human's scent for miles," a man answers, his tone like the cracking of a whip. His voice has a wilder sound to it—almost like it's pulling against the limits of his throat with every word.

"Shut up. Both of you," another male says. His voice is lower than the others, but he sounds younger somehow. Crueler. "We don't have time for this."

We hear them walk away, their footsteps on the tile reverberating through the room. They stop, and the sound of sniffing fills the air. I shudder at the horrible noise. Dean's breath is hot on my ear as he rests his forehead on top of my head. He is shaking. I am too.

I look down at the blade strapped to Dean's boot. He follows my gaze, and his grip on me tightens.

With one free hand, I reach up, digging my nails into the skin of his forearm. *You promised*, it says.

The Vessels move to the next door, the dead leaves crunching under their feet.

18

Dean lets out a slow breath as he nods against the back of my head. He knows what I mean. It is the promise we'd made to each other when this first started. I didn't ask it of Harlow, because I knew it would scar her more deeply than she already was. But I would rather be dead than be the husk of a person the Vessels would leave behind.

I'd made Dean promise that he would kill me before that happened.

He'd made me promise the same.

"Over here," the female says, crossing the foyer to our side.

The Vessel's breath rattles as she inhales, breathing in the air right outside our door. She runs her nails over the wood, and the scratching noise grates on my bones.

My head swims, and I grab Dean's arms as he pulls me closer to his chest. He isn't breathing now. I'm not risking it, either.

The metal of the blade looks so cold, its edges sharp. I wonder if I will have the strength to do it, if I need to.

But I know that if it is going to be the last few moments of my life, I am right where I've always wanted to be. In Dean's arms, his heartbeat reverberating off my spine, the warmth of his skin under my fingers.

Then, as abruptly as she came, the female Vessel steps back, her footsteps fading, along with the others'.

Hope floods me, raw and painful, as Dean lifts his head, straining to listen.

We are quiet for a minute, then two. Three, not daring to move.

Dean's arms drop, and he chances a peek with his mirror. He

looks around, then back over his shoulder.

"They're gone," he whispers finally.

"That makes no sense," I reply. And it doesn't. Vessels are usually thorough in their brutality.

"I'm not about to second-guess a miracle. Are you?" he asks, motioning for me to follow him.

We creep into the foyer, careful to avoid leaves. The urge to run is thick in my veins, and it takes everything I have in me not to give into it. I want to sprint as fast as I can, shrieking until every last bit of terror that coats my lungs has been shaken off by sheer force.

In an instant, something shifts. The air feels charged somehow, like someone has flipped a switch. And everything feels wrong.

The hissing sounds like it's surrounding us, but I know it's just the echo, rolling over each other as it rocks off the walls.

Dean spins, pulling the daggers out of their holster, even though I know it's useless. With just two of us, there's no way we could take on one Vessel—let alone three.

I almost turn back to our hiding spot, but the footsteps are growing louder, and I know we won't get lucky twice.

Then, Dean's hand is in mine, and he yanks me toward the collapsed fountain. He steps in, swearing at the cold.

The muck in the water is dark enough to hide us from view, and it will mask our smell.

But I freeze at the sight of the small waves soaking the legs of his jeans. My chest seizes, and I shake my head.

"Get in the water, Char," he pleads. "It's the only way."

I know that, but it doesn't matter. I can't get in the fountain. I'll panic like I always do, and they will find us. They will find Dean—all because of my uncontrollable terror.

I can't let that happen, so before he can grab me, I turn and dive behind a limestone statue of a lion tackling a horse and clamp my hand over my mouth.

The sound starts from outside the northern doors. Dean shoots me one more pleading look before he ducks gently under the water, careful not to make waves. The female Vessel marches inside, her steps decisive. I inch my mirrored bracelet around the corner of the limestone base.

She is beautiful, even in her heartless new form. She has a scar across her cheek, and one side of her head is shaved. The rest of her dark hair falls in waves down her back, and her lethal red eyes are upturned and lined with eyeliner. The mirrors can block the Crimson, but they do nothing against the naked fear that grabs me the second I see her hateful eyes in the glass.

"The orders can wait for one more fucking minute while I find them. I know they were here," she snips, eyes roving the foyer. I pull my hand back. I thought it would make it less scary to see that she still looked human somehow. That maybe it would be better than being chased by a wraith draped in black robes.

But nope. It is just as scary.

The first male speaks as the female stalks to our previous hiding place and tears the door open. A ripping sound fills the

21

room and echoes off the marble, and she hisses. She's pulled the door straight off the hinges. She growls in irritation and throws the door to the side. It lands on the tile with a loud clap that makes me jump. "If we find the Chosen One, then we won't need to scavenge like this anymore, Lemmere. You're not seeing the big picture. And Caine won't care if you see it or not. If we're not back at the gate in two minutes, you'll never be hungry again."

The woman, Lemmere, hisses as she slams the door to the viewing room.

"If she even exists," she bites back. "How many times have they thought they've found them before? And it all ended the same, didn't it? A pile of bones, picked clean before the crows could even get to it."

My stomach twists, and I clamp my teeth around my top lip.

I want to look over again, just to make sure that Dean is still there. I don't know how long he can hold his breath, but I pray he can hold it a little longer.

"I smell them. I know they're in here somewhere," Lemmere snaps.

If I had been in the water, they'd have left by now.

Leave, I beg silently.

Lemmere huffs but follows the male back to the doors. "This won't matter if we aren't allowed to hunt at some point," she says. "None of her orders will pertain to us if we aren't *alive*."

My mind pricks, questions tinkling like shards of glass at her words.

"You'll be worse than dead if you mention insubordination again," the man orders through a wet-sounding snarl.

Lemmere chuckles. "Oh, I love watching you try and pretend you still give a shit about orders, even in your condition, Richtor. It's like watching a wild boar try and use a fork."

The Vessel named Richtor starts another growl, but quickly swallows it. "We search, as ordered. Then we find the food," he commands.

I breathe easier as the door creaks. They are leaving.

Despite my terror, questions bloom in my chest.

I know the legend they're searching for. We all know— *the Chosen One*. A myth—the one who can end the Crimson and all the sorrow it's brought. But the *her* they were talking about . . . she was different. She was giving them orders, and they were obeying.

Who is ordering the Vessels? I chance a movement, pivoting slowly in the same moment that a slight breeze rolls through the foyer. It's nothing—a whisper. But that's all it takes. The squeaking door stops abruptly, and I twist, edging my mirror around the edge of the statue.

In the reflection, I watch as Lemmere turns on her heel, her red eyes positively alight with glee as she zeroes in on the fountain.

"I told you, Richtor," she sings, walking slowly back to the fountain. Richtor doesn't argue, because he can't talk. His eyes have gone a shade darker than Lemmere's—the color of spoiled blood. His lips twitch, curling over his teeth as he slinks toward the fountain where Dean is hiding. He's hungry, and whatever reason he has is slowly slipping.

"Come out and play, little human," Lemmere says, kicking a leaf as she makes a show of tiptoeing toward the murky water. I know he must be almost out of breath. I'm surprised he lasted this long.

It is in that moment, staring into Lemmere's bloodred eyes, that I realize I can't do what Dean had asked of me. I can't kill him.

And I also can't live with myself if I don't fulfill my promise.

The panic of those two things, combined, makes me jump to my feet.

"Over here," I choke out, hoping that Dean is still underwater and can't hear the stupidity coming out of my mouth. If I survive this, he will kill me.

Lemmere and Richtor both look up, startled for half a second. A deadly playfulness sparks in their eyes, and Richtor's lips peel back even farther.

"I'm here," I repeat, my voice catching in my dry throat.

Lemmere jumps from one edge of the fountain to the other with lethal grace. Vessels don't just have immortality and heightened senses. They are also extremely strong and freakishly agile. You know, all the things you'd hope the things hunting you wouldn't be. If the painful demise into a mindless hunk of cannibalistic meat wasn't inevitable—a fate Richtor is closer to than Lemmere, it seems—it almost wouldn't be a bad deal.

I look down, eyeing her in the mirrors strapped to my wrists and thighs. The reflections move together—dozens of Lemmeres inching toward me. My heart pounds in my chest as I chance a look to the level of the fountain. Richtor is on the edge of it. I just need him to step off, to get away from Dean.

He jumps down and comes alongside Lemmere, who isn't moving.

"This is where you run, little one," she purrs.

And I am all too happy to oblige.

I whip around, sprinting down the hallway, shoving past half-hinged doors as I book it toward the exit.

I hear them behind me, Lemmere's snarl ripping off the marble like a living thing as they pursue.

It is only when I reach the far doorway that empties into the main courtyard that I realize I don't really have a plan.

No. I don't have a plan at all. I tear down the courtyard, under overgrown olive trees snaking around the trellises that used to separate the walking paths.

"Charlotte!" Dean screams from behind me. The sound of feet skidding on gravel rips through the air, and I raise the mirrors on my arms to look behind me. Dean jumps over the railing of the stairs, running toward me as he pulls his iron blade from its sheath. Richtor spins around, his terrifying grin widening as he takes off toward Dean.

Lemmere stays locked on me, and I take off once more.

I turn left and launch myself over stone benches before

skidding to a stop as I reach the balcony that overlooks the museum's front entrance. I ignore the laughter that bubbles up from Lemmere's chest as she slides to a stop against the railing.

"Running out of options, darling," she croons.

I sprint toward the stairs on the far northern side, still without a plan. Even if I get to the cobblestone road that leads down to PCH, I will still have to—eventually—turn and face her. That, or just run straight into the ocean.

I am almost to the stairs when Richtor appears, leading Dean by the point of a knife. Dean's eyes are shut, and I keep my eyes cast down, watching in horror through the mirror as Richtor runs his tongue up Dean's neck.

"Get out of here, Charlotte! Go!" Dean cries, and I hear the choked fear in his trembling voice. Even though he has his eyes glued shut, he knows I'm there. A figure moves in the edge of my vision.

Lemmere stalks toward me. Through the reflection, I see her tilt her chin down as a fake pout forms on her lips.

I back up, stepping into an alcove that overlooks the frothy, whitecapped ocean, and feel the stone railing behind me. Lemmere is a foot away—too close to use the mirror. I lower it and shut my eyes tightly.

"I had a sister like you once," Lemmere says lowly. "Such heart. Bravery. Guts."

She leans in, and the smell of her invades my nostrils. Rosewater and rust. I fight the gag that rises in the back of my throat. Her breath washes against my temple. "They told me that the strongest ones taste the best. I didn't believe it until I tasted her."

"Let her go," Dean growls. I can hear the panic in his voice.

Lemmere clicks her tongue disapprovingly. "Well. That's cute. True love in the face of the end of the world. And aren't we in the right place for a good ol' Greek-style tragedy?"

"We're just friends," I choke out, immediately feeling completely ridiculous. It's not like it matters. Neither of us is going to get out of here alive. Force of habit, I guess.

Lemmere chuckles. "Honey, if you were going to walk out of here, I would tell you that you need to work on your lying."

"Go to hell," I hiss, and I feel her fingers around the side of my face. Her hands are like fire, burning my skin.

She takes in a deep breath before letting out a slow sigh. "Open your eyes, love," she whispers.

I hear Dean struggle, and feel Lemmere step closer to me. I wondered what would be worse—to be eaten or turned. Now I'm too scared to think. Her lips brush the shell of my ear.

"I'm starving, and you smell so good—a campfire mixed with the bite of snow-covered pine trees. But maybe that's a little shortsighted. Maybe we could use your fire, especially now."

I have no idea what she is talking about, but I can't ask questions even if I were able to think of one—my panic shuts my throat tight.

"Open your eyes," she orders again. I squeeze them tighter,

my face spasming from the effort.

Her voice is sharp against my lips. "Open your eyes, or I gut the boy."

"Char, don't," Dean calls out. His voice falters, and I know he is biting back pain. I know Richtor has probably pressed the knife into his skin.

"You'll let him go if I do?" I whisper.

Her laugh tickles my face. "Of course not. But I won't spill his intestines on this imported Italian tile and make you watch as he slowly chokes on his own vomit."

Bile spikes up the back of my throat, and fear slides through my veins.

I know Dean is shouting, but I shut it out.

He would do the same.

I open my eyes, but can't bring myself to look at her gaze. I focus on her bright mouth. This close, and I still don't know if it's from lipstick or blood.

"I remember there was a time when I would have lamented snuffing out bravery like this," she whispers. Her words are laced with the memory of sadness, like she is recalling sadness as one would recall the temperature of any given day. There is no emotion attached to it. I don't know if it's what happens to every Vessel, or if they have to kill off their human side in order to feed the way they do.

She opens her mouth, and a glow lifts from the back of her throat, like she is lit from within.

I don't know how this part will work. I just know that I'll

do it to save him, and then Dean will have to do what he's promised.

I wonder if it will hurt, and I wonder if wondering that, in the scheme of things, makes me a coward.

But God, I hope it won't hurt.

Chapter 3

THE DAY THE CRIMSON FINALLY TOUCHED US, WE were at Santa Monica High School for one of Vanessa's gymnastic meets. I remember the day like I remember a nightmare. The reel is cut in odd places, and I know there were memories left on the cutting room floor. I don't care, though. I know that there are things that I don't ever need to see again.

When the research ship, the *Magdelena*, went missing, no one really cared. It was one of those "well, this is odd slash tragic" news stories that ran at the end of the hour before they started back up with the important political news and lottery numbers. "Pirate Queen" was even trending on Twitter. It was something for the conspiracy theory YouTube channels and Reddit threads. The footage from the researcher on board was creepy, sure. But probably a hoax.

There were checkpoints on the off-ramp of the 10 Freeway

that day, but no one told us why. Maybe the police manning it didn't even know themselves yet. Maybe they did, and they didn't believe it.

The reel in my mind cuts to the gym meet. To the smell of sweat and chalk, and the hardwood bleachers. The instrumental version of "The Bird and the Worm" playing over the mounted speakers as I watched Vanessa.

Vanessa, with glitter gel holding even her smallest flyaways in a tight bun. Her velvet and sequined leotard, and the way she looked at me as I sat on the floor next to the mat, as I always did. She sprayed her grips with a water bottle and ran the leather strap along the inside of the chalk bin. She grinned at me, and I nodded. She walked over.

Help? she asked, holding a hand out. She needed me to tighten the Velcro straps of her grips. I pulled them with a *rrrrip* and rewrapped them.

Good? I asked. She nodded. I looked up at my family. Harlow sat in the bleachers, her back against the railing as she read a book.

You got this, Van! my mom called from next to her, blond hair catching the stadium lights.

That was the last moment when things were okay. I wish I had memorized it. I wish I'd had the weird sixth sense that told me to keep it close, to burn it into my memory. But even now, the recollection is bleached and faded. I remember the next part, though. How my father clenched his jaw and lowered his phone. He whispered something to my mother.

31

What? I saw Harlow ask.

But my mom never answered. Vanessa jumped onto the springboard. She swung from the lower bar, bringing her legs up to leverage herself up and over.

Flawless. That's what she was. A force to be reckoned with.

She was in the middle of a handstand on the high bar when the first scream rang out. It was bloodcurdling. For half a second, I thought it was an injury. Someone dismounted sideways or under-rotated on their tumbling pass.

People started running toward the door, but Vanessa had no clue. She never let anything distract her while she was doing a routine. She swung around the bar, executing a release move.

I glanced up at my family. They were standing, my mom's eyes wide as she focused on the door.

Harlow looked down at me then, not waiting for my parents to act.

Get her! she screamed. Something in her voice told me not to ask questions. It was full of something I wasn't used to from Harlow: terror, pure and unfiltered.

I moved, jumping up onto the platform and racing for the bars. And then I saw it.

People, streaming into the stadium. People. But . . . not.

It was the first time I ever saw a Vessel.

Their eyes were red, their steps even and smooth. They poured through the door, grabbing people and pulling them to the ground, their open mouths glowing as they tore into flesh.

For a second, I froze. Just a second. Whatever survival

instinct I had clicked in that moment, just as Vanessa reversed her momentum and swung back around the high bar, readying herself for her dismount.

A female Vessel walked slowly toward her, those bloodred eyes fixed on Vanessa.

I don't know how we survived, knowing now how we were always one glance away from death. My mom would've said it was divine intervention, had she made it through the night.

VANESSA! I screamed, launching myself forward. I grabbed her around the waist as she came around, sending both of us careening into the metal-and-wire cable that kept the bars secure to the gym floor. We rolled, and Vanessa landed on top of me.

Something warm and sticky soaked my shirt, and I turned in time to see a Vessel, leaning over one of the coaches, his fingers digging into the man's throat. He looked up at the bleachers beyond, his eyes glassy with intoxication as he smiled and bore down. The man stopped moving as the Vessel squeezed tighter and more blood pooled, inching across the wood floor.

What the hell? Vanessa said as I scrambled to my feet, slipping once in the blood, and pulled her with me.

Run was all I said, my eyes locked on the female Vessel still slowly walking toward us.

Vanessa, breathing hard, grabbed my hand as we ran, getting lost in the shrieks and shouts as everyone pushed to the exit.

I don't know how we found my parents. Maybe they found us.

Somehow, we got to the parking lot. Somehow, we got to

our car. I got in the back, my hands sticky with chalk and blood. I didn't move. I could hear the words my parents were speaking, but I couldn't give them meaning.

He was dead. That coach was dead.

Those things killed him.

They were going to try to kill us. My father weaved in and out of traffic, but when we got to the highway, it was dead stopped. We were trapped. My father whipped the car around. Even in my foggy state, even in the shock, I recognized the streets as he navigated through stopped cars. We were heading to the marina.

I don't know, even with years to think about it, how the world ended so fast for us. We went into the gym and the world was one thing. We left it, and it was on fire. In the space of a minute, I went from not believing in monsters to seeing them firsthand. I clenched and unclenched my sticky, blood-soaked hands. The blood dried and cracked.

There were bodies in the street as the Vessels stalked down the road. The barricades shut off roads, funneling everyone directly into the wave of Vessels that walked down the highway.

They thought they were protecting us, but they just damned the whole city, my dad said.

Helicopters and jets sounded overhead, and someone said something about the National Guard.

It gets fuzzy here. The smoke and the screams and the awareness that we were inches from something cataclysmic.

We can get to your mother's by boat, my father's voice said to my mom. He was right. The roads were too congested—we would never get anywhere.

We pulled up next to the dock. A man stepped out of the shadows next to us, knocking on my mom's window.

Excuse me, he said.

It was polite. I remember that. It didn't sound like death.

And we didn't know then what we know now. The Crimson had just bled across our city. It wouldn't be until a couple weeks later that we understood how it was transmitted.

Sometimes I stall the memory at this point. Sometimes I imagine that I knew then what I know now and screamed at my mother to close her eyes. I tell my father to close his. I tell him to punch the gas.

We pull away, and no one dies. No one turns. My family is still whole.

But that's not what happened.

I saw it—the moment the man leaned down and looked at my mother. His eyes were the color of a radiant Southern California sunset—the kind that turns the sky all different shades of purple.

This is where everything in my memory deepens—where the ink is still wet, all these years later.

For a second, I was relieved. His eyes were violet, not red. I thought the red eyes were the only ones you had to look out for. The man flicked his eyes to my father.

My mother started screaming. She put her hands to her face,

35

muffling the cries and somehow making them more terrifying.

My father gasped in pain and leaned over the steering wheel, flooring the gas pedal. The man fell back as we lurched forward, disappearing into the shadows once more.

He stepped in, ruined our lives, and then disappeared. There was no warning. No follow-up. And sometimes that just happens. A collision—no sense to it, no purpose.

"Get to the boat!" my father yelled, his eyes shut tight.

Vanessa tried to lean forward, but Harlow pulled her back, something like understanding slinking across her face. My mother curled up in the passenger seat, sobs racking her shoulders.

I heard the click as Harlow opened the door. The sounds of the shrill terror wafting over the city rolled into the car like a thunderclap.

"Mom? Dad? Come on!" Vanessa yelled as Harlow pulled her from the car.

My parents didn't move. His eyes still closed, my father reached over and grabbed my mother's hand. He squeezed once. Harlow reached into the back seat, pulling me, digging her hands into the collar of my jacket and yanking me out of the car.

I tried to fight back, but she shoved me. I don't know how she knew, or how she stayed so strong.

The shuffling of feet sounded on the street beyond, and Harlow and I looked. Hundreds of Vessels walked toward us, filling the marina.

"Go!" my mother cried from the front seat. She opened the door and stumbled out, her eyes still shut. Then she turned and opened them, keeping her eyes fixed on the Vessels walking down the street.

My father stepped out of the driver's side. "We will buy you as much time as we can."

I didn't want to comprehend what was happening.

"We can get help!" I yelled, reaching for my mother's hand. She pulled back.

Vanessa sobbed harder, and the Vessels creeped closer. I knew they were fast when they wanted to be. They could have overcome us by now, if they chose to. But this wasn't about overcoming us quickly. They were having fun.

I backed away, following Harlow while still walking backward, but Vanessa refused to move. I heard the boat engine start behind us.

I pulled Vanessa toward the dock, ignoring how she clawed at my arms. Harlow helped me heave her into the boat, and we jetted away from the dock, the force of the engine knocking us back. None of us said anything then.

It could have been minutes or hours. I don't remember.

"We have to go back," Vanessa yelled, standing. Harlow didn't even look back, but kept her eyes on the dark water ahead. Above us, the moon turned inky. The blood moon—a total lunar eclipse that casts the moon in a red shadow. I'd seen one once with my dad, but this one felt different. The dark around us felt thick—alive somehow.

Harlow turned her head, just slightly, and spat over her shoulder. "There is no *back*, Vanessa. Mom and Dad are . . ." She didn't finish, and I was grateful.

"We can find a way to fix it!" Vanessa yelled.

"We don't even know what the hell is happening, Vanessa!" The boat jumped a wave, and Vanessa lost her balance for a moment before steadying herself.

I shut my eyes, letting the stain of the bloody night wash over me.

I should have said something. I should have reached for Vanessa when the boat hit another wave and I saw her lose her balance once more. I should have yelled at Harlow to look out as Vanessa lurched forward, knocking Harlow sideways and sending the wheel careening left.

The world spun.

And then there was darkness. Cool, all-encompassing darkness as I sank down, and down, and down into the water. The boat had thrown us all at the abrupt turn.

The water wrapped me up as it had a thousand times before. I waited for the comfort—for the peace. But the hands that once embraced me tightened. And tightened.

There was no sunlight rippling in a refracted dance above me. No laughter skidding over the waves like a pebble.

There was only darkness.

Darkness and death.

I kicked my feet, but I didn't know which way was the surface and which was the fathoms. I didn't know if I *wanted* to know. Nothing in the surface world would make me feel any better, and while I knew that—self-preservation took over and I started thrashing as heat bloomed in my lungs. I needed air.

I needed air.

I needed the surface, no matter what horrors awaited me.

But the air didn't come.

My lungs screamed, and they felt like the sound Vanessa made when I wrenched her from our mother.

A current pulled me sideways, yanking my hair out of the elastic band. I kicked harder, and black spots filled my vision.

They were dead.

I was dying.

I scrambled, letting out a scream that sent little bubbles spinning past my face.

Then, just as the black on the edge of my vision pulled in toward my pupils, I broke through. Sputtering and coughing, I thrashed against the waves.

"Char!" I heard my name and turned. Harlow was swimming next to the boat, her hand tight around the rope secured to the bow.

"Where is Vanessa?" she cried.

A new vise spun tight around my lungs as I twirled, treading water.

Vanessa. There was no Vanessa.

"Nessa!" I shrieked.

"We have to find her!" Harlow yelled before she dove under

the surface. She disappeared, and terror spiked through my chest.

All too soon, Harlow broke the surface again and looked at me.

"Charlotte! Look! Dive down and look!" Her words hit me like arrows, and I bit down hard, clenching my jaw against the panic that felt like a rampant fire loose in my chest.

Vanessa. I had to find Vanessa.

I ducked under the water, but didn't make it more than a couple of inches before my lungs spasmed, the terror pulsing through them. I sucked in involuntarily, and sputtered as I shoved upward. I heaved as I broke the surface.

Harlow looked at me as she came up from a deep dive.

"Charlotte! What the fuck are you doing! We have to find Vanessa!"

"I'm trying!" I shrieked, raising my arms and sending myself underwater once more.

And once more, the terror that seized me once I was under was unbearable. My hands shook as I fought to get above the surface, but something stopped me. There was something touching my foot. I opened my eyes, trying to see below in the pitch-black waves. I felt it again. Something touched me.

I tried to reach down—to grab whatever it was. I prayed that it was Vanessa.

A finger grazed mine. I let out a scream and tried to dive farther. I tried to reach her, but she sank lower, and I couldn't. I wasn't sure if it was the water or my fear that stopped me more.

I shoved upward again.

"Harlow!" I screamed. "I found her! She's here, Harlow! Help!"

"Get her! I have the boat, Charlotte! We need the boat!"

"I can't!" I breathed. The feel of the water around my feet, the swirling darkness wrapping around my body, was already sending me over the edge of another panic attack. I tried to go under, but I froze.

My sister was drowning, and I couldn't move.

Harlow screamed out a string of curses, and then there was a splash of water as she swam.

She dove, the splashing around us sounding in the dark for a moment before there was silence.

Silence as I treaded water, waiting for Harlow to come up. Waiting to see if she found Vanessa.

I screamed into the night, a terrifying sound of fear and helplessness. The sound of it was foreign even to me—I sounded like a wounded animal. I tried to go underwater again, but the fear kept me afloat.

Then Harlow broke the surface, and I cried out as I saw Vanessa in her arms, her dark hair plastered against her face.

"Help me!" Harlow cried, and we swam back to the boat. I got in first and then reached down. It took everything I had to pull Vanessa back into the boat. I set her on her back, and it was then I realized she wasn't breathing.

Harlow heaved herself into the boat, spilling onto the deck.

"She's not breathing!"

"What?"

"She's—she's not breathing, Harlow!" I shrieked.

Harlow skidded forward on her knees, putting her ear to Vanessa's mouth.

I couldn't tell if she was whispering out a prayer or a curse. Knowing Harlow, it was likely she was doing both.

I pulled back against the inside edge of the boat as Harlow pumped on Vanessa's chest.

One two three four five six seven eight. Mouth to mouth. *Again. One two three four five six seven eight.*

I wrapped my hands around my hair and pulled on the roots.

Vanessa wasn't breathing. She wasn't breathing because I couldn't dive down and save her. I couldn't save her, and those few extra seconds could have been the difference.

One two three four five six seven eight, Harlow pumped.

"Don't you fucking dare, Nessa," Harlow choked out. "Don't you fucking dare."

A sob ripped from her throat as I pulled my knees to my chest and let out a small cry.

"Don't!" Harlow snapped, her eyes wild as they found me through strands of wet hair hanging in her face. The low light of the blood moon made the hatred in her gaze glitter. "Don't you even cry, Charlotte. She's not dead. She is *not dead.*"

Harlow reached down, feeling for Vanessa's pulse.

I saw the look of terror that she tried to hide when there was nothing.

There was nothing.

Harlow started the compressions again.

"Harlow," I whispered, bringing a shaky hand to my mouth.

"Shut up, Charlotte," Harlow bit out.

Vanessa's face was blank, her eyes closed as she lurched under Harlow's hands. Her bun had come undone, and I could still see the faint trace of glitter in her scalp.

She was dead.

My sister was dead, and it was my fault.

The horror of it mixed with a self-hatred so deep I swore I could feel it rattling my bones.

I did this.

I let her die.

My heart didn't break then. I knew what that felt like. This . . . this was different. This was a hollowing out, a remaking. It was as though I didn't have a heart at all. Because a heart was something that was only useful if it could love.

I'd never thought I was a particularly brave person. But I didn't realize I was that much of a coward.

I sat there, watching my older sister give everything she had, scraping her nails across the billowing cape of the death that was slowly walking away with my sister in its arms.

Harlow's jaw clenched as she pumped.

She didn't stop all at once. For fifteen minutes, her hope died slowly. Each moment still punctuated the night with a grunt, a ruthlessness that we later learned cracked Vanessa's ribs.

When Harlow stopped, when she fell back against the deck, her wet jeans slapping against the fiberglass finish, her face stunned and blank, I went still.

Harlow didn't say anything. She didn't rage at God or scream. She was just . . . quiet.

And that was more frightening than anything I had ever seen. Harlow was a fighter, but in that moment—she had given up.

The waves pelted themselves on the side of the boat, and the lapping sound mixed with Harlow's harsh, ragged breathing as we both froze, unwilling to be the first to speak in the new world that stretched out—the world where half my family was gone.

I don't know how long we sat there, too cold and numb to shiver as both of our lips turned blue, eyes fixed on our sister's body. But it was long enough that when Vanessa lurched, I thought something terrible was happening—that it was a different part of whatever horror we'd just witnessed on land. She coughed twice, eyes bulging with panic at the water in her throat. They were *her* eyes still.

Harlow shoved herself up, helping Vanessa roll onto her side. Harlow hit Vanessa on the back, letting out a triumphant cry as Vanessa heaved. Harlow pulled Vanessa against her chest.

I know Dean is screaming, but the blood rushing through my ears drowns him out.

And then, Lemmere lets me go, and I crumple to the tile, the sharp pain in my wrists snapping me back to myself as the burning in my lower back ebbs and I can hear again. I lift my mirror and pull out my knife, ready to fight. Lemmere lets out a shriek, turning just in time to see an iron arrow run through the back of Richtor's head. Dean doesn't hesitate, but shoves Richtor's body back and pulls a blade from his sleeve. In the space of a breath, he throws it, end over end, until it hits Lemmere in the shoulder.

Richtor hisses, pushing himself back upward. Vessels can only be killed by beheading them with an iron blade, but from what we can tell, they still feel pain. We use arrows at the Palisade—it usually buys us a couple of seconds when we need it most. But this time, the arrow just seems to piss him off.

Lemmere curses, the breath making heat waves as it rolls past her lips. She is about to lunge at him when a blade runs through her from behind. Her head topples, landing on the blood-soaked tile with a sick thud. The body follows, revealing a lithe figure all in black, the lower half of her face obscured by a black mask. Richtor rushes the killer, but she wastes no time in tossing the blade to Dean, who has a better angle. He catches the blade in midair, twisting it with skill and ease before swiping it across the air, severing Richtor's head from his body.

The blood slinks across the tile toward me as the sound of dozens of raiders sounds on the stairs.

I avoid tilting my mirror, because I'm pretty sure whose angry gaze will meet mine. The boot moves closer, rolling Richtor's head over so that it's facedown. He's dead, but dead eyes can still pass the Crimson.

I stare at the brackish blood as long as I can before looking down at the reflection to confirm who just let out the irritated noise.

I know that I will have nightmares for months to come. The feeling is still seeping back into my legs, and my lungs burn from the aftershocks of adrenaline.

But it doesn't really matter that I just literally stared death in the face, because it is still freaking terrifying to look up at the raiding commander's rage-filled eyes as she pulls her mask off her face and tucks it under her chin. Harlow wipes the fine mist of blood off her defined cheekbone with the back of a gloved hand. It smears upward, an obscene shadow of the perfect contour she used to paint on in our bedroom mirror before shows.

"There had better be a fucking excellent reason for this," Harlow hisses.

Chapter 4

TWO RAIDERS—MAX, WITH HIS TWO MISSING teeth, and Glenn, his graying hair cropped short—come up behind her. She eyes Dean, who wipes her sword on his pants as he answers the question before she asks it.

"Only two Vessels chased us, but there was a third," he says, tossing the sword and catching it by the blade before handing it hilt-first back to Harlow. She snatches it and looks to her men.

"Sweep the perimeter. If it's still here, end it," she says. Her bleached blond hair flutters in the ocean breeze, her smoky black eyeliner making her death glare even scarier.

"He didn't sound like he was progressed, but that one was, so I wouldn't rule it out," Dean adds, pointing to Richtor's corpse as he makes his way over to me.

"Use a mirror," Max calls, and Dean waves him off.

"She's fine," Dean replies. Still, I go a step further and shut my eyes tight as he approaches, relief flooding me as the reality of what we just survived hits me. He puts his hand under my chin and tilts it up. I keep my eyes closed, and Dean sighs.

"You don't know I'm fine," I whisper.

"I'll risk it. It seems we're doing that today," he shoots back.

I open my eyes, keeping them downcast. The memory of my mother's shriek echoes through the back of my mind, the perfect accompaniment to the fear singing in my blood. But a still sort of reassurance cuts across my thoughts: I don't feel any different.

Dean angles the mirror strapped to the back of his wrist, and I look at myself.

There are spots of dark liquid on my cheekbones and in my eyelashes. Blood.

But my eyes are normal—the irises a weird mix of green and brown. My mom used to say they looked like a sunlit forest. Dean eyes me in the reflection. "What the hell was that?" he asks.

I don't know what to say—I don't have an explanation I can use. *I love you* is the only thing that makes sense, and it's the one thing I can't say.

"She alive?" Harlow asks, her voice a blunt knife as she strides over to us.

It was never hard to tell when Harlow was mad. She was never that great at hiding it. When our parents told her she couldn't get her belly button pierced for her sixteenth birthday, she told me she was going to be mature about it in an effort to show them that she should be allowed to make her own decisions. But when they didn't change their minds within the fifteen minutes she'd allotted for her patience, she went out and bought cigarettes instead. She chain-smoked the whole pack, threw up, and left the butts on the front porch in a pile.

So I don't exactly expect subtlety from her. Yelling, maybe. But the silent treatment is way worse. She doesn't say a word to me as the raiders look through the rest of the museum. There is no sign of the other Vessel—the one with the cruel voice.

That distinction seems almost silly, now that I know how cruel Lemmere was. I tell Harlow what I heard them saying—something about orders from *her*. Her face remains blank as she nods once, then motions for me to head down to the caravan of cars waiting on the stone driveway.

Dean sits in the front seat of the Range Rover, and I climb in the back. Harlow drives south, leading the convoy back to the Palisade.

"So stupid," she breathes, wringing her hands on the steering wheel like she's trying to choke it. I look out over the storm-covered ocean, trying to find words. She's right. Even with mirrors, we were taking a huge risk. There are many dangers in the world now, and most of them aren't Vessels.

Because one of the worst parts about this virus—this curse—is what it's done to the people who don't have it. And it all hinges on one simple, awful fact: there is a way to survive the Crimson, if you get it. Once you're exposed and the countdown begins in your iris, staining it from purple to red, you have one day to change your fate, and only if you do the unthinkable: pass the Crimson on to three Curseclean—people who have never been exposed to the Crimson before. Do that, and your iris turns yellow. We call a yellow iris Xanthous—and it means that you're immune to the Crimson for the rest of your life. The Curseclean you've infected become Exposed, and the purple countdown begins for them, a sick cycle with no conceivable end.

And if they don't find a way to pass it on? If the purple counts all the way down? Then the color goes from purple to an angry red, and the person—as you knew them—is gone.

They're Vessels.

I guess the closest thing we had to compare them to in the beginning was the undead in horror films. But that didn't quite fit. They're not the grunting, mindless creatures that teetered across our screens. At least, not at first. For a while, they're still . . . *them*, just hungry. That phase lasts longer for some than others, though we don't know why. There are tales of mothers and brothers and husbands who turned but stayed with their families even after, a black sash over their eyes and a lock on their doors. They could still talk and reason—and they said they'd rather die than hurt anyone. The families didn't have the heart to do what needed to be done, because they still sounded so much like they were before.

But the hunger always wins, in the end, and their promises don't count for much when they break the lock. I wish that was the worst part about the Crimson, but it's not. The loophole of this curse created more monsters than the actual Crimson. They're called Runners—traffickers who capture and sell Curseclean to those who can pay to save their own lives and become Xanthous. The Runners spread the curse, then lock the Exposed up in a cell and wait for the Crimson to take over. The blindfolded crew then goes about the task of killing the Vessels the only way they can be killed—by beheading with an iron blade.

Eventually, Dean takes a deep breath. "The headdress was there, Har. Right where Charlotte said it would be."

"I said *no*," she barks at him. "Not with Maddox Caine so close."

I blanch, wondering for the thousandth time if Harlow can read my thoughts. "Maddox Caine?" I blurt, forgetting too late that that intel probably wasn't for me to hear. Maddox Caine— one of the most notoriously violent Runners on the western seaboard. Her cruelty is matched only by her body count.

Harlow meets my gaze in the rearview mirror, and I see the irritation in her level stare.

Yeah, I wasn't supposed to hear that.

"That's classified. So don't tell anyone," she orders.

I roll my eyes. Who would I tell?

Harlow twists her grip on the wheel and turns to glare at Dean again. He knew.

"We talked about it, and I said no. See, as your girlfriend,

I would expect you to respect that. But as your *commander*, I demand it. Now everyone will look at me and expect some sort of follow-through here, Dean. And what am I going to do? Put my boyfriend in the stocks for a day?"

"Sure," he says, shrugging. "Though I wanted to point out that when I brought up bondage that one time, you said you were *not* into it."

I snort, despite myself, and then shrink down in the seat as my cheeks flush hot and I try to turn it into a cough.

Oh, I don't want to know that.

"I'm not joking right now." She turns her head, shooting daggers at me before turning back to the road. "And don't even get me started on you."

Dean glances at me in the rearview mirror, and I stare out the window.

"That's three aware Vessels at once. *Three*," Harlow says, and I hear the confusion in her voice. "And two were in that pre-mindless state. They're staying there longer and longer." She chances a look at Dean. "We're missing something here."

Harlow slows down as we pass a motorcade of cars. They all have the same insignia spray-painted on the door—a flame surrounded by a circle. Enforcers—the envoys from the Torch sent to gather intel and give aid to the rest of the country.

"They're going the wrong way, aren't they?" I ask, craning my neck to watch as they pass, the sand and dirt spinning up in clouds behind their wheels.

"They're pulling back," Harlow says, her voice low. I whip

around, my fingers gripping the back of the seat. I meet Harlow's gaze in the rearview mirror.

I open my mouth to ask more, but she looks forward again, straightening her shoulders. That much information was a gift—sister to sister. But she won't tell me any more.

I reach down and pull the headdress out of my backpack, fingering the cool metal through the fabric I'd wrapped it in.

You'd think we would have learned our lesson about treasure, Dean had joked. And he was right.

You'd think.

Most people heard about Anne for the first time when the Crimson was spreading. When we realized that "obviously fake" footage from the research ship wasn't fake.

But I knew about Anne long before then. My mom would tell me there was a reason for it—that it was destined, or some shit. She's always had more faith than I could ever understand. It was that kind of faith that wanted to help the man who knocked on her window. That kind of hope that got her killed. It's that kind of hope I can't afford. So the truth of it is that my sisters and I knew about Anne de Graaf because my dad was a history professor who specialized in Atlantic studies in the sixteenth and seventeenth centuries. In short? He was a pirate specialist. Every summer, we'd travel to Boston for an annual convention of pirate buffs. That's where we first heard about Anne: the French maiden who challenged her husband's killer to a duel, won, and then took his ship for her own.

The pirate conventions were cool when we were really young. Leo, a burly man with a salt-and-pepper beard down to his belly button, would always make us balloons shaped like swords. We'd eat funnel cake from a truck and watch our mom inspect old coins as our father pored over antique maps and argued with other scholars about trade routes in the Spanish sea. We'd step into Madame Menagerie's fortune-telling tent and gape at the old books and maps she had on an impressive display. Her real name was Shriver, and she'd laugh with us, putting on a heavy fake accent as she grabbed our hands.

You will be the muse that launches ships, she'd say to Vanessa. *You will lead armies, and men will fall at your feet*, she'd say to Harlow, who'd roll her eyes but love the sound of that.

And you, your faith will save the world.

I would nod, forcing a smile on my face even as I would think to myself that if I needed any proof that fortune-telling was bullshit, I just got it.

An older woman named Carolyn would always bring us frosted lemonade from her RV and let us sit under the canopy her husband, Ed, set up. She claimed to be related to Anne, through her mother's side.

She would pucker her lips, mention how the lemonade needed more sugar, and then rehash the story of Anne's death, though my sisters and I knew it by heart.

Her ship was overtaken by Spanish privateers. After a harrowing fight, Anne's crew knew they were overrun. There was no escape. And, for pirates, no quarter. The captain of the enemy ship took a liking to

Anne. He said she had kind, gentle eyes. He wanted to take her back to Spain with him. He promised riches. He promised comfort.

But what he was really promising, all women know, was a cage.

Vanessa always had the grace to look mildly concerned during this part of the story, which nicely balanced Harlow's obvious nail-picking indifference.

And Anne was not one for cages. She'd already climbed up from the pit of Tortuga, where she was sent as a child along with hundreds of France's other unwanted children. She'd earned her life through blood and sweat. No way she was going to let some royal mustachioed ass-kisser take it from her. So she climbed up on the bow of the ship, and he was enraged that she dared turn her back to him—on what he offered. He called to her and ordered her to look at him.

You will look at me when I'm talking to you, he said.

Carolyn would pause, letting the anger build in all of us. No matter how many times we heard it, that part always made my shoulders tight with rage.

Look at me.

I'd heard it before. All women have.

So Anne did look at him, Carolyn continued. *And she said—*

And we'd join in, because we'd heard the story so many times.

You will not choose my end, for this heart is mine.

And, with a sword's flourish, she threw herself into the sea, where no man dared follow her.

She took no guff, Carolyn would say.

That's one way to put it. Because Anne didn't just give herself to the sea. She *cursed* it. The members of her crew told the story for years to come—how her eyes blazed red as she stood on the stern of the ship, hands on the ropes. How the sky darkened as she shouted, and how her throat seemed to *glow* with the weight of her rage as she spoke the fateful words:

Come find me in the depths! she screamed. *Write redemption on my bones. What bid my heart now turn to stone.*

Some people said it was just a legend—something nice her crew invented to make her death seem more fitting. Others said she was simply driven mad in those last few moments.

Either way, the legend was born.

T-shirts with the phrase were hung at booths—*Come find me in the depths.*

Plays with kids in pirate costumes carried on the legend. Harlow and I would walk by the stage at the center of the festival and see the children's program ending with a little girl, no more than six, yelling the fateful lines through the lisp of her two missing front teeth.

Nothing could make Harlow laugh like hearing *Write redemption on my bones* coming out of the mouth of a kid.

"This place is ridiculous," she'd say, even as a genuine smile slunk up her darkly painted lips. Because there was something in the words that stretched across the oceans and through the centuries: the power of a woman tightening her grip around her life, even as the world sought to pull it away from her.

Magic wasn't real. We all knew that. But the story haunted me, and I'd think about those words as I wandered through the convention hall alone. Still, they echo through my mind.

You will not choose my end, for this heart is mine.

Harlow could get up in front of hundreds, plug in her guitar, and sing. Her lyrics were personal, and her voice was like liquid metal. Vanessa could launch her body toward a vault, power over it like some sort of ninja, do two and a half flips, and stick the landing.

At night, I prayed that I could be brave like them. Like Anne.

And every day, I woke up just as I had been the day before. It was easier to believe that her strength, just like her magic, was just a fantasy.

But that changed the year some amateur treasure hunters aboard the SS *Magdelena* found the remnants of a ship that legend said belonged to Anne. And that would usually excite people like my dad, who *lived* for finding shipwrecks. But he shook his head gravely when he told my mom about it over dinner. Some members of his department had asked the treasure hunters to allow them to study the ship, but they'd refused.

The way they talk about her, Gabby, my dad said. I didn't know if he was talking about Anne or the ship, and honestly? I didn't really want to.

They found treasure, all right. Coins and jewels and gold. But they found something else—more than they bargained for. A rib cage, perfectly preserved in the midst of the coral and brine—and in the middle of it was something no one expected: a ruby, the size of a heart.

Se racheter was carved in the fourth rib. My dad told me it was the French word for "redemption."

That night he was up till dawn. I remember seeing the shadow of him pacing under the door. Everyone had written Anne off as a legend. A myth.

But now there was evidence that she was more than that.

The scientific community begged the treasure hunters to wait—that they could have the ruby, but could they *please* let them examine the rib cage first.

But the treasure hunters didn't care. The very next day, they put on their diving gear and went down to get the ruby. And when they found that the ruby was too big to fit between the ribs, they did something my dad couldn't believe—

They snapped them in half.

And after they'd taken everything of obvious value, they left.

Scientists came in after that to pick up the scraps that the hunters had discarded. The ribs were the most interesting part. They thought it was art—something done in Anne's honor that could confirm her historicity.

They didn't realize it wasn't art *about* her.

It *was* her.

And the carving on her rib? After testing, they determined it had happened *before* she died. No one could explain how that was possible.

They could not have known what they were unearthing. Not when they brought it to the surface, and not when they popped champagne and congratulated themselves for the biggest treasure recovery in thirty years.

All that was ever seen of the *Magdelena* was a video recording—the captain's log that was wired to the nearest station. The cartographer was the first to show symptoms—purple around the iris.

The last emission from the *Magdelena* was from one of the treasure hunters. His singsong voice was high, lilting, laced with manic laughter, the purple in his eyes like seeping ink from a broken pen. They played it on the news, and my mom listened to it once before announcing that she wouldn't let it be played in her house again.

> *Come find me in the depths*
> *Write redemption on my bones*
> *What bid my heart now turn to stone*

> *The greed will seep*
> *The poison run*
> *Until then breathes*
> *The Chosen One*

Then, the tape went dark. The speakers filled with static. Then screams. Then, one last sentence:

> *She is reborn by water on the night of blood.*
> *Find her, and she'll find where the heart lies.*
> *She alone is the end.*

More laughter, then static.

And when some researchers found the *Magdelena*, they found an empty ship—the ruby, now called Anne's Heart, was gone.

I always thought that if I found out magic was real, it would be to the tune of some sweeping musical score.

But that's not what happened. When I realized magic was real, I felt sick.

From the looks of it, we all did.

Because, unlike the rest of the world—we'd heard that rhyme before.

Chapter 5

HARLOW AND DEAN KEEP ARGUING IN A COMFORT-
ing thrum, one that I tune out as we wind up the hillside. We
turn a corner, and I peer around a line of overgrown trees. A
wall of mismatched wood rises at least fifty feet high. As we
pull closer, I can see guards pacing along the barricade. I recognize a couple of them—Tace and Marvin are on the western
side, mirrored bands covering both their arms.

Harlow presses on the brake, and whatever argument they
are having pauses as a line of bodies swarms out of the slowly
opening gate. They all carry huge blades, their mirrored bands
and bracelets glinting in the sunlight.

Harlow opens the console between the driver and passenger
seat and pulls out three strips of thick black cloth. She tosses
one to Dean and then sends one back to me. It lands in my lap.

Dean sighs, and Harlow shoots him a death glare.

"I know, I know," he says, reaching it up and tying it over his eyes.

I know better than to argue. This is how we stay safe.

Someone hits the hood of Harlow's car with an open palm, and we all open our doors.

"Hands up, guys," a deep voice says. I recognize it—Kyle.

I tie the cloth around my eyes. Years ago, the darkness would have scared me. Now there's a strange comfort in it. For a moment, while I'm completely vulnerable—I'm also safe.

"In a minute I'm going to pull the blindfolds off you. You're going to keep your eyes down, do you understand?"

Dean sighs. "Kyle. We do this every damn day."

"She doesn't," Kyle replies, and his black jacket lets out a soft *swoosh* as he obviously gestures to me. "And I'm not going to stick a knife to someone's throat without being *very* explicit."

"You don't have to put a knife to her throat at all," Dean growls, a low threat in his voice. "None of us would do anything to put this place at risk—"

Irritation spins in my gut like nausea, and I shake my head. "I'm fine, Dean. All of you. I'm fine. I don't want any special treatment. This is the protocol."

I don't need him sticking up for me, especially not in front of Harlow. I don't need the way his gruff voice makes my knees weak and my heart flip over. I don't need it *at all*.

"Dean. You're first," Kyle says. I hear the soft whisper of fabric, then a pause.

"Clear," Kyle says finally.

Then he steps closer to me.

"You ready, Char?" Kyle asks me. I nod. He reaches back and pulls the blindfold from me. I keep my eyes shut tight, and I feel a guard step forward behind me, reaching around to position a blade a few inches from my neck.

"You may look down," Kyle says.

Slowly, I open my eyes and look down. Kyle holds a small mirror at my waist level. He tilts it, catching my gaze in the reflection. The warmth of his brown eyes stares back at me, inspecting my irises for a moment before he nods to the watchman standing next to me.

"Clear," he says, and the guard steps away from my back, taking the knife with him. I let out a sigh, trying to make it as quiet as I can. I'm sure everyone can see the fear on my face, but that doesn't mean I want to make it obvious.

I watch as they pull the blindfold off Harlow. She looks down, her eyes shut.

"Commander," Kyle says by way of invitation, his wide hands holding the fabric with an odd sort of reverence. Harlow opens her eyes and peers down into the small mirror. He nods to her. "You're good."

She claps him on the wide shoulder as she walks past, signaling for me to follow her.

I follow her, my eyes locked on her leather-clad shoulders as she saunters ahead of us. Her shoulders are meant for this—straight back, even. With the weight of the world resting on them, without a care.

I should know by now that those are the moments when Harlow shines—the ones when fear overtakes everyone else and she alone manages to keep her feet. It was that way in those days after the Crimson first started and we built the walls around this place, making the Palisade. We'd heard that eye contact through a mirror was safe—but Harlow was the first one to test it, earning everyone's respect in the process. She'd always liked being the one to do things other people feared.

As we walk through the settlement, people incline their heads toward my sister. They ask her questions—clarifying shifts and double-checking perimeter watches, and I look around at our settlement, which is a small portion of the neighborhood we were able to wall off. Our old school is at the middle, with a block of houses in every direction.

When a woman with black curly hair and hole-filled jeans calls to her, Harlow turns to look at me. "Check on Nessa?" she asks, reaching a hand out to me. It is force of habit that I reach back and squeeze, but I am thankful for it. Sometimes I need to feel like a sister, and not a soldier.

I know we aren't done discussing the headdress. She'll rip into me later. But right now I have to find Vanessa, and I have a feeling I know where she'll be.

My younger sister is perched on the balance beam, the dim light from the stormy sky filtering in through the high gym windows. The morning feels like days ago, but it's still only early afternoon. She stands at the far end, high on her toes with her arms up by her ears. She takes a deep breath, lowering her arms as she bends in a slight crouch before launching herself backward. Her hands find the four-inch-wide beam, fingers splaying perfectly as her legs open in an even split in the air. One foot finds the beam again, and she rotates upward before throwing her body back once more, executing the same move but bringing her feet to the beam at the same time before throwing her body up into a backflip.

I've been at enough meets to know this combination by heart. Back handspring step-out, back handspring into a back tuck.

Vanessa wobbles slightly but keeps her balance. She wears a black sports bra and tight spandex shorts, and her stomach glistens with sweat. Only in the end of the world would my little sister still have six-pack abs.

"I'd give it a nine-point-four," I say, my voice echoing through the gym. She pivots on her toes, eyeing me as she turns.

"Ridiculous. My feet were flexed, I could feel it," she counters. Vanessa will never be satisfied with her performance. She is a perfectionist to the core. Her brown eyes drop to her feet, as if she can figure out why they've personally betrayed her.

I walk into the gym, my sneakers squeaking on the wooden floor as I eye the balance beam. Our school used to have a gymnastics team, and Dean had found the beam in the storage locker when we'd set up camp. Vanessa had shrieked with delight, even though Harlow and I weren't sure about the structural integrity of something that had been packed away for years. But

65

no matter how hard we'd tried to talk her out of it, Vanessa had kept pleading with Dean to set it up.

I spot the bruises on the back of her calves. "Harlow warned you about the beam, Ness."

She glares at me as she works her way to the far side of the beam. "Harlow has no room to talk about things being 'too dangerous,'" she snips, stopping to take a deep breath. She lunges forward, twisting into a round-off back-handspring double layout. She over-rotates the landing on the eight-inch pad lying on the floor and winds up on her back.

"Dammit," she huffs, hitting the mat with her palms. I step on the mat and look down at her. Her eyes flash. "Don't even say it." She adjusts the straps of her sports bra, revealing the red mark on her side. It has the puckered look of a fresh scar mixed with the beauty of a tattoo.

Se racheter, it says.

She sees my glance, and quickly readjusts the bra to hide it.

"I don't have to say it. You already know. Don't put me in the middle, Ness. I hate lying to Harlow and she's already pissed at me enough right now," I continue.

"Harlow isn't the boss of me."

"She's the boss of everyone," I shoot back. "And I kind of agree with her on this one. Staying in shape is one thing, but if you get seriously hurt, Nessa—"

"Losing my edge is worse than getting hurt," she argues. "I am not going to start from scratch when this shitstorm ends. You think Natalia Drake stopped training?"

I stick my hand out, but she doesn't take it. She just glares up at me until I let it fall to my side. Natalia Drake, Vanessa's rival on the balance beam—the one gymnast who always came at least a tenth of a point from my sister's score.

"I don't even know if Natalia Drake is still alive. And neither do you," I snap.

Something flickers in Vanessa's eyes, a ripple in the dam that holds everything back. It is a feeling I understand well, even if I don't work it out by throwing myself around on a narrow piece of metal covered in leather.

"She's alive," Vanessa says, pushing herself to her feet. "And she's nailing her double-back dismount." Vanessa shoves past me.

I don't know what to tell her, because I've said it before. It's what we all know, a truth that hurts Vanessa too much for her to really look it in the face. It is a truth her guarded face dares me to say right now.

She doesn't like that we worry about her. It reminds her that Harlow and I almost lost her once.

With a lithe, feline movement, Vanessa swings back onto the beam. I block the dismount mat, staring at her. She glares back at me, a strand of dark hair falling out of her bun and into her eyes.

She lifts her arms, arching her back in a quick stretch, but I see the quiver in her, the unsteadiness that I've just kicked up. The truth is, I don't want her to lose the fire that made her one of the best gymnasts in the state. I don't want to see her drive leached out of her by this place. I want her to remember Natalia Drake, and to keep doing the thing she loved. The world demanded she give up, and she didn't. The same tenacity that made her come back over and over after falling off the bars or beam is the same tenacity that would get her through this. And I wish I had the kind of faith she did—that this is all just a shit-storm that will eventually blow over.

And if my plans succeed—the ones I've been busting my ass to see through for the past several months—then maybe this whole thing could be a hiccup in her life. Maybe it is too late for Harlow and me to be normal again. Maybe this whole thing has marked us past what we'd be able to return from fully. But I do hope, somewhere deep in the part of me that still can hope, that Vanessa will keep being Vanessa when this is over.

Until then, the more she *acts* like it, the better.

Because I heard what the Vessels said. I felt the sickness crawling up my throat at the thought. They were looking for the Chosen One, and they were only miles away.

I step back off the dismount mat, and Vanessa's shoulders relax slightly. I mean, Harlow is already pissed at me. I don't really want Vanessa on my bad side, too.

Footsteps sound behind me, and I turn to find Kyle, a grim expression on his face as he hovers in the doorway. Next to him is Alan, one of Dean's closest friends and the arms specialist of the Palisade. His dark skin is covered with sweat. He ties his braids into a ponytail as he cocks an eyebrow at me.

"The Council wants to see you," he says, giving me a

warning look when I roll my eyes.

I nod, turning to watch Vanessa as I back toward the door.

"Your right knee was bent," I say, and a grin spreads across my sister's face before she gets back on her toes, ready to try again.

I turn, letting the smile slip off my face.

The Council's voices are muffled through the door as we walk into the hallway. Kyle motions for me to wait as he walks inside.

After looking over my shoulder to make sure no one else is around, I inch forward, leaning as close to the door as I dare.

"The movements are more calculated now," a deep male voice says. "They are centralizing or something. Traffic at the Blood Market has almost doubled in the past month."

The Blood Market. The words send a small chill over my shoulders. The Blood Market is where the Runners take Curse-clean to sell to the highest bidder.

The Torch has tried for almost a year to take it down, but they can't get close.

"Well. We're going to have to put more watchmen on the walls, then. If Runners want to sweep through here, then they won't catch us by surprise," a familiar female voice answers. Harlow. "But if we're facing Runners *and* Vessels like the kind we saw today—three, working together, almost all fully aware—we will have to figure something else out."

I don't realize I'm leaning on the door to listen until Kyle pulls it open and I stumble inside, barely catching myself before careening to the floor. I look up and find the faces of the Council staring back from behind a line of tables in the middle of the school's massive cafeteria. Harlow sits next to a man with graying hair and dark skin—Malcolm, the leader of the Palisade. On the other side is James, a woman with a lean face covered in a line of scars across her light skin. Next to her is a seat where my grandmother had sat up until three months ago. It's still empty.

There's a door in her heart that's closed. Nine and thirteen.

I blink, shoving the memory of those words as deep as it will go.

Dean stands in front of a crudely made wooden table, and he casts a glance over his shoulder at me as I walk farther inside.

Of course Harlow would tell the truth about today in her report. Of course she couldn't just cover for me for once in her fucking life.

"By all means, come in, Charlotte," Malcolm says. I can't read the emotion in his deep voice, but I know I don't have anything to fear from him. He was voted to this position for a reason—he's one of the best men I've ever known. Though that means that he'll be impartial now, and the fact that he was a friend of my grandmother's—more than a friend—won't factor in when he considers punishment.

I stand next to Dean, stopping myself from giving him the same look I'd given him a thousand times over the years when we got caught doing something stupid.

"You had permission to go check the nets down at the

shoreline, Charlotte," Malcolm says, his voice vibrating through my lungs. I nod.

"Normally, I'd go over the bylaws that your own grandmother helped draft, but we don't need pomp and circumstance. You both know that you jeopardized more than your own lives today. What I want to know is *why*."

I bite the inside of my lip. My plan isn't ready yet.

"I was being dumb," I say, raising my eyes only slightly. I hope they buy this. Dean is still by my side.

I hear the clink of metal, and my eyes dart up just in time to see Harlow drop the headdress on the table in front of her. My heart sinks.

"Careful with that!" I cry, stepping forward. Dean grabs my arm, pulling me back.

Malcolm looks at the headdress and then slowly turns back to me. "Charlotte Holloway." He breathes my name like a curse. "Please tell me this isn't what I think it is. Tell me you didn't jeopardize your lives for one of your puzzles."

Heat singes the back of my neck as Malcolm's words cut through the room.

Puzzles.

Like I'm a kid on the floor of a playroom. I cock my jaw to the side. I can't tell him why I really needed it, because then I'd have to tell him *how* I know all of that.

I feel Harlow's glare from across the room, and I don't dare meet it. I know she knows what I'm really looking for, and why. And she knows that I can't explain myself.

"I thought . . . ," I croak out, my voice sounding small as it gets swallowed up in the vast quiet of the room. I look up, seeing the disappointment in Malcolm's eyes as he sits back in his chair. "At one point, Anne had that headdress. It was in the hull as she docked in Bordeaux." All that is true.

I hope Harlow will jump in. That she'll stop me from having to stumble over a lie that will make me look like an idiot. But when she doesn't, I know I have to jump in. "I thought it might be of some . . . use. It was stupid. I just . . ." I take a deep breath as I look to Malcolm. "If the Vessels are staying like . . . *that*, like the ones we saw today, then we're in trouble. And if they're centralizing . . . *mobilizing*, then we have to do something. Even the Torch Enforcers are pulling back. So I know it was a long shot. But I can't just sit here and hope we figure something out."

I look up, meeting Dean's eyes for a fraction of a second before he looks down.

"Har—" he starts.

"That's 'Commander' to you, Sergeant," Harlow bites out. Dean falls silent for a moment, absorbing the blow as the air in the room thickens with tension.

"Commander," he starts again. "We broke the rules. But Charlotte's right. We have to change something, and soon." Dean looks around to make sure the only people in the room to hear his next words are the ones who are supposed to be there.

Malcolm stands. "That isn't for you two to decide. You are not Lou," he says, his voice booming through the room as he invokes my grandmother's nickname, immediately cutting off the argument rising in my throat. "Our troops had to go in, blind, to save you," he continues, his voice more subdued now.

"We didn't ask them to do that," I retort, knowing that it's a stupid thing to say even as the words slip past my lips. Malcolm's gaze darkens. He looks down at me. "Know your place, Charlotte. And it's not leading futile, renegade missions. From now on, you're needed in the garden. Dean, you're needed on the wall. That will be all," Malcolm says by way of dismissal. I don't look back at Harlow as I turn on my heel and walk out of the room, shoving the crash bar down harder than I need to—hard enough that my teeth rattle.

I know it's the apocalypse, and everything has already come crashing down.

But even in this brave new world, I still feel like I'm the other sister, referred to in the possessive: Harlow's shadow. Vanessa's keeper.

Because my older sister is a commander.

And my younger sister is the Chosen One.

Chapter 6

I MOVE THROUGH THE COURTYARD, STOPPING AS I walk past a small mess hall and see a group of people crowded into the common room—it was once a teacher's lounge. A voice wafts over the crowd gathered inside. I look through the window at the mass of people gathered around a small flat-screen propped up against the wall. It has a crack that leaves a neon-green line down the middle of the screen, but it works, thanks to the feeble generator Malcolm lets us use for these broadcasts.

On the screen, a woman sits at a desk, her suit jacket clean and pressed. She reads from a list of names, pausing only slightly between each one.

I stop for a moment, listening to the words as they slip past her perfectly lined lips.

Somewhere, people's lives are changing as she reads.

In the Torch, the world is almost . . . normal. And if you can afford an application, you can enter the lottery.

"Anyone getting any life-changing news?" I whisper to Marjorie, an elderly woman who always wears an army-style utility vest over her flowery blouses. She shakes her head slowly, and the familiar smell of her AquaNet hairspray fills my nostrils.

The camera pans over, leaving the woman reading the list to show a man standing next to her. His blond hair is swept out of his vivid yellow eyes, a reluctant smile on his handsome face— Abel Lassiter, the leader of the Torch.

"I know they have reliable electricity and health care there, but damn if I wouldn't be excited to win just to see that jawline up close," Marjorie whispers loudly, elbowing me in the ribs. Two girls in front of us turn around to give Marjorie a nod. Someone else lets out a "mmm-hmm" in agreement. Sergei, our cook, leans backward in his seat, resting it against the wall. His tattooed arms are bigger than my thighs, and he holds them out for balance as the chair pivots.

"Abel Lassiter is a former navy fighter pilot, top of his class at Johns Hopkins, and one of the world's top virologists. His mother was an engineering genius who designed walls that withstood the apocalypse and saved Western civilization. But you're going to sit here and ogle his *looks*?" Sergei asks, disappointed.

Marjorie and the girls turn back to the screen for a moment, watching as the lottery ends and Abel thanks the woman before walking to the podium to speak to the press gathered there. He brushes a hand through his hair absently as he looks over his notes.

"Yup," Marjorie answers decisively, and the other girls nod in agreement.

Sergei sits forward, and his chair thuds as it hits the ground. "I thought women were supposed to be better."

Marjorie picks at her nails. "It's a brave new world, Sergei."

I lean against the doorway and watch on the TV as Abel adjusts the microphones on the podium. Marjorie isn't wrong, and she's clearly not alone. From the moment he stepped out beside his mother, Genevieve Lassiter—the architect of the Torch—Abel was of particular interest. It was weird, but it was almost like we had our own royal family. The Lassiters were people we could follow. Hope was a rare medicine, and we took it where we could. Hearing that the Torch was succeeding—that our way of life was not completely gone—was hope.

Genevieve had been fearless and brilliant, and her son was self-made. And not even a postapocalyptic hellscape and the threat of flesh-eating monsters could stop the thinned-out press corps from pointing out that Abel Lassiter wasn't bad-looking. The fact that he was a leading virologist was just icing on the cake. He vowed to find a cure for the Crimson.

But things are a little different now.

A few months ago, Genevieve went out with her fleet, and wasn't seen again. Abel took some of his best men and went searching, but she was gone. Her boat had sunk off the coast—a Vessel attack. When Abel returned and took up his place as the general, he was changed. The twinkle in his eye had sharpened, and his smile was not as easy. He brought Admiral Marsali into his circle—the patriarch of an old military family—who led the Torch's navy with an iron fist. He didn't smile on camera, and had no interest in mincing words. *This is about survival* was all he'd ever say. He had two children—twins—though they kept out of the limelight. Until Abel fell in love with Admiral Marsali's daughter, Evelyn.

It was a fairy tale, and even Harlow—who wore Marvel shirts with "Hulk Smash the Patriarchy"—couldn't help but roll her eyes and begrudgingly admit that they were adorable.

Evelyn had studied nursing before the Crimson, and she looked at Abel Lassiter like he was the only man in the world. He, in return, looked at her like she showed him that there was good in the world worth fighting for.

Evelyn disappeared six months ago, when she led a supply run to one of the more unprotected settlements south of Portland.

No one has seen her since.

Abel puts on a brave face—we all see it. But every drawing—every announcement—he looks a little more broken. The circles under his eyes look a little darker.

I listen to his voice while my fingers play with the splintered wood peeling from the doorframe and force myself to pull out of the sad thoughts surrounding Abel and Evelyn.

"General, any comment on the new reports of the Vessels . . . changing?"

Abel stops, his expression hardening. "People have been scared for a long time. But fear isn't what drives us anymore. If the Crimson is shifting, then we will shift with it. We will do whatever it takes to defeat this thing."

"Any progress on the acquisition of the subject of the prophecy? The so-called Chosen One?" another reporter asks. My stomach drops, and my hand stills on the doorframe. Abel sighs and then laughs softly.

"Chasing a ghost is not high on our list of priorities right now. As we all know, my mother put her hope in such things, so I respect those who put theirs in it," he says. "But I'm a man of science, and I will continue to work to find a cure and push infrastructure. A majority of our settlements are surviving without even one working generator. But we hope the construction of our new power rig will change that. That is our priority."

The Rig. The first big construction project of its kind since the Crimson started. It's just off the coast, and when it's finished, it will provide reliable power to the whole western seaboard.

"Any updates on when we'll be allowed to know the specifics about it? Maybe . . . visit?" a hopeful reporter asks.

Abel smiles. "Not until we know it can withstand the strength of our enemies. If the Vessels start putting their assets on a news channel, maybe I'll think about evening the playing field."

Chuckles and noises of joking disappointment roll through the crowd.

Another question arises from the crowd. "Sir? Any news of Evelyn?" Abel freezes for half a second, but pushes on, pretending he didn't hear.

I've heard enough.

I nod to Marjorie before taking off across the courtyard.

I am almost back to the house when footsteps sound behind me. I turn around to see Harlow running toward me. I roll my eyes and turn back around.

"Charlotte," she calls. I keep walking. I don't want to talk to her.

"You couldn't have my back? Once?" I hiss. "You know why I had to find that stupid headdress. You *know.*"

Harlow leans closer. "And I told you that it was a dumb risk. How would we explain that, Charlotte? 'Oh hey, guys. Suit up. I know we need antibiotics and baby formula and *food,* but Charlotte thinks my sister's nonsensical slam poetry nightmares told us to go on a mission to retrieve a fucking *necklace.*"

"It's a headdress, and we're past being able to explain things. We have been for a long time," I shoot back.

Harlow's eyes narrow for a second at my words, and she swallows hard as her eyes dart to her feet. I'm right, and she knows it.

"They were looking for Vanessa," I whisper finally.

Harlow goes still, and then she raises her eyes to mine. "How do you know?"

I look around to make sure no one is within earshot before I whisper back. "That's what the Vessels were discussing in the

Getty. They said *she* sent them. Who are they talking about, Harlow?"

Her first instinct is to dismiss my question—I see it in the way she takes a deep breath.

"I heard what you were all talking about with the Council," I say. "I know there's more going on than you want us to know." The naked irritation on her face quickly gives way to something I'm not used to seeing: fear.

Without a word, Harlow pivots on her heel and stalks toward our house. She pauses for a second and motions for me to follow, and we cut over an empty sidewalk and under a row of overgrown palm trees. Her stride is long and practiced, and I struggle to keep pace with her. When she speaks, her voice is low and quick.

"Some of the Vessels are staying aware for a lot longer than normal," she starts, her eyes scanning around us to make sure—for the seventieth time—that we're alone. "And they're working together."

"Everyone knows that," I reply, coming to a stop. "There's no need for the ghost protocol shit—they literally just asked Abel about it at the Torch lottery broadcast."

Harlow halts in her tracks, turning to face me. Irritation ripples over her taut expression before she tilts her head back, letting a humorless smile slink over her dark lips. She drops her chin, and I hold up my hands in surrender.

"Sorry. Continue," I say, taking a step to close the gap between us.

Harlow catches her tongue between her teeth, a thing she only does when she's really debating something. "Not all Vessels are staying in that state. We don't know why some degrade into mindless flesh-eaters, and why some stay like . . . before. But enough are staying aware, and they're starting to mobilize, and . . . they're following someone. They're calling her the Vessel Queen. We've been examining their movements for the past couple of weeks. They've commandeered ships and made outposts. It's like—"

Harlow stops, taking a deep breath before locking onto my gaze.

"It's like they're looking for something."

I step back, shaking my head at the thought. "They're looking for Vanessa. I told you, they want the Chosen One. I heard them."

"They could be mobilizing for any number of reasons. They could be planning an attack," Harlow says, her voice quiet and even, like she's trying to convince herself.

"Or it could be both. She's the only one who can end the curse. They'd want to get her out of the way before attacking." I look up at my older sister. "We have to go to the Torch."

Harlow's eyes widen, and she's quiet for a second, like she's waiting for the punch line. When one doesn't come, she scoffs. "What? No."

My shoulders stiffen at her easy dismissal. "What other choice do we have?"

Harlow steps closer. "Any other choice that doesn't involve

putting Vanessa's life on the line. All we have is the ravings of an asshole on a tape. She has night terrors—that's it. I'll need more than that to risk putting a target on Vanessa's back."

I don't back up, even though I know that's what she's expecting me to do. We've had this conversation before, and it always ends up in this place—we can't leave, because it's dangerous. We don't even know if we'd survive the journey to the Torch. Even if we did, we don't know if they'll believe us and let us in. We don't know what they'll do to Vanessa if they *do* believe us. What if they believe that killing her will solve this? What if *they* decide to put her in harm's way? Harlow and I know the truth about this—there's no un-telling that secret, once it's out.

So we can't let it get out.

"*This* is the safest bet," Harlow says, gesturing around us. "*We* are the only ones who are going to protect her. Unless you pull some stupid shit again like you did today."

The black around her eyes is smudged, making her blue eyes stand out even more. For a second, I thought we were in this together—that she was trusting me with a secret. But it's just like it's always been. I step back. "You," I say, turning away and heading back to the house.

I hear Harlow's footsteps behind me. "What the hell does that mean?"

I whip around. "You said *we* are the only ones who can protect her, but you really mean *you*, right?"

"What the hell is this about?" she whispers.

I never told her. I never explained to Harlow what had

broken in me the day I found her and Dean pressed up against the wall of the bathroom at the public pool.

"I just wanted to help," I choke out.

She presses her lips together, and I know she doesn't know what to say to that. That hesitation, that thought that she didn't trust herself to say what she was really thinking, was worse than her anger.

"Keep your pity," I spit.

"You don't want my pity? Fine." She shifts her feet. "If you *ever* put the man I love in danger again, then I won't stop the Council when they want to have me beat the shit out of you in the square as punishment. Do you understand?"

Her breath washes over my face, the bite of her words stinging in every way she intended. I make myself meet her eyes. She shoves something into my hands, and I look down. I feel the familiar edges. It's the headdress, wrapped in an old T-shirt.

"I understand, Commander," I say, my voice flat.

I spend the rest of the afternoon in the garden, refusing to take the gloves Marjorie offered me as I pull up weeds. It's almost harvest time, but the plants are brittle and bare. I yank weed after weed, loving the slow throb of the sunlight on the back of my neck as my skin burns. My fingers blister, but I don't stop. Malcolm walks by. I glance at his worn hiking boots as they pause just beyond the perimeter, and then I toss a handful of weeds before him as I look up at him. He surveys the sad state of the dry patch, taking a deep breath before meeting my eyes.

I glare back, not saying a word as his eyes fall to my bleeding hands, then to the empty basket beside me.

It's late in the day by the time I walk back to the house. It doesn't look any different than when my grandma was alive. The same plants sit in windowsills. The wind chimes still sound the same when the wind whispers through them.

For a while, we lived in this house, the four of us. There was hope then. That it could be like it was before, at least a little bit. That we could scratch a strange little home out of the scraps the Crimson left us. That maybe Vanessa wasn't as marked as the new scar on her rib seemed to make her.

That hope disappeared as the dreams got worse, going from soft whispers to strange words she'd spit out like broken teeth in the middle of the night, and she told us about Grandma's death before it happened. *There's a door in her heart that's closed. Nine and thirteen.*

And the next week, our grandmother died from a heart attack at 9:13 in the morning. She grabbed her left arm and fell over in this tomato patch.

As Harlow and I dug the grave in silence, handkerchiefs over our mouths, we knew.

Since then, walking back to my grandmother's house doesn't feel like coming home. I keep waiting for it to get easier, because people say it does. Maybe it did, before the end of the world. But I don't know how grief is supposed to work now.

A voice stops me as I reach the top of the porch.

"You need to disinfect those cuts," Malcolm says, perched in my grandma's favorite porch chair.

"If you came here to lecture me," I start, "Harlow already beat you to it."

Malcolm stands, groaning as he puts his hands on his back. He acts like an old man, but we all know better. I've seen him lift sandbags during rainstorms. He's seventy-four pushing thirty.

"I don't need people being nice to me," I add, my voice just louder than a whisper. Malcolm doesn't say anything, and I know he's waiting for an explanation. I exhale sharply as I walk down and sit next to him. "Someone being kind is just . . . pity now. Maybe it wasn't before. But whenever someone is nice to me, it just means they think I'm too weak to handle things on my own."

Malcolm pulls a small vial from his back pocket and pops the lid. The smell of isopropyl alcohol wafts up, and he motions for me to give him my hand. I sigh, knowing better than to argue. His rough fingers find my wrist.

"I disagree with your entire premise. Start to finish—terrible." Malcolm used to teach college English, and I often forget until he says something like that. "Kindness, in this world, is the only thing that shows that we're worth the survival we're fighting for. You should accept it as the precious and rare thing that it is. We can't save humanity if we lose ours."

"Okay, professor. I'm wrong. I recant, blah blah blah-*hooooowww!*" Malcolm squirts some alcohol over my cuts, and the sting rips up my arm. I glare at him, knowing he's enjoying it at least a little. "You did that on purpose," I whine.

A smile curls up his lips, moving the white hairs of his beard. "I did."

"I fucked up," I breathe.

"Language," he growls.

I lower my hands. "I should have known, Malcolm. I'm not Harlow. What the hell was I thinking?"

Malcolm reaches over and, with gentle but firm fingers, finds my chin and turns my head to face him.

"Language." He doesn't let go. "No. You're not Harlow. You're not Vanessa. I've watched you all for years, Charlotte. You look up and see Harlow and look back and see Vanessa and then look down at yourself and wonder what good you are."

I swallow the tightness in my throat and make myself meet his brown eyes.

"You are Charlotte Holloway. And that means something."

"Well. If you have a working thesis about what that 'something' could be, I'd love to hear it, Doctor," I joke.

He lowers his hand. "Nope. You get to do all that work yourself, love." Malcolm pushes himself off his knees as he stands, letting out another exaggerated groan. "I'm getting too old for pep talks. So get your shit together."

"Language," I shoot back. He leans down and kisses the top of my head before ambling back toward the street.

◆◆◆

The house smells the same—a hint of bacon and dryer sheets, even though the dryer hasn't worked in months, and we haven't had bacon since the Crimson took over and we worked to build the perimeter around what is now the Palisade.

But it's like the walls are holding their breath, waiting for a return that will never happen.

My grandma's chair sits in the corner. No one has sat in it since she died. Her purse, still full of coupons and Tic Tacs, hangs on the hook by the door.

I walk into the back room I share with Vanessa, the one we always shared when we came to visit. The bedspread is a strange rust-orange cowboy print, and there are collectible plates with different Old West scenes mounted along the wall.

We talked about changing it up when we first made the Palisade. My grandma was fine with us making it our own. But then she died, and the idea of boxing her things up was just too much.

I toss the headdress onto the bed as I slink to the floor, exhaustion weighing heavy on my bones as I peel the T-shirt back and stare at the gold. I can't believe just this morning I was talking Dean into going with me to get it. He agreed because he's Dean, and he knew it was important to me. We risked our lives for this thing—more than we've risked our lives for anything up until this point.

The storm gathers outside as I reach under the mattress and pull out the notebook I keep tucked deep beneath it. I flip it open, tearing past the strange drawings and words etched in the margins.

I don't know when exactly I started writing down the things

Vanessa said in the middle of the night. It was after the night of the blood moon, but before my grandma died. I realized that Vanessa didn't remember the things she said or the shapes she drew out with her finger on the wall. She'd sit up, have what Harlow now calls an "episode," and then fall back asleep like nothing happened. I'd ask her about it in the morning, but she'd have no recollection.

I started keeping a record, thinking it would eventually make sense—maybe she was telling us something that could help.

The words blur as I flip through the pages.

Find him on the dark blue, 3A, the one with the teeth.

She said that three times, two weeks ago.

Then, she stood up and ran her finger over the wall over and over, her eyes still closed. I sat back and watched, sketching out the shape as best I could.

The way out, she said, hitting a fist to the wall twice before crawling back up to her pillow.

I turn the pages, running my fingers over the grooves the pen left in the paper.

His love pulls his loose threads. Loose threads loosely stitched. You'll see it before she does.

Glimpse to the water and you'll see fire.

Then, a week ago, she said something else.

Bordeaux. Bordeaux in the box. See.

Over and over. I woke, grabbed the notebook, and wrote it down. The next morning, as I helped Sergei wash the canned green beans, I kept thinking about it.

I'd heard that name before. It bothered me until lunchtime, when I remembered that I'd seen it in the museum—the head-dress was nicknamed the Bordeaux. Rumor was that it had belonged to Anne. And I knew where it was.

It was the first thing Vanessa said that might mean some-thing for the Curse—a riddle I felt I had solved. For a couple of days, I fought the rising hope that built in my chest—*maybe there's an answer.*

My fingers find the page with the words etched on it: *Bordeaux. Bordeaux in the box.*

I reach back and grab the headdress, bringing it into my lap. The soft gold shimmers in the low light from the window, and I lift it, angling it so I can look into the rubies. The dark red stares back, flat and lifeless. I turn it in my hands, running my fingers over the edges. I'm looking for words. Or numbers. Coordinates. A map. Something. *Anything.*

But it's just a headdress.

I don't realize how big the hope in my chest has grown until it crashes down into my lungs, taking all of my breath with it.

It was for nothing. That whole mission—that risk—was for nothing.

I drop the headdress, letting it clatter to the carpet with a dull thud as I gather my knees to my chest.

Your faith will save us all, Madame Menagerie had said.

I'd written it off, but maybe part of me hoped it was true at the time. That I'd find some great reason for all of this. Some point.

I lie down on the floor, looking up at the cracking plaster on the ceiling.

I don't hope we'll rebuild some kind, good world. I don't think this is a tapestry that's being woven—one I'll understand once it's done.

I think the only point of all of this is to survive.

Chapter 7

THE NIGHT AIR BITES AT ME AS I WALK OUT, AND I wrap my sweater closer as I step quietly across the driveway to the logs that now ring the fire pit in a semicircle. Vanessa sits alone, staring into the flames. I sit next to her.

She has dirt on her nose, and I know she probably went straight from her impromptu gym session to working in the garden. Vanessa doesn't do well with sitting still.

"You should get some dinner while it's . . . ." She thinks. "I won't say *edible. Available* works better," she says softly.

I snort.

"You okay?" I ask. She turns to me, her eyes finding mine. The light glitters in her brown eyes.

"Promise me you won't ever do that again, Charlotte," she whispers. I don't know how she knows. Harlow wouldn't tell her.

I take a breath, but Vanessa holds a hand out to stop me from explaining.

"I don't know what this is, inside me," she starts, "but you all are risking your lives being around me enough as it is. I can't have you trying to act on things I say. If something happened to you . . ."

I pull her into a hug. She fights it for the briefest moment, then sags against me.

"I hate this," she whispers into my shirt.

I hold her tight, resting my chin on her head. "I know."

"This wouldn't happen if we just told the Torch," she starts, and my arms go still around her. "Just *tell them* where I am. We won't be able to end this if I'm hiding out here like a child."

I pull her back, keeping my grip on her shoulders as I give her a soft shake. "You *are* a child, Vanessa."

Dean walks up then, a plate in his hands. Vanessa stands.

"I'm going to bed," she says, turning. She stops, looking at me sadly. "No one is a child anymore, Charlotte."

Before I can say another word, she's gone, walking toward the house.

Dean doesn't say anything as he sits next to me and hands me my plate. Two sad-looking Vienna sausages roll on the plate, bumping into a little scoop of garbanzo beans. We are running low on supplies, then. No one eats Vienna sausages on purpose.

I shake my head, but he doesn't take the plate back. "You missed dinner."

"I dodged a bullet," I say, looking at the plate and back up to him. He snorts and sets the plate on the log next to him.

It is quiet, the sound of the fire crackling mixing with the distant thunder that rolls over the ocean. I look out. The clouds over the water are light purple, churning and rolling over each other like smoke. But the air between the whitecapped water and the clouds is black, and seems to go on forever, like a mouth opening to the abyss.

The water is unforgiving. Wild. Hungry.

I turn to look into the flames, losing myself in the comfort of the heat and light.

"You didn't tell her," I say finally.

Dean rubs his hands together. "Tell her what?"

I look at him. His blue eyes look green in the firelight, his jaw shadowed. Pity sucks when it comes from Harlow. But coming from Dean? It's almost unbearable.

"That I didn't get into the fountain with you. That the Vessels tracked my scent," I say.

"It was a mistake," he says. He is throwing me an out. A way to pretend that the fear inside me hadn't been strong enough to almost kill me. Kill us.

"It wasn't a mistake, and you know it. I froze, just like I always do." I look back at the fire.

"You watched your younger sister almost drown, Charlotte. That will mess anyone up. I don't blame you one bit for being scared of water. Harlow understands that."

"It's not scared," I whisper, hoping the words are swallowed by flame. Dean reaches over and wraps his arm around my shoulder. It's a kind move—a platonic one. Something he would do for a sister. Which is what I am to him. My heart twists in my chest. "Scared is an aversion. Scared is . . . *I would rather not*. This is something else. This almost got you killed, Dean."

He drops his arm slowly and turns to the fire, leaning his elbows on his knees.

"You were the one in the clutches of the Vessel," he says quietly. "Because of me. Because you thought you could save me."

I know he didn't tell that part to Harlow, because there is no way that she would have lessened my sentence if she had known.

Death before the willful Crimson.

"Why did you do it?" he asks again.

I think about lying for a moment. Just long enough to turn to look at Dean.

The question crackles in the air between us, heavy as it rides the heat of the flames.

My Dean, even if he doesn't know it.

Thoughts flutter through my mind like snow. I know if I catch one on my tongue, it will disappear. I can't tell him that I love him. That I've loved him for years. I loved him when we fought on Halloween night when I was fourteen and he hurt my feelings by assuming I wanted to trick-or-treat when I asked to go to a party with him and Harlow. I loved him when I was fifteen and he punched out a guy who snapped Vanessa's bra at the movie theater. I loved the sound of his laugh and the way he sang off-key in the car. I loved him the whole time he'd been falling in love with Harlow.

I love him even though it feels like I am breathing splintered glass when he looks at me like he is looking at me now.

"You're my friend," I say finally. The simplicity of the words sounds false, like a chord struck wrong on a piano. I wonder if he can hear it.

Dean narrows his eyes for a second, and opens his mouth like he is going to say something. He reconsiders and then takes a breath. But before he can speak—

"Okay," Harlow's voice cuts in. "So tomorrow's supply run is going to be focused on finding more canned goods to save us from having to eat these little, tiny"—Harlow plops down on the log across from Dean and stabs a sausage with her fork, holding it up to the glow—"penises," she says at last.

Dean purses his lips as he glances down at my plate. "I hadn't thought of them like that," he whispers, his voice low.

"You wondered why I skipped dinner?" I ask.

Dean stabs the sausages with my fork and holds them out to me. "Hey. Food is food." He pops them into his mouth and smiles.

Harlow makes a face. "It's not the shape that gets me. It's the 'meat product' ingredient on the label. What is that exactly?"

"It's delicious, is what it is," Dean replies.

Harlow lowers her fork and regards me across the fire.

"Vanessa inside?" she asks. I nod. This was as close to closure as we were ever going to get.

We good? it asks.

My nod is a quiet acceptance of the tenuous truce. *We're good.*

Harlow nods and tosses another stick into the flames. The conversation dies, the air around us filling up with unsaid things.

Sometimes I wondered what would happen if I filled that void with the truth that fills my chest to the brim. What would happen if I opened my mouth and told them both. I wonder what kind of gasoline that would pour over the fire between us.

"Tomorrow. I'll need you to take lead," Harlow says to Dean.

"I'm out of the doghouse? Just like that?" he teases.

"If you weren't the best shot in the compound, you wouldn't be leaving this place for a month. But we've got orders, and I need you having my back." Her gaze is ruthless as she glares at him.

"Baby, I'll have whatever side of you I can get," Dean drawls, a smirk curling up at the corner of his lips.

"I'm serious," she bites out, and Dean's smile freezes. He straightens, almost imperceptibly.

"I'm sorry," he says. A sergeant to his commander.

The thunder rolls closer, and a bolt of white-hot lightning illuminates the horizon.

She looks to me, then back to Dean. "You two scared the shit out of me. I saw that Vessel, and—"

"Harlow," Dean cuts in. He leans forward more. "I'm sorry." A boyfriend to his girlfriend.

Harlow's glare softens. "I want to stay mad at you."

"I know. It's the worst, right?" His coy grin is back, his eyes raking over her.

Welp. That's my cue.

I stand as Dean gives me a nod, and Harlow walks around the fire and chucks her Vienna sausage at Dean's head. He catches it in his mouth.

I turn, hustling into the shadows at the sound of Harlow's shrieking laugh as Dean pulls her into his lap. They were always that way. Harlow is obsidian—sharp and cool. Dean is the fire.

"Next time I'll know better. I won't bring her out," he whispers. I hear it, just over the hissing of the log cracking and falling to pieces in the flames.

I halt, the words like weights on my feet.

I won't bring her. Like I'm a kid. Like I need his protection. Like I can't handle myself.

I can't even get mad at him for thinking that. For treating me like I need protection.

Because I do.

I froze, and it almost cost us both our lives.

Their laughter falls silent as I walk inside, toeing off my shoes by the front door. I creep down the hallway, stopping for a moment to check on Vanessa. She is sprawled out on her bed, her headphones still in. I wrap them up and pull the duvet over her shoulders.

Out of habit, I glance out the window above my bed. Harlow's fingers are tangled in Dean's hair as she twists in his lap. I duck, heat rising in my cheeks as I put my head on the pillow and press the heels of my hands to my eyes.

My tears taste like the ocean.

It's not that I don't dream. I dream a lot. But they've always been shallow—a tide pool of memories and bits of shimmery thoughts and remnants of a boy's smile or a weird line I heard in a movie.

But this feels different.

This is a memory, soaked in sadness and thick with the feel of sunscreen and salt.

I'm on the ocean, but the fear that usually coats the back of my throat is gone.

I'm on the boat, the one we had when we were kids—a small speedboat my father called the Batmobile.

It didn't make sense, and Harlow told him as much, but he didn't care. It was a small boat—so small that whenever we took it out of the marina and into the harbor, the slightest wave would send us all flying. We spent many summer days on that boat, eating melted peanut-butter-and-jelly sandwiches and pushing each other off the bow into the water.

I'd let the water pull me down until the sunlight was nothing but a dappled promise lofted above my head like the underside of a cathedral's belly. The water was quiet, a place where my thoughts drifted alongside me like my sun-lightened hair. The ocean was laughter ringing off the surface.

In the dream I feel the water coursing over my skin, coaxing the blood in my veins and the air in my lungs. Back and forth, in and out.

Swish, swish. Swish, swish.

Somehow, this dream pulled me back to a time when the water wasn't a thing of nightmares. Back when it was home.

Swish . . . thump.

Thump thump thump thump.

My eyes fly open, and I'm back in my bed.

I roll over in bed and pull the pillow over my head, cursing the proximity of my bedroom to Harlow's. Things are bad enough without me having to *hear* her and Dean.

Thump thump thump.

I throw the pillow down, irritation boiling in my gut as I sit up, ready to scream at them both for waking me up in this totally disgusting way.

But I freeze at the sight in front of me.

Vanessa is at the foot of my bed, her dark hair falling over her shoulders as she hits her head softly on the wall. Her hands are carved like claws, her nightshirt swishing around her thighs. I watch her, swallowing my scream back down.

Thump thump thump.

She's sleepwalking again.

"Nessa," I say, sliding out from under the covers as smoothly as I can. We know all the rules about sleepwalking and night terrors by now. Don't startle them awake. Don't yell. Just gently try and guide the person back to bed, and usually muscle memory takes over.

I reach for Nessa's hand, but she yanks away with startling force without breaking the rhythm of her head on the wall.

"Vanessa," I say louder, grabbing her hand. She spins around and drops to her knees on my bed, bouncing once before going still.

"Let's go back to bed," I whisper, and she looks straight at me.

I freeze, wondering for a moment if she's woken up. She tilts her head, studying me with those unseeing eyes, and I fight the urge to scream for Harlow.

"The silver whole brings the storm to the sea, the mirror on velvet brings the ships to their knees," she says quietly.

My stomach plummets, and angry tears spring up in my eyes. I bite them back and clench my teeth together so hard that I wonder if the grinding sound alone will wake Harlow and Dean. I put my hands on Vanessa's shoulders.

"The black veins lead to the heart," she says.

Her hands find mine then, like she's begging me to listen, even though she's not awake.

"Follow the black veins. Home will lead you to it."

I don't know who chose her for this. I spent my life going to church and believing in a creator with a grand plan. But I can't imagine why the fate of the whole world has to rest on my sister's shoulders. My sister, whose only concern up until two years ago was how to best keep her leotard from riding up during her routines. My sister, who hasn't even kissed anyone yet.

The fact that all this seems pointless—as well as painful—just stirs the anger in my gut. I shake her shoulders to get her to stop saying nonsense.

"Wake up," I order.

I used to think that Anne de Graaf was the coolest figure in history—a rebel, a trailblazer.

But in these moments, looking into Vanessa's glazed eyes . . . I hate her more than I've ever hated anyone.

Leave her alone. You've already destroyed the world. Leave this girl alone.

"Vanessa," I bark, and it startles her. Rules be damned— these aren't normal nightmares. She blinks once. Twice. Then she's awake.

"Go back to bed," I say, forcing lightness into my tone. She looks around, realization slinking over her expression as she climbs back into her bed. Within ten seconds, she's asleep again.

Everything is still, save the rain pelting the window. Outside, the fire pits are dark. I pull the notebook out from under my mattress and scribble the words in it, pushing so hard that the pen tears through the paper. I close it and toss it aside before curling back up into bed.

But I can't sleep.

There is this feeling, this heaviness that coats the air with dread.

It's a feeling I've worn often, and learned to wear well. I had long since stopped listening to it.

Something is wrong.

I've been feeling that since I was seven. *Something is wrong.*

It's a knot in my stomach that only medication could ease.

I stopped the meds before the world fell, and I wasn't about to add one more thing to the list of needs around here. I don't even know if Harlow would be able to find any.

It's the apocalypse. I assume everyone has an anxiety issue.

I try to go back to sleep. I try to tell myself that it is just dread.

But I can't.

I slink out from under the covers and creep down the hallway. I'm wearing an old T-shirt from my single, ill-fated season of soccer from four years ago. It still fits, and the team name, "GRASS-KICKERS," is emblazoned on the front— and I'm sporting some of Harlow's old cheer shorts with "U WISH" stamped in glitter paint across the butt. It's not my best look, but they're comfortable, and that's all I care about.

Lightning flashes, adding to the edge of panic. I push Harlow's door open, stopping at the sight of her curled up with Dean in the covers, both asleep.

His hand rests possessively around her waist, and she has a palm on his bare, muscled stomach. I turn away. I am not about to wake them.

I go to the kitchen, pulling a water bottle from under the counter and marking it on the sheet of paper nailed to the wall. We have to keep track of what we take. Outside, I see the perimeter wall from the kitchen window, with three guards stationed at the overlook.

I recognize the navy windbreaker. Kyle. He stands near

Davis and Elk, two guards with swords strapped across their backs.

I take a deep pull from the water bottle, trying to force the cool liquid to rinse the dread from my throat as I shut my eyes.

I lean over the kitchen sink, forcing myself to swallow.

I don't know what makes me look up just at that moment.

But I see Kyle fall, the shouts landing seconds after. Someone—something—beyond the wall just took him down. A scream sounds through the night, and the loud *pop* of a grenade. I drop to the floor, the water bottle spilling over the cracked kitchen tile.

I force myself to breathe as the image of Kyle falling replays in my mind on a loop. I have to do something.

I shoot up, careening down the hall as I scream Harlow's name.

Someone is coming. Some*thing* is coming.

And I don't know which one is worse.

I crash into the doorframe, and Harlow is already up, her walkie-talkie screeching out as the men at the wall call to her.

Dean tosses her blade to her, and she strings it over her back in one fluid movement, seamlessly pulling up her dark jeans and slipping her unlaced combat boots on.

Vanessa is in my doorway then, her eyes wide as she peers over my shoulder through the window. People are running down the street, armed and ready.

"Shit," she whispers, understanding crossing her face. She disappears, and I know she is getting ready.

We've prepared for this. We've survived it before. If it is a rogue band of Vessels, we'll cut them down. If it is a small group of Runners looking for Curseclean, we'll cut them down, too.

And if it's the Vessels we've been fearing? a voice in my head asks, and terror trickles down the back of my neck. I shove the bubbling dread down as I run to my room.

The Palisade isn't going to fall. We won't let it.

I pull my shoes on before tying my hair back. I grab my mirrored bands and secure them to my wrists and forearms. I think for a second, and drop to my knees near the bed. I grab the Bordeaux and the notebook, and throw them in a fanny pack that I strap to my stomach under my sweatshirt. Harlow and Dean leave her room, and I follow. Vanessa is behind me, a black hoodie pulled over her head.

Harlow turns. "Charlotte, stay here."

I blanch. The fear in my chest is a knotted vine, but I can't just stay and wait. I would rather face it. Vanessa and I protest at the same time.

"Hey, I don't need a babysitter, Harlow! Are you kidding me?" Vanessa cries.

"At least let me help Kyle. I saw him fall, Harlow—" I start, but she whirls on us, her eyes sharp.

"Get Vanessa to the bunker and stay there. That's an order. Both of you."

I shoot a pleading glance to Dean, but his expression is taut as he checks his knives and mirrored straps. This is a battle now. Any trace of the silly Dean is wiped away, and he isn't about to disagree with his commander.

They leave, not bothering to close the door behind them. A swell of chaos rips across the night, and I bite back the terror that ripples over me in response. I turn to my little sister, her dark eyes stark against her pale face.

There is defiance there, and I feel its twin spinning in my bones. I want to sprint out in the darkness—to show that I am more than the fear that chokes me.

But I stop, knowing that there is a good chance that I am not better than that. That Harlow is right to send me out of harm's way.

A blast rings out and I duck, pulling Vanessa close to me.

An orange glow slips in through the open door, and we look out the window.

My heart staggers to a standstill as the realization washes over me. They've blown the front gate over.

Runners never risk attacking an armed settlement, and there are plenty of drifting people to keep the Vessels fed.

There was no logical reason for the attack. Except—

I turn to look at Vanessa, her gaze reflecting the light as she stares out the front door.

Unless they know she's the Chosen One.

She opens her mouth, but I don't give her time to think. I wrap her frozen fingers in mine and pull, yanking her behind me as we run through the house. I snatch a blindfold and a mirror off the back counter, and then we barrel out the back door. The rain is lighter, more of a misting than an actual rainfall.

Still, I'm soaked in seconds.

I give the blindfold to Vanessa. She starts to argue, but I glare over my shoulder. "Now."

Fear overtakes her irritation, and she puts it on.

The bunker is along the edge of the perimeter, three houses from us. If we stay low, I can get her there. I can get her safe. We slip through the backyard, the wet grass whipping across my shins. I chance a glance at the fence. Figures wreathed in shadow slide through the opening, and the ring of blades sounds through the night. Shouts echo, and I wonder which voices belong to Harlow. To Dean.

My stomach tightens at the thought.

I'll get Vanessa to safety, and then I'll go back. I can help.

I hold the mirror out in front of me as Vanessa and I sprint along the edge of the back fence, ignoring another burst of orange light that blows up the night. Ignoring the screams that ripple through the air.

"Charlotte, we can't just hide," Vanessa whispers, her breathing ragged, though I can't tell if it's from the sprint or the sobs she's holding back.

My hand tightens on hers as we follow the cement water run. "We will listen to Harlow, Vanessa," I hiss over my shoulder. By the time I get her to the bunker and in the arms of Marjorie and the others, she won't have a say about me taking off to join the fight.

The wooden fence to my left ends, and the emptiness around us makes my chest tighten. We're out in the open.

A wet rustle sounds from the side of Marjorie's house, and I careen to a stop just in time to see a hooded figure step out from under the overhang. A black bandanna is tied around the lower half of her face. I look down, but not before I see the flash of a blade. Vanessa and I run, but another figure steps out from the shrubbery behind the fence, blocking our path.

I feel the edge of the blade at my back.

"Hello, sweetheart," a deep, sensuous voice croons behind me.

Chapter 8

I TURN, MY EYES SHUT, VANESSA'S TREMBLING fingers clasped in my fist.

"Please," the woman says. "If I wanted to kill you, I would have. Open your eyes."

I'm not stupid. I keep my eyes shut. But she raises the blade and holds it to my throat, pressing the metal to my collarbone, and I don't have a choice. She is right. She could kill me either way. I open my eyes and look to Vanessa—they've taken her blindfold off, too.

The woman's yellow eyes meet mine, and my breath catches. It isn't the startling shade of yellow against her pale skin that throws me. It's not that she's Xanthous, or that she presses the blade deeper against my skin as my jaw sets.

It's that I recognize her.

Maddox Caine.

The most notorious Runner on this side of the Pacific. Here. In our compound.

Her jet hair is cropped short. A scar cuts through the edge of her right eyebrow, stark against the smoky coal she smudged around it. Her full lips curl up in a smile as she takes in my horrified look. Her nose turns up slightly at the end, giving her an elvish look.

"Let her go," Vanessa says from behind me, but I redouble my grip on her wrist, begging her to be quiet. They can't figure out who she is, and that will be a lot easier if Vanessa doesn't draw attention to herself.

Even though it doesn't really matter, and I know that some-where deep in my bones.

If Maddox Caine is here, it's probably already over.

Maddox jerks her chin, and a second blade presses into my back.

"Move," she says, and three figures in black appear behind us. None of them use mirrors or blindfolds—there's no need to. They're all Xanthous. One grabs Vanessa, and the other flanks us, blade out. We walk across the grass, between Marjorie's and Sergei's houses. When we reach the main street, I see the full horror the night has wrought.

The mist of the lightly falling rain creates bright, hazy halos around fires that light up the night all around us. Screams fill the air, thickening the terror blooming in my chest.

Ahead, at the perimeter, the gate hangs off its hinges. Bodies lie in the street, unmoving.

My eyes scan the foggy dark, desperately looking for Dean and Harlow. I can't see anything. The guard grabs my shoulder.

They will plunder everything and burn our homes. Then they will march every Curseclean person down to their ship— the *Devil's Bid*. And we will be shipped off to the Blood Market, to be sold as food to Vessels or as answers to Exposed.

"Girls!" a familiar voice screams. I look over just in time to see Malcolm racing toward us, his machete at his side. His shirt is soaked, and blood drips down his arm. I can't tell if it's his.

He eyes Maddox. "Let them go," he says.

Maddox lets out a snort laugh and clasps her hands in front of her. "That's going to be a no, old man," she says. "Turn around if you want to survive this night."

Malcolm smiles now, and it's hollow. Hopeless. It looks wrong on him, and it makes my stomach churn. "You think I'm stupid? You think I don't know where you're taking all of us?" He twirls his machete.

Maddox freezes then, looking back at Vanessa and me for a moment before turning back to Malcolm. "See, that's where you're wrong. Turns out, lucky for you—we aren't here to restock."

A chill that sweeps through me as my darkest fear is confirmed. There is only one thing more valuable than Curseclean.

I look to Vanessa, her dark hair hanging in her eyes, the terror in them unmistakable.

A dark understanding flickers in my gut. No. It's not possible.

"Liars," Malcolm spits. "You're Runners. You're only here for one thing."

Maddox levels her gaze at Malcolm once more. "Usually? Yes. But we've been hired for a different reason. We're looking for someone. Been looking in these parts for a while. You kept this little haven hidden for a long time—you should feel very, very proud of that. If we hadn't found two dead Vessels on the tile of that museum and used our hounds to track that smell back here? You would have stayed that way."

Ice grips my spine, and it feels like the world falls out from under me.

My fault. This is all my fault. This whole invasion. All this destruction. My fault.

I don't have time to shout as a man with a wide, crooked smile comes out of the shadows behind Malcolm. I open my mouth a half second too late, and the scream comes out not as a warning but like someone is wringing terror from my bones as the man runs Malcolm through with a spear.

I hear Vanessa shriek next to me, the shredding sound enough to wrench another yell from me as my knees give way. The guard behind me keeps me upright, his wiry fingers digging into my arms.

The man behind Malcolm yanks the spear back and steps around Malcolm to join Maddox.

"Malcolm!" I cry. The old man meets my eyes as he brings his hands up to the wound in his stomach, touching it like he almost doesn't believe it.

Tears mingle with the rain as I pull, trying desperately to break from the guard's grip.

"No," I breathe, watching helplessly as the light in Malcolm's eyes dims. Watching helplessly as he slumps to the ground.

The air feels stagnant and heavy as I heave it in and out of my lungs. The guards pull me to my feet, and Maddox looks down our fire-lined street once more before motioning for the guards.

"We got the other," the bald man—the one who murdered Malcolm—says. Maddox motions to the guards, and we're moving again. Vanessa sobs as she looks at Malcolm's body, and tries to twist out of the guard's grasp.

Malcolm is dead. The man who had let us in here. Who had given us shelter when we had nothing. The man who had loved my grandmother lies dead in the street, his blood mixing with the rain and pooling in the gutter.

And it's all my fault.

As we walk, part of me is grateful that the poison of those words won't fully mix with my blood, my eyes turning to fix on the back of Maddox's neck, where a tattoo in a language I don't understand sits inked over her vertebrae. I know the reality of it will hit soon enough, and I can't fully fathom the damage it will cause. I don't know what will be left of my soul when the tidal wave hits.

I thought we would keep going forward—toward the gate. Toward the ship, and the Blood Market.

But they pull us into darkness, shoving Vanessa and me into the school auditorium.

Only one light is on, casting a strange shadow into the cavernous room. In the middle, a girl sits. I see her white-blond hair first, her head dipped toward the ground as she crouches on her knees before two men who hold blades dangerously close to her neck.

For a moment, she looks so small and helpless that I don't recognize her.

"Harlow!" Vanessa shrieks beside me. My voice snags in my throat, but I let out a small whimper of relief at the sight of her. At least she is alive. My eyes scan the edges of the auditorium, looking for Dean. He's not here.

I shut my eyes for a moment.

Survive now. Then find him.

I have to deal with what is in front of me.

Harlow looks up at the sound of us entering, and I gasp at her face. A bruise blooms over her cheekbone, and blood drips from her nose.

The guard spins me around and shoves me to my knees, pain screaming up through my legs as I hit the floor. Vanessa lands hard next to me. Everything is quiet as three more of Maddox's guards filter in, and she follows. She shuts the door, the slam echoing through the room.

"Do you know what is interesting, ladies? May I call you ladies? Madames? Job, what is the proper way to address the subjects of a prophecy?"

Maddox looks to the wall, where the bald man who had killed Malcolm now stands, cleaning his spear. He shrugs.

"I told you. I don't know what you're talking about,"

Harlow grinds out, defiance glittering in her eyes. I wonder, for a moment, if Maddox had told Harlow how they found this place. I wonder, for a moment, if my sister knows I am the reason all of this is happening. If we live through this, if we can ever piece our lives back together after tonight, I know that this is something I can never escape. My cowardice the night Vanessa almost drowned had marked both of us, but at least no one had died.

Tonight that isn't true.

Maddox kneels in front of us. "Come on, now. I've been honest with you. The least you can do is cut the bullshit. We've been looking for quite some time, you know. And then . . ." She smiles. She's not going to tell us how she found out.

"The answer to the Crimson, sitting here all this time." Her voice holds a note of incredulity as she steps back. "But not for long."

I look at Harlow, a question in my eyes. *What are we going to do?* I beg silently.

And for the first time since before I can even remember, the fear reflecting in my big sister's eyes tells me that not even she knows.

"You would turn against your own kind?" Vanessa asks. She's caught on. We're buying time. I force myself not to look out the windows, to beg the shadows to move. To beg help to come.

Maddox leans down then, her eyes feral. There's no smirk, no hint of the cat toying with mice. Just amber ice and a sneer.

"Even before Vessels existed, humans have *never* been my kind. The world has done nothing to deserve my allegiance. It's done everything to earn my judgment."

Those cold eyes glance to Harlow, the unnatural color even more unsettling from the side.

"Tell me which one of you it is, and this won't have to hurt," she says. I try to hide my surprise, and know Harlow does the same. Maddox knows it's one of us, but she doesn't know which.

She doesn't think the fact that we are sisters could mean anything. She assumes our survival instinct will override any loyalty. That kind of thing was for the world long past.

Everything seems to slow down. I can feel the stillness on my left as Vanessa braces herself. If she gives herself up to the Vessels, she could be the destruction of the entire world. She's the only one who can find Anne's Heart. And then, the only one who can stop this. Without her, the curse has no end. The weight of humanity's fate balances in her mind, tethered to the lives of her sisters. I can feel her slow intake of breath. On my right, I feel Harlow's fingers inch for her boot, for the blade she keeps tucked in there.

She will swing for Maddox, and she'll die.

World-ending surrender on one side, and life-ending violence on the other.

I sit between them, the answer like an ember on my tongue. A thought unspools in my mind. It's a half-formed idea, the spark of madness. It grows, fast-moving tendrils of wildfire, lashing against the edges of my terror.

I breathe in faster, my voice finding air before either of my sisters can move. Before either of them can ink their names on their death warrants, I sign mine.

I shove myself to my feet, and the guards around Maddox spring into action, pulling their blades from their hilts and their guns from their holsters.

Maddox narrows her catlike eyes at me, and I look down at Harlow.

Only years with her allow me to see the shock flickering over her face. She swallows hard, the question in her eyes flashing almost as fast as her strategic mind can figure out what I've just done.

"I'm the Chosen One," I breathe.

Chapter 9

MADDOX'S EYES FIND MINE.

I don't look at Vanessa or Harlow, but I hear Vanessa take a breath, and I pray she isn't about to try and contradict me. But she doesn't get the chance, because another explosion—a louder one this time—rips through the night.

The wall behind us caves, and everything erupts into chaos. My ears ring, and I fight to see in the blaze of light and rubble. Vanessa and Harlow are on the other side of the chairs, with Harlow shielding Vanessa from the blast. Harlow's eyes find mine, and she scrambles to her feet.

"Torch Enforcers!" someone yells, and I hear Maddox let out a rage-filled curse as she grabs my arm and yanks.

Harlow starts to run after me, but another blast hits the building, and she falls.

"Get her safe!" I scream over my shoulder. Maddox looks

behind as she drags me and stops to lift her gun and point it directly at Harlow, who glares in defiance. I shriek, pulling at Maddox's iron grip. She holds fast.

"You're lucky right now. We have what we came for, and don't have time for any more. But if you follow us, I swear you won't get lucky twice, and I'll blow your head off." Harlow looks at me, her eyes shining with rage and tears.

"Get her safe," I repeat, and she gives me a shallow nod. Behind her, Vanessa realizes what we're doing—that we're letting this happen, and she screams as she rushes forward. Harlow grabs her, putting a hand over her mouth as she drags her toward the opposite door.

We run through the dark, Maddox's fingers like a vise around my arm. I catch a glimpse of the Torch Enforcers on the main street—their gray suits working side by side with our people. Maddox keeps us to the shadows and out of sight, though I can see everything. I bite the tip of my tongue to keep from crying out as they lead me through the ruined husk of my home. The houses are burned out, and bodies litter the street. Maddox steps over them like nothing.

Kyle lies still in the street, his eyes open as the rain pelts his body. I don't realize I've stopped walking until someone shoves me from behind. I step over my friend, fighting the urge to reach down and close his eyes.

"Move," Maddox orders, and I rake my eyes over the bodies, searching for Dean.

I take in the still forms of friends and neighbors—people

who have shared our fire and fought with us to make a new life out of the shadow of a dying world.

People who have died because I led Maddox here.

I step over another body—Sergei—and walk past the gate.

I am numb for the whole ride, which lasts an hour or ten minutes, I don't know.

Maddox opens the back door before I even realize we've stopped moving, and she yanks me from the van with one pull.

"That way," she says, and I look around. The rain has let up, but only a little. And we are at the opening of a pier—one that used to be a tourist attraction. At the end amidst the shadows of the dark water and flurry of whitecaps is the *Devil's Bid*—the ship that transports Curseclean to the Blood Market.

I turn around, weighing my nonexistent options.

Harlow will have gotten Vanessa to safety by now. They'll be headed to the rendezvous point that every member of the Palisade knows by heart. Every second I'm with Maddox is another second they have to get away. Something catches my eye about fifty feet down the beach, beyond the pier. I didn't see it when I walked up. There is a line of people standing by the rocks, guards surrounding them. Some have guns, and some hold torches aloft. I peer into the ocean just as another boat, smaller than the *Devil's Bid* but still one for cargo, drops anchor just beyond the shore.

"What is that?" I ask as one of the guards steps forward, casting light on the people. They are tied up. Captured. Then I see him.

His arms are secured in front of him, the guard pointing the muzzle to his back to keep him from fighting. Alan is in front of him, straining against the bonds that keep his wrists tied together.

"DEAN!" I scream, yanking myself from my captor's grip. I sprint, hearing my guard swear loudly behind me as I take off running.

Dean's eyes search the pier, confusion until he finds me. His eyes widen, fear and rage filling his face.

"Char!" he screams back. I book it, not knowing anything other than the need to get to him. I take off down the strip of sand that runs parallel to the abandoned highway.

Dean. My Dean, tied up with dozens of other men I've never seen before, blood smeared on his face. He pushes against the guard, who responds by hitting him across the face with the butt of the gun.

I scream his name again, my mind racing. They are taking Dean. They are selling him, along with dozens of other Curse-clean.

A weight hits me from behind, and I see black spots in my vision as I hit the ground, a rock digging painfully into my thigh. Dean roars as Maddox flips me over, braced on top of me.

I kick as hard as I can, all the blood and hate from the past hour distilling inside me as a single rage-filled scream.

Maddox presses her blade to my throat as her gaze glitters with barely constrained rage in the moonlight.

For the first time, it doesn't scare me. "Let them go!" I shriek.

The guards catch up then, one holding a stout torch. Maddox hefts me to my feet, turning me to face the group as she presses her blade to my throat. A rowboat pulls up to the shore, and the guards behind the Curseclean usher them forward.

Dean fights, and the guard has to press the muzzle of the gun to the back of his neck to get him to move. He does, his eyes fixed on me as he steps into the surf.

"You said you weren't taking anyone else!" I cry.

Maddox runs a hand through her hair. "Sure. That wasn't the *plan*, per se. But I'm never going to turn down an opportunity to sell more cargo. Especially when *that* guy was a *particular* pain in my ass," she says. "I've never seen a man fight with a metal straw, but he managed to stab *two* of my best guys."

Behind me, one of the Runners whimpers, as if to confirm.

I press against her blade, and warmth trickles over my collarbone.

Maddox whips me around and shoves me backward, right back into the guard's arms. She looks back as the crew rows the Curseclean back to the ship, an insufferable smirk slipping back over her mouth.

"Oh. I'm sorry. Was that guy . . . yours?"

Hatred rages in my chest like a fire. If I was Harlow, I'd kick her ass. I'd wipe that smirk off her face with some sort of spin-kick she'd never see coming.

"You think you've seen it all, little princess? You think it couldn't get any worse than your boy getting shipped off to die?"

Maddox pushes a tongue past her red lips and runs it over the blade still slick with my blood.

My jaw clenches so hard I feel like my teeth will crack as she leans closer, her voice hissing past her teeth in a menacing whisper.

"It can get worse. I can devote all my time and energy into finding your sisters and gutting them like fish. You threaten me again, you pull a stunt like that again? You'll understand that there are corners of the darkness that you've never walked. There are horrors that have barely reached your imaginings, let alone your realities. So I couldn't give a *shit* if you're the Chosen One. I had the sea when the world was standing, and I have it now that it's on its knees. It makes no difference to me. Defy me again and I will make you pay."

I watch as the ship weighs anchor. I watch as it pulls out into the harbor with Dean in the hull. I watch as the man I love slips into the waves, his life as forfeit as mine.

"Fuck you," I breathe, a laugh riding my voice.

She lets out a small sigh of annoyance before lashing out and clocking me across the face.

The last thing I see is her pitiless eyes before everything goes black.

Chapter 10

I WAKE ALL AT ONCE, PANIC BITING UP THE BACK of my throat. There's a small stream of water hitting me in the face. I sputter, gasping as I arch off the concrete beneath me. I roll over, coughing and choking, my fingernails scratching the floor of the cell.

A cell. That's where I'm at, and I realize it as I look around.

It's small—no bigger than a walk-in closet, with bars on either side. I shove myself up, my head throbbing from where Maddox hit me. I'm still in my pajamas, and they're bloodstained and damp, with a splotch across the center of "GRASS-KICKERS." And all my mirrored bands are gone.

Maddox stands on the other side of the bars, an empty cup in her hand. Two of her guards stand next to her, smirks on their faces. I immediately flip my eyes to the floor. Daylight streams in from the barred door above, and I wince away from it.

"She wakes," she croons.

The memories from the night before come flooding back, drenching my mind with a fresh wave of terror and dread.

My sisters got away.

Malcolm is dead.

Dean.

"Where are they taking him?" I bite, shoving myself up. I scramble to the bars as Maddox slips back—just out of reach. Her smile widens.

Maddox steps forward. The streams of soft sunlight fall on her raven hair, making it look blue. "You already know."

The Blood Market. My lips quiver, and I press them between my teeth. Dean's going to the Blood Market.

"Wow. You've got it bad. So much concern for him, and not one question about where we're taking *you*?" she asks.

I meet her eyes, trying my best to hide the fear in them.

"Not somewhere I'm going to survive," I whisper. "You wouldn't be taking the Chosen One to the Torch—Runners aren't welcome there. So the only other option is that you're giving me to them."

Maddox purses her lips, impressed. "You know how much they'll pay to get rid of the one thing that can stop them?"

I don't answer, and she leans closer. "A *lot*," she whispers.

"How did you know where to find me?" I ask, hoping that she'll be in the mood to brag. But instead, she leans back.

"Curious, huh? Well. I think you're in luck. You and I? We can help each other."

124

I clench my hands on the bars and look around. The floor of the cell is a strange yellow linoleum that's peeling up at the edges and covered with mystery stains. It smells like it was once a fishing boat. I angle my eyes toward the ceiling—the bars look newly installed. The salty air wafts in, ruffling Maddox's black shirt. I'm not stupid. Things can absolutely get worse.

But not by much.

I turn to Maddox, a weird calm slinking over my shoulders as I imagine Dean next to me. His wide shoulders and deep, reassuring laugh. I let rage gather in my bones, overwhelming the fear.

"I'm not doing *shit* for you," I say finally.

Maddox sighs, gesturing for her guards to open the cell.

"Fine. We'll do this my way." Maddox pivots, heading up the stairs toward the deck.

The guards grab me by my arms and haul me after her.

I blink against the bright light as we step out onto the surface. We're on an old, repurposed fishing boat, and the harsh winds are whipping through the rigging. Maddox's crew fills the deck. Some are cleaning, while others tie bands of rope. I shiver, thinking about what it will be used for. They all stop to watch as Maddox saunters over to the railing. The guards push me after her.

I look down at the dark, churning water, frothing white where the *Devil's Bid* cuts over the waves. My heart beats faster as I picture the guards throwing me to the fathoms below.

She closes her eyes and takes a deep breath, letting it out

slowly before turning to me. "Where is Anne's Heart, Chosen One?"

I blink at her, trying to figure out her play without giving away the fact that I don't know anything. It makes me wish I'd taken Dean up on his offer to teach me poker.

"You're going to double-cross them," I say tentatively. "I don't know how long you'll survive if they go to get it and it's not there."

Maddox snickers. "I didn't survive this long without backup plans."

"I'll tell you, and you'll let me go?"

Maddox laughs now. It's an easy sound, one that might be pleasant under different circumstances. "Oh no, no, no. You're gonna die. But I'll give *this* back."

She pulls my notebook out from the band of her pants and holds it up. My throat constricts, and I reach for it in a blind panic. Maddox rears back, taking the notebook with her. The pages whip frantically in the wind. "I'm keeping the necklace. It's got to be worth something."

"Give it back," I cry.

"I tried to read it, and"—she lets out a low whistle—"if you weren't going to be torn limb from limb in a couple days, I'd suggest getting some professional help."

I look at the notebook as she holds it out over the edge of the boat. "I don't know what all this means, or why it's important. But clearly, it is. So tell me where to find the Heart."

If I tell her somewhere fake, she'll realize I've lied. They'll go after Vanessa and Harlow. That's going to happen anyway once the Vessels get me, but Maddox just said it will be a couple of days. That time could be the difference between them getting away and them getting caught.

Everything I know is on those pages, but I'm not going to survive long enough to figure anything out.

Still, the thought of losing any lingering hope of cracking the code and saving the world feels like a kick to the chest.

Maddox sees the conflict on my face, and I feel a decision click into place. It's better that it's gone forever than in her hands. If I'm going to die, then it's best that the notebook is gone.

"No," I say.

Maddox narrows her eyes and then throws the notebook over the side. I let out a small cry as it flips, end over end, landing in the bubbly ocean below.

She walks by me, stopping to whisper in my ear. "I was going to leave before she ripped you open. But now? I might just watch."

Maddox jerks her chin, and her guards drag me back to the cell. They toss me inside, and I don't fight, because my mind is reeling from the word she said.

The *Devil's Bid* isn't just bringing me to the Vessels. Maddox Caine is delivering me to the Vessel Queen herself.

Chapter 11

I LOSE COUNT OF THE DAYS.

Every couple of hours, they bring me to the deck to hose me off, and leave me to dry by tying my hands to the railing. I shiver, looking down at the water as I press my cheek to the metal and breathe. That's the only measure of time I have now, and it's the only positive thing I can really focus on. I'm breathing.

Above, a gull screeches, and I watch it dive into the water, the white foam stark against the gray-blue of the waves. I taste the salt on my tongue and close my eyes. It reminds me of movie popcorn. Of the times when I would snuggle in the dark next to Harlow and get lost in a story. Back when I wished I could go on an adventure of my own.

I would have wished for something different if I knew it would be like this.

The only thing that gives me hope is that every minute I keep this up is another minute I draw the attention away from Harlow and Vanessa, giving them a chance to get to the Torch.

And maybe Harlow will realize where Dean is. And maybe she'll have time to go save him.

Even if that's a long shot, the thought that they're far away gives me peace as I sit and shudder in the wind. If anyone could pull that off, it's Harlow.

Maddox asks me, each time, if I've changed my mind. Each time, I'm quiet.

Maybe the sixth time—maybe the tenth, I don't know—she pulls her dogs from their kennels below. She brings them to where I'm zip-tied to the railing with my arms over my head, each of them pulling on the rope she's looped around their collars. A bag hangs from her belt loop, and it swings against her legs as she climbs the steps. They look like they're German shepherd mixes, and they're friendly enough as they sniff my feet and lick my toes, but I turn my body as much as I can, holding my breath.

"Ragnar and Pollux. Cute, huh?" she asks. I tense as the bigger of the two, Pollux, leans in. He smells like a dog, and I try to reconcile that otherwise comforting smell with the terror that's spinning in my chest. He sniffs my nose, and I go very still, which is hard to do when I'm shivering so badly. Satisfied, the dog turns away, and I breathe again.

Maddox sinks to the deck next to me, and then, without a word, pulls a hunk of raw meat out of the bag. The dogs snap to attention, rapt expressions fixed on the still-bloody hunk. She tosses the meat to the floor, and whistles once. The dogs rush forward, ripping into the meat with startling ferocity. Maddox rests her arms on her knees, silent as she watches her pets shred the flesh. I peer out from behind my elbows, trying and failing to control my quivering muscles.

Pollux has blood smeared over his snout, and Ragnar growls as he pulls at what I think is a tendon.

I realize, as I look at the pinkness of the meat, that it might not be an animal.

"You know being eaten by a carnivore is actually designed *not* to hurt that badly?" Maddox muses. I keep my breathing steady as she tilts her head, surveying her beasts. "Their teeth are made for killing. If this thing was alive, Ragnar would've bit the throat out before starting in—and it would've been quick."

Pollux gets too close, and Ragnar snarls viciously. The smaller dog backs off.

"But human teeth are different. We're omnivores. We *can* eat meat, but a bulk of our teeth are flat, for crushing plants." She turns to me, pulling her lips back with a finger to show me. "So, being eaten by a human is . . . a lot worse than this." She gestures to the dogs.

I feel the fear uncoil in my throat like a living thing, and I force myself to shut my mouth and close my eyes. The sounds still rocket through my chest, and I can't help but imagine what it will feel like to be torn apart. I open my eyes, because the reverberating sound of tearing meat and growls is worse on its own.

Maddox leans her head back, resting it against the railing.

"I'll make you a deal. You tell me where the Heart is, and I'll kill you." She turns her head to me, keeping it tilted back.

"Won't the Vessels kill you for that?" I ask. The second I loosen my jaw, it clatters together in uncontrollable shivers. I glance up—my fingers are blue. Maddox shrugs. The meat skitters too close to us, and she kicks it away with a heavy boot. The dogs follow it.

"We have an understanding. I'm more valuable to them alive than dead. I'll just say you threw yourself overboard. They still get what they want. No Chosen One."

Ragnar hits bone and latches on, his jaw working and letting out a soft squelching sound with every bite.

Maddox flicks open her knife and stabs it into the deck between us. Her blade teeters back and forth, and I watch it through the puffs of steam my breath leaves as it slips past my lips.

"It won't hurt," she whispers. Her words are soft, and my gaze travels up her toned arms, stopping at her eyes. I try to imagine her in a world before this, but it seems like she was built for this chaos. Even her softness wouldn't quite fit any-where but here, in a situation where the kindest thing she can think of is slitting my throat.

I open my mouth, not sure what I'm going to say. My teeth click together.

But I don't get to say anything, because someone calls to her and points over the water. I see it—a small boat. It almost looks like a ferry. My blood goes cold with the hungry look that passes across Maddox's face, her hunting instincts kicking in.

Maddox pulls the knife from the deck and stands, giving a motion with her hands that all her crew seem to understand. They move in sync. A deadly, well-oiled machine.

"Think about it," she says. "Once we pass the coastline, there won't be any turning back."

They take the boat with a sort of lethal efficiency, leaving me tied to the railing as they usher dozens of people into the levels below. I thought the sound of the meat was bad, but it's nothing compared to the despairing cries from people who recognize the name of this ship. People who know where they're going now.

After what feels like hours, someone comes and pulls me to my feet. They take me below, and I trip into my cell. I keep my eyes down, hating the feeling of helplessness that comes without my mirrors. I sink to the floor, staying as close to the corner as I can.

"You okay?" a female voice asks. I keep my eyes to the ground.

There's movement in my periphery, and she speaks again from the cell next to mine.

"Hey. Use my mirrors. We're safe." I lift my eyes slowly and see that she's kneeling, sticking her arm through the bars. It's wrapped in leather straps, all covered in bits and pieces of glass. In the reflection, I can see her—a pale girl with a tangled mass of blond hair and yellow eyes staring at me through the bars.

She tilts it so I can see the other person in the cell with her has the opposite coloring—she has dark skin and sharp cheekbones and leans on the bars, facing the stairs. Even without her turning toward me, I can see that her eyes are the same stark color. Xanthous.

"You good?" the blond girl asks. I nod once, and she lowers her arm.

"Why do you have those if you're safe?" I ask softly before I can stop myself. She shrugs.

"I wasn't always." She considers this for a moment. "And, you know, not everyone is."

I turn to look forward, trying to process this. Kindness feels odd. Misplaced somehow. Malcolm's words sound in the back of my mind. *We can't save humanity if we lose ours.*

I shake the thought away, because I can't hear his voice without seeing everything else, like the moment I lost him.

"You okay?" the blond girl asks.

Her companion doesn't even bother to look and see who her companion is talking to before chiming in.

"Rielle, we're all on a Runner ship. You can assume that everyone here is decidedly *not* okay," she says.

"I was talking about her blue lips, Lucia," the blond girl, Rielle, says, her tone mocking. "And the fact that she was tied to the railing before we got here. That's an oddly personal way to treat Curseclean."

I wrap my arms around myself as Lucia moves closer to the bars. She's Xanthous, but that doesn't make her safe. "Where did they pick you up?" Rielle asks as she pushes herself back to her feet and pulls her sweatshirt over her head.

My survival—and the survival of those I love—seems to be solely predicated on the lies I tell and the information I now withhold. I don't know what is safe to say anymore and what isn't. Rielle tosses something through the bars, and her sweatshirt lands softly in my lap.

I stare at it for a second, almost like I'm waiting for the catch. I want to refuse it, because I don't know what she wants in return. But I'm so cold I don't really care. And we can't be far from my fate, at this point. It won't matter what they know.

"Malibu," I say quietly. "A little south of Malibu."

Lucia raises her dark eyebrows. "And Maddox Caine raided Malibu and took only . . . you?"

I nod. The mixture of hunger and thirst and cold has me feeling lightheaded. "She took me. But another ship took other people. They took Dean."

I feel them move but don't look. I don't have the energy.

Lucia turns away, and Rielle lowers herself again, her weight leveraged against the bars until she's crouched next to them beside me.

"Is he your boyfriend?" she asks. My eyes dart over to her—the mess of blond curls covering the right side of her face as she tilts her head.

She meets my eyes, and she can read confusion on my face. "The boy," she clarifies.

"Dean," I offer again, tucking my knees to my chest and

pulling the sweatshirt over them. The warmth wakes me up a bit, and I feel the blood in my hands again.

"He is," Rielle says, crossing her legs in front of her as she pulls a lock of her hair through her fingers. "I can tell by the way you talk about him."

A prickly feeling starts in the back of my neck—an awareness that this girl might not be prying just because she's interested. Everyone has another motive these days.

"He's not my boyfriend," I counter, irritation taking over. "He's my *sister's* boyfriend."

Rielle tilts her chin down, a smile curving up her lips conspiratorially. "Okay, well I want to hear *that* story," she says.

"Shut up, both of you," Lucia says from the corner of her cell, bringing her watch to her ear like she's trying to see if it's still working.

"Come on, Lucia. It wouldn't kill you to learn to make friends," Rielle hisses over her shoulder.

"It could, actually, yes. Have you learned nothing in the end of the world?" Lucia retorts.

"We're not friends," I cry incredulously, pushing myself to my feet, my eyes still on Rielle. Her brows are knitted together in something like confusion, and I feel a pang of regret. I lean forward. "We're on the *Devil's Bid*. You've been captured by Maddox Caine, and you're Xanthous. You are of no use to her."

Rielle flicks her eyes to Lucia, whose eyes narrow slightly at the harshness of my words. But they don't argue, and I look around to make sure no one else can hear. "The lock on the door leading to the deck sticks, and they usually don't pull it twice to make sure it's shut. So the *second* they open your cell, run for it. There's a clear shot to the railing on the left-hand side." I look up to the standing girl, the one named Lucia. "Haul ass, and jump over. It's your only option."

Just then, as though I'd summoned her, the metal door on the far end of the brig swings open. It lets out a low groan as Maddox steps inside, flanked by two guards. She walks down the line of cells, her gait as smooth as any predator's. I scoot away from the bars. I don't want her to know we were talking.

My breath catches in my throat as her eyes fall on me, her taut expression unreadable.

Did she figure out I've been lying? Or is it finally time?

"But that's the thing," Lucia breathes out quietly, lowering her wrist from her ear as she steps back, eyeing the ceiling of the cell. "We weren't captured."

That's the exact moment Maddox stops walking suddenly, and her eyes aren't on me.

They're on Lucia and Rielle.

Maddox's eyes widen.

"What the *hell* are you doing here?" she shouts, and then everything goes dark.

Chapter 12

THE BRIG ERUPTS AS I SHOVE MYSELF BACK INTO the corner of my cell. Metal creaks open, and the sound of boots scuffing on the ground mixes with Maddox's shouting orders and the other prisoners yelling.

The dark makes everything feel louder, the terror and confusion of the murky shadows amplifying every sound. We're in a metal tube atop an endless ocean. We're *locked* in a metal tube atop an endless ocean.

Panic brushes up against the back of my throat like a flame, and I shut my eyes tight against it.

Not now.

But the panic is there, making everything move slowly and too fast at the same time. I push myself up, feeling around the cell for the door. If there's any chance of me getting free of this place, it's happening right now—and I won't let it slip away because I can't control my own mind.

I walk around the cell, my hands brushing against cold steel in the dark.

The lights snap back on, and I spin around, squinting against the light as I take in the scene through Rielle's mirror. I'm facing Lucia and Rielle's cell. A crack sounds, and Rielle pulls Lucia against the bars as the ceiling above them caves in. A man lands in front of them, hood pulled low over his eyes, plaster and debris landing in a rolling cloud at his feet.

Maddox raises her gun and points it at him.

"Get the girl. No matter what happens, don't let her out of your sight," Maddox orders her guards, not taking her eye off the man through the sight of her gun. He raises his head slowly.

One of the guards behind Maddox pulls a set of keys from his pocket, but the other objects.

"Captain," the one with the green bandanna starts. "It could be dangerous."

Maddox goes still and then turns toward the guard.

"You're questioning me?" she asks, her face incredulous. Being doubted throws her off-balance, and it's the moment the guard was waiting for. He throws out a foot, catching the other guard behind the knee before snatching the gun out of his hand and knocking him out with the butt of the gun. Maddox turns, pointing the gun at the man who is most decidedly *not* a member of her crew, but Green Bandanna is too fast. He grabs the muzzle and twists, and Maddox loses her grip.

The prisoners in the other cells let out a raucous cheer, but Maddox isn't going down that easily.

She lets out a roar of frustration and lunges, dodging the man's swipes as she spins and lands a solid kick to his gut. He groans and she pulls the gun, still in his grip, over his head, clocking him with the barrel as he refuses to let go.

I chance a glance at Rielle and Lucia, and the stranger now standing in their cell.

He's pulled something from his pocket and is fastening it to the cell door. As the fight between Green Bandanna and Maddox rages, he looks to me. I catch his eyes in the mirror. He's Xanthous.

"I'd step back if I were you," he says, his voice muffled by the black fabric draped over the lower half of his face.

I lurch backward as Maddox lands another punch, this time to Green Bandanna's jaw. He falls, and she wipes the back of her hand over her nose, which is now bleeding. He's got at least a hundred pounds of muscle on her, but they are evenly matched.

A low whining tone revs up from the contraption secured to the door, and then a loud *bang* sounds through the brig, followed by a plume of smoke. Lucia coughs, waving her hand in front of her face. Seconds later, as the smoke wafts away, I see their cell door, hanging like a broken jaw off the hinges.

Maddox looks, her mouth opening in rage as she sees what they've done. It's a half-second mistake she can't afford, and Green Bandanna knocks her backward, catching her off guard just long enough to fasten her wrists with zip ties to my cell bars. He pulls the keys out of his pocket and opens my cell.

"Come on," the fighter says through the dark fabric. He tosses the keys to Rielle, who runs down the block, opening cell doors. Prisoners barrel down the hallway, making for the stairs that will lead to the deck. The fighter turns, pulling the door on the far end shut and sticking a mop in the handle. They bang on the metal, and the sound echoes through the ship.

I don't move. It's not fear that makes me stop, but the realization that just because these people hate Maddox doesn't mean that they are my friends. It doesn't mean they are any better than her.

They could be worse. They could be rival Runners, plundering Maddox's cargo.

"You're dead." Maddox laughs lowly. There's only a hint of rage in her words, like this is a poker hand she's lost and not an all-out invasion of her ship. "If you take her, they will find you. She will cost you your life, Marsali."

Marsali. The name pulls on my memory, but I don't have time to place it.

She lets out a hateful snicker as Rielle strides over to the other man, reaches up, and snatches the green bandanna off his face before kneeling down and stuffing it in Maddox's mouth.

"I think you've talked enough," she says, bopping a finger on the end of Maddox's nose. Maddox growls, the sound terrifying even through the ball of fabric. Straightening, Rielle looks at me.

"You coming?"

I don't move. I know I'm dead on this ship. But I might be dead with them, too.

"Thomas, help get them to the stern," the man Maddox

called Marsali orders, and Rielle follows Lucia to the stairs, leaving just the two of us. He lifts one hand, tugging the black fabric down over his chin.

I look at him. Without the black bandanna over his face, I can tell he's probably about Dean's age. His broad shoulders are covered in a dark blue hoodie still peppered with debris from the ceiling, and his boots are wet as he steps closer.

I take another instinctive step back, and he cocks an eyebrow at my blatant distrust.

As if I wasn't just locked in a cargo hull like an animal, which would give anyone trust issues.

He glances down at Maddox, who has the green bandanna still stuffed in her mouth.

"This one? This is the special one that will bring me death and destruction?" he asks, his eyes trained on her as he steps into the cell with exaggerated care. He tilts his head, the light catching the shadows under his high cheekbones, sloping down to a strong jaw covered in dark stubble.

He looks back to me, narrowing his yellow eyes. "Color me intrigued."

I needed to be Vanessa earlier, but now I need to be someone else. Right now, I need to be strength. I need to be a razor's edge covered in viper poison and angled toward anyone looking to mess with me.

I need to be Harlow.

What would she say now?

Harlow.

"I'm not here for your intrigue," I shoot back, straightening my shoulders like it will somehow infuse my voice with authority or something. As though any sort of good posture can undo the fact that I have mascara dripping down my face and "U WISH" stamped across my ass. I hate how he runs his eyes over my body, like he's thinking something similar.

"Who are you?" he asks quietly, a smile twisting up the side of his mouth.

The door bangs and shudders once more, and I know Maddox's crew will find a way in. I don't have much time.

"Seth!" someone calls from the stairs. "Let's move!"

Seth. Seth Marsali. Son of Admiral Marsali—from the Torch. Evelyn's twin brother.

Seth steps closer, and I fight to hold his eyes, lacing defiance in my gaze as he steps closer. I'm backed against the wall of the cell—I can't go anywhere.

"You do you, princess. Come or don't, but whatever you're going to do, do it quickly." He turns away.

My eyes flick to where Maddox is tied—

Where she *was* tied.

Seth sees it the same time I do, and whips his head to look back at me, a question in his eyes.

The plastic restraints lie forgotten on the floor, and Seth follows my horrified stare for half a second before the gun cocks behind him. He turns to find a muzzle in his face, Maddox grinning with blood in her teeth.

"What do you think your daddy will do when I chop up his favorite disappointment and use him as chum?" she purrs. Her voice is lethal, even when it's absent of rage. Because there's no rage in her now. She isn't *mad* about this. She sees it as sport. This—from all the lives in the cages to her freshly broken nose—is all a game to her.

And blowing Seth's brains all over me will be her version of "checkmate."

I can't have anyone else die because of me. I look around, desperately searching for anything that could help, but the cell is bare.

"I think you'll be doing him a favor," Seth replies evenly, grinning humorlessly. If he's scared, he's not showing it. "He might even throw you a parade, and I know how much you hate being cast in a positive light. Probably best to let me go."

Seth steps to the side, and Maddox mirrors him. I stay at the bars, watching them circle until she's standing in front of me.

"I don't think that's gonna be the way this goes," she muses. "Though I do so regret the thought of losing that *face*. It'd be like shattering the Winged Victory of Samothrace. Even if you aren't really my type." Another crash thunders against the door. The crew has found some sort of battering ram, it seems. We don't have much time. "But there's more where that came from, right? And I think your sister and I would get along better."

Seth's grin freezes, and a deadly, killing calm sweeps through the cell.

"There are a thousand reasons to kill you, Maddox. But mention Evelyn again and I'll only need one."

Maddox raises the gun. "And our repartee was going *so* well."

With a final shattering noise, the door finally gives way,

and the sounds of shouts rip down the corridor. Seth seizes the moment of distraction and lunges, knocking Maddox's arm upward and shoving her back.

"Go!" he screams as we scramble through the door. We barrel down the hallway just as the door bursts open, and Maddox's crew spills inside. I hear the metallic click and brace myself for the gunshot, but it doesn't come. Maddox swears loudly, and it sounds like a strangled growl.

"*Get them!*" Maddox screams.

"Time to go," Seth says, and I don't argue. I follow him up the stairs, and he stops just long enough to slam it shut behind us. We race up the curving wooden steps, Seth right behind me, and spill through a narrow doorway and into the rainy night. A fight is raging on the deck, most all with blades of some kind. Up on deck, Thomas and Lucia hold off Maddox's crew while Rielle stands by a rope tied off the edge of the stern. The rope stretches off the back of the *Devil's Bid*, secured to something I cannot see through the fog. Prisoners slide across, their lives suspended over the black water.

"Hey, Lucia, Thomas! Wrap it up!" Seth cries, sprinting toward the rope. I freeze as the sound of the door opening at the bottom of the stairs rings through the night—screeching metal and a raging Maddox.

Fear roots me to the spot. I can't step off the deck and over the water. I can't. The terror clouds my mind, pulling my rational self deeper and deeper into a tailspin with no end.

I feel hands on my shoulders, and then Lucia is dragging me behind her.

"How the hell did you even survive this apocalypse?" she seethes, yanking me behind her, up the steps to the stern of the ship.

Maddox and her men erupt onto the deck, a wave of simmering rage emanating off her like a living thing.

"I don't think so, sweetheart," she says, eyes locked on me.

Thomas steps in front of her, blocking her path as Lucia pulls me toward the stern.

"Come on!" she says, grabbing the rope and swinging off the edge. Rielle follows, like they've done this a thousand times.

"Thomas!" Seth shouts to Thomas, and Thomas turns, jumping onto the railing of the ship and giving Maddox a mock salute before leaping into the darkness. She seethes, turning to me.

"Go!" Seth orders, but I freeze.

Maddox gets closer.

"You need to go *now!*" he orders, but I can't move. Maddox's hateful eyes practically spark with bloodlust as she starts up the steps.

She'll kill me. It doesn't matter what the Vessels hired her for. She'll finish the job now.

I turn to look at Seth, his hair soaked and windblown, his jaw tight as he regards me with something between incredulity and naked irritation. I have no other choice. The fear snakes up my spine, but I launch myself out and grab the rope. My skin screams as pain rips down my fingers. I look down.

The water glitters black, like the gaping mouth of a devouring monster. I let out a scream as my fingers slip and I let go to redouble my grip.

Seth grabs the rope and swings down beside me.

"Hold on!" he yells.

"What the hell do you think I'm doing?" I shriek.

He lets go, dangling by one hand as he pulls a knife from his boot.

"Hold on harder," he shouts back.

I don't even have time to scream before he reaches up and slashes the rope, sending us plummeting to the unforgiving darkness below.

Chapter 13

I SLICE THROUGH THE INKY BLACK WATER LIKE A razor, so smoothly I don't even feel the impact.

I open my eyes as the frigid water squeezes air from my lungs in a string of bubbles. Looking up, I can see the glowing light off the stern of the *Devil's Bid* mixed with the slight glow of the moonlight refracted through the dense fog.

The surface slips farther from me, my hair dancing around my head like it's caught in the wind.

And I can't move.

I can't thrash—I can't kick back the shadows that seem to reach up for my feet, thirsty for the panic that leeches deeper into my veins with every passing second. My chest burns, and I can't tell if it's my lungs begging for air or the complete and utter terror unfurling in my bones like propane finally catching a spark.

There was a hope, somewhere tucked in the back of my mind, that maybe I'd built this up. Maybe, if I could just make myself go under, that my body would respond well. That the fear I'd awakened the night of the blood moon wouldn't actually be as strong as I'd feared.

I was wrong.

I'm so scared I can barely move, except to tilt my head to watch the light from above slowly fade.

Fight. Fight. Don't go down like this.

The voice is a screech in the back of my mind. She's buried under the rubble that used to be my life, and I can barely hear her.

Fight. You aren't ending this way.

I kick once.

Twice.

The fear roars in the back of my mind, leering back and rebounding. A fresh wave of hot panic lashes at my spine, and I cry out from the pain.

Then, a vise grip clamps down on my wrist and yanks me upward.

Up, up, up.

We break the surface, and the fight overtakes the panic. I gulp down lungfuls of damp air, my mind clearing.

I'm alive.

"Hold on to me!" Seth orders, and I wrap my arms around his shoulders. He tugs twice on the rope, and then we're being pulled through the water so fast there's a wake behind us.

Someone on the other boat is pulling us up.

Seth lets out a groan as they pull us out of the water and up along the back end of the other ship.

I cling to him, and his fingers dig around my waist. We twist as the rope hauls us up, and I see faded lettering on the side of the ship.

The *Ichorbow*.

My chest seizes. The *Ichorbow*—almost as notorious as the *Devil's Bid*, but not quite.

It's another Runner ship.

For a second, I almost let go, because the thought of being skin to skin with a Runner makes me want to throw up.

But the thought of the yawning deep beneath keeps me clinging to Seth, even as I curse myself for being such a coward. Behind us, the *Devil's Bid* is fading as the *Ichorbow* pulls ahead.

Rielle and Thomas meet us at the railing and pull us over. Seth lands on his feet, but I spill onto the deck, hacking up a lung as the adrenaline from the panic attack slowly ebbs from my limbs, leaving me shaking.

Rielle drapes a blanket over my shoulders as I peer up through drenched hair. I can't stay on my knees. I look weak enough. My legs shake as I make myself stand. The *Ichorbow* is a sailboat, which explains why we're going faster than the *Devil's Bid*. In this wind, it's easy to clock more knots than an engine.

God's engine is all we need, baby, my dad used to say.

Seth whips around, eyeing me with wide, piercing eyes.

"What was *that*?" he asks.

I look around the deck. Lucia stands next to the railing, wringing out her black hair. Rielle hands blankets to the other prisoners. Thomas, who somehow managed to *swim* from one boat to the other, mans the wheel.

Harlow. I need to act like Harlow.

"You cut the rope!" I shoot at him. Maybe he thinks I'm a weak swimmer. Maybe he thinks the stormy waters were too much for me. Maybe he didn't pick up on the fact that I was a deer in the headlights. That I literally sunk like a stone.

"Yes I did. If you'd moved your ass a little faster, I wouldn't have had to," he shoots back.

I clamp my jaw down tight against my chattering teeth. If this is the *Ichorbow*, then it doesn't matter what I say. We've gone from one Runner ship to another.

Rielle lights two torches on the railing, illuminating the deck and sending a huff of steam up past the sails.

"You are going to stand there and act like you're some sort of hero? It would be more merciful for you to let me drown."

Seth stalks across the deck, the muscle in his jaw twitching. "What the hell are you talking about?"

Water streams down his face, his soaked shirt tight against his heaving chest. His yellow irises catch the firelight.

And I remember another story—one that got lost in the flurry of reports about Evelyn's disappearance. Seth Marsali, her twin, abandoning his position in his father's fleet. Going rogue. His father gave a statement, disavowing his son.

I never knew who captained the *Ichorbow*, but now I do. And it makes sense. What better way to rebel against the Torch than to become Runners?

"You're a monster. A traitor," I spit. Seth closes the distance between us.

"You don't know what you're talking about," Thomas growls from across the deck, but Seth shakes his head once before turning his focus back to me.

"And what are you?" Seth asks. "Besides a princess with piss-poor self-preservation skills?"

I shiver, but catch the light glittering off something tied to his belt.

I clamp my jaw together for a moment, and then, so quickly I don't even register myself doing it, I shirk off the blanket and lunge.

By the time I snatch the knife from his sheath and press it against his neck, his entire crew has their own weapons drawn.

Seth freezes as I press the metal to his corded throat. His shoulders are huge against my small hand—the hand I'm trying desperately to keep from shaking.

I've never held a knife against someone's neck before. A bigger part of me is terrified to know what I could do with one flick of my wrist. Another part, a part I'd be ashamed to admit, is thrumming with the thrill. The control. His blood pushes beneath my blade, and I could spill his life on my bare feet. I could watch the light drain from his murderous eyes.

It's like he can sense what I'm thinking, because when I look up at his face, he raises his chin a fraction of an inch.

A challenge.

I step closer.

Lucia appears behind me, as quiet as the wind whipping over the deck. She makes no noise, but I feel the tip of her blade run down my spine.

Seth glances at her over my shoulder. I don't know what he sees in her face then, but he narrows his eyes for half a second, and the knife eases off my skin.

"What did Maddox want you for?" he asks plainly, raking his eyes back to mine. "You were her only passenger. You must be worth something."

My thoughts are spinning, my heart hammering in my chest as I try to think. This is a game of chess, a dance on thin ice where one wrong move sees me plummeting to my death. I had no choice but to pretend to be the Chosen One in front of Maddox. I had to save Vanessa. But now? I have no reason to believe they won't slit my throat right here if I tell them I'm the Chosen One.

"I don't know."

"Liar," he retorts.

"I'd rather be a liar than a murderer," I seethe.

"So you admit you're lying?" he retorts.

Shit, I walked right into that one. I raise my chin, defiant.

"I don't see you arguing the fact that you're a murderer."

"Well, it seems you're pretty set on that. I doubt I could talk you out of it," Seth bites.

Seth opens his mouth, but then shuts it again.

Lucia snorts behind me, and I see Rielle's eyes narrow from her spot beside Thomas. He runs a hand through his jet-black hair. His dark eyebrows furrow over Xanthous eyes that glow, the color unnaturally bright against the rest of his Korean features. It looks like he is about to say something, but Seth talks over him, tilting his head like my blade isn't still at his throat.

"I actually don't think I'm planning on talking to you anymore about anything, princess." His eyes harden. He reaches up, and gently—surprisingly so, for how he's glaring at me—puts his hand on mine and lowers my blade.

If I were Harlow, I'd cut him just for daring to challenge me. But I'm not. He called my bluff. Seth gives me one more once-over before turning away. He walks across the deck, and I follow.

"Where are you taking me?" I ask, looking out over the water like it will give me any clue as to where the hell we're going. As if I can even tell the direction we're heading in.

A thought blooms in the back of my mind—if we're heading to the Blood Market, then at least I'll be closer to finding Dean. But he could have a deal with private contractors. He could be taking me anywhere.

A heavy feeling settles over my frame. Seth looks back at me, but doesn't say anything.

"Hey!" I shout. He stops. "I didn't ask you to blow up my cell. I didn't ask you to literally drop me into the ocean, and I didn't ask you to yank me onto this shitheap of a boat. The least you can do is tell me where the hell you're going to sell me off."

His muscled shoulders tighten at my words, his fists clenching at his sides as he slowly pivots to face me.

"You seem to know everything. It won't hurt you to have to
figure this one out."

It doesn't take long for them to show me below deck. I thought
I'd be shoved into another cell, but instead Lucia just gestures
to a cot in the corner of what looks like a pantry. She must read
the question on my face, because she rolls her eyes.

"Feel free to jump over the railing and try to swim for it. We
all saw how *that* went."

And she shuts the door.

Shaking, I lower myself to the cot, my legs trembling. I
don't know if it's from exhaustion or fear. Probably both. I pull
Rielle's sopping sweatshirt over my head, letting it *plunk* on the
floor next to me. Cold bites at my skin, and I shiver uncontrol-
lably.

I don't want to cry, because I know that if I start, I might not
be able to stop.

I was scared on the *Devil's Bid*, but at least I knew where I
was headed. At least I knew—even though it was horrible—
what fate awaited me.

Now?

I have no clue.

I'm in the grips of Seth Marsali—a loose cannon by any
measure. I have no clue what he's going to do with me.

I close my eyes, but all I can hear is the sound of Dean

screaming my name as I barreled down the beach toward him. All I can feel is the crushing weight of Harlow's arms as she squeezed me.

I press my heels to my eyes. I don't have the notebook anymore.

I shut my eyes as the first sob rips through me, shaking my shoulders as I let the tears fill my eyes—fill me.

My parents. The world. Dean. My sister, and the fate that waits for her like a noose around her neck—the fate she never asked for. My grandmother, and the way they placed a towel under her jaw when she died to keep her mouth closed. The fact that I can't blame that on the curse—that would have happened anyway, eventually.

Malcolm. How he thought the world was worthy of hope and humanity and ended up dying in the street.

Grief is a fist around my windpipe, and it's almost worse than being underwater.

"I'm so sorry," I whisper. To no one. To everyone.

Then the door opens, a small squeak echoing throughout the tiny pantry. I look up to find Seth Marsali holding a tray with a cup of water and two bread rolls in one hand and clothes in the other.

I wipe my eyes and shove myself up.

He raises the tray wordlessly.

I don't take it. "You wouldn't want your cargo to spoil, is that it?"

He sets the tray on one of the shelves before holding the

clothes up, irritation spreading over his face as I don't reach out for those, either.

My clothes are still wet, and I've been covered in goose bumps since getting on Maddox's ship. I'm pretty sure my legs are numb from the cold and those black leggings look lovely and warm, but I'm not about to tell him that.

"I'm not cold," I add, at the exact moment my teeth decide to betray me with an involuntary chatter.

Seth nods gravely. "I can tell." He tosses the clothes at me, and I don't catch them. They fall to the floor.

We stand in silence. His lips are a thin line as he glares down at me, and I glare right back.

"You think I'm going to fall over in gratitude and tell you things," I say finally. "I've seen enough movies, Marsali. It's not going to work."

"Right. Well. You've just given away that there are things to tell."

I raise my eyebrows. "Are there? I think we both know I find you repulsive enough to enjoy wasting your time."

Seth nods. "I don't doubt that, princess—"

"—You can *stop* calling me that at *any* point, by the way. Your crew is not around for your misogynistic asshole routine."

"If I was a misogynistic asshole, I wouldn't give you those clothes to change out of because that shirt is practically see-through when wet. In fact, if I was a misogynistic asshole, I would not have said anything at all."

I move just a fraction of an inch to cross my arms over my

chest before I stop. No. He's trying to make me second-guess myself, and I'm not going to. Harlow wouldn't. Harlow would pour water down her front and then kick his ass.

"I'm not a princess," I shoot back, because it's all I can think to say.

"Fine. Tell me your real name, then."

My nostrils flare. No way in hell I'm telling him that, and I've hesitated too long to make one up. Seth nods like he expected my resistance to that.

"Which brings me back to my original question," he says, pushing off the door and stepping closer to me. "What did Maddox want with you?" He gestures to me at *you*, as though the general unimpressive state of me will really drive his point home.

Me.

Me, the one who is neither a captain nor a rebel.

Me, the one who doesn't quite know, the filler between two more interesting people.

I don't know what to tell him.

I'm Charlotte. I'm no one.

"You'd have to ask Maddox. Because honestly? I think I was a mistake." There is more truth in those words than anything I've said all night, but I doubt Seth believes me. He's quiet for a moment as he regards me.

"You know what this ship is," he breathes, his bright, yellow eyes finding mine. They are cold—not a hint of warmth or kindness there. Those are the eyes of the captain staring down a threat. "Then you know what the captain of the *Ichorbow* is capable of. I am asking you a question, and I won't ask it again. Believe it or not, I can be a pretty reasonable man."

I lift my eyes then, meeting his with a rage that burns through the fear. I don't know where it comes from, and I don't question it. I would rather be pissed than terrified, and Seth has given me all the fuel I need to not feel scared, even if it only lasts for a few minutes.

He lets out a soft, humorless laugh. Then, without another word, he turns and opens the door. He shuts it behind him, and I stare at the cold metal.

Eventually, I will have to face the spilled blood that will forever stain my memory.

But right now? I need to fight. I need to find a way to get to Dean, and then get to my sisters. I don't care how impossible it is—and it is pretty impossible.

I need to make it out of this, because for the first time in too long I've decided: I'm not dying this way.

Chapter 14

I SPEND THE NEXT TWO DAYS IN THE ROOM. I SLEEP more than I'd like, but I know my body needs to recover from what it went through on the *Devil's Bid*, so I don't fight it too much. But when I am awake, I'm running through what I can remember from the notebook. I stare at the ceiling and whisper them to myself, over and over.

I can almost feel my mom's fingers in my hair, telling me to relax.

It will all be okay, she'd say, and I'd believe it. She had a way of believing so much that it felt contagious.

But she's not here, and hope has never been as catching as fear. I sit up, racking my brain for an answer, because thinking about the prophecies keeps the memories away sometimes.

Find him on the dark blue, 3A, the one with the teeth.

His love pulls his loose threads. Loose threads loosely stitched. You'll see it before she does.

I remember the shape she made with her hand, and the two fists. *The way out. The way out.*

Veins lead to the heart.

I know better than to hope that they'll suddenly make sense, but it doesn't stop the little pulse in my chest that keeps whispering. *Maybe. Maybe now.*

Someone leaves food outside my door, though I always wait until I hear the footsteps walk back down the hallway before I reach out and grab it.

Somewhere on the third day, shouts sound from above.

I peer out of the small circular window that rests just beneath the edge of the ceiling in the pantry. All I see is gray mist—it brushes up against the glass like curious fingers.

It's so thick that seeing through it is impossible, yet somehow I know we're almost *there*.

I just don't know where *there* is.

It's like I can feel a shift in the air, a strange pull as the ship turns ever so slightly to the right. Something feels electric, like we're brushing up against the edges of a tangle of live wires. I stay perched on the edge of my cot, up on tiptoes, desperate for something. Anything.

Seth didn't come back after that first encounter, and despite the fact that my door remained unlocked, I didn't venture out.

Partially because I did, in fact, cave in the middle of the first night and pull on the leggings and the gray knit sweater he'd left, because I was *freezing*. I didn't want to give him the satisfaction, though I honestly doubted he'd spared me a second thought after he'd left the room.

The door behind me opens, just like I had a feeling it would.

I turn around. Rielle holds up a pair of black boots. Thick soles, pewter buckles, scuffed toes.

"I guessed size seven," she says, tossing them onto the floor between us. "We dock in ten minutes. I'd get those on. Seth isn't going to wait for you."

She turns, and I jump off the cot. "Where are we?"

Rielle runs a hand through her thick golden hair and looks at me, a challenge in her yellow eyes. "Come up and find out."

Before she leaves, she drops one more thing on the shelf near the door—mirrors, secured with leather and rope, buckles and knots. She's left me her mirrored bands.

The sound hits me first—the raucous shouts mixed with loud cracks that I pray are fireworks. It's still dark below deck, so I feel my way to the staircase, the boots Rielle gave me soundless on the wood.

The air whips my hair off the back of my neck as I step onto the deck, the world glowing pink and purple through the hazy fog. Seth and Thomas stand at the wheel, and the other prisoners from the *Devil's Bid* are huddled at the stern, peering toward the source of the noise.

Seth spins the wheel, and we roll across the dark water. We slice through a gap in the fog, and my breath catches in my throat as I move to the railing, my hands shaking as I grab the wood.

I've heard about the Jawbone—a metal city propped up on stilts just over the horizon, hovering between rumor and myth. No one I have ever known has been here, the stories always unconfirmed. Some people say it's a converted oil rig. Others say it's a repurposed lookout from World War II.

Whatever it was, it's something else entirely now.

Rusted steel juts from the waves, eight different pods of varying heights surrounded in latticework balconies, creating an octagon-shaped port. The mismatched heights and oblong structure are what gave it its name—it looks like a grim smile, a grin emerging from the waters. I've seen towns smaller on my family's road trips to Mammoth in the winter. I thought it would be more menacing, honestly.

But it sounds like we're slowly sailing up to a giant frat party.

Several ships are tied to the metal, docked at odd angles, flags of dozens of countries hanging over the edge. Dozens of strands of multicolored bulb lights dangle over the open water in the middle like they had been strung up by a careless spider.

People sit on the edges of the balconies, their feet hanging over the jet-black water that sparkles with the pale lavender and blush reflection of the lights, amber bottles in their hands.

I secure my mirrored wraps, making sure that the glass is facing up. I exhale on them, wiping them clean with my shirt—something I've seen Harlow do before an excursion. It feels weird to be the one doing it now.

I watch as Seth hands the wheel to Thomas and walks down the steps toward the stern. He doesn't even bother looking at me.

Just as well. If he thinks of me as something forgettable, then I won't have to worry about him suspecting that I'll figure a way out of this situation.

Lucia purses her lips as the ship bumps against the dock. Her eyes flick down to my new mirrors. "You don't think they have screening protocol?" Lucia asks next to me. She smirks, tucking her own necklace of mirrors into her shirt.

"I don't trust protocol," I say quietly, watching as the ship bumps up against the dock.

Lucia nods at me. "You're not as stupid as you look."

Harlow had taken me to a couple of her after-gig parties over the years, and I'd been around more than one celebration after the raiders found an untouched stash of beer tucked in the back of a ransacked grocery store.

So I know what a rager looks—and smells—like. But the Jawbone is next-level. The tinge of alcohol mixed with the faint whiff of urine and the smoke from a grill somewhere makes me press the back of my hand to my mouth as I follow Rielle down the dock and across the bridge.

Lucia was right—two women with mirrored holsters strapped over cargo pants stop us and do a screen before letting us down the rest of the ramp that leads to the main structure. We walk closer, and Lucia stays back, the mirrors secured in leather strips around the backs of her hands clinking against the metal of her belt as she eyes me. Maybe they think I have some grand master plan in place, and I'm getting ready to make a daring escape.

As of right now? I've got nothing. I can't even jump off the bridge and into the water, because I'll sink like a stone.

Maybe that's kinder than the fate that awaits inside, a voice says.

Out of habit, I keep my eyes down on the water teeming below the grated walkway, the glow of the lights beneath sending strange shadows up to the surface.

We stop, and Lucia grabs a shoulder before I walk straight into Rielle. There are two knocks and then a voice.

"Tell Monte I'm here," Seth says.

There's half a beat, then the sound of a heavy lock being pulled.

"Eyes cast," a gruff voice says. The sound of a metal blade rings through the air, and I know they're going to screen us again as we walk inside.

I chance looking up only to the level of Seth's boots as he steps up to the door, pausing for a moment before continuing. I lift my eyes slightly, enough just to peer through the door, and it's unlike anything I've seen since the Crimson started. It's shadow and firelight, the smell of cigarette smoke and burning wood wafting out like a fog.

The cacophony of clinking glass and music rises as we get closer. A shadow falls over us, and I look in the reflection on the water. We're beneath a tall guard tower. Boots walk up beside us, and I hear the sound of a fist on the metal. A door squeaks open.

"Long night?" one high voice asks.

There's a slurping sound, like someone taking a deep pull

of coffee. "Nah. No Torchies," someone responds. They're guards, and it sounds like they're changing shifts.

"This fog isn't gonna help, though," the first one says before both voices disappear into the tower and the door shuts once more.

Rielle steps up and then inside.

My turn.

"Up," the man orders, and I lift my eyes. He's beside me, a mirror lifted as he checks. I catch a glimpse of my reflection.

My hair is wild, eyes even wilder. I tuck my unruly locks behind my ear.

"Go ahead, love," the man says, lowering the mirror so it shows him. I look at him—he's older—probably as old as my dad would have been. Bushy beard, thick around the middle.

He nods at me tentatively, like he's not sure what will happen to me if I step inside.

That makes two of us, but I don't have the luxury of thinking too hard about it, especially since Lucia is behind me then, shoving me into the shadows. A deep, rhythmic beat shakes the room.

Slowly, I raise my eyes. It's bigger than I thought—wood paneling lofted to a point above our heads. It almost looks like a hunting lodge.

I follow Rielle, who follows Seth deeper into the fray.

A hunting lodge that was commandeered by a gambling ring.

Fire pits with different-colored flames sit in the middle of tables directly under mirroring skylights cut into the ceiling, pulling the smoke into the night. People surround the tables, cigarettes and all manner of pipes in their hands. A woman with yellow eyes and closely cut black hair blows smoke in rings as she looks me up and down. I shake my hair loose from behind my ears, rethinking my attempt to look less wild. It can't hurt to look a little wild here.

I turn around, and find only Lucia behind me. The rest of the people in the brig with me must have been told to wait somewhere else. A bar sits on the left side of the room, and a woman with a bright purple braid pours clear liquid into metal cups before sliding them to two men in leather jackets sitting on the barstools. The room is packed, the body heat steaming up my cold mirrors.

Shouts erupt at a far table, and I turn sharply at the sudden sound. A woman with long strawberry-blond hair raises her hands in triumph. The men around her groan and throw bottle caps—their chips—into the center of the table.

"Her name is Hilary," Rielle says, and I jump. I didn't realize she was there. She smiles conspiratorially as she motions back to the woman. "She was a high school English teacher before the Crimson, and now she comes in here, cleans these dudes out, and takes supplies back to her settlement." Rielle looks to the far wall, where I see an assortment of wares, available for trade-in at the end of the night: iron blades, bullets, mirrors, and some jewels.

This place is for underground survivors. Rule breakers of the highest order. Rielle walks, and I follow.

We weave through the fire pits, toward the far end of the hall, where we disappear through a corridor, the dank, musty smell of stale seawater filling my head as all my other senses go dark.

Two more knocks, and a door opens.

This room is smaller than the hall, and quieter. The walls are red velvet, and the floor—

I stop for a second, choking out a scream.

The floor is glass. Beneath, the gray ocean, lit by the flood-lights, churns.

Seth doesn't stop as he strolls across it—he's been here before. I force myself to look up—to keep my mind off the fact that I'm hovering above the abyss. I know everyone has been screened, but I'm not stupid enough to think that makes me safe.

Which basically means I can't look anywhere, really. The thought frees me, in an odd way.

A series of wide, circular tables sit under an iron chandelier covered in half-melted candles.

Beneath it, at the center table, sits the most beautiful woman I've ever seen. Her red hair is twisted around one shoulder, cascading down the front of a black dress that doesn't suit this place at all. Her arms are covered in tattoos, and rubies glisten from elegant settings around her fingers. She has mirrored fin-gernails, and gold-edged glass panels secured to the inside of her forearms with sterling bands. It's beautiful, something done for aesthetics first, and survival second. I haven't seen anything like it.

People sit at the table with her, black cards tucked in their hands. Jewels are scattered across the table—emeralds and sapphires. They aren't fighting for bullets or blades. This must be the high-end room.

If there was ever going to be a time to escape, it's here. I just have to find the right time. But with Rielle on one side of me and Lucia on the other and Thomas back in the main room, my options are limited.

"You're late," the woman drawls, leaning forward on her elbows as she lays her cards facedown on the table.

Seth stops. "I told you I'd be here within the week, Monte."

The woman glares at him, her golden eyes lined with bronze. The others leave the room, walking past us without so much as a glance. She's Xanthous, though she doesn't look like a Runner at all.

What could she be after?

"Cutting it close is as good as late," she says, picking up an emerald and rolling it between her index finger and thumb. "I thought you might have changed your plans. Gone after bigger fish, as it were."

Seth widens his stance and grins. "Come on. Ain't no bigger fish out there that could make me turn my back on you, gorgeous."

Monte tosses two sapphires into the pile. She smiles and licks her top lip.

"Not even Abel Lassiter?" she singsongs, setting a card down.

I go still, and I see Seth's shoulders stiffen at the name of his presumably dead sister's boyfriend. The difference between living and dying in this world is often based on what you know and what you don't. But not even Seth can pretend not to care about the name that just crossed Monte's lips.

"What?" he asks. The word is choked and thin.

Monte raises her perfect eyebrows. "You didn't hear? Abel Lassiter's ship went missing yesterday. Went to check on the progress on that Rig of his, and never came back."

I chance a look at Lucia and Rielle. Rielle looks backward at Thomas, her expression tight. They didn't know.

Seth's hands are fists, and I hate the water-through-my-fingers feeling that overwhelms me: that I'm getting half the picture. Seth abandoned them. He *left*. Betrayed Abel and Evelyn. Why would he care?

I watch the way Seth takes a deep breath and then unclenches his fists. He loosens his shoulders.

"They're getting bolder," he says. His tone has a practiced air of ambivalence, but it's too late. He already showed that the news rattled him. Monte sits forward, almost like she's amused by the attempt.

"Well. Our reasons are less exciting. We got held up," he says, looking back at me.

"Do you have what we agreed upon?" she asks.

My stomach clenches as I look over. Lucia has a hand on her knife, and Rielle casually spins her blade between her fingers. If I'm part of this transaction, there isn't going to be much I can do about it.

Seth pulls a piece of paper out of his pocket and tosses it on the table. "The tech shipment will pull out in two weeks from the eastern docks. Those are passcodes and the names of the guards working that morning."

Monte snatches the paper up with her pointed nails and opens it, eyeing the writing on it before dragging her gaze back up to him expectantly. "This is all you got for me? Not much to go on, Marsali. That, mixed with your tardiness . . ." Monte picks up a jewel from the center of the table and twists it between two fingers.

I bite my cheek as Monte turns her yellow eyes to me.

Seth shifts slightly, moving in front of me just enough to make Monte's smile widen.

"She goes with the others," he says. "They're waiting for her."

They're waiting for her.

"A tech shipment isn't what I was hoping for," Monte says, her eyes sharp. "You and I both know I wanted to hit the main depot. But *she* could sweeten the deal. She certainly looks sweet enough."

Seth's eyes go flat.

"Or perhaps you have something else?" Monte croons as the jewel in her hand catches the light. She's playing with him, and she's winning.

Seth sighs and reaches back into his coat, and I gasp when he pulls out a familiar piece—the headdress.

Rielle grabs me, pulling me back before I can say anything.

"That is *mine*," I hiss over my shoulder at Rielle, pulling loose from her grip.

"Seth didn't know that. Thomas grabbed it from Maddox's quarters before we left. Let it be—one wrong move gets you killed," she whispers.

The questions bubbling at the back of my throat feel like they're going to drive me mad. But, for now, the tension in the room has dissipated. It becomes clearer as Monte reaches into a hidden pocket in her gown and withdraws papers. I risk a glance: coordinates. But of what, I'm not sure.

"And will you be staying?" Monte asks, her eyes moving slowly up and down Seth before flicking to Rielle.

"You mean will I be losing everything I have at your table again? Sadly, no," Seth says, the edge in his voice barely notice-able through his playful tone. "We're heading north right after we see the girl to her place."

I step out from between Lucia and Rielle. "I'm not a *thing*. I won't be spoken about as though I'm not here," I bite out.

Monte smirks as she pushes herself to her feet. Seth turns, glaring at me.

I said no talking, the look says.

Monte runs her tongue over her top teeth as she steps around the table. "Well, Seth. I know you had plans for her elsewhere, but I know for a fact that there are several Vessels who would be very happy to get a taste of *that*," she says.

Monte's grin deepens as confusion colors my expression.

She's about to say something when the door opens, and Thomas slips through the doorway.

"Seth?" he asks, an incredulous laugh riding his voice as the sound of shouts and crashes spill down the corridor behind him. "We've got a problem."

The door snaps open, throwing Thomas forward. He catches himself, pulling a knife from his boot as a man with stringy blond hair barrels through the doorway, rage etched on his pale face. Behind him, three men the size of small trees lumber inside.

"Seth Marsali, you prick," he seethes, pointing to Seth.

Seth falls as still as granite. The man glares back at him, spittle caught in his patchy beard.

"Geramond. I didn't know you'd be here. Did you know he'd be here?" Seth asks, turning to Monte. She shrugs, looking down at her nails.

"No one knows anything!" Geramond roars. "I've been stranded at Port Cadre for three weeks. Because you *stole my ship.*"

Chapter 15

"TECHNICALLY, YOU STOLE IT FROM THAT MILLION-aire yacht club guy when the Crimson hit Catalina, Geramond," Seth says.

If Seth isn't the captain of the *Ichorbow*, or if he has only been at the helm for a couple of weeks, then he isn't the notorious Runner I thought he was. I was wrong, but *how* wrong, I don't know.

"I paid for that privilege in blood, you asshole," Geramond responds. "I took that ship by the code." He runs the back of his thumb across his throat. "As you can see, I'm still alive, and out a pretty penny since you took my livelihood."

"Livelihood," Rielle says, her words clipped. "Is that what you call selling Curseclean?"

"Careful, girl. There are no judgments here," Monte breathes coolly.

A grin flicks up the side of Rielle's mouth. "Oh, I'm not judging. A man has to make a living. Especially a man who has to pay for any sort of human interaction," she spits.

"Watch your mouth, whore, or I'll watch it for you," the man next to Geramond, a slim reed of a man with graying hair, chokes out.

Seth takes a dangerous step forward just as Thomas lets out a generous string of curses.

But it's Lucia who puts a knife to the man's throat, quick as a breath. No one else saw her moving down the wall.

"Say that again," she hisses.

"That's enough," Monte says, taking a decisive step forward and putting her hands out on either side of her, palms up. The light glints off her mirrors, her nails, her gems. "Marsali. You stole his ship. You owe him recompense." With a swivel of her head, she pins Geramond to the spot. "That's the price according to the charter," she explains. She moves closer to Geramond, her steps smooth and lethal. The room falls silent. "But call another woman a whore in my presence and I'll throw your tongue to the depths. I'll let you choose if it's still attached to your head when I do it." Her words are clipped, her teeth bared behind bloodred lips. I don't doubt her. Honestly, something tells me she's done it before.

Geramond saunters toward Seth. "I'll take back my ship, and then I'll take your cargo. You walk away with your life."

Prickles of ice flood my spine. Cargo—the other people on the boat.

And me.

Seth's voice is low and measured. "I don't think so. I've already secured plans for them, and I don't think it would look good for this establishment to condone the breaking of a previously agreed-upon contract."

Geramond shakes his head, revving up for a comeback when Monte holds up a hand. "Enough."

Both Seth and Geramond look to her as she stands. "Geramond, if the cargo is spoken for, it's spoken for."

The man seethes, but says nothing. Seth doesn't show any reaction, almost like he's waiting for the hammer to drop.

Which it does.

Monte sinks to her chair.

"But, Marsali, you took his ship. And that complicates things."

She drums her mirrored nails on the polished wood of her chair.

"To the pit, then?" she asks.

The pit.

I look to Rielle, whose skin has tightened against her skull. Even Lucia, who still stands behind Geramond with murder in her dark eyes, looks afraid.

Seth turns to Geramond. "Winner gets the ship," Seth says.

Geramond snorts, a sneer curling up on his thin lips.

"Winner gets it all."

I walk with Rielle through the dark. Lucia joins us somewhere between the glass room and metal walkway, and I yank my arm from Rielle as I stare down Seth's silhouette ahead of me. My mind races, looking for a way out.

I didn't make it this far to lose my life now.

We emerge out on the railing, overlooking the inner circle of the Jawbone. Seth and Geramond continue down the catwalk, but Rielle and Lucia pull me to the railing.

"I don't want to be bartered like a cheap watch in a poker game," I snap.

"And I don't want to hear that my Benefit cream isn't available on the black market anymore. Bad things happen to good people," Rielle says.

I'm quiet as I look around at this little, teeming city over the water. I could run. I could turn and sprint back the way we came. I wonder how far I'd get before Lucia pounced. I look over the edge of the railing. Below, the floodlights illuminate the pod's steel legs, though they go so far down that they're lost to the shadows of the deep. I swallow the knot in my throat and lean back. There's nowhere to go.

"What does Seth mean, *we're spoken for*? Who did he make a deal with?" I ask quietly. People pour out of the metal pods, filling the catwalk around us, all facing the illuminated circle of water below.

Lucia's face is tight as she searches the crowd and finds who she's looking for—Thomas. He stands with the other survivors from the *Devil's Bid*. They look as confused as I do. Thomas gives her a nod, and she nods back, relaxing.

Rielle stares forward, the light dancing on her face with the water.

The clinking of chains ripples through the night, and the rumble of applause splits the cold air. Chains from the edges of the surrounding pods are pulling something up from the water. I crane my neck forward to get a better look.

A latticework metal platform rises, cutting through the light as the chains roll up on a levy. The crowd gets louder as it emerges from the ocean, water spilling over the sides as the platform stops, suspended over the water below the railing.

"What the hell?" I breathe. Rielle bites her nails.

Across the way, Monte steps out of her heels and onto the lowest rung of the railing.

"Knaves!" she calls, and the crowd screeches in approval. "We have a disagreement. Geramond de Levlier challenges Seth Marsali to the right for ten units!"

Units.

"Units?" I hiss, looking to Lucia. "Is she talking about *me*?" I ask. "Is that how she refers to *people*?"

Lucia silences me with a look, and I turn back to face the platform, my fingers digging into the railing. Next to Monte, I see Seth. He pulls his shirt over his head, the scars on his shoulders visible even from this distance. He looks like one of the sculptures from the Getty Villa, with wide shoulders tapering down to a narrow waist. His face is drawn.

Next to him, Geramond does the same. I didn't realize how huge that man was, back in the red room. But he's almost twice Seth's size.

With one seamless movement, Seth eases over the railing,

facing the water. He spans the three-foot gap between the suspended platform and the catwalk with one jump. The platform creaks and sways at the weight.

"You know the rules!" Monte yells as Geramond leaps across the gap. Seth almost loses his footing at the jolting weight, spinning as Geramond chuckles, the chains rattling as he steps closer to the center of the platform. "First blood wins. I don't care how much or from where."

I freeze as realization sets in. They're going to fight.

Geramond is built like a tank—his arms seem like they're bigger than my entire body. Seth circles the edge of the platform, the light pouring up from beneath the waves making strange patterns on his torso. He moves like a soldier—shoulders back, fists loose and ready. His muscled chest and abs are both peppered with bruises and scabs. He has strange, uneven tan lines, probably from his time on the water. They face each other. Geramond grins, and Seth tips his chin down, readying himself.

Monte lets out a *whoop*, and the fight starts.

My breath catches in my throat as Geramond roars and charges Seth. Seth is quicker, ducking a right hook and rolling over the metal.

"Shit," Lucia breathes as Rielle spins, bringing her hand to her mouth as she leans back against the railing. It's just started, and she already can't bear it. I don't know what his plans are for me or the others from the *Devil's Bid*, but I was wrong about them once. I have too much blood on my hands—I don't want any more.

"Take me to Monte," I say, turning to Rielle. "Just offer me. I'm special—you heard Maddox."

The crowd cheers as Seth lands a kick in the center of Geramond's gut, but it barely fazes him. He backhands Seth, sending him sprawling. Seth rubs his palm over his nose. No blood. He's still in the fight, and the crowd goes wild.

Geramond picks Seth up by one hand, lifting him high before spinning to throw him to the platform. Seth maneuvers quickly, getting out of his grasp—but just barely. I get what Lucia and Rielle are seeing now. Geramond isn't playing just to win. He's playing to make Seth pay for humiliating him.

He's playing to kill.

"Seth isn't going to walk away from this," I whisper, and Lucia's eyes snap to mine. There's defiance there, but not enough to come up with an argument. She knows I'm right. "Whatever you were getting for me, it can't be worth your captain's life."

I look down, my eyes traveling along the catwalk before falling on the ships docked at the far end of the settlement. The *Ichorbow*'s purple flags snap in the cold wind.

"He's the captain," Lucia grinds out.

I look over at the pit. Geramond has Seth pinned.

"Not if he's dead," I reply. "But I have an idea. A new one."

Lucia's eyes dart to Rielle's—a decision.

"Speak very quickly," Rielle says.

Chapter 16

WE SLIP BACK THROUGH THE GLASS ROOM, NOW empty, and then through the now-empty tavern, Rielle and Lucia running beside me.

My plan is bonkers, and they know it. But it isn't crazier than standing there and watching their friend die. And maybe, if I can save his life, they will consider letting me go.

Maybe.

We spill into the night, the fog thick around us.

The *Ichorbow* is the first ship in the port. "There," I say, moving toward the ramp.

"I don't think so, baby," Lucia says, putting a hand on my shoulder. "I'll do it. You're staying with Rielle." Before I can argue, she's taken off toward the ramp, disappearing from sight as the fog swallows her whole.

I hear three grunts, then three splashes as whoever was

guarding the deck is thrown into the water.

"She's good," I whisper incredulously, more to myself than anyone else.

"You have no idea," Rielle agrees from beside me.

Moments later, Lucia runs back down the ramp—the grenade launcher in her hand.

"Far side. There's a speeder tucked on the edge. I'll grab it and meet you at the eastern edge."

Lucia shakes her head. "No. Too far. We can take this one," she says, motioning to the ship next to the *Ichorbow*. It's beautiful—a small, cream-colored yacht. My eyes fall to the purple lettering on the side. Lucia and Rielle walk toward it.

Glimpse of Paradise.

Something in me tilts, and nausea creeps through my gut. Vanessa's words echo in the back of my mind.

Glimpse to the water and you'll see fire.

I can't shake the chill that goes down my spine. "No," I say firmly. They both turn at the sound of my voice. "Not this one."

Lucia rolls her eyes and keeps walking, but Rielle stops, her curious gaze fixed on my resolute expression.

"Why?" she asks softly.

"Because. Something bad is going to happen to it," I say, almost automatically. I have no proof of it—no way to substantiate this beyond the strange whisper in my chest that tells me we need to stay away from it.

"We don't have *time for this*," Lucia hisses, and Rielle holds her hand up.

"We'll take something different, Lucia. The one at the end," Rielle answers. Lucia doesn't argue, but lets out an irritated groan as she slips down the dock, the grenade launcher perched on her shoulder.

Rielle and I run across the tavern, through the dark corridor.

I stop as my eyes find the pit. Geramond has Seth pinned, his hands around his throat.

I don't know why the sight of it makes me rage. Seth belongs in this world, this underground place of traded lives and shadowy dealings. He asked for this fight.

He's planning on using me as a *bargaining* chip. I shouldn't feel anything other than smug indifference at the sight of him turning purple.

A wicked blast rips through the night. The crowd's cheer dims as confusion settles over the catwalk, all eyes turning toward the dock. A second blast sounds.

Rielle cups her hands over her mouth. "TORCH EN-FORCERS! TORCH ENFORCERS AT THE DOCK!" she screams.

Chaos erupts. People run, some jumping over the railing into the water while others shove through the door. Rielle pulls me to her, tucking me close to her body behind the door as the panicked crowd pushes into the dark. I peer through the crack in the door, catching sight of the pit as Geramond lets Seth go. Monte strides across the catwalk on the opposite side, shouting orders to men manning the Gatling guns on top of the tin roofs.

Geramond is shouting orders, too, but to his men on the catwalk, motioning toward the ship. Seth hauls himself up to his knees, coughing as Geramond looks over his shoulder. With one look to make sure Monte isn't there to see, he kicks Seth once in the stomach, sending him sprawling. A cry rips from my throat at the sight, my hands flying to the door, even though the crowd rushing inside on the opposite side keeps Rielle and me pinned against the wall.

Seth tries to stand but can't get his feet. *Come on*, I urge. He shoves himself up, staggering to the railing, but I don't get to see if he makes it, because Rielle pulls me behind her.

I think we're headed out toward the pit, but she leads me deeper into the dark.

My stomach tightens. Maybe, despite what I've just done to help, they will still be content throwing me into the hull of another ship and pocketing whatever profit they can.

Rielle pulls open a door, motioning to the ladder inside. It disappears into the dark below, and I hesitate.

"What's down there?" I ask. Water. Ocean. Death.

The only thing worse than being underwater? Being underwater in a metal box.

My throat clenches at the thought, my mind zeroing in on the panic until everything around me fades into a dull roar.

But Geramond's shouts of rage pull me back to the moment, as does Rielle's insistent touch on my back.

"Go," she says.

And it's not an order. It's not even angry. It's a plea. Despite the show she put on in the glass room, she's as scared for him as I am. I leap to the ladder, speeding down into the darkness. She follows, pulling the steel door shut above us. With a clang, we're locked below.

Chapter 17

MY BOOTS HIT THE FLOOR, THOUGH I CAN'T SEE IT in the darkness. The air is damp and stale, and it's everything I have in me to not let the panic wring the air out of my lungs. I can hear the shouts and roars sounding above us—the chaos that's reigning in the Jawbone. Rielle jumps off next to me and lets out the same soft birdlike sound that she did earlier.

It's silent for a moment, and then the same sound—a response—echoes from across the room.

There's a *hiss*, and Rielle lights a match next to me. A soft glow lights up the room.

Though it's not as much a room as it is a janitor's closet. Across from us, no more than three feet away, is Thomas. I don't know how he got there—but I'm learning that Thomas has a gift of appearing and disappearing that I will never under-stand. Rielle steps closer, and the light catches Seth as he leans against the wall, his hand cupped over his ribs.

"What the hell were you *thinking*?" Rielle cries, stepping closer. She gingerly lifts Seth's shirt, and even in the low light I can see the dark bruises blooming on his side.

"I was thinking adrenaline would make up for a fifty-pound difference in muscle mass. I was mistaken," Seth grits out. I stand back, the pads of my fingers splayed against the metal wall as I take in the sight of his face—it's swollen and split. The flesh over his left eye looks like overripe fruit, and he spits a stream of blood into the shadows.

"Where's Lucia?" Thomas whispers, and as though he timed it, another blast ripples through the night.

"She'll meet us on the starboard side," Rielle says. "The others?"

"Already on Desmond's ship," Thomas replies. "Seth was right. They weren't thinking as much about the other passengers once she walked into the room. Perfect distraction."

I open my mouth to ask what the *hell* they are talking about, but another round of shouts and feet pounding above us quiets me.

"You could have gotten yourself killed," Rielle seethes, lowering Seth's shirt more roughly than she needs to.

"But I didn't. I take it this half-cocked plan was Lucia's idea?" he asks.

Rielle looks over her shoulder at me, and Seth follows her gaze, meeting my eyes for half a second before the match dies. Darkness swallows us again before another breath of orange light blooms in Rielle's hand. I didn't think he'd be grateful, but I am surprised by the anger simmering in his eyes.

"You let her talk you into practically destroying this place?" he asks, his voice low.

Rielle moves to answer, but I cut her off. "I'm not about to let Runners decide my fate."

"Stop calling us Runners," Thomas snaps. His eyes flash at me. The contrast of the Xanthous irises against his dark eyebrows is striking.

Seth pushes himself up, wincing as he balances.

"In a moment, there will be two knocks on the other side of this wall. It's a pressurized sublevel loading dock. A woman named Katrina will take you to a ship. It's captained by one of our contacts, Desmond, and chartered for Mexico. There's a Curseclean safe house there."

"Safe house?" I ask. The word doesn't compute.

Seth cocks an eyebrow. "Safe house. We're not Runners. We're . . . the opposite."

I shake my head. That makes no sense. There is no good out on the water. The ocean is bloody. The worst of humanity. There isn't any hope this side of the Torch anymore. I watch the sputtering light die in Seth's yellow eyes, then reignite as Rielle lights yet another.

"How do I know you're not lying?" I ask, even though there's something in my gut that tells me he's not.

You don't know what you're talking about, Thomas had said the first night on the *Ichorbow*.

"Why wouldn't you just *tell* me that?" I bark, stopping as I look up, praying no one heard me.

"Because," Seth counters quietly. "We can't risk anyone finding out. We don't tell people where they are until they get there. In case the ship is overtaken and things don't go as planned."

I swallow. It makes sense, but I think of how scared I've been for the past day. How I was sure I was about to be handed over and killed. I don't know if my knees are shaking from relief or rage.

"You can't just *do that* to people," I bite out as another match dies. I stop as a thought hits me.

Mexico.

I can't go south. I need to get to the Blood Market. North. I need to get to Dean.

"I can't," I say.

Seth cocks his head. "Can't what?"

"I can't go south."

"Yes, you can. You will," he counters, stepping closer. He takes a match from Rielle and lights his own.

I shake my head. "Take me with you."

Seth smirks, and it spreads across his face. I haven't seen him smile yet, and it takes me by surprise. He laughs. Softly at first, and then in earnest. He puts a fist to his closed mouth.

I cross my arms, irritation sparking in my chest as Seth exhales slowly.

"That was a good one. Really."

"I'm not kidding," I clarify. I don't have much time. That knock will sound any second. My mind spins, grasping for anything.

Seth looms over me, his eyes meeting mine as he raises a finger. "First of all? You're Curseclean. That basically means you're dead if you stay out here long enough. Second? I seem to remember you freezing up and sinking like a stone barely twelve hours ago. I can't afford that kind of liability on my ship."

I look to Rielle and Thomas. I don't expect them to vouch for me at all. But the pity I find there is familiar.

It's the same look Harlow and Dean gave me that night. It's the look you'd give a bird with clipped wings that thought it could fly.

The spark of rage burns brighter, a wildfire of anger seeping across my chest. "Okay, wiseass. But ten *minutes* ago, I stopped you from becoming nothing but a smear on the pit floor. And I saw the coordinates when Monte handed you the paper. You can't afford to send me away."

All traces of humor slip from Seth's face. The muscle in his jaw ticks as he glares at me.

"You're headed north. And you're going to take me with you," I finish.

"That wasn't for you to see." He glowers.

"But I did see them. Now what are you going to do?"

Seth's calculating, his bright eyes searching my face as the two soft knocks sound on the other side of the metal door.

"You're going to go with them. You're going to forget what you saw. You're going to go live safely in Mexico and never mention me or my crew to anyone. Do you understand?" He says it quietly, so quietly that I can't tell if it's a reassurance or a threat.

"I can't go south," I say, not bothering to hide the desperate plea in my voice.

"Why?" Seth asks. It's direct. His eyes search mine, unblinking. A challenge.

I blink, faltering as the words don't come. He rips his eyes from mine and stalks to the door.

I can't go south. Dean will die if I go south.

Seth reaches for the handle, and the words fly from my throat before I can talk myself out of it.

"I'm the Chosen One."

Seth goes still as the words fill the space between us. Rielle sits up, and Thomas puts his hand on her arm.

Seth looks over his shoulder. "What did you just say?" he asks.

The knocks sound again, more impatient this time.

"I'm the Chosen One. I know where Anne's Heart is, and I have to get to it. Before anyone else does."

Seth pivots, facing me fully. "That's a sick joke," he says, his voice as low and dangerous as I've ever heard it.

"It's not a joke," I say quickly. "You wanted to know why Maddox had me in her hull? Why she said I was special? That's why."

More knocks. Seth ignores them, his gaze fixed on mine, and I can see his mind racing, weighing his options.

If I played this wrong, if they *aren't* the people I'm hoping they are, then they'll take me straight to the Vessels. Or if I played it wrong and they're smarter than they look, they'll avoid this shitshow altogether.

But if he is who he says he is—the kind of person who would fight to keep people out of Geramond's clutches, the kind of person who would chance a raid on the *Devil's Bid* just to free Curseclean, then maybe he cares.

Maybe he's the kind of person dumb enough to hope.

Knock. Knock.

"I need to go north. I need to get to the Heart so I can end this. You can take me there."

"Where is the Heart?" he asks.

"You think I'd still be alive if I trusted anyone with that information?" I retort.

He narrows his eyes, and I know I have him there. He didn't trust me enough to tell me he wasn't a Runner. I would be a fool to trust someone, *especially* someone I just met, with that kind of knowledge.

The lie is acrid on my tongue, and it only tastes worse as Seth steps closer to me, blinking as he cocks his jaw to the side.

"You didn't say anything," he starts, though it's not an accusation. It's him putting it all together.

Weaving the lie I'm spooling out between us.

"Would you? If you were me?" I ask.

Seth moves then, wrenching open the door. I can't hear what he says in those few muffled seconds, but when he closes the door and looks at me, there's an expression of resolution on his face.

He doesn't say I'm coming with them. There's no grand proclamation. The shadows headed south slink from the doorway and disappear, and then we're alone.

"Let's go," he says. And we do.

Chapter 18

EVERYTHING IS STILL CHAOS AS WE SLIP THROUGH the close metal corridors that snake like a maze. Above us, in the heart of the Jawbone, screams and the clamor of swords ring out against the splashing that's coming from—I'm assuming—people jumping into the water. There are no Torch Enforcers, but they don't know that, and the fog is lending itself nicely to the confusion—which is what we were hoping for.

Seth opens the hatch and slips into the night, motioning for me to follow. I do, coming out into the cold air and onto a slim metal outcropping just below the western edge of the Jawbone.

The fog is so thick it's almost impossible to see more than ten feet out. If I really try, I can see the dark, looming silhouette of ships tied to the dock.

Rielle and Thomas climb out next to me. Rielle puts a finger on her lips, and I nod. Above us, boots pound on the latticelike metal, rage booming in voices as the chaos reigns. Every knave on this godforsaken metal fort is armed and ready for a fight with Torch Enforcers—we've shouted *fire* in a crowded theater, and everyone is too panicked to realize that there isn't one.

Their shouts fade as they walk back toward the center of the Jawbone.

Moments later, a dark form slinks over the water, cutting through the curtain of cloud coverage.

It's bigger than any boat I've ever been on.

And Lucia is at the helm.

She lets out the same *coo* that Rielle and Thomas used earlier, and then Rielle and Thomas step toward the end of the platform and dive into the water, cutting through the surface like arrows: soundless, barely leaving a wake. They both emerge twenty feet away and swim to the ladder carved into the ship. I watch them climb up the side.

I freeze, my mouth locked tight as I realize what's happening. If they see me falter and sink, they might think twice about helping me. Seth already thinks I'm a liability.

The boat keeps drifting closer, by some miracle and small mercy. This whole metal hellscape was built for ship access. I can feel Seth's eyes on me, and the question lingers in the air between us as the ladder gets closer.

He's watching me. Studying me.

What kind of Chosen One created by a ruby found in the middle of the ocean can't *swim*?

When the ship is three feet from the metal platform, I can

see the cuts in the wood that make the ladder. I can't wait for it to drift closer, because it might not.

With one more look to Seth, I leap into the darkness.

My fingers catch the rung of the ladder, and my chest slams painfully against the side of the ship while my legs splash in the water. I can only imagine how ridiculous I look, but I'll take anything that keeps me from having to swim.

I climb, the mist surrounding me until I reach the edge of the railing. I roll onto the deck and vaguely register Rielle and Thomas drying off near the mast. But I don't see Lucia until I feel the blade at my throat. Her eyes burn bright as she looms over me.

"They said you told them you're the Chosen One, and I know you're a fucking liar," she seethes.

"Lucia," Thomas calls—a warning.

Lucia shoots them a glance but doesn't lift the knife.

I swallow, and the dull blade scrapes against my skin. I open my mouth, but then Lucia's weight is wrenched off me. I breathe, the frigid air filling my lungs, and roll over. Rielle, still sopping wet from her swim to the boat, pulls Lucia off me and presses her knee to Lucia's chest.

"Get *off* me!" Lucia bites, not letting out more than a deadly whisper, because we are still right next to the Jawbone. I sit up and wipe my hand across my throat, checking for blood. I don't feel any.

"We have a chance to end all of this, *all of it*, Lucia, and you are *not* going to let your shitty, murder-y attitude ruin this for us," Rielle shoots back, leaning forward to be heard.

Lucia bites the air, inches from Rielle's face. The click of her teeth sounds across the deck.

"Enough," Seth's voice sounds from the railing as he reaches the top of the ladder. His boots make a thudding sound as they hit the deck, and Rielle looks up for just a half second, but it's all the time Lucia needs to bring a leg up and across Rielle's chest, switching the momentum until Lucia is on top.

"Thomas," he says, and Thomas strides to the wheel.

"That's what *I* said," Lucia says, standing quickly and pointing the edge of her knife at me. "Enough of this one. The *Chosen One*? Seth, do you hear how ridiculous that sounds?"

"I hear it."

"Then what the hell is this?" she barks.

Rielle leans back and kicks up, landing on her feet. She swats the back of Lucia's head with an open palm. Lucia glares at Rielle, who just makes a *what are you going to do about it* face before walking over and extending a hand to me.

"Deck drop!" Seth calls from the helm. Without another word, Seth, Lucia, and Rielle all drop to their knees on the deck. I follow suit, turning to look at Thomas, whose hands are on the bottom half of the wheel.

There's a slat in the railing, and I peek out. We're sailing away from the Jawbone. Next to us, *Glimpse of Paradise* cuts through the water. The dread in my chest rises.

"Bank left," I whisper, looking to Seth. He narrows his eyes at me.

"*Get away from that ship. Now,*" I beg. Seth considers for a second and then tilts the wheel. We pull away from the yacht.

The chaos is dying down, the noise of shouts and crashing metal lessening against the night. Up ahead, a giant mass of flames blooms and cracks on the water. It's a ship, engulfed in fire. We pull past it, the destroyed boat shifting just enough to reveal the name on the stern.

The *Ichorbow.*

Seth, crouching next to me, turns to glare at Lucia over his shoulder. "Why do I have the feeling that you had something—no, *everything*—to do with that?"

Lucia fingers her mirror chain and shrugs one shoulder. "I had to fire the grenade launcher to start the ruckus. Might as well be pointing it at *something.*"

Rielle snorts out a laugh, and Lucia grins in her friend's direction. "Classic," Rielle breathes.

A sound like a thunderclap rockets through the night, and we all duck. A blast of heat rolls over us, and the orange blaze gets brighter. I pull myself up and peer over the railing.

Far across the water, *Glimpse* is on fire. There is nothing around it—no conceivable reason why it should have exploded.

My breathing quickens, and I hear my heartbeat in my ears.

"Looks like an engine malfunction. If they feed it bad gasoline long enough, it corrodes," Thomas says, gesturing for Seth to take the wheel so he can take a closer look.

"What the hell?" Rielle asks. I turn to look at her, and there's awe on her face. "You knew."

Glimpse to the water and you'll see fire.

Vanessa's words were right. I look back to the ship as the fire overtakes it.

It's the first time Vanessa's words have changed something— the first time I've understood them *before* something happens. A small thrill blooms beneath my ribs. I turn to look at Seth, who regards me with an unreadable expression as he turns the wheel, taking us farther from the Jawbone and farther into the fog.

Soon, the only sound around us is the lapping of waves against the ship and the creaking of the wood beneath our feet. The fog fades, and the dark sky stretches above us, the moonlight bright on our faces. I stand, making my way to the railing. The water is smooth, like glass.

"She could have made that happen," Lucia says finally. There's no rage in it, which is almost scarier that way. "Planted something." It's cold and calculating, like I might as well not even be here.

"Right. Between being completely under your watch and . . . *being completely under your watch*, I snuck over to a ship I didn't know to plant a bomb I didn't have," I snap.

Lucia sits back, crossing her arms over her chest.

Honestly, I don't blame her for not believing this. I hardly believe it, and I've seen and heard way more shit than an exploding ship. Even in the face of a curse like the Crimson, the idea of a Chosen One is a lot to swallow. The bright stars glimmer around the full moon as Lucia and Rielle argue. Thomas tells both of them to calm down, and Rielle tells him what he can do with his advice. I look up at the night sky and take a deep breath. That was lucky, but they don't know that.

Everything has fallen to shit so many times, I'm starting to learn to appreciate the small things when I can, like the sight of a full moon and the crisp, cold air in my lungs.

I stop as the thought hits me. Full moon.

This time, I don't have a weird, nauseous feeling. I don't have some weird, inexplicable insight. I just remember what Vanessa said the night the settlement fell.

The silver whole brings the storm to the sea, the mirror on velvet brings the ships to their knees.

Rielle bites the inside of her cheek as she looks at me.

The silver whole brings the storm to the sea. A silver whole.

I look up. The moon is full tonight. Something clicks into place—a last hope I grab with a whole fist. They're still arguing as I shove myself to my feet.

"There's going to be a storm tonight," I blurt. Seth looks at me for a moment before raising his eyes to the crystal clear sky. Not a cloud in sight. "A bad one," I add.

"You're not even good at *pretending* you're not full of shit—" Lucia starts, but I pin her with a glare.

"If I'm wrong, then you can do what you want. Leave me alone in whatever pit-of-the-earth way station you want. But if I'm not? You take me with you." I look at Seth. He clenches his jaw as he considers. It's a lot to ask, but I *know* I'm right.

"And, just clarifying the terms here," Lucia says. "If you're wrong, we toss you overboard."

My throat tightens at her words, and I know she's watching me to see how I react to that.

"Fine."

"We're not throwing anyone overboard, Lucia," Seth cuts in, his eyes on the sky as he walks to the middle of the deck, scanning the stars like he can find proof of my words there. Or something to damn me.

He lowers his gaze.

"We'll wait, then, *Chosen One.*"

I don't know if it's the look of taut regret on his face, or the way he spits the words like they're a mouthful of sour milk. But I know, in that moment, despite everything that just happened, everything he just saw—and despite the looks of irritation he keeps giving Lucia—Seth Marsali doesn't believe a word I'm saying.

Chapter 19

LUCIA SHOWS ME TO MY ROOM WITH A GRUNT, BUT after a couple of hours, I give up sleep—somewhere between paralyzing fear and nagging hopelessness. Whichever time that was.

The air in the room was too thick, too filled with my own breath.

As I step out onto the deck, the night air bites straight to my bones and I don't fight it. I let out a low hiss and let the sea air lift the hair from the back of my neck. Goose bumps prickle along every inch of me, and I close my eyes.

I look out off the back of the stern, the moonlight illuminating the white, frothy wakes that cut over the black abyss.

"As much as you dying would solve a lot of my problems, I don't think hypothermia is the way you want to go," a low, smooth voice sounds behind me.

I turn. A small fire burns in a metal pit secured to the deck, and Seth sits on a stool next to it, an open tin can in his hand.

Shivers rack my body as I eye him. He motions to the fire with his head, and I walk over. His eye is less swollen, and it's looking more like a normal bruise. But closer, I can see that his lip is still split, his knuckles still bloodied.

I sigh in pleasure as the heat seeps through my skin, and Seth pulls a folded blanket from under his stool and tosses it to me. I wrap it around my shoulders and sit on the stool opposite.

The fire crackles between us, embers catching the wind.

"Couldn't sleep?" he asks finally, digging his fork into the tin can.

I shake my head. "The door doesn't lock, and I keep imagining Lucia duct-taping my hands together and gleefully tossing me to my doom." It's a joke, but it's also not.

Seth rolls his eyes.

"No one is tossing you into the ocean, princess," Seth says, bringing a forkful of green beans to his mouth. He stops before they reach his lips and holds them out slightly. An offer.

"No thanks," I say softly, and then his words register. "And you can stop calling me princess, you know."

"You would prefer 'Chosen One'?" he asks. His eyes are sunset-tinted in the glow of the fire, and they bore into me. It's a joke, but it's also not.

"Charlotte," I correct. I don't trust myself to say more.

He holds my eyes for another beat and then shovels a bite of green beans into his mouth.

It goes quiet again, the wind sounding like a low hum rippling over the water. The fire dances in the wind.

"The whole country thinks you're some traitorous frat boy, you know."

Seth's fork freezes on the way back down to the can, and his eyes find mine. "You're a shit conversationalist, Charlotte the Chosen One."

"*Charlotte*," I grind out. "What I mean is . . . I wish they could know they were wrong. About you." My eyes fall to the flames.

Seth scrapes the fork over the tin ridges. "It wouldn't matter."

"What are you talking about? Of course it would. There isn't anything good this side of the grave anymore, Seth. I've seen it. The best-case scenario is some sort of horrible illness that takes you out before you turn into a monster, your *loved ones* turn into monsters, or you're all *eaten* by monsters. You could give people hope."

"I thought that's what you were for?" he asks. It's a simple question, but it cuts through my chest like a razor. Especially because, in this moment, he's not saying it ironically. He's not saying it to get a rise out of me. He means it. Hope is as foreign to him as it is to me, and he's circling it. Poking it with a stick. Seeing if it's still breathing, and refusing to get excited until he knows it's the real deal.

And I'm exploiting that.

Sickness spins in my gut as the full weight of what the hell I've done settles on my shoulders. I've done something here.

I've pulled a thread I can't un-pull.

My mind grasps for something—anything—to redirect the conversation.

"Did Evelyn do this, too? Before . . ."

Something shifts in him, and I see it. Shields up, the massive swipe of raising them extinguishing any flame of hope he'd manage to bring from kindling to spark.

"No. She didn't get the chance."

My mouth moves soundlessly as I search for words, but none come. Everything I've been fearing—losing Harlow and Vanessa—he's been through. I should know what to say here.

But words fall short at the look on his face.

"So you were remade by water on the night of blood. That's what the prophecy said, anyway," he says. It's conversational, not inherently a challenge. But I see the look in his eyes, and I know he's testing me.

"Yes." It's clipped, a word cut from the chunk of other things I can't say and tossed at him.

He tongues his molars, cocking his jaw to the side as he regards me. He shrugs. "And what does that mean? Was it some sort of ceremony? Did some priests in robes anoint you or some shit?"

"No." My shoulders square. I may not be the Chosen One, but it's not a lie that there *is* one. And Vanessa's been through hell for it. My hackles rise, the blood filling my cheeks.

He sits up. "You understand how ridiculous it sounds. Like the hope invented by people who wanted to give their kids some sort of way to cope with the apocalypse. And the 'Chosen One' sounds like a trope from a C-list made-for-TV movie."

His voice, that *word*, grates on me, and I feel the anger blooming through my bones.

"More ridiculous than red-eyed creatures? Wake up, Cap, we've been in a bad fantasy movie for a *long* time."

Seth laughs then and sniffs against the cold. The tip of his nose is red, and for the first time since I sat down, I wonder how long he's been out here. If he thought it was safe to sleep at all. "It's nothing personal," he says.

"You're calling me a liar. That feels pretty personal."

For a moment I can't believe how righteous I can sound while actively being in the wrong. It's a talent. A shit one, but I'm almost impressed, honestly.

"I wasn't calling you a liar. I was asking for information. But if you're asking, yeah, I take lies pretty seriously. I'd even say *personally*," he shoots.

"So you're all about honesty, then? Mr. *I Stole a Man's Ship and Said It Was Mine*."

Seth holds a hand up. "I never told you I was the captain of the *Ichorbow*. You assumed."

I laugh this time, and it's humorless. My breath is visible above the heat of the flames.

"Fine. You want honesty? Then give some. Why the hell did you take me with you if you don't believe in the Chosen One?"

The air is thick between us, and the fire crackles, unaware of the fight raging over its head.

And then, in that moment, Seth is caught off guard. His eyes meet mine, and we're at a stalemate.

"I don't know," he says finally. He swallows hard and clamps his jaw tight. There's an emptiness in his words, the shadow left in the space where a promise should be.

I stand, knocking the stool over with the suddenness of it. Then, I'm striding across the deck, the blanket falling off my shoulders.

Maybe I should tell him. I should just tell him the truth. I saw the look when I said his sister's name. He knows what it's like to love, I think.

I'm looking down at the deck right when I see the first pebble of rain plop against the wood.

It doesn't register at first. Not until the heavens crack open above my head, and the clouds I was too angry to notice roil across the air, thunder ripping through the night. Rain pours, soaking me in seconds. I turn just in time to see the fire wink out in a puff of steam. Seth doesn't move for a moment, like he can't quite believe it, either.

The silver whole brings the storm to the sea, the mirror on velvet brings the ships to their knees.

Vanessa's sleep-drunk voice sounds in my memory. The soft look on her face as she stared out the glass, unseeing as the words poured out of her mouth.

Seth stands, squinting as he looks up into the falling rain. When he meets my eyes again, there's something I haven't seen yet in his gaze. It's not an apology. It's not something reassuring. It's something I remember feeling with Vanessa: disbelief.

One right thing is a fluke. But two?

"I drowned that night," I call. "That's what it meant by *reborn*. I fell beneath the water, and I died."

If he feels like an asshole, he doesn't give that away. If he's sorry for doubting me, he keeps that hidden, too.

But I've just proven him wrong.

It doesn't feel as good as I'd hoped it would.

Chapter 20

WHEN VANESSA SAID THE STORM WOULD BRING the ship to its knees, she wasn't exaggerating.

All night, the ship rocks on the water, tossing about like a leaf. I try to help, but Rielle just shouts at me to stay in my room. That it's safer for me there.

I wait for the fear to come. The winds are howling so fiercely that it feels like the walls holding me above the murky depths are made of plywood, ready to splinter at a moment's notice.

But the fear stays away, or maybe it never left. Maybe fear has become so mixed in my blood that it's part of me now. Maybe I've been low-grade panicking since the night Maddox took the Palisade, so this doesn't feel like the end of the world.

And even if it is, I've already survived the end of the world a few times.

◆◆◆

Sometime before dawn, there's a sharp knock on my door. I pull it open. Seth stands in the doorway, completely drenched. His face is drawn. The swelling has gone down, but he has purple rings under his eyes.

"Where?" he asks.

I blink sleep from my eyes, trying to figure out what the hell he's talking about.

"What's our heading?" he clarifies.

"Where are we?" I ask, looking over my shoulder at the window. The sky is clearing, and the soft pink blush of sunrise is just starting to inch over the horizon.

"Off the coast of Oregon," he replies.

I step aside, motioning for him to come in. He closes the door behind him. He puts his hands in his pockets and shifts his feet. It takes me a moment to place the body language. Is he . . . uncomfortable?

"What?" I ask.

Seth presses his lips together and rolls up onto his toes before going utterly still.

"You're the Chosen One," he says. The words have come out as a taunt so many times from him in the past twelve hours, so I don't know what to do now that it sounds genuine.

But the words are raw as they slip past his lips, and they tear me down to the studs. He believes it. The whole of him, all the muscle and heat and the water dripping down the column of his throat, is stretched as tight as a bowstring in the presence of what he thinks could be the end of this hell. Hope, on Seth, is a lethal thing, a beautiful razor glinting in the low light.

If I'm honest? I didn't think much when I said it back at the Palisade. I just knew I couldn't watch them take Vanessa. And I didn't think much again when I said it at the Jawbone. The lie was just locked and loaded in my mouth, and I spit it out at the first sign of trouble. I've been using it as counterfeit currency, waiting for someone to hold it up and inspect it.

I realize as I sit, staring at Seth Marsali as he wars with his own pessimism, that I didn't think it would pass the first inspection. But here he is, and this lie has legs now. I'm watching it stand. I'm watching it breathe. I'm watching it stretch and move.

If I say yes now, there is no turning back.

I nod, my body responding before I can stop it. Because that's what I was going to do. I was never going to risk my only chance to get Dean back—to get to the Torch, where I know my sisters will be. I don't care what it costs me. But the way Seth's face tightens, the way I'm breathing hope back onto a fire that was long since dead, makes me think that the cost of this very well might be his life—and my soul.

He leans against the door. "So you know where Anne's Heart is."

"Yes."

"You don't have to tell me. I wouldn't. But I have to know where we're going. I need a direction."

"North, still. Just . . . head for the Blood Market. That'll be close enough."

He nods, and I see him calculating. Thinking, like a captain does.

"Where was Maddox taking you?" he asks carefully. I need to tread carefully here. One wrong word, one misplaced lie, and this all falls apart. I don't know how long Dean has, to begin with. But I can tell the truth about this.

"The Vessel Queen," I say. "Because I guess that's a thing now."

Seth runs a thumb over his lip and stands. "Yeah. We've known about it for a while. It takes longer for things to reach the shore, I think." He paces through my small cabin. "Did she say anything else? Did she mention Abel at all?"

I hear the sorrow in his voice, and I shake my head sadly. "No. I'm sorry."

Seth bites his thumbnail. "They wouldn't kill him. Whoever took him—Vessel or Runner. He's too valuable."

"He's your friend?" I ask.

Seth lowers his chin once. A nod.

"Is he as great as everyone says?" I venture.

Seth considers my words. "He's better," he says finally.

I don't know what to say to that, but Seth spins on his heel, cutting the awkward silence with more calculations.

"So the Vessel Queen will be looking for you," Seth says, looking at me like he's trying to gauge how afraid I will be at the thought.

I steel my gaze. "Yes."

Seth pulls a piece of plastic from his back pocket. Inside, the paper Monte slipped him is safely folded against the storm.

"We're headed north, Charlotte. And I'll take you there. But I need you to think about this carefully. The Vessels have been on the move, and we didn't know why. But now we do. They've been looking for you—you're a threat to their power. Maddox won't be the only one who knows the Chosen One has been found. If we go up there, it'll be dangerous. More dangerous than ever, now that Abel is missing. The Vessels *and* Runners will know that the Torch is in chaos without him."

"There isn't another option, Seth."

"We have to make a supply stop just north of Crescent City. There's a safe house there. We leave Curseclean at that location all the time. Someone usually shows up every three days to smuggle them south, to safety. You could—"

"I am not running." I look down, bracing for his *no*.

He takes a breath as he considers me. "Then I'll see it through," Seth says.

I can't help it then. I look up, my eyes meeting his.

"I'll take you north. I'll stay with you until you find Anne's Heart, Charlotte, and you end this."

I didn't plan on that. I figured they'd leave me on the shore, and I'd be able to slink off, buy Dean's freedom, and disappear.

This is going to be more complicated than I thought, but it's kindness. Which is also complicating, for different reasons.

Seth nods once and then turns to the door.

A thought rips through me, and the words fly past my lips before I can think.

"One condition."

He stops, looking back over his shoulder. "I didn't know we were bargaining."

"If you weren't doing this for me, would you be looking for Abel? Would you be saving more people?"

His gaze hardens as he shifts to look at me. We're allies, but we're not quite friends. He doesn't trust me. And for good reason. But I need to know this.

"Abel would want me to see this through. And ending the Crimson saves everyone on *all* Runner ships."

He turns to leave, and my hand flies on its own to grab his forearm, trying not to fumble as I discover that it's thickly corded with muscle. He stops, looking down at my grip on him.

"I won't let you stop helping people so that you can help me," I say, and I mean it. Down to my marrow, I mean it. I want to save Dean more than I want to keep breathing, but if I sacrifice others' lives in this lie, then I'm no better than a Vessel or one of the Exposed people who pay to become Xanthous. And if Dean thought his life came at the price of others', then he'd never recover. The Dean I love would be gone.

"We'll head north. But you'll still help people and look for Abel along the way."

Seth is quiet as he looks at me. He's infuriatingly hard to read.

My eyes flutter as I exhale, the force of my plea racking through me. "Please, Seth."

My voice shakes something loose in him. I see it in the way he turns, the way his gaze starts as calculating, then shifts, and I know he understands. "We won't ignore any calls."

I nod and let him go. He stops at the door.

"You're not what I expected, Chosen One."

My head jerks up at the nickname, ready to see a sneer. But as Seth turns back to the door, I think I see a soft smile on his lips.

Chapter 21

I TRY TO SLEEP, BUT MY STOMACH GROWLS, AND I realize I don't know how long it's been since I ate.

I slide my feet into my boots and slink out into the narrow hallway. The canteen is on the other side of the ship. As quietly as I can, I creep to the door and crack it open. I slip inside, slowly shutting the door behind me. I'll just grab a can of beans, or a couple of Triscuits or whatever they have, and run back to my room and just hunker down until it's time for my entire Liar McLiarson plan to come crashing down on top of my head—

I turn, stopping as I find Lucia and Thomas sitting around the tiny breakfast nook, Styrofoam cups on the table in front of them. I freeze.

I don't think that Rielle likes me, per se, but at least she hides her complete contempt. So, of course, she's nowhere to be found. Of course.

"What do you want?" Lucia asks, and Thomas gives her a

glare over the edge of his cup. "What?" she barks.

I cross my arms over my chest, but it still feels like I'm running into battle without armor or something.

"I was just . . . hungry."

Lucia leans back against the burnt-orange leather seat, sticking a toothpick in between her teeth. Her crop top inches up, revealing a muscled stomach. "If you're expecting a sort of 'Be Our Guest' sort of thing, you've got another thing coming."

"Think," Thomas says, swirling the contents of his cup.

"What?" Lucia snips.

"It's 'you've got another *think* coming,'" he says, downing the rest of the liquid.

I slowly inch toward the Formica counter, where a small pack of saltines sits, half-eaten. I'll grab those and disappear before Lucia can skin me alive via verbal lashing.

"That makes no sense," Lucia says, her voice closer to me than it was half a second ago. I jump, spinning to find her standing behind me.

Thomas rolls his eyes behind her. "You don't really care, do you?" he asks.

Lucia shakes her head. "Nope," she replies to Thomas, then whips her yellow eyes to me. "And what do you think you're doing?" she asks as I look in the cabinet.

"I am of no use to you if I pass out from low blood sugar," I say.

A smirk slides up the side of her face. "You're of no use to me with or without these four-year-old crackers."

Thomas uses the distraction to reach out and snatch the rest of her Snickers bar, and Lucia slowly turns her head to him, giving him the scariest death glare I have ever seen.

"You wouldn't dare," she whispers lowly.

"You're going to have to pick. Save the Snickers bar or give Charlotte a hard time. You can't do both."

Thomas holds the chocolate up, dangling it between two fingers as he slowly lowers it to his lips. He puts it between his teeth and narrows his eyes at Lucia. I kneel down, sorting through the cabinet. There are saltine crackers, a couple of bottles of Gatorade, and several MREs.

"You ass," Lucia grumbles. I look over as Thomas chuckles.

"Come and get it," Thomas replies, though he keeps the chocolate between his teeth, so it comes out *cah ah geh ih.*

Lucia presses her mouth to his, taking the candy bar from him with her lips.

He laughs, and she shoves him. Lucia chews the chocolate and wipes the back of her hand across her mouth. They remind me a lot of Harlow and Dean. The thought pulls at my heart in more ways than one.

"Stop watching us, perv," Lucia snaps, and I jump at the sound of her voice. I grab the crackers and stand. The sooner I get out of here, the better.

Thomas lightly smacks the back of Lucia's head, and she whips around to slap him before she saunters over to me, still chewing on the candy bar.

"Can't sleep?" Thomas asks, and Lucia looks back at him, disgust plain on her beautiful face. Thomas tilts his head at the look—a challenge. He's not going to treat me badly just because she does. Lucia rolls her eyes as she turns back to me, pulling out her knife. She means it to be intimidating, but I've been through enough now where it really doesn't faze me.

"Too much on my mind," I answer, ignoring Lucia.

"Not as common an affliction as you'd think," she chimes in, running the edge of her knife under her thumbnail. Now it's Thomas's turn to roll his eyes. "Good one."

"So you two are . . ." I motion between them, and Lucia crosses her arms.

Thomas waits to see if she'll answer, but she's silent. He puts his palms flat on the table. "Yes. We've been together since before the Crimson. We were part of an act in Vegas." Thomas answers my unasked question. "Knife throwing. I was talking to another girl and Lucia chucked a throwing star into the side of my grande Americano. We've been together ever since."

Lucia's eyes soften despite herself, and she looks at Thomas. My chest pangs at the affection there for a moment before she turns to me. I force myself to meet her eyes. That's one thing I learned from being Harlow's sister all these years. Never show weakness during confrontation.

"Look. You don't like me. I get it. You can put the knife away."

Lucia laughs. "I don't *like* anyone."

"That's true," Thomas quips, and Lucia ignores him.

"But I don't care about that," she continues. "I don't trust you."

"It doesn't matter what you think. Seth trusts me, and he's the captain," I say. All the teasing, the swaggering, slips off her face. She leans forward, stabbing the wall next to my head. I flinch. Lucia braces herself on the handle, her yellow eyes seeming to glow as she pins me against the wall.

"I've been around the world's best bullshitters, and I can smell *them* from a mile away. You're not that good. You're hiding something, *Chosen One*," she whispers. "I know girls like you. You probably ruled your school. You're probably used to getting your way, and you think you're going to wrap Seth around your finger like all the others. And maybe you could, if I wasn't here."

Rage bubbles up in my blood, bringing color to my cheeks. If I could tell her. If I could tell her how hellish middle school was. If I could tell her what it was like to grow up in Harlow's shadow. In Vanessa's trajectory. The anger simmers, and I glare at her.

She leans closer, and her breath tickles my ear.

"I'm going to find out what you're hiding. And when I do"—she pulls the blade from the wall—"I won't miss."

I've earned every threat she can muster—even her hatred. But I won't let her know that. Not with Dean's life on the line.

So I turn my head and bring my lips to her ear.

"You can try," I whisper back.

I push past her, shoving her shoulder with mine as I scoop to grab the crackers off the floor. I chance a glance at Thomas, who is eyeing me, his forearms braced on the table. He points to the crackers in my hand and then shakes his head. I look down, confused. He grabs a protein bar from the cabinet over his head and then tosses it to me. I catch it with one hand, and I thank God that I didn't drop it.

"She's not kidding. Those crackers are four years old," he warns. I set the sleeve down on a shelf next to the door, cringing.

"Thank you," I say, fully expecting Lucia to throw a

comeback in my face. But she's quiet as I leave, and I can feel her eyes on my back, almost as sharp as the daggers she wants to plunge there.

I slide the canteen door closed behind me, and it clicks shut just as a door ahead and to my left slips open. Seth slinks out, pulling his green sweater over his head.

I've seen Dean without his shirt. I am pretty sure I can remember each individual time, because it's branded so deep in my synapses that I can see his tanned torso when I close my eyes. I'd like to think that I can keep my cool around beautiful people after all these years of practice. But when Seth turns and sees me, his hands still bunched in the sweater over his chest, I stare.

Because I love Dean. I know that down to the marrow of my bones. But I'm also a human with a pulse who knows some things. And Seth Marsali is *something*. I've seen him shirtless before, in the pit, but that felt different somehow. It's hard to admire someone's physique when you're trying to figure out how to get through the day without dying. Now? In the middle of the night?

I can't help it. It's just so . . . *there*.

His muscles stretch as he freezes, one arm in the sleeve. His pants are slung low on his hips, and his torso is a collection of the variation of possible bruise colors—everything from buttery yellow to an angry-looking green. The dip in his shoulders leaves a shadowed hollow—the same one I used to admire on Dean.

I nod, lifting the protein bar by way of explanation. But it slips from my fingers, clattering to the ground.

I kneel down to get it just as Seth does. He gets there first, lifting it off the floor and handing it to me.

"Sorry," I say. His lips curl up as he pulls his other arm through the remaining sleeve.

"For what?" he asks.

For staring. For lying. For—

I shut my thoughts down, because if I start down that road, I don't know how long it will take me to stop.

"I didn't mean to be a creeper."

He looks over his shoulder at the door to my room. "You can come out whenever you want, you know. You're not a prisoner."

I stop. I didn't think I was, but I didn't really consider myself free, either.

Seth runs a hand over his hair. "You know, we have real food. Did Lucia not tell you?" Seth looks over my shoulder like he's about to walk into the canteen, but I step into his line of sight. The last thing I need right now is for him to go stir that pot.

"I'm good. Really. I just needed something in my stomach."

Seth looks down at the protein bar and winces. "Arctic White Chocolate. What does that even mean?"

I snort and look down at the all-caps font. It has a lightning bolt going through the *t* in *Arctic*. He reaches for it, and his fingers brush mine. I quickly pull my hand to my side.

"Are you sure you want to risk this?" Seth asks, and I look up. He's not glaring at me. Not looking me up and down like I'm going to combust.

This is nice. A normal conversation, almost. I don't know when I last had one of those.

"We have some mandarin oranges in there," he says. "I'd hate for the Chosen One to die on my watch from some weird, protein-bar-specific foodborne illness."

"I like the mystery," I say, holding up the bar. "Makes me feel brave. It's like Russian roulette, but with your intestines."

Seth cocks his head, questions riding up the side of his mouth as he smirks. They fill the crinkles around his eyes as he squints, and a soft laugh rises from his chest.

And I want to crawl into a hole and die. It doesn't even have to be big. It can be a small hole. I'll just curl up and cover my eyes and never make human contact again. I just talked about rampant diarrhea. In front of Seth Marsali.

In front of Seth Marsali, who just had his shirt around his neck. No wonder I can't tell Dean how I feel. My skills around the opposite sex range from vacuum hickeys to discussing bowel movements.

"Where did you come from, Charlotte the Chosen One?"

"Delaware County, originally," I say dumbly, which just makes his smile widen as he looks down.

"That's not what I meant."

And those eyes find mine, squinting like he's searching me for answers. And I realize that I don't remember how long it's been since someone looked at me with a question in their eyes.

I've been Harlow's sister since I was old enough to sway to the sound of her sirenesque voice. I've been Vanessa's guardian since the day I had the blood of her first scraped knee on the pads of my fingers.

I don't remember the last time I was *Charlotte*.

When that name stood in isolation, searched and seen on its own.

"What—" he starts, but he's cut off by the sound of the door behind him creaking open. Rielle looks around the doorjamb, her short nightshirt barely reaching the top of her lean thighs. Her tumble of blond curls falls over a shoulder as she hands a folded map out to Seth.

"Marked it," she says, and he grabs it, nodding thanks.

Rielle sees me standing there, and her eyes widen as something dawns on her.

"That reminds me! Seth! You never showed her!" Rielle hisses, dipping back into the room for a second before returning with her hands behind her back. She pivots, like she's trying to hand whatever she's hiding to Seth without me seeing.

Rielle nudges him when he doesn't play along, and Seth rolls his eyes as he moves the map to a free hand and angles his body toward her so that he can grab it.

"Ta-da!" Rielle says, holding her arms out as Seth pulls the headdress from behind him. Whatever half smile that's creeping up my mouth disappears as my mouth drops open. Seth holds it out farther, and I take it.

I must look as confused as I feel, because Seth shrugs, clearly trying to counteract Rielle's dramatic flair. "I heard you. When I handed it to Monte. I figured it was important—"

"So he snagged it before we got out of the Jawbone!" Rielle finishes with a flourish. Seth gives her a look, and she puts her hands on her own shoulders as she bounces on the balls of her feet.

Emotion swells up in my throat as I look down at the gold in my hands.

"Thank you," I mumble, because I can't find the right words. I look up at Seth, and I know he can see the sincerity in my eyes. "Seriously."

He nods, and I look from him to Rielle.

And suddenly, realization washes over me. Seth was just in there. Undressed.

Heat floods my cheeks as I mumble something about an early morning, which, of course, makes no sense. We're literally all living on a boat together. I don't have a pressing engagement I can fake.

I rush into my room and slide the door shut behind me. I'm exhausted, but I don't fall to the cot. I can't. Something in me is still tight, a wire ready to spring. My feet pace as it builds. I spin, pressing my body against the wall before sliding down to a crouch, my forearms braced over my knees, the headdress in my hands.

Dozens of thoughts fight for my attention, but one rises above the rest as I tuck the headdress in one of the bags I found below deck—the one I've been using for my stuff.

I didn't know how I was going to get Dean back once I got to the Blood Market—but now I do.

But the relief of that answered question wars with something else as I lie back on the bed.

I tasted something in those seconds before Rielle opened the door. Before she reminded me of what it was like to be the awkward third wheel.

For a moment, I was seen.

Even if it isn't by the man I love. And even if I was leaning toward it for the attention, or the sheer contact, or whatever the hell other reasons lie at the bottom of my murky, limping heart.

And I liked it.

Chapter 22

I'M UNDERWATER AGAIN.

The panic stirs in my chest with a violent twist.

Moonlight cuts through the waves, illuminating the twisting yards of kelp and sand.

I kick, trying to propel myself upward to break the surface, but I don't move.

I look down, and the terror rips up my throat.

There's no weight tied to my legs. No logical reason why I'm stuck here. I kick hard again, but still I don't move. I thrash my arms, but my fingers curve into claws and cut through the water pointlessly. It's like I'm on land, trying to fly.

My scream shoots bubbles around my face, swirling and obscuring my vision.

But I see her then. Even through the sand and dappled moonlight.

Her dark hair floats about her head, dancing with the rhythm of the waves, but her eyes are still as she watches me. Her dark vest secures a cream-colored gown around her chest, leaving the skirt to swirl around her, revealing bare legs.

For a moment, she just stands there—watching me as my lungs burn.

And then, she walks closer.

Walks, not swims.

Her feet kick up the sand on the ocean floor, and one hand flits to her chest, working the buttons on the vest.

I don't know who she is, but I know no human can do what she's doing.

I try to swim backward, to get away from her. But I'm stuck.

She reaches out again, her hand curling into a claw, her bloodred lips part, and her throat is alight. I think I recognize her.

I thrash, scraping and clawing at the water in sheer desperation.

Charlotte.

Her fingers are inches from my chest when I hear my name, louder this time—and it's not coming from the woman.

Charlotte.

I blink, and I'm awake.

The rain is lessened now, just a smattering of fat droplets hitting the deck around me.

And it's Seth over me, his face tight with tension.

"Charlotte," he says, worry creasing his brows as he helps me sit up.

I look around. We're on the deck. It's dark—sometime

between two and five, if I was to guess by the placement of the moon.

My fingers sting, and I look down. They're bleeding. I was scratching at the wooden deck.

"I was . . . dreaming," I say softly, still gazing down at my messed-up fingers.

"Shit. That wasn't dreaming, Charlotte. That was a nightmare. A night *terror*." His voice sounds strained.

I blink as I stare into the fog slinking over the water. I shake my head.

"I don't have night terrors. My sister does," I say before I can stop myself. My voice sounds far away. *Get with it. You have to be on guard*, I remind myself.

Seth moves his head so that I'm looking at him. I haven't seen real concern on his face before, so I don't know whether to read it as caring or irritation. He's shirtless, and the cold coaxes goose bumps over his shoulders. I realize that he's also barefoot, and even in the dim light of the gas lantern, I can see the dark circles under his eyes.

He stands, lowering his hand to help me up. I take it, and he hauls me to my feet.

"Come on," he says.

He takes me to the canteen and turns on one gas lantern on the table.

"Sit down," he orders, and I listen. There's a blanket on the bench behind me, and I pull it around my shoulders, shivering.

Seth kneels next to a cabinet and pulls out some bags and ceramic mugs.

"I woke you up," I say. It's not a question. I can tell by the hair matted on the back of his head.

"I'm a light sleeper. Especially when I hear someone screaming like they're being murdered," he replies, emptying powder into the mugs.

I shake my head. The dream was so real.

"I never used to dream like this," I whisper, more to myself than to him. Like I can figure it out if I say the words out loud. It makes sense that the terror of what I've seen and been through would catch up to me eventually. Especially if I spend most of my waking hours keeping secrets.

Seth pours water into the mugs and sticks them into the microwave. He steps back as the mugs turn on the plate inside.

"Have you lost someone recently?" he asks. No frills, no dancing around my feelings. Just a blunt question.

"I don't know anyone who *hasn't* lost someone recently," I say, aware that I'm sounding defensive.

"Yeah, but not everyone has night terrors. That should say something."

"Thanks," I say, trying to shove as much sarcasm into one syllable as I can.

The microwave beeps, and he opens it. He pulls the mugs out, wincing at the heat as he carries them to the table. "I studied psychology before. I saw a lot of PTSD at the Torch. Many of the patients had night terrors like that."

I look at him, unsure what to say next.

He's never mentioned his time at the Torch. He's never mentioned that he lived there, and that his family is basically royalty.

I haven't really stopped to think about the fact that he gave up the life I've been fighting for.

"What's it like there?" I ask quietly. I've seen pictures—streetlights that still work. Kids playing on scooters in the street. Mirrors are for putting on lipstick and going to class or on a date.

Seth slides the mug over to me. "It's like . . . what life was like before."

I look down. I don't know what I was expecting, but it wasn't this weird . . . *sludge.* Seth snorts at my expression.

"It's a mug brownie," he explains, blowing on his.

I laugh as I lean down to smell it. It does smell like a brownie. "I didn't know we got baked goods at the end of the world," I say.

Seth shrugs. "It's not the end of the world, Charlotte. That's what you're here for."

I look at him, ready to roll my eyes. But he looks back at me steadily as he twists his plastic fork, no teasing in his bright gaze as his golden eyes search my face. After forever and not long enough, the fork clatters against the edge of the ceramic, and he looks back down to the mug. I need to change the subject. Now.

"I'm sure the last thing you need is someone waking you up with bloodcurdling screams."

Seth shrugs as he puts another bite into his mouth, thinking as he chews. "It could be worse," he says, swallowing.

I hold up my bloody fingers. "Worse than losing your shit in front of strangers?" I retort.

The planes of Seth's face look sharper in the low light, and his yellow eyes blaze in the single flame of the gas lantern. He's silent for a moment, weighing his next words carefully before he looks at me.

"When my sister disappeared, I didn't sleep for two weeks," he says softly. "And when I heard they found her body . . ." He swallows hard. "Well. Now I'm a light sleeper."

Everything in me stills. Two weeks ago, I couldn't imagine Seth Marsali even *talking* to me, let alone telling me something like this.

The whole country mourned Evelyn, but I never really stopped to consider what it would be like to lose her as a sister. A *twin*.

"I'm so sorry," I whisper, knowing full well that even that is a sad excuse for a response. I don't know what else to say.

Seth nods, poking the brownie with his fork. Normally, I can't read him. I have no clue what he's thinking. But right now, in this moment, I can see the sadness on him like a weight he carries on his bare shoulders.

"There's always that joke about one twin being the better of the two, but . . . she really was."

I'm opening my mouth to say something when Seth sits up, whipping his head to the window. In one swift movement, he kills the gas lantern and motions for me to get down. I sink low on the bench as he crawls next to me, peering through the glass into the dark.

"What is it?" I ask. He motions for me to sit up and points through the window.

I twist, allowing my eyes to peek over the edge. On the horizon, I see it—a dark ship cutting over the water. My breath catches in my throat.

"Vessels," Seth says. I don't ask how he knows. He's been on the water long enough that I trust his judgment.

"Should we hide? Set sail and pull closer to shore?" I hiss, though I know it's a silly question. Seth shakes his head.

"We just need to be still and hope they don't see us. They're hauling ass fast enough that they might not be looking for prey right now." His voice is soft—distracted—as his golden eyes track them across the dark horizon.

I'm quiet, listening to his breathing for a moment before he relaxes against the bench.

"They're not stopping," he says finally, but he doesn't turn the gas lantern back on, even as we both sit back up.

A thought lurks in the back of my mind. I don't want to ask him, but I know it's not something that can wait until we're taken over.

"In my settlement, we have a code. *Death before the willful Crimson.* I could trust that my people would . . ." I swallow, knowing that I can't easily take the words back once they're out. I find my courage and push on. "If they try and get me . . . please kill me first, okay?"

Seth's face tightens, and his eyes darken.

"I don't want to ask that of you, but I have to. Will you?"

The moment is thick between us as he stares at me wordlessly. I grasp for something . . . anything . . . that will make it at least a little bit lighter.

"I'd ask Lucia, but I'm pretty sure she'd shoot me just as a precaution," I joke.

It takes a moment, but the corner of Seth's mouth turns up. He nods once.

It's all I need.

We sit there, in the dark, for I don't know how long. Seth doesn't move from the window, a vigilant captain unwilling to take his eyes off the predator-ridden waters.

Neither of us says anything, and the mugs on the table go stone-cold.

Chapter 23

I STAY UP UNTIL DAWN TRYING TO PULL OUT ANY of Vanessa's other prophecies from the corner of my mind to put them on paper.

A thought unfurls in the back of my mind—a question I've had since the Jawbone.

Did Vanessa know this was all going to happen? Somewhere, in the part of her that the Crimson woke up—did she expect it?

The dream about the storm could have been something she needed as she escaped north with Harlow. But the *Glimpse of Paradise* . . . that was just for me.

I hear my mom's voice in the corners of my memory. The warmth of her shoulder on the shell of my ear as I leaned on her on the porch swing and she talked.

Everything conspires to fulfill the plan, she'd say.

She said *everything*—the good and the bad—and it made

sense when the bad was a terrible grade or a mean friend. Even losing the boy I loved to my older sister. It's harder when it's this. When it's the screams of the dying and the blood of people I love trickling into the gutter.

I want to remember her voice now. I want to believe that this all has a point. That maybe I'm supposed to help Vanessa when we find each other again. That she gave me the tools to survive in this.

I want to believe that maybe, in the end, even my darkest lies will serve a purpose.

When I wake, it's about noon. I pull my hair back into a ponytail and step out onto the deck, which is now awash with sunlight. I don't hear anything for a moment, and then—

A splash, and a scream.

It takes two seconds for it to register, but my feet are moving, and I'm racing down to the bow of the ship, skittering to a stop.

This isn't what I expected, and it takes a moment to process what I'm seeing: Rielle, standing on the railing, a bright red bikini on her tanned, toned body.

"What is this?" I shout, the words bursting free from my chest. I didn't realize how scared I was until the relief hits me like a wave. "I heard a scream."

Seth sits with his back to the rigging, an apple in hand. He looks up when he sees me, and I can't read the expression on his face. His bruise is almost gone, and the cut on his lip is healed. "Diving contest."

Lucia's voice sounds from below. "Bull*shit*. That was at *least* a nine."

Seth inspects the apple. "I told you. Your knees were bent slightly, and the angle of your dive wasn't straight. As captain and head judge, I have to deduct."

"It was a *cannonball*, you ass!" Lucia shouts. Seth smirks and takes a bite of his apple.

I don't know if we're going to talk about last night. Or what last night means. If we're slowly becoming friends or if we're just not enemies anymore.

Rielle looks over her shoulder, and I don't even hide the fact that I'm checking her out. I don't use the term "perfect" often, but she is quite the specimen. She knows it, too, from the way she's grinning at me.

"Want in on this? I got a spare in my room," Rielle says, motioning to her bikini and giving a little shimmy.

"Perfect ten," Seth jokes, and Lucia splashes him from the water below.

"I'm good. I just . . ." I motion to the pad of paper and pencil. I was going to come up here and think. Maybe a change of scenery will jog my memory. "Why are we stopped?"

I look out—we're closer to the coast than we have been in several days. I can see the leaves of the trees dancing in the wind, and I shiver. I don't know how Rielle and Lucia are actually getting in the water right now.

"We needed to restock. We have a station tucked just beyond those trees, but it's safer for one person to go. Less of a scent for

Vessels to track, now that we have a Curseclean on board," Seth explains through another bite of apple.

"Vessels will eat anything," I say, almost defensively.

Seth points a finger at me. "But they'll always prefer Curseclean, and they know the Chosen One is Curseclean."

"Yeah, but that could change," Lucia quips.

"No, it can't," I say firmly.

Rielle and Seth share a glance, and the playful tone feels like it loses its footing, snagging on the words hanging in the air. I take a deep breath and peer at the shore. "So Thomas drew the short straw this time?"

Seth smirks. "Nope. I did. Hanging out with them is a pain in the ass. But we have to sit here and wait anyway, and since it's the first not-cloudy day in like a month, these two couldn't help themselves."

Lucia hauls herself back up over the railing, her black one-piece almost as scandalous as Rielle's bikini. It plunges deep in the front and back, and she wears it well.

"In your dreams, Cap," Lucia says, twisting her hair out a little too close to his boots. "He's just jealous that I repeatedly beat his ass with my double-back twist."

Seth looks to the sky like he's pleading for help. "That's not a double-back twist! You can't just fling yourself into the air and call it a double-back twist!"

"Everyone be quiet! I have to concentrate," Rielle demands, lifting her long arms above her head. She takes a deep breath and then jumps, feetfirst, into the water.

I walk to the railing, looking over into the water. It's more blue than black, since we're closer to the shore. For the first time in a while, I feel the longing that used to tug on me back in the summers before all this happened. I miss the water being a friend.

Rielle emerges, spitting a mouthful of water before looking up. "How was that?"

Lucia rolls her eyes next to me. "That isn't anything! That's like stepping into the ocean! So . . . perfect ten for *stepping into the ocean*."

Rielle glares up, indignant. "That is too a thing! It's called a pencil jump—look it up!"

"And how would I do that, genius?" Lucia shoots back.

"You're both ridiculous," Seth sighs, the apple dangling from his hand.

I don't know if it's the sunshine, the shallows, or the company, but he's the opposite of the taut, on-guard captain I saw last night.

Lucia reaches out, grabbing the apple with one hand before crunching into it.

"Okay, smartass. You go." She gestures to Seth. "Show us what you got." She wipes the apple juice off her chin with the back of her hand.

"Hard pass. You two are terrible judges," he replies. "I'll get ten points from Rielle for getting wet and three from you because I didn't break my neck."

Lucia opens her mouth to argue, but I tap the eraser of the pencil against the pad as I speak up.

"I'll do it."

Lucia looks to me. "And what are your qualifications?" she asks, and I assume she's half kidding. I straighten my shoulders.

"Well. My sister was the number one level-ten gymnast in the state, and I was at every competition, so. I know a thing or two. I can for sure tell if something is a *twisting double-back*."

Lucia purses her lips, finally smiling at my minor correction and veiled challenge.

Rielle laughs. "Oh *hell yeah*, she's got the jargon and *everything*."

Seth's mouth curves up into a smile as Lucia and I turn to him.

"All right. We got the Summer Olympics happening right now. She's our judge. Let's do this." Lucia hits her hand on the railing and climbs up.

"This is us killing time waiting for Thomas before we commit more crimes," Rielle says, reaching the top of the ladder and swinging her feet to the deck.

Lucia hoists herself up on the railing. "The world has gone to shit. I say this is a redo of the 2020 Olympics—it's the Olympics. You ready?" she asks me. I nod, lifting a hand to shield my eyes from the sun.

Lucia turns around and goes up on her toes. I bite the inside of my lip, surprised how the little movement fills me with longing. *Vanessa.* I shake the thoughts away. I can't afford to start crying now. Not after last night. Seth probably already thinks I'm fragile enough.

Lucia jumps backward, bringing her knees to her chest as she twists and flips once, then twice. Her twist is only one-fourth of a twist, though, not half. She plunges into the water. For a moment, I think about giving it to her. It won't hurt to maybe not have her hate me.

But something about Lucia makes me wonder if she under-twisted on purpose, just to see if I really know anything.

She breaks the surface and looks at me expectantly.

"A one-fourth twist double-back," I say. "I give it a nine-point-four. Your legs came apart a little at the end. But other than that, it was good."

Lucia regards me for a moment, and I wonder if she's just plotting what swear words she's going to use to tell me off. But she purses her lips and gives a small nod. "I'll take it."

"Nine-point-four. Not bad," Seth says, sliding off the railing. He pulls his shirt over his head. I don't think I'll ever get used to seeing that chest. I wasn't in the mindset to admire it last night, but I am now. And I do, as he climbs up onto the railing.

"Double front," he says, looking down at me.

I cock an eyebrow. "Proceed," I say. He turns, his back muscles rippling in the sunlight as he raises his arms above his head. Then he jumps, tucking his legs in and executing a perfect double-front flip.

Rielle and I laugh, and even Lucia claps when he breaks the surface, flicking the water out of his face.

"How was that?" he calls.

"I don't know. His toes weren't pointed," Lucia says.

Rielle smiles, catching on. "Yeah. And I think he over-rotated."

I make a show of thinking about it before I lean over the railing. "Nine-point-three," I call down, and Seth smiles knowingly, nodding as he runs a hand through his wet hair.

"I sense a prejudicial judging panel," he calls up.

I smile as the sunlight warms my face and Seth climbs back up over the railing. He points to Lucia, who shrieks and warns him with a *don't you dare*, but he grabs her and throws her over his shoulder and jumps in.

Rielle joins, and I find a comfortable perch on the railing. I've written down everything I can remember, but my hand still idly holds the pencil. Soon, I find myself sketching. I sketch Rielle as she climbs out of the water, fingers adjusting her straps. I sketch Lucia as she dunks Seth. Somewhere in there, I loosen my mirrored bands and set them next to me. I look at my skin, and the indentations the glass has left over the soft blond hair.

The wind whispers across the deck and rustles my paper, and for a moment . . . just a moment, I'm still.

And I know this can't last. I know.

If the Vessels don't catch me, then the Runners will. If I escape them both, then my own lies will have the privilege of finishing me off.

But right now, just for a moment, just for half an hour, I'm a teenage girl again. And I'm listening to squawking laughter and splashing waves.

And I don't ask why they don't ask me to jump in, because

I'll have to fully realize that they probably remember what happened last time I went in the water. And I don't let myself wish I could slip into Rielle's extra bikini and show off my own flawless double-back. I don't let myself imagine what it would be like to feel Seth's eyes on me.

I don't.

I look at the words on the page, trying and failing not to glance down at the captain in the water.

It's less than an hour later when the sounds in the water below go silent. Fearing the worst, I look over the edge. Seth, Lucia, and Rielle are looking in the same direction. I follow their line of sight, and my heart seizes in my chest. A small fishing boat bobs in the water, not even two hundred yards away. Seth turns to Lucia. I can't hear what he's saying, but I know by the way that his jaw sets that the fun is over. He swims to the ladder and climbs up in the amount of time it takes me to slide off the railing. His eyes are lit as he walks quickly to the stairs, disappearing below. Lucia is next, her expression matching his.

Rielle is last.

"What's going on?" I ask.

"We don't know. Could be a scouting ship. Could be a family in trouble. Either way, we're not going to just leave it."

My heart leaps. It's a complete long shot, but there's a chance that Harlow, Vanessa, or Dean could be on that ship.

I pull the mirrored bands back on as Seth and Lucia emerge from below deck, iron blades at their sides.

Seth stops when he sees me pulling the bands over my arms.

"You're staying here. Rielle?"

Rielle pauses as she reaches the top of the stairs that lead below deck. Seth points at me, and she inclines her head.

My chest tightens. I can't just *sit here*. I need to *do* something. If Dean is on that boat, or Harlow, or Vanessa . . . I look to the blades on Seth's belt. I can't explain it—but the need builds inside me like a dam.

"No," I bark, shoving myself to my feet. Seth reels around, his expression drawn.

"This isn't a discussion," he growls.

I step forward, meeting his eyes. "It's not. I need to go with you, Seth." I glare at him. "I *have* to go."

It's low, and I feel the shift in his understanding. I'm letting him believe that it's a Chosen One reason. I'm letting him believe that this is prophecy-level stuff.

He moves closer to me, his breathing harsh. His eyes stay fixed over my shoulder on the boat that's coming closer every second, but his words are just for me. "You come with me, you do as I say. No arguments, no hero shit. Got it?"

I nod, and he turns back to the ladder without another word.

We ride the dinghy over the whitecaps, Lucia sitting at the motor. She kills the engine as we get closer and shoots me a look over her shoulder. She raises her blade, as if to check that I'm armed. I lift the machete Seth handed me before we left, and she looks away, satisfied.

The boat is small enough to go from bow to stern in about fifteen steps, and the sides are rusted and dented. I look at the name—*Heaven Sent*—and run the words along everything I remember, but nothing clicks. We drift closer to the metal ladder that hangs over the side, and Seth grabs it, pulling our raft closer.

I am the last one up, and climb over the railing without making a sound. I keep my eyes downcast, watching the world in the cracked reflection of my mirrors. Seth and Lucia walk toward the bow, blades drawn. Rielle stands in front of me, knives in both hands. There's a lot of luggage—duffel bags and suitcases. I walk past a rolling pink carry-on with Disney princesses on the front.

It's covered in blood.

I look up at Rielle, and I see the tenseness in her shoulders.

Something bad happened here.

The sound of the waves lapping against the side of the boat mixes with our footsteps as Seth makes his way to the cabin.

He looks back at us as he reaches for the door handle, lifting his blade once, twice, and—

He pulls the door open and immediately takes three steps back, coughing and retching. Lucia swears, covering her nose with her forearm. It takes a couple extra seconds for the stench to reach Rielle and me, but when it does, it's so bad that I almost pass out. It's a mix of rotten meat and waste, all locked in a hotbox and cooked. My eyes water as I whip around, pulling my shirt over my nose and mouth. When I look back, Seth is taking a tentative step inside the cabin. Lucia pulls her tank top over her head and ties it around her face, then follows Seth in nothing but shorts and a hot-pink sports bra.

I move to follow, but Rielle grabs my arm.

"Don't," she says softly. I turn to her, ready to argue. But the look in her eyes isn't concern—it's something else. She's not worried about me getting injured. She's sparing me from whatever is inside the cabin. Part of me says that I should push on. That if the bodies in there are Dean or Harlow or Vanessa, I want to know.

But the smell is overpowering, and I can't imagine what it looks like in there. If the people I love are in there, then I'm better off not knowing.

It's quiet for a second, and then Seth and Lucia come back out. Seth lowers his blade, his shoulders sagging. He has a paper in his left hand, and he stares at it.

Lucia pulls the shirt off her face and leans forward, bracing her hands on her knees. She walks over to the side, leans over, and vomits.

I don't ask. I don't need to. I can tell by the way Seth paces by the railing that there are no survivors.

"A log of their distress calls. They hailed Torch Enforcers six times a day for *two weeks*," Seth says, whipping around. "No answer. And you know why?"

He crumples the paper and throws it to the side. I've never seen this kind of fire in Seth's eyes before. It's something past rage. It's despair, lit from within. His breathing is ragged; his hands ball into fists before opening again.

"Because it was a couple of families. Blue-collar parents,

from the looks of it. And . . ." He stops, blinking for a second. Tears bite the back of my eyes as I see him struggle to find the words. His voice cracks, and he cocks his jaw. "And *kids*. And he would have told the Torch Enforcers to leave it alone. To focus on *the big picture*."

"Who?" I ask quietly. Rielle turns away and runs a hand through her hair. I look up as Seth's eyes find mine. A dark, hollow laugh rips from his throat.

"Who? My *father*. You want to know why I left? Why Evelyn *left*? Because we found out how my father and Genevieve were dictating who the Torch helped. People with money. Skills they deemed necessary. Young people. Politicians. Bureaucrats. Abel has been trying to reverse that since he took power, but . . ." Seth gestures to the boat. "And now that he's gone . . ."

Seth shakes his head and turns away. I don't even realize I'm crying until I taste the tears that slip over my lips. I open my mouth, but the words die in my throat as I see a shadow rise up in the tinted, distorted window of the cabin. For half a second, I think it's Rielle, coming back around. But it limps slowly toward the door. A terrible, croaking sound rips from its throat, and every step it takes makes a bubbling sound, like it's stepping through puddles of blood.

"*Seth!*" I shriek as the Vessel careens onto the deck. Seth spins around, lifting his blade as Lucia shoves herself upright.

"Charlotte! Look away! *Now!*" Seth screams, and I drop my gaze to my mirrors as I raise my knife. Rielle runs back up the side of the boat as more croaking grunts join the fray. There are more Vessels. Lucia ducks as what used to be a man in a mechanic's jumpsuit lunges for her. She switches the blade between her hands as she comes back up and swings it wide. The Vessel's head falls to the deck with a sickening *thud.*

"Rielle!" Seth calls, cutting off a head as he kicks another Vessel into Rielle's swinging blade. It falls to the deck. I can't count how many there are—they are moving too fast, and it's hard to tell in my small, cracked mirrors. But it would only take one to end me.

I hear it before I see it, and I smell it even before then. Heavy footfalls sound behind me, and I tilt my wrist to see it in the reflection.

It used to be a woman. She's wearing a flowery dress, and has a crucifix necklace stuck in the decaying flesh above her breastbone. Her eyes are a violent, hateful red. My hands shake as I redouble my grip on the blade.

I've never killed one before. I've never had to.

I hear Seth scream at me, but the Vessel's grunt drowns out what he's saying. I shut my eyes tight, lift my blade, and swing as hard as I can.

I feel some resistance as the sword hits, but the grunting stops and my arm follows through. Blood hits me in the face as I hear a disgusting *thunk,* followed by a dull thud. The Vessel's head and body. I keep my eyes shut as my heartbeat pounds loudly in my ears.

The sound around me fades back in, and it's just the ocean again. No grunts. No screams.

I open my eyes slowly, keeping them down. My mirrors are covered in blood, and I wipe them on my pants as I turn and check the rest of the deck in the reflection.

Seth's in front of me before I know what's happening, and I jump as his hands touch my face. I shut my eyes and let out a small shriek.

"Charlotte, it's me," he says softly. "You're okay."

I open my eyes, blinking as Seth's yellow gaze searches my face, his palms cradling my jaw.

"Are you hurt?" he whispers, wiping blood off my cheek with the pad of his thumb. I shake my head.

"Deep breaths," he murmurs, and I meet his eyes as I force myself to take several slow lungfuls of air.

I look in his eyes as I exhale. I did it. I killed a Vessel. I didn't freeze. I did it. And Seth Marsali is holding my face. He's so close that his voice vibrates my rib cage when he talks.

He lowers his hands slowly, then steps back.

And I don't say anything, even as we climb back down the ladder and ride back to the ship.

Even as I find my notebook by the stern, sit with my back against the metal, and let the blood dry on my face as Seth stalks down the stairs. We return, just the four of us, but somehow the boat feels empty.

Chapter 24

THOMAS COMES BACK WITH SUPPLIES, AND WE lift the anchor. We all jumped in the water when we got to the ship to rinse off the blood that was caked on all of us, but I still change my clothes and splash water on my face. I'm not sure I'll ever feel clean again. No one really feels like talking, and for hours, we don't.

The sun is set when Rielle finally finds me in the crow's nest, the wind so cold that my face feels numb from it. Her hair is wet, and she smells vaguely like flowers. I wonder if Thomas found body wash on his supply run.

"I take it they never officially announced how Evelyn died," she says finally.

I shake my head as I watch the waves beat against the front of the boat.

"Vessels," she answers. I nod. It was never official, but I

think most of us assumed.

"He thinks it's his fault," Rielle says at last.

The thought feels like a kick to the chest. "What? Why?" I bite out.

Rielle sighs heavily. I'm quiet as she bites her top lip, lost in thought. It slides between her teeth. "I'm from the Torch, too," she says. My head whips to her, and she smiles softly. "I'm sorry, did my lack of refined fucking manners not give me away?"

She's kidding, but there's something about this story that has a scar to it. I have enough of those myself to sense them.

"My parents called me to the living room one night, before the Torch," she starts, and her voice is quiet and small-sounding. "And they told me they had something for me. They put a blindfold on me. I thought it was a new bike," she says, raising one shoulder and smiling even though her eyes are filling with tears.

"They sat me down and I heard them bring this person in. I could hear her breathing. They sat her in front of me, and then they . . . they took my blindfold off."

She cracks her knuckles and looks down, rattling off the rest of the story like she's tearing off a Band-Aid.

"And it was a man. My father's age. His eyes were . . ." She takes a deep breath. "They were the deepest, scariest red I've *ever* seen. Like blood that was at its boiling point."

I remember Lemmere, and the Vessel on the boat.

"I didn't know what to do. I felt this . . . *burning* in my eyes, and I knew. I knew I'd been infected."

The memory of my mother hunched over in the passenger

seat, palms to her face, screaming . . . I blink and focus on my breathing. I can't allow the panic to take over, not now. I want to hear the rest of it.

"They infected you on purpose?" I ask. Saying something drowns out the sound of my mom's terrified shrieks as they play in my memory.

Rielle nods. "I screamed at them. I asked them why the hell they would do something like that. I shut my eyes, and they told me not to worry. That they had a solution."

My stomach clenches. I've grown up around Curseclean and the idea of Runners. But I've never met anyone who used them before.

"Then they brought three more people out. One was a burly guy with sleeve tattoos. The other . . . she looked like my school librarian. One was just a kid."

Rielle can't hold the tears back any longer. They streak down her cheeks, mixing with the salt of the ocean.

"They were Curseclean. And my parents sat there on the couch next to me as they forced these people to meet my eyes. To take the Crimson so that *I* could live."

Words don't work as I think about what she's telling me. The shame she's inviting me to see. I fight to keep my face blank, to stop myself from crying, too.

"And I was a teenager. I didn't think to tell them no. And for a while? That thought made me feel better about what happened afterward. How they tied the blindfolds back on those people and shuffled them outside. But since then, I realized that they didn't have to force me to do anything. I was . . ."

She sucks on her bottom lip. "I was *so scared*, Charlotte," she says, looking at me for the first time since she started the story. Her yellow eyes burn. "I traded their lives for mine."

I feel hollowed out as I lower my gaze to the hands she has clenched on the railing so tightly her knuckles are white.

Rielle just told me her deepest shame. No prompting. No lies.

For a second, I wonder what would happen if I tell her the truth. If I let her in to see my darkest truth just as she's let me in to see hers.

But I don't. I can't. Dean's life is still at stake.

"You were a kid," I whisper. "This is on your parents, and Anne." I bite out her name like a bitter afterthought, and Rielle shakes her head slowly.

"See? I don't get why people think that. Especially women. We should be better than that."

I laugh before I can stop myself, and she tilts her head like she's waiting for my explanation. "Come on, Rielle. This isn't slut shaming. She cursed *the world*—"

"—and we loved it," Rielle shoots back, her voice taking on the edge of someone who has sharpened their opinion over a long time. "I saw the T-shirts. I heard the stories. We loved her 'womanly rage' until it was too messy. Until it became real to us. Maybe we deserve this. Maybe it's about time."

The words hit me somewhere deep and send something spinning.

We loved her rage until it became real to us.

She takes a deep breath through pursed lips, and I look over at her. I expect her to apologize, but I don't know why. She doesn't, though. She reaches out and grabs my hand, and I don't pull away. "I appreciate you trying to absolve me. But I don't think I can be absolved. I don't want to be. I knew what I was doing. We all did. Those moments show who people really are."

Below us, Seth comes above deck. He walks to the bow. Rielle watches him.

"I want you to know that when Admiral Marsali tried to inoculate Seth against the Crimson just like my parents did me, they had to put a gun to Evelyn's head to force him. He would have rather died than hurt other people, but couldn't kill her. That's the only reason he's Xanthous. And it haunts him every single day."

Rielle takes a deep, shuddering breath and lets it out slowly. She wipes her tears with the back of her hand. "I spent years trying to make it right—met someone who hated the Torch as much as I did. Together, we were going to change the world. But . . . that doesn't always work out."

I look down. Of course. Seth. I remember the image of her slipping out of his room.

"I didn't tell you this so you could feel bad for the shitty person I am," she says finally, her voice stronger. "I'll sail this ocean and try and save as many people as I can with the evil gift I now have. It's the *least* I can do. But Seth? He does this for Evelyn." I understand. It was the same reason I wanted on that boat today. Rielle's voice brings me back to the moment. I feel sick. I lean down, putting my head between my arms. I think about the promise I made him make last night. It's the same kind that haunts him now. "But also because Evelyn believed that the world could be better, even after all of this. So when he sees things like that, like today"—she takes a breath—"I think it makes him wonder if the world can be saved."

I look down at Seth as he stares out at the dark, still water, and I wonder the same exact thing.

The sky is clear, the stars like spilled glitter on black velvet. And for once, the night is warm. I forgot my boots, but I don't really need them.

I don't really realize I'm hoping he's out here until I see him standing at the stern.

Walk away, a voice in my head tells me. Nothing good can come from me getting more involved. But the thought that I made him promise something so painful when he's already carrying the weight of Evelyn's disappearance makes my heart hurt.

"You should be asleep," he says without looking back. "Sleeplessness is a contributing factor for night terrors."

I creep up next to him. He's wearing a gray long-sleeved shirt, and the mirror on the long chain around his neck hits the railing with a soft *tink*.

"You okay?" he asks softly.

The memory from the boat plays in the recesses of my memory. The feel of the blade in my hands. The resistance as it met flesh. The blood.

His hands on my face.

I nod. "Yeah."

"You did well," Seth offers. "Held your own."

I incline my head, a *thank you.* He returns the gesture and then looks back over the water.

I remember what I thought when he first yanked me on board the deck of the *Ichorbow.* How much I hated him. How I thought he was a monster and told him so over and over.

Everything he's done, he's done to stem the guilt that eats at his core.

I can relate.

So I don't know what we are: friends, or just allies. And it doesn't really matter, since neither will survive the realization that I've been lying through my teeth this entire time. I steel myself and walk up beside him, trying my best to convince myself that it won't hurt when that happens.

"But you can't have night terrors if you don't sleep. So. It's just a matter of commitment."

Seth smiles and looks down.

My gut twists, just a little, and I remember how it felt when Dean looked at me. *Dean.*

I glance away, reminding myself that I had to *make* Seth keep my company. And that Rielle was in his bedroom two nights ago.

Seth's smile is crooked as he looks up at the stars. "So you're just really committed to avoiding all your deep emotional traumas, is what you're saying."

I smile back. "What can I say. I lettered in emotional dodge-ball."

Seth considers the words. "Emotional dodgeball. Huh."

It's now or never. I swallow hard. "Rielle told me about Evelyn. About what you're doing for her."

If it's an overstep, I can't tell. Seth's face is unreadable, and I plow forward.

"And I know it's none of my business. I just wanted to apologize if what I asked of you in the canteen . . ." Seth turns to catch my eye, and the pain I see there almost knocks the wind out of me. *Please kill me first*, I'd asked. "If it hurt you. I shouldn't have asked that."

Seth considers my words as he looks out over the wakes rolling from the back of the ship.

"Did she tell you about my father? About what he did?"

I nod. "Basically."

Seth exhales. "He put the gun to my head and told me to look up. I couldn't. I thought the fear would be worse, but . . . it wasn't. But then he put the gun to my head and told me he'd kill Evelyn. So I looked up. I gave the Crimson away. And every day I have to look in the mirror at these eyes and know what I did to earn them."

"You did what you needed to do," I say, hating how the words sound like something I tell myself all the time.

"You didn't," Seth says.

The only sound is the lapping of the waves as Seth studies the line where the sky meets the sea.

"Why would you tell them who you are?" he asks finally.

"Maddox, I mean. She couldn't prove it, I'm assuming. Why admit it?"

I don't know if I'm just tired of lies, or if his honesty broke something in me. But the truth slips past my lips.

"I was trying to save my sisters," I say. "I figured if I could just draw Maddox away, they'd have a chance to escape. And they'd find Dean and . . . get away. Get to safety."

"Who is Dean?" he asks, his voice quiet.

"One of my best friends. My sister's boyfriend."

"That's dumb," he says, and I shoot him a death glare.

"I'm aware," I bite out.

"Not that you shouldn't care about other people, Charlotte. It's just that your life is worth more than a bargaining chip. For anyone."

"It's not worth more than my sisters. It's not worth more than Dean," I snap, my voice rising too much.

The understanding washes over Seth's face, and I know he's seen me. He understands.

"Hell of a price to pay for someone else's boyfriend," Seth replies softly.

I fidget with the hem of my shirt as I search for the right words. By the time I find them—*it's not like that*—it's too late.

"Ah," Seth says, leaning back, his hands wrapped around the other side of the railing. "You're in love with him."

"Don't *ah* like you know the situation," I snip.

Seth straightens, holding his hands up. "You're right. I shall never *ah* again."

"Good," I shoot back. "Because I'm not."

It's quiet for a moment, the roar of the boat on the ocean the only sound filling the night.

"Does he know?" Seth asks.

"God, no," I say absently, then immediately regret it as I whip my head to Seth. A grin spreads across his lips, and I know he got me. All of the secrets I've guarded without so much as a slip, and he pulled this out of me in under a minute. Fucking hell.

I drop my head to the railing and groan, and Seth lets out a soft snort.

"Wow, Charlotte the Chosen One. You're shit at this."

You'd be surprised, I think, shoving the thought down as I stand up.

We look out at the water together, and I rub a hand down my face. "Yeah. Sure. Fine. I love him."

"For how long?" Seth asks.

I shrug. "Since as long as I can remember, I guess. He lived next to my grandma, so I'd see him a couple times a year when we visited. We grew up together."

"And he fell in love with your sister," Seth finishes.

"It wouldn't make sense if he hadn't," I say immediately.

I feel Seth turn to look at me, a question on his face. I take a deep breath and let it out through pursed lips. "You'd love her, too, if you met her. Beautiful. Fierce. Smart. And she can sing like . . . like nothing I've ever heard. Her band, Nevermind, opened the Jingle Ball the year before everything went to shit."

"This is your older sister?" he asks.

I laugh. "Yeah. And then my younger sister is—"

"The gymnast," Seth finishes. I stop, remembering that I talked about Vanessa earlier, during the diving contest. I nod slowly. "Yeah."

He leans his forearms on the railing. "You have to tell him," he says finally.

The laugh that comes out of me sounds frantic, almost manic. I bite my lip and turn to Seth, my eyebrows arched as high as they'll go. "Yeah. *That's* a hard pass. How would I even start that conversation? *Hey, Dean, my oldest friend. Mind if I put my mouth on your mouth? Oh hey, older sister, the military badass who can kill me with one hand, I was just professing my undying love to your boyfriend,*" I joke.

Seth pushes off the railing and turns to me. "Well. I think you'd have to talk to her first, obviously. But being honest is better than shoving it down, especially if you don't know what could happen if you took the chance."

I want to laugh at the thought. I can't believe I'm thinking about this. I can't believe I'm *talking* about this. With *Seth Marsali.*

"It's not even Harlow, though. Even if they broke up . . . I wouldn't be able to tell him. I wouldn't know where to start."

"It's easy. Watch." Seth meets my eyes and takes a deep breath. I press my lips together, trying not to laugh as he prepares. "Dan," he starts.

"Dean," I correct, rolling my eyes as I comb my wind-wild hair out of my face. Seth waves me off and then brings his

fingers under my chin, turning my face up to his.

He's quiet for a second, and everything in me stills. The wind whips around us as Seth's molten eyes bore into mine. The rough skin of his finger grazes the bottom of my jaw, and I fight back a shiver.

"I want you," he says, his voice low and gravelly. The air in my lungs feels hot all of a sudden, and I breathe out as my heart stutters in my chest.

The words burn the air between us, and I nod.

"That's pretty good," I choke out.

He slowly lowers his hand from my chin and then shrugs one shoulder. "Keep it simple," he says, leaning back against the railing and propping his elbows on the top bar. "Even if everything falls apart, if you're honest? Your sister will respect you. And she might be pissed, but she'll have your back. That's what sisters do."

I hear it as soon as he does, and I see the shadows crossing his face again. *That's what sisters do.*

It goes quiet again. I speak, even if it's just to pull him back from that mental ledge he's walking on right now.

"You're a good one, Seth. And Evelyn would be proud of you."

He breathes in deeply through his nose. For a moment, I think I pushed it too far. But he blinks and turns back to the water, his eyes still fixed on me.

"You shouldn't think too highly of me," he murmurs, and the hurt in his gaze sears me like a brand.

"Well, I do. And I'm the Chosen One. So. It's kind of a big deal," I joke, desperate to try anything that will ease the pain on his face.

He nods, blinking too many times as he turns back to the waves. When Seth glances at me again, his eyes are bright with tears. The sight of them sucks all the air out of my lungs, and my eyes burn. I draw my eyebrows together and give him a nod—a salute from one broken thing to another. He straightens, wiping his face quickly with the back of his hand. "You are. But I have to say, as a diving judge? I question your credentials."

I smile then, heat unfurling in my chest. "Don't hate the player. Hate the *game*."

Seth's mouth drops open in surprise as he holds his arms out. "You're not the player! You were the *judge!*"

I shrug, giving him a *who, me?*

Seth points at me. "Rielle and Lucia talked you into a lower score. Admit it."

I laugh at the desperation on his face, and I hold up my hands.

"Fine. It was a nine-point-seven."

"I knew it," he says as he turns back to the water before leaning closer. "Nine-point-eight," he challenges.

"Don't push it, Marsali," I reply, smiling as I walk back to the stairs.

I don't look back, but somehow, I know he's smiling, too.

Chapter 25

THE WATER IS CALM.

I think that's what puts me off first. It feels like there's an electrical charge in the air, humming so low that it thrums through the nerves in my molars.

I emerge from below deck, hugging my jacket to me as I look over the horizon. The sky is a flat gray. I can't see the edges or soft folds of the clouds. It's the shade of the steam coming off my breath, and the water is like black glass.

The crew is on the starboard side, looking out. I walk up behind them as they talk in hushed tones.

Rielle twists her hair in a knot and ties it back.

I'm about to ask what the hell is going on when I see it—

A ship, a little closer than the horizon line. Lucia propels herself down from the mast, a set of binoculars in one hand. She hands them to Seth, who has appeared behind me. He peers through the lenses.

"Cobalt," he says. He hands the binoculars to Rielle, and she looks. The word feels odd. I replay it in my mind—*Cobalt.* It's like I've snagged on it somehow. "A passenger ship, last docked at the Jawbone last month."

"Vessels? Or—" I whisper.

"Runners," Seth says from behind me.

Even from this far, I can see the hull. I can imagine the inside—rooms converted into cells filled with Curseclean. Headed to the Blood Market. My fingernails bite into the wood. The fear that lashed at the back of my neck a moment ago is washed away by something else. Something more useful. Rage.

"Do they have people on board?" I ask.

"Only one way to know," Seth says. The walkie clipped to Rielle's belt lets out two bites of static. Rielle sends three pulses back.

"Thomas wants to know what direction we're headed."

I look back and am surprised to find Seth looking at me, a question on his face.

"You promised," I say.

He clenches his jaw and then looks to Rielle, inclining his head slightly before turning and stalking toward the ladder leading to the lower deck.

Rielle sends one burst over the walkie, and I turn to follow Seth, ignoring the look of pure irritation coming from Lucia.

Seth walks down the stairs.

"Seth."

He's walking down the hallway. I don't know if he's

purposely ignoring me, or if he's just so focused he can't hear me. But I say it again, louder: "Seth."

He stops, opening the door to his room.

"What can I do?"

His brows knit together as he looks at me, trying to process what I'm saying.

"I want to help," I clarify.

He blinks. Once. Twice. Then he shakes his head.

I open my mouth to argue, but he takes a step forward. "You are going to go in your room and lock the door. And you're not going to open it until you hear my voice telling you to come out."

Rielle calls from above deck, and Seth walks into his room. I don't ask for permission. I follow. "I'm not going to hide like a child. I showed you—I can handle myself."

It's a small cabin—the same size as mine. I don't know what I was expecting—in the movies the captain always has the biggest room.

"This isn't a small boat with a couple Vessels, Charlotte. It's a ship that requires at *least* seven people to man. You're not going to hide like a child. You're going to hide like the Chosen One who could destroy the world if you fall into the wrong hands," he says, pulling open the drawer of a small desk and pulling out several knives. He lifts his shirt, revealing a holster and two sheaths clasped to his belt.

On the wall, right above the desk, a picture is tacked up with one clear thumbtack.

Evelyn. Her smile is wide and easy as she stares into the camera, the freckles on her scrunched nose melding together as she grins.

I'd seen her picture before. But never realized how much they looked alike.

Lucia calls down into the lower deck: "Two minutes." Seth looks out his window as he shoves the drawer shut before walking past me.

I know I should listen. I should go shut my door. But the thought of hiding in the room while Rielle and Lucia and Thomas fight at his side makes me feel sick.

I'm not helpless.

"Seth," I call again as he steps out into the hall. He blinks, remembering that I'm there.

"Your room, Charlotte. Lock the door. Don't open it until you hear my voice."

I hesitate, but I know there isn't much time for him to stand here and argue with me.

"That's an order," he says, his voice shifting just enough to know that I can't talk him out of this.

I watch him walk back up the steps, then turn and walk back into his room.

I don't need to talk him out of anything—he just won't see me.

I jump onto his bed and look out the window.

The ship must have been coming for us as we were coming for them, because it's within spitting distance now. My breath catches in my throat. If this ship I'm on was once a fishing vessel, then this thing must have taken down whales. It's huge, looming outside the window like a wall.

The *Cobalt*.

My mind buzzes, like it's trying to recall a tune, or like it's trying to grab onto the tendrils of a dream.

All of a sudden, I remember.

Find him on the dark blue.

Dark blue. Cobalt is dark blue. My hands shake as I put the pieces together, but I'm pulled back to the scene outside the window.

A man in a gray hoodie stands at the railing of the *Cobalt*. I can't see his eyes in the shade of his hood, and I look down at my wrist, adjusting the mirrors on the leather straps. I'm not taking a chance.

He yells something, and it's muffled through the window. But in the reflection of my bracelet, I see the smirk on his face as he shouts something to our ship. This isn't good. I look for a latch on the window, hoping to push the glass out and listen, but it doesn't open.

Ropes dart from the *Cobalt* to our ship, grip hooks fastened to the end like angry, cruel hands. They make a *thud* as they latch onto us above my head, and I duck, looking up.

They've got us.

I look out through the reflection in time to see the man in gray kick a board between our ships. A plank.

"What?" I gasp out loud.

Then, Seth walks across, his hands up.

I hit the window, a shout ripping from me as I watch, helpless. The man in gray kicks out the back of Seth's knees, and he falls to their deck.

They tie his hands behind his back, and I spin around and launch myself at the door.

I yank it open and peer out. The hallway is empty. I creep down toward the stairs, realizing too late that I don't have a weapon. With one pivot, I'm racing toward the canteen. I pull two knives out of the drawer and race back down the hallway, up the stairs. I chance a glance around the corner, onto our deck. There are three people on board that I don't recognize. A girl with red hair braided down her back, a man with a neck tattoo of a lipstick mark, and a guy wearing black gloves with mirrors sewn onto the backs. He's Xanthous—I can see that from here. So he's probably stolen those gloves from one of his victims.

I tiptoe around the edge of the door, keeping away from them as I grip my knives. I slink, crouching down as I run under the window of the captain's galley and around to the bow, then slide, keeping on my knees as I look through the window to the other side. The captain's galley is empty—Thomas isn't there. On the deck of the *Cobalt*, Seth is still on his knees, his face unreadable as the man in the gray hoodie paces in front of him.

My mind races as I look around. Braid and Neck Tattoo stand sentry at the edge of the plank, blades drawn.

They're scary, but I doubt they would deter Lucia.

No. There's something going on here that I'm not seeing.

As if on cue, I see someone slip out of the water and start scaling the side of the *Cobalt*, a knife in her teeth.

Rielle. Lucia is right behind her, her eyes lit—there's not a hint of fear in them.

They planned this, I understand. And my stomach feels like it's going to fall out of my butt as I fully realize—*they planned this*. And I'm on the deck, right where Seth told me not to be.

I thought I was helping, but it's entirely possible that I'll cause a bigger problem.

Shit, I mouth to myself, rolling over to try and slink back the way I came. But Gloves steps toward the starboard side. If he looks left, he'll see me braced against the side of the captain's galley. I scramble back, hiding by the bow.

I shut my eyes for a moment and lean my head back.

Shit.

I have to think of a way out of this.

But before I can, a hand comes up and clamps over my mouth.

My hands fly up, but Thomas slides up next to me, a finger to his lips.

I nod, and he lowers his hand. Noiselessly, he motions for me to scoot away from the fiberglass edge. With a flick of a wrist, he opens a small storage cabinet. There's a coil of rope, but other than that—it's empty. He motions for me to get inside.

Fear slides up the back of my throat, but he shows me the

inside of the door. *It opens from the inside*, his look says.

I nod, sliding inside. He points to my chest.

Stay here, the look says.

I nod.

He looks over his shoulder in time to see Lucia and Rielle scramble over the edge of the railing of the *Cobalt*. He closes the cabinet door, and it goes mostly dark.

Thomas's voice rings out then, and it sounds nothing like him. "Check the captain's pockets! He has two knives sewn inside them."

Footsteps then as Braid and Neck Tattoo run across the deck, no doubt to grab Thomas. I listen to the footsteps as they round the side of the captain's galley.

I hear a scraping sound scratch across the deck. They're dragging Thomas, who they think is surrendering. I can't help it—the whole thing is so brilliant, I smile. Seth acts like he's looking for a truce while Lucia and Rielle, both strong swimmers, scale the boat. Then Thomas pretends to panic, giving them inside information. Once they're distracted, the other two strike. That's a variation of the plan that they executed on the *Devil's Bid*.

I wait for the screams—for Lucia and Rielle to take the crew down. The ship is huge, but even I could see that the crew was not as big as one a ship that size would normally demand.

The scream starts, but it's not the one I expect.

"Bitch!" a male voice roars. I hear a sickening thud that sounds like flesh hitting wood, then a sound that shreds my

heart into a thousand pieces.

Thomas screams then, his voice raw with terror. "LUCIA!"

Something has gone wrong.

Something has gone terribly, terribly wrong. The terror in my chest doesn't subside as I twist the knob and peek out from the cabinet. There's no one there.

I crawl to the corner and peer around—I have clear sight of the *Cobalt* from this angle.

A man with blood dripping down his ear holds Lucia pinned in front of him, her blade against her own throat. I look over the glass partition. Thomas is in a similar position on our ship— Braid has a machete against his collarbone, and she's moving it up and down slowly, like she's playing a cello. The look on her face is too bright—too gleeful for there to be a hope that she'll think twice about spilling his throat onto the deck.

"Let her go!" Thomas cries, and Lucia struggles.

Seth stands, and the *Cobalt*'s crew all draw their weapons. The man holding Lucia tightens his grip, and Seth holds his hands out as he lowers himself to his knees once more. "Let her go. Let her go, and you can take me."

I bite the tip of my tongue at the thought.

The man in the gray hoodie laughs. "*You* were the one that started following us. We were content to keep sailing, Marsali. But now we've got a problem—one you alone won't be able to fix."

I turn my knives in my grip so that they're tight against my forearms, and an idea blooms at the back of my mind.

I slide against the fiberglass, shoving myself back around the

270

way I came. With one movement, I'm on my feet, running crouched as I come back to the wood awning above the stairwell. Braid, Neck Tattoo, and Gloves are all watching Lucia.

They think they've seen our play. They think we're out of cards. But I see Rielle—perched in the crow's nest, the butt of a crossbow tucked against her shoulder. She's waiting for the right moment.

And I can give her the right moment.

I tuck the blades into the back of my sports bra. I'd seen enough of the crew to know that they're all Runners and, therefore, all Xanthous. Which is good, because I won't have time to check eyes if this works.

If.

Such a small word to balance my life on, but there's not really a choice. My eyes flick to the *Cobalt*. Most of the crew is situated on the deck facing us, but there are three who are focused on something else—a door. It looks like the same kind of door that this ship has, the one that leads below deck.

We were content to keep sailing, he'd said. That's because they have a full hull.

There are people down there.

Find him on the dark blue, 3A, the one with the teeth.

I remember Vanessa's words, and my mind reels. *Cobalt.* Dark blue.

Who is *him*?

A strange, wild hope bites up the back of my throat. Could it be Dean?

I look back at the ramp. *Focus*—I have to get through this.

Fear spits adrenaline into my veins, and the burn of it coats the back of my throat and the inside of my eyelids. There isn't a part of me that doesn't hurt. There isn't a part of me that isn't entirely taut with fear.

But if this crew falls, then I have no way to get to the Blood Market. If the *Cobalt* takes us over and finds me, then I'm dead anyway.

That thought gives me the strength to stand.

I lift my hands and step out from behind the stairwell.

"Wait!"

Braid looks over her shoulder, and Neck Tattoo spins, raising his machete with a shocked expression on his squished, brutish face.

I feel every one of the *Cobalt* crew turn their gaze to me, to my thin arms above my head. I don't have to fake the fear on my face—that just comes naturally.

"Charlotte! What are you doing?" Thomas seethes.

"Shut up," Braid orders, digging her blade tighter against his throat.

But it's Seth's gaze that hits me right in the chest. The man with mirrored gloves puts his hand behind my neck, his thumb and forefinger digging into my skin so tightly that I wince despite myself.

"Take me!" I call.

"And why would we do that?" Gray Hoodie calls.

I look up, meeting Seth's eyes as I take a deep breath.

"Because. I'm Curseclean." I don't take my eyes off Seth's.

The crew of the *Cobalt* lets out a low ripple of laughter. It starts with Gray Hoodie and spreads until the man with the gloves is chuckling. The girl with the braid shoots me a pitying glance as she laughs harder.

"You're not bad-looking, sweetheart, but *one* Curseclean isn't going to do much. I mean. *We* could come up with an arrangement, maybe?" His voice is thick with implications that make my skin crawl as his eyes rove over me. "But it does beg the question—what's a Curseclean doing with you lot this far north?"

He steps closer, his eyes narrowing as though he's trying to solve a puzzle.

"You know, they're saying some crazy things now. About the Chosen One being found. One of Maddox Caine's crew got drunk at the Jawbone a little while back . . . said they had her in the hull for a bit."

I try my best to look unimpressed. Confused. Anything other than scared. Gray Hoodie cocks his head.

". . . said she was a pretty little thing that wasn't too bright. And that she got away with some self-righteous assholes who like to mess with our way of life." He punctuates his words with a swing of his sword. I swallow back a litany of curses and move my eyes to Seth's. His jaw tightens as his gaze bores into mine.

Do not.

Do not, the look in Seth's eyes tells me. I can feel it pulsing off him. But I swallow hard.

And I chance a quick look at Rielle, who can see me through her sight. And I hope she can see the plea in my eyes like I can see Seth's.

I look at Gray Hoodie. His eyes are yellow, too, though they look wrong. Too yellow, almost—almost neon. It makes him look like more of a monster than he already is.

"Yeah. I'm the Chosen One."

Gray Hoodie's face tightens as my words sink in. He's quiet for half a second, and then—"Bullshit."

"Maybe. But the mark on the inside of my wrist says otherwise," I say, the lie sliding off my tongue like butter. I'm getting used to it. I don't even think I sound half as uncertain as I feel.

Gray Hoodie considers. And then he steps forward, curiosity getting the better of him.

Right into Rielle's line of sight.

Rielle pulls the trigger, and the arrow spears Gray Hoodie's shoulder. He screams, falling down. Thomas shoots to his feet, throwing his head back. It connects with Braid's nose with a sickening *crack*, and she lets out a primal howl as blood splatters the deck.

At that moment, the door to the lower deck bursts open, and dozens of prisoners spill onto the deck, armed with what I assume are stolen weapons. Rielle and Lucia had set them free.

The Curseclean descend upon the crew of the *Cobalt*, fighting for their lives.

I don't have time to second-guess myself. I reach behind me, pulling the knives out from the elastic of my sports bra. With one swipe, I do what I'd seen Harlow practice a thousand times—I run the blade along the back of Gloves's knees.

I feel the tendons snap like rubber bands under the serrated edges, and I have to bite back the bile that rises in the back of my throat. The sound that comes out of his mouth rips through me like a physical blow, and I know before he's even hit the deck that it's a sound that's been imprinted on my bones.

I fall backward, and it takes everything in me to not drop the knife as blood oozes over my fingers. The man writhes on the deck, and I feel Thomas's hands on my arms as he hoists me to my feet.

We're running, and I don't ask questions. Thomas's hand is slick with blood, and I don't know if it's his or Braid's or Gloves's or someone else's. I follow, my eyes raking over the chaos unfolding on the *Cobalt*'s deck as he leads me back across to our ship.

My eyes search. *Him.* That had to mean something. Vanessa loves Dean like a brother. If her Chosen One–ness was going to give her visions about one *him*, it would be Dean. But I don't see him.

Lucia kicks a man square in the chest before spinning and loosing two blades straight into another man's throat. Rielle slides down a rope from the mast and crouches next to her, firing arrow after arrow until her quiver is empty. Then, she pulls a blade from her boot.

I look over at the deck—I didn't see Seth get away.

A strange new wildfire lights in my chest as I realize that I need to.

I need to know he's safe.

Bile rises in my throat again as my eyes search, raking hungrily over the tangle of fighting bodies until I see him. He's at the other end of the ship—the bow parallel to ours. His face is smeared with blood, his teeth bared as he fights a man with two blades.

It's then that I realize we're back at the stairwell, and Thomas is trying to usher me inside.

"No," I mumble, craning to look over his shoulder as I try to pull my arms from his grip.

"Charlotte, they know who you are. You need to *hide*," Thomas shouts, letting go of my arms to put his hands on the side of my face.

The closeness startles me, and I meet his eyes. There's no anger there—just desperation.

"You need to *hide*," he says again. "They know we're with the Chosen One, Charlotte. We'll be fine. But Seth will only worry about you. Get below."

At the mention of Seth's name, I look back again to Seth as he fights on the *Cobalt*.

I see it just as it happens.

The man has Seth against the railing, and Seth is so focused on the man in front of him that he doesn't see the opponent slinking up from behind. He doesn't see the man lifting a harpoon by the hilt—a stick of unforgiving iron.

The air gathers in my lungs, but gets caught somewhere in my throat as the man with the harpoon brings it down, cracking Seth over the back of the head. Seth staggers, grabbing the railing before the man in front of him shoves him with both hands.

And then he tumbles over the bow and into the black waves below.

Chapter 26

I DON'T SCREAM, BUT THAT'S ONLY BECAUSE I CAN'T breathe.

Seth cuts through the water with a sickening splash, and the air *whooshes* out of my lungs as I shove past Thomas.

Seth, I finally scream, surprised that the sound is coming from me.

Thomas scrambles behind me as I sprint to the bow of the ship, my eyes searching the dark water. He understands, because the terror on his face is real as I turn to him and panic grips me as the reality of what just happened slices through my mind. Seth is unconscious. He's unconscious in the water.

Time is already running out.

I whip around, falling to my knees as I rip the cabinet door open so hard that it almost comes off the hinges. I lug the rope out.

"Help me!" I cry, and Thomas is there, lifting the rope. I tie a knot onto the railing and then grab the other end. I don't think as I wrap the rope around my center.

Thomas tries to stop me, but I slap him off, casting a glance across the way. Lucia lets out a wild yell as she swings her blade at a Runner, while Rielle ushers two Curseclean out of the hull. We're the only ones who can do this.

"He's unconscious. He can't climb, and I'm not strong enough to pull us up. I can grab him. I'll tug twice. Then you pull."

"Charlotte," Thomas starts, and I see the hesitation in his eyes. They talked, I know. I know Seth told him about what happened the night they took me from the *Devil's Bid*.

I froze, and there's no promise that I won't freeze again. In fact, that's what I'm thinking. It's the reason my fingers shake as I finish the knot around my waist.

It's the reason I don't say anything as I climb over the railing. The water was calm earlier, but it isn't now. It churns, almost like the violence above is calling to its likeness below.

I look over my shoulder at Thomas. He knows I'm right. He can't go in, because I can't get them out.

If I don't jump in this water, Seth dies. I wish I could tell myself that the thought of him slipping below the waves is enough to propel me forward, but it's not.

It wasn't when Vanessa was under, either, and she's my sister.

"Shove me, Thomas," I order.

"What?" he calls, incredulousness coloring his voice. I

want to be strong enough to let go on my own, but terror has taken over. I sank last time. All I have to do now is just sink again. I don't have to swim. I have to go deep, find Seth, and tug twice.

"Shove me, dammit!" I screech, and Thomas listens. Two wide hands find the center of my back, and my head snaps back as Thomas pushes me off the edge of the railing.

The water is as cold as it's ever been. As it wraps around me like a fist, the terror it conjures up in my bones is as bad as I expected. I'm freezing and burning at the same time, the bubbles from my terrified screams fluttering against my cheeks and nose like taunting kisses.

I thrash, the unending weight of the ocean pressing into my nose and throat, demanding the air from my lungs as the price for my intrusion.

I kick against the water.

Once. Twice.

Three times.

The bloated bellies of the warring ships hover over my head, obscuring the already low light. I can't see well. It's all bubbles and light shafts. I feel like I'm being swallowed, and the panic swells.

But I kick again. I push against the water as the voice tells me that I am too afraid to move.

No, I'm not.

I'm swimming then, my arms reaching, searching. I can't

lose him. I won't lose him.

The thought crashes into me, wringing more bubbles from my lungs and sending the fear scattering.

I won't lose him.

And then I feel him. Cold, unmoving fingers brush against my arm. I let out a shriek, and my lungs burn. Not from fear, I realize, but from the need for oxygen. How long have I been down here?

I wrap my arms around Seth and reach up, pulling twice on the rope as hard as I can. I dig my fingers into him so hard that I'm sure he's bleeding. The rope lurches, dragging me so fast that I almost lose my grasp on Seth. I redouble my grip and wrap my legs around his waist.

He's not moving. I shove the thought away, tightening my legs around him so hard that my muscles scream. We break the surface, and air floods my lungs as I let out a loud gasp. Seth is limp in my arms, and I shake him. Nothing.

The rope bites into my middle so painfully that I cry out, but I don't let go. I won't.

They pull us up, up, up, and then we're at the railing. Lucia is there, reaching over. Rielle grabs my shoulders as Thomas and Lucia and a couple other people I've never seen before hoist us onto the deck.

I cough, sputtering and shaking as Rielle flips Seth onto his back. She tilts his head and puts her ears to his lips.

The look on her face tells me what I already knew—he's not breathing.

She starts compressions, and I don't move. I don't know if I even breathe. Blood mixes with seawater as Rielle pumps, and I remember the man and the harpoon. My fingers still shake as I work the knot, pulling the rope from my waist. The rope burn on my skin is so bad that it burns, the stinging from the salt water only registering as I look at it.

I've seen this before.

Flashes of Vanessa and Harlow flicker in my memory. The way Harlow's face was set. The way Vanessa's limp hand lurched with every compression.

But Vanessa was alive. Vanessa lived.

"He's bleeding. Can you tilt him? I can compress it," I bite out, though my teeth are chattering so hard that I don't know how I get the words out. Rielle nods, pressing her lips together as she tilts Seth, and someone hands me a T-shirt, which I ball up and shove against the back of his head. I inspect the wound—it's more to the side of the head than on the direct back. A shallow scalp wound—the type that bleeds a lot but isn't as scary as it looks.

"Rielle?" Thomas whispers, and Rielle shakes her head.

And I can't look at her face. I can't see what I saw in Harlow that night. I can't see the hopelessness in them.

I press the shirt against the wound and I pray.

The words slip out before I can stop them.

Please, I'm whispering. *Please*.

If there's a plan for all of this, Seth has to be in it.

"Please, God," I whisper. I pull myself closer to him, letting my fingers of my free hand find his jaw. Water drips from the edge of my nose and lands on his lips. "You're not done here yet. Not like this."

I believe like I wanted to the night Vanessa was on a ship just like this. I should have fought then. Hope is worth something, and I feel it—a defiance, a wild spark in my chest.

I look up, expecting Rielle's expression to be full of pity, or sadness. But her gaze is lit from behind, and her mouth moves quickly, though I can't hear what she's saying. She nods once, urging me on.

And then Seth coughs, and Thomas lets out a string of swear words as Seth turns, spitting up water, and Rielle pats him on the back, hard.

He's alive.

My mind is spinning, fighting with my heart as a small weed blooms between the bricks. A small thought I don't want.

I push back, shoving myself to my feet as I turn to look at the deck.

My feet are so cold I can't feel my toes. I look around as the Curseclean find each other on the deck, hugging and crying. My eyes rove over the faces, desperate for something familiar. Someone familiar.

Find him on the dark blue. This has to be it. It has to. Dean has to be safe.

Seth talks to Rielle, her hands in fists against his back as she embraces him. She sets her forehead against his, closing her eyes as she says something to him. The sight is like a spear through my chest, and I whip around, my eyes desperately raking over the deck, looking for him.

Dean.

He should be here.

Lucia is behind Thomas, crouching with one hand on the railing, relief plain on her face. She stands, wiping her nose with the back of her hand before turning to face the dozen people huddled in the center of our ship. I walk over to her.

"Are there any other people on the *Cobalt*?" I ask.

She shakes her head. "Rielle said there were empty cells down there still. If there were more people, that's where they'd be. I mean, there was a locked hall, but that's where they'll put the Exposed, if there are any—"

"So we just leave them down there?"

"What else can we do, Charlotte?"

I don't wait for her to finish. I stalk across the deck until I find Gray Hoodie, still hunched over his mutilated leg. He spits a curse at me as I kneel down next to him. I feel Lucia come up behind me.

"Charlotte. We have to go. They hailed another ship as we approached—more Runners. It could be Maddox."

I ignore her as I lean closer to Gray Hoodie.

"How many Exposed are there?" I ask. He groans, breathing in gasps of air through clenched, yellowing teeth.

"Go to hell, you stupid *bitch*." He turns, and his sweatshirt lifts slightly as more blood from the wound gushes onto the deck. And I see it, hooked on a belt loop—a ring of keys.

I reach out and snatch them. He tries to stop me but howls in pain when he takes his hand off his knee.

"Come back here! *Come back here!*" he screams as I step

away. He struggles to get up, like he's going to follow me or something, but Rielle shoves him back to the deck with her boot before taking off after me.

I hear Seth call my name, but I don't turn back.

Lucia runs up beside me. I expect her to try and stop me, and I'm ready to fight. But her shoulders are set as she strides alongside me. "We have to move quickly."

"Char, we have to go," Rielle calls.

"Get them back to the ship, and get ready to haul ass," Lucia hollers.

3A, the one with the teeth.

I feel the spinning in my gut. *Dean. Hold on, Dean. I'm coming.*

I sprint to the stairs and tear down below. "Where was the locked hall?" I cry.

The levels have numbers etched on the walls. *1. 2. 3.*

I know where it will be before she answers. "Three," Lucia answers.

My heart is beating so hard it feels like it might shatter my ribs. I stop at the third level and pull out the keys.

There are at least thirty. We don't have the time.

Then, I see it. A key with serrated edges that come to perfect, symmetrical points. The key almost looks like a mountain range. Or teeth.

My heart staggers in my chest.

"This one," I breathe, pulling it loose with shaky fingers. I slip the metal into the lock and twist. It takes both my hands before the lock turns with a deep, booming *click*.

A thrill rushes through me, and I let out a sharp gasp as I pull the door open as hard as I can.

"Let me check first," Lucia says, pushing past me. I lift my arms and survey the hall through my mirrors, then lower one arm to grasp my knife from the back of my pants.

The hall inside is dark, and the air is musty and damp, like it's been closed for some time. The doors on all sides are closed, their windows blocked out with black plastic. Lucia pulls a small flashlight from her pocket and illuminates the shadows.

"Dean?" I whisper sharply. It's silent, and I step farther inside. "Dean!" My voice echoes and Lucia whips around, her finger to her lips.

But besides the soft hum of the motor and the trickle of water, there isn't a sound.

Then, I hear it. A groan, from the back.

"Dean," I breathe. My feet move on their own, and Lucia has to struggle to keep up. I skid to a stop at the last door and yank it open, keeping my eyes fixed on my mirrors.

He's huddled in the corner of the room on a thin, dirty mattress. His hair is greasy and hangs over his forehead, and he holds his hands up to shield his eyes as Lucia directs the beam to his eyes.

His yellow eyes.

"Dean," I whisper, lowering the mirrors. But as I drop to my knees in front of him, I see the confusion on his face.

All at once, my heart sputters to a stop. Because it's not Dean in the cell.

It's Abel Lassiter.

Chapter 27

"HE HASN'T EATEN OR SLEPT IN ABOUT A WEEK, I'D guess," Thomas says. "But other than that? He's fine. No signs of torture or permanent damage."

We're sitting in the kitchen an hour later. It took Rielle, Thomas, Lucia, and me to get Abel off the boat—he was too weak to walk by himself and, truth be told, he had no reason to trust us.

Seth wanted to help, but Lucia said she'd kill him, so he paced the deck until we brought Abel over.

Abel, who pulled free from my grasp to hobble toward Seth, who, in turn, launched himself at his friend with such fierceness it brought tears to my eyes.

Abel trusted us then. We got him clean clothes and some water. Seth found him a bed as Thomas revved the engine as high as it could go. Lucia disabled the *Cobalt*'s rudder, so they're dead in the water. I watched the ship disappear over the horizon, and I've kept my gaze out the window since then.

Vanessa's prophecy wasn't about Dean. It was about Abel.

We saved the leader of the free world. That means something. And Seth isn't dead—that means something. I feel different now, like a bone has been set. It still aches, but there's a rightness about it.

But I thought I'd be holding Dean tonight. I thought, for a few brief minutes, that I'd hear his laugh. I'm having a hard time letting that thought go.

"I'm going to go to bed," I whisper. Rielle rubs my back as I slip across her lap and out of the booth. "Will you check on Seth?" she asks.

I stop, lowering myself on her knees as confusion slips over my face. I don't know if everyone knows about Rielle and Seth, and I don't want to broadcast something private. "I figured you would. When you, you know. Went to bed," I whisper.

Rielle's brow furrows, and then she lets out a snort laugh. "What?" Realization slips over her features. "Oh. *Oh*," she says, shaking her head. "No. Seth is like . . . he's like my brother. You thought . . ." She makes a face across the table, and I turn to see Lucia and Thomas holding back smiles.

"What?" I ask. Lucia presses her lips together as she stands, gathering her dishes.

"Seth is . . . not my type," Rielle says gently, cocking her eyebrow meaningfully.

"Oh," I say, twisting to look down at Rielle. I realize what she's saying. "*Oh*. I just assumed, when you said you met someone in the Torch, that it was . . . Seth."

A small flicker of sadness crosses her expression, and she wrinkles her nose. "No, babe. She and I . . . we had different ideas about how the world should be saved."

"Sorry," I say quietly, and Rielle wraps her arms around my waist and lays her head on my shoulder. I wrap my arms around her.

She gives me a squeeze, and my heart swells. I didn't know I could love someone like I love my sisters. But this—Thomas, Rielle, Seth, even Lucia—this is real in a way I haven't felt in a long, long time. She lets me go, and I'm barely out the door when I hear Lucia cackle. *"Seth?"* Rielle hoots, and I slip out into the hallway to the sounds of their laughter.

The Curseclean have filled up all the extra rooms, and even spilled into the hallway. I maneuver around them. Seth comes to the bottom of the stairs, and I stop when we lock eyes.

But then a familiar voice calls my name.

"Charlotte?"

I turn.

Alan, huddled among the passengers, his brown eyes wide. I'm walking toward him before I even fully realizing I'm moving. He was with Dean, that night on the beach. They were loaded onto the same ship.

"Charlotte! Shit, what are you *doing here*?" he asks, rushing forward to pull me into a hug, and I notice angry red cuts on his dark skin—a remnant of the fight above.

"Where is Dean?" I ask, my heart stuttering in my chest.

A thousand terrible scenarios play out in my mind, things that could easily explain his absence.

I pull back from the hug and look Alan in the eye, searching for a hint of pity or sorrow.

"Where is he?" I ask again, fisting my hands in his shirt.

"He's fine. He's *okay*, Char—" He grabs my wrists, and I realize how hard I was holding him. Alan speaks slowly, trying to break through the terror that has a hold on me.

"We escaped the next day—several of us. Any of us willing to risk the waters for a chance at life. We traveled together for a week or so, and then we found Vanessa and Harlow at the rendezvous."

I stop, everything in me stilling. Vanessa and Harlow. They got away. I've been holding that hope in the back of my chest, not willing to look at it for weeks. I could not even entertain the thought that they weren't both safe.

I would have lost my mind. More than I already have.

My knees give out, and Alan kneels with me. "They're alive," I breathe. All of them. My sisters. Dean. They're alive.

"They're headed to the Torch," Alan says. "We were all going to go together, but we got separated. And, well. I guess I picked the losing road." Tears slip down my cheeks, and I wipe them off with the back of my hand. I nod.

"Charlotte. They're saying . . ." Alan lowers his voice. It's so soft, it's almost reverent. "They're saying you're the Chosen One." I don't meet his eyes, afraid that he'll say something. That he'll call me out.

"She is," a voice says from behind me. I turn, looking up at Lucia. I wait for a smirk or a snide comment, but she doesn't give one. It's just a tentative expression, caution wrapped in hesitation. I stare at her.

It's like an uneasy truce. She was with me when I found the keys. I push myself to my feet, and I see it in her face—she knows what I did for Seth, and she knows that Abel is safe. She's not my friend. Not yet, but as of this moment, it doesn't seem like we're enemies.

That is, unless Alan gives her reason to believe that I'm lying through my teeth.

But he lets out a small laugh. "That's why Harlow never wanted you to go on supply runs," he says, and it's everything I can do not to bristle at the connection. "That's why she was so pissed when you and Dean ran off the day we got raided. Wow. It was all there—I just didn't see it. She was so scared that you were going to get caught or hurt. She treated you like glass."

I force a small smile, even as my insides are churning. Yeah. Harlow acted like I was made of glass. But that's because she'd seen me shatter. I nod, and Alan nods, too, like he's just figured out a riddle.

I bite my tongue as heavy footsteps sound behind me. Seth walks up behind Lucia, leaning on the wall as he stares down at me. I look away because I don't trust what he'd see in my face right now.

"Dean was so worried about you, Charlotte," Alan

continues. "He was sick with it. We all saw you run for him across the beach that night. And then that Runner tackled you. We just . . . we didn't know what was going to happen."

I feel Seth's eyes on me, and I glance up. It's everything I have to hold his gaze as something flickers across his face. Recognition. Understanding.

And underneath? Anger. It's been simmering since I stepped out earlier. He has plenty of reason to be, because I didn't listen. I didn't stay safe. I came out on the deck. Then I announced that I was the Chosen One. And then I jumped off the ship after him. So, it's safe to say I kind of went my own direction on that one.

I straighten my shoulders, a wordless conversation ripping between us as Alan keeps talking: "Charlotte Holloway. The Chosen One. Whoa."

I need to move. I can't stand here anymore, especially now that I hear murmurs behind me. All around us, people whisper.

The Chosen One.

Her?

She can end this.

I slip into my room and close the door behind me. I'm alone for two seconds before it opens. I pivot, expecting Rielle. But Seth closes the door and meets my eyes. Blood stains his white shirt, which is still soaking wet, though the bleeding on his head has stopped.

"What the hell was that?" he seethes.

I match his gaze, defiance flaring in my chest. I don't say

anything as he stalks closer.

"I told you to stay down here," he whispers dangerously.

Something in me snaps. "Well, it's a good thing I didn't, because you would be flotsam wrapped around the *Cobalt*'s rudders if I had. *You're welcome*, you ungrateful asshole—"

Seth's eyes light up as he advances on me, but I don't step back. This is my room. My *life*, and my decisions. I'm tired of being treated like glass.

By Harlow. By him. By *everyone*. I can take care of myself.

Seth shakes his head. "It doesn't matter what happens to me, Charlotte. Don't you get that?" he barks.

"I didn't get caught. The world is still safe."

His eyelids flutter for a moment as he processes my words. Like I've said something strange.

But that's what he meant, isn't it?

Seth does the right thing. And caring about me—about helping me save the world—is the right thing.

But for a moment, just a moment, I let myself read into the way his jaw ticks as he clenches it shut, and the way he opens his fist slowly at his side. I let my eyes search his face.

"Don't ever do that again," he whispers, and his voice breaks—it's not an angry sound. I stop, looking up.

I was cold a moment ago, but the look in his eyes sends a jolt of heat up my spine. I drop my gaze to his lips—the salt in the cracks of his dry skin. Water drips down his shoulders.

I want to shove him back and tell him to leave, but my hands are stuck at my sides, pinned by the simmer I see in his eyes.

The rage has cooled, hardening like molten metal into something different.

And that's the thing here. The shadow with no name—the coiling at the base of my spine. I don't want to know why it hurt to breathe when I couldn't find Seth on the deck of the *Cobalt*. Why my eyes raked over the crowds of people, searching for him. And how it felt when he'd gone in the water—like my lungs were brittle, all of a sudden, and my scream would shatter them.

I finally find my words.

"The last time I checked, we were partners. You don't tell me what to do," I bite out.

"You're right," he says. His eyes drop to my lips, and he swallows. "You've saved all of us. Saved Abel. You don't need my permission. You never did."

I open my mouth to shoot something back, but his eyes find mine again, and the look in them steals all the breath from my lungs.

"So. I'll just ask, then," he murmurs. I've never heard his voice this soft before. It's like fingertips threading through my hair. It's the heat of a fire on freezing skin. He leans in, and I shut my eyes as his breath slips over the dip in my shoulder.

"Please, Charlotte." His beg is no more than a whisper. "Never . . . *never* do that again."

"Because I'm the Chosen One," I breathe.

He pulls back, his amber eyes finding mine, and I must be imagining the look of hunger I see there.

"No," he says finally. It's a tortured sound.

He leans closer, and I feel his breath hit my lips. I don't know what will happen if I tilt my head up. But I feel a thrum in my chest, and my head feels light. My hand moves on its own, and I grab the side of his soaked shirt, bunching my fist in it as I lean closer.

Seth's breath hitches as the space between our bodies disappears. The tip of his nose brushes against mine, and my knees shake. His hand cups the side of my face and travels to my neck, and I don't know what's happening, but I want it to keep going. Maybe it's adrenaline from the fight. Maybe it's knowing that Dean is alive, and that this charade has to end soon.

Or maybe it's just because Seth Marsali does something to me, and I haven't really wanted to admit it.

I brush my lips softly against his and then pull back.

I can't believe I just did that. I look up at him, my mouth opening and closing as I struggle to find words. None come, and I feel his hand tighten around the back of my neck as he presses his mouth to mine.

I've been kissed before. Once at the movies, and a few times with a couple of guys in Harlow's circle. Even at the settlement, I'd had a couple of make-out sessions in the empty classrooms. But those were something born of need. My basic physical need, and a deep, unyielding need to try and get over what I couldn't have.

But kissing Seth is different. Because with him, I don't think about anything except the soft feel of his lips, and the warmth of his tongue as he slants his head, deepening the kiss. I twist my hand, wrapping his shirt tighter as I try to pull him closer. I wring water out of the fabric, and it pelts the top of my shoe.

He lets out a soft moan, and his hand slides down my back as we kiss harder. Faster. I pull back slightly, fighting for breath, and he drags his other hand up into my hair and it's like he can't stand not touching me. I sink into the kiss again, loving how his stubble is scraping my face raw.

I could lose myself in this kiss. As we back up and my calves hit the bed, I know I could lose myself in him. In this. And I want to. I don't want to think about anything else. I don't want to think about Dean, or the lies I've told, or how this can't last.

And I realize, all at once, how much it means to me, and how much it's going to hurt when I lose it.

I let out a soft cry as I wrench myself free, stepping backward until I trip onto the bed.

"I can't," I whisper through deep, staggering breaths.

Seth is frozen, his chest heaving. He blinks a couple of times, like he's snapping back to reality. His breathing slows, and he takes a couple more steps back, toward the door.

"It's him, right?"

This isn't about Dean. Not at all. But that's an easier answer than the truth.

"Yeah. It's . . ." I need to burn this bridge. I need to make sure that whatever embers he's just kicked up in me don't catch fire at two in the morning, when I know he's across the hall. "It's him."

Seth takes a deep breath as he runs a hand through his hair.

He nods, swallowing hard.

"Okay," he says. Like that's sufficient. Like one syllable will cauterize whatever gaping thing he's just opened up in my chest. There's a beat, and then he slips back out through the door without another word. It's everything I can do not to sink to the floor as his footsteps fade.

Chapter 28

THE DAYS BLEND TOGETHER, SWIRLING INTO ONE just like the blue of the sky and the sapphire of the ocean at the horizon. I become a ghost, haunting this ship and fading into the background as much as a Chosen One can. Seth spends a lot of time with Abel, helping him get his strength back up.

The bow becomes a balm to my soul, the frigid sea air biting into my skin as we tear north.

Rielle tries to talk to me a few times, but she can see the faraway look in my eyes and knows that I'm not in the mood to talk.

And I'm not.

Dean is safe. He's with my sisters.

There is no reason for me to be going to the Blood Market, especially since I will be leading Seth, Lucia, and the others into danger for no reason.

I'll walk them up to a place filled with Runners and count-less other dangers just to turn around, shrug, and tell them I have nothing. That I'm a liar.

I sit in my room and stare at the papers where I've scribbled down the prophecies, begging them to tell me something, any-thing, as I listen to the rhythmic beating of waves outside my window.

I count the footsteps as they track above, and I'm getting better at knowing who is who.

The decisive walk belongs to Lucia. She doesn't stop once she's got a destination. The ones that scrape slightly are from Rielle, because she's constantly turning to answer questions. Thomas rarely makes footsteps, because he's always swinging from the rigging to the railing and not even bothering to touch the deck.

And Seth's steps—they are heavy. I hear them in my chest, because he walks like he has the weight of the world on his shoulders. We haven't talked since the night we took the *Cobalt*. Part of me wants to believe it's because he's focused on Abel and the plans they're making to get him back to the Torch, but I know there's something deeper. Something changed that night.

Thud. Thud. Thud.

I shut my eyes.

I didn't expect to need to pull the plug on this plan so early, but now I'm faced with the reality that I always knew was coming.

There was going to be a time when I had to admit what I've

done. A time to run. I hoped, as everyone does, that when the time came, I would be ready. That I would handle it well.

But it's here, and I've opted for the postapocalyptic version of teenage cowardice: a note.

And once we pull up to the safe house, which Thomas tells me is somewhere in the redwoods just on the border of California and Oregon, I am going to leave.

It's almost dawn as we reach the shore of Damnation Creek Beach, and the feel of the rock-covered coast under my boots is foreign enough that it takes a moment for me to remember how to walk. The air is crisp, the sky clear as gulls let out sharp cries from overhead. The smells of damp earth and tang, pine, and salt weave through my hair as the wind whips it over the goose bumps rising over my skin. I look back at the ship—the one I won't be seeing again.

I stumble, my boot catching on one of the rocks. I stop myself on one of the smooth black stones, thanking God that it wasn't one of the razor-sharp ones that jut from the shore like daggers.

Seth appears next to me then, crouching to grab my elbow.

"You okay?" he asks quietly. I don't need to look at him, because I know what I would see. He'd have his captain's face on—the one that he's had on for the past several days. The one that matches the blades slung over his back I see out of the corner of my eye. His voice is professional. Detached.

I nod, pulling my elbow back against my side.

In front of me, Rielle ties her hair into a knot as she talks to Alan. Abel walks in front with Thomas. The rest of the Curse-clean lace up their boots and zip up their jackets against the harsh gusts.

Lucia ties the rowboat behind us, and I look up the steep trail. She comes up beside me. "It's about six miles to the safe house. Mirrors up. If you see outsiders, shout it down the line," she says.

I'm relieved to be back on the shore. Land, where my lies were born and where they can die. We walk, and the burn that bites my calves feels good after days of sitting. I need more of it.

I push on, slowly making my way to the front of the pack next to Rielle as we press deeper into the redwoods, the trees rising on either side of us like giants. Everything in my heart feels dark and dreadful, poisoned by the lies I've told, but the beauty of this place coaxes wonder out of my weariness.

I find myself smiling as I spot a family of deer grazing in a clearing just off the trail. Butterflies flit on the wind, completely unperturbed by the oily, evil mess man has made of the world under them.

"Is that a smile?" Rielle asks, her cheeks flushed as she looks over at me. The sunlight breaks through the clouds, making shadows across her beautiful face. Her yellow eyes sparkle as she grins over at me.

"Yeah. I guess," I say softly. This is almost over. I'll leave, and then this whole crew will be able to get on with their lives. Abel Lassiter is safe, and he'll be able to call the Torch from the

301

safe house. I'll find my sisters, and Dean.

No one else will have to get hurt.

"Dean is safe, I hear," Rielle says, and I look down at my feet.

"He was a couple weeks ago, at least," I say. I have tried to dampen the hope in my chest—to lessen my expectations so that if I'm wrong—if everything isn't okay—I won't completely fall apart. But that was a pointless effort. Dean and Harlow are together and safe. There's nothing they can't do together. They'll keep Vanessa safe. They'll all be fine.

"I still want to hear that story," she says, half joking. "How long have you been in love with him?"

I search for words, remembering my talk with Seth. How I'd left, and how the skin of his touch burned even hours later. My love for Dean is a refuge, all of a sudden, and the look of Rielle's face is asking me to lean into it. So I do.

"I don't know," I say, the words feeling good in my mouth as I let the memories roll in the back of my mind. Dean, his shoulders peeling from sunburn. The weight of his body on mine as he picked me up and threw me in the pool. The way my veins vibrate to the sound of his voice.

"Oh bullshit. Everyone knows the moment they realize they're in love with someone," Rielle says, smiling.

Seth is quiet behind me, though I hear his rhythmic breathing.

"Maybe Charlotte doesn't want to talk about her Dean," he says, his voice hoarse. It's the first time I've heard him talk this whole trek. I chance a look over my shoulder at him, irritation filling my gaze.

302

His eyes bore into mine, and I glare right back.

Don't be a dick, it says.

I check to make sure Alan is outside hearing range.

"Her Dean?" Rielle asks, her voice dripping with *awww how cute*. "Is that what you call him? Your Dean?"

Not on purpose. And Seth knows that.

I feel his presence behind me, thickening with every step.

"Yeah," I say, louder. Seth has no right to be a jerk about this. It was one kiss, when we were both fired up from almost dying.

It was more than that, and you know it, a voice in the back of my head says. I grind my teeth. Seth is still being an asshole, whether it meant something or not. And it's easier to be mad at him than to be anything else, so. If he's offering an out, I'm going to take it.

"So?" Rielle asks. "When did you know?"

I force a smile onto my face, and Rielle elbows me.

"Come on, Charlotte. The world is shit, and I love remembering that there are good things still happening in this world. There are still moments of goodness and love and all that sappy shit."

I do remember the moment I knew. I remember the feeling of swelling in my chest—a tightening that felt like it was going to shatter me into a thousand pieces.

"We were swimming at the public pool," I say. "It was night."

"The two of you?" Rielle asks, her eyebrow cocking. "Oh, I know where this is going."

"*Just* the two of you?" Seth asks, and I shoot him a look over my shoulder that says *don't be an asshole.* "You sure there weren't more people there?" he presses.

Rielle rolls her eyes. "Whatever. Don't listen to Seth. He's just jealous because he hasn't gotten laid since the end of the world."

"Shut up, Rielle," he snaps.

I remember the way his groan sounded as it rattled the back of my throat, and the grip of his hand on the back of my neck. I shake the thought away and turn back to Rielle.

"It was just us," I clarify. And it's true. Harlow said she was over swimming, but Dean and I weren't. We stayed in as she went to take a shower in the girls' bathroom. "And I just knew."

Heat spreads across my chest as I remember. I was close to him as we joked about nothing and everything. I splashed him, and he splashed me. He lunged, pulling me close before picking me up over his shoulder and falling backward in a mock wrestling move.

I realized that, in that moment, I was drunk on him. I wanted to stay pressed to his skin as long as I was breathing. I wanted all of him.

"And he told you how much you meant to him, right?" Seth asks, and I look back at him.

Asshole, my gaze shouts. He meets my eyes defiantly.

"He didn't have to," I bite out.

Seth narrows his eyes. "But he *has* told you what you mean to him, right?"

"Geez, Seth," Rielle breathes. "Lighten up."

I clench my jaw and then step to the side of the path. Rielle gives me a questioning look, but I motion to my boot.

"I'll catch up. Gotta tie my shoe," I explain. Rielle nods and bounds ahead. I kneel down, pretending to redo the knot of my laces.

Hot, vicious anger claws up the back of my throat. I need to be able to believe that the kiss didn't mean anything. I thought he would just let it go, and let me do the same.

This is going to be harder than I thought it would be, and it's easier to blame him.

A shadow stretches over me.

Seth holds out a hand to me to help me up, and I ignore it. The group has moved on, and I stand, lengthening my stride. The last thing I need is to talk to him.

"Charlotte," he calls, and I ignore him. I hear his heavy footfalls behind me. "Charlotte."

I whip around, letting the rage fill my eyes. "You're an asshole, Marsali."

He holds his hands up. "I'm sorry. I just . . ."

"You just what?" I shoot.

Seth looks over my shoulder. The group is continuing, slowly hiking out of earshot. He sighs, and I see him deflate a little.

"I shouldn't have taken it so far. That was out of line. I just . . ." His voice falters, and I stop in my tracks, turning around to face him. He sighs. "I want to make sure you're okay. And I'm doing a shit job at trying to talk to you after—" He doesn't finish the sentence, but the memory of the kiss floods back, bringing heat to my cheeks. I look away.

"Well, I don't need you to make sure that I'm okay, Seth," I snap, "because we're not *friends*."

The words fly past my lips before I can taste them. Before I can roll them across my tongue and decipher them as bitter. As lies.

Seth freezes, his yellow eyes boring into mine. He lets out a small breath. A humorless laugh. It hit him right where I wanted it to.

"Fine."

"Fine," I spit back, the falseness of it conjuring nausea in my gut.

That's when I hear a small, shrill noise roll down the line and blood rushes in my ears. The whistle.

Something is coming.

Seth doesn't hesitate. He grabs my arm and pulls me into the brush as Rielle signals for the Curseclean to hide, and they all jump off the road. Seth pulls on my arm, and I lose my balance. I topple, and he falls with me.

"Shit," I hiss, feeling his arm around my waist as we both careen to the ground. I twist, landing on my back.

He lies on top of me, his elbow braced on the side of my head.

"Shit," he growls.

The sound—a *crack*—splits the air. We both go still. The wind whispers through the trees, but no other sound rides the breeze. Still, neither of us is willing to chance a movement.

"I'm sorry," he whispers. His eyes find mine—and there is sorrow and regret mixed with the fear. He's not talking about landing on me.

He shifts like he's going to move, but I grab his waist as another *crack* rips through the woods.

"Don't move," I breathe.

His solid chest rests on mine. Heat blooms in my rib cage, sending goose bumps over my collarbone. I wonder if he can tell. If he can feel.

Fear wars with something else; something deeper that has started to churn in my gut.

"If I tell you to, you run. Run as hard and fast as you can. You get to the ship. Do you understand?" he murmurs.

My hands go rigid, my heart thundering against his chest.

"We talked about this," Seth whispers, feeling my reluctance.

"*You* talked about it," I bite back, swallowing the tightness in the back of my throat.

"Run south. Cut across and back down the path. Get to the water. Get to safety."

The thought of leaving makes me sick. I yank my hands free and bring them down to his sides. I pull on his shirt, turning my head so that my lips are at his ear.

"If I run, they'll kill you all on sight and take the Curse-clean. If I stay, then we have a bargaining chip. We can find a way out of it. Like with the *Cobalt*."

He's quiet for a moment, and I know he doesn't like what I just said.

"A bargaining chip? Are you insane?"

"I won't let them hurt you," I answer back, and he lifts up to look me in the eyes.

"I can protect them," he says, his voice strained.

I blink, swallowing hard as my eyes flick between his.

"I won't let them hurt *you*," I repeat, emphasizing the last word.

And it hurts, how much I mean it. It hurts, how his face tightens as he looks down at me, how I can see his thoughts racing. It's the truth I've been dodging for the past two weeks. It's the truth that brought me to the deck under the full moon. The truth that sent me plunging into the sea. It's the truth that has kept me awake in the middle of the night, aching for a touch I've never felt.

Seth is still, our hearts thundering against each other.

A whistle cuts through the air. One low, two high. All clear. But we don't move.

"I'm sorry," Seth says again, quieter this time.

"*I'm* sorry," I reply, and he'll never know how much I mean it.

Seth shifts, just a little, and he's going to get up, but stops as his body aligns with mine. I look up at him, his yellow eyes heavy-lidded as they meet my gaze. Restraint tightens his jaw, and his eyes drop to my lips. *We should go. We need to go. I need—*

But I know I'm hours away from never seeing him again,

and it brings a sort of fluttery panic to my chest. I'm going to lose him soon.

I need this.

My hands slowly inch up his ribs, and he closes his eyes as he drops his forehead to mine, and something like a shudder makes his hips settle gently into me, bringing his lips even closer to mine. It's a shallow movement, but I gasp, a jolt of electricity licking up the back of my spine.

I don't know what we're doing, but I know I don't want it to stop. I let out a shallow breath, hitched as my mind unhinges from the darkness that has kept it tethered to reality.

I want him to steal the breath from my lungs. Our faces are so close.

This is a glass moment hovering above a marble floor, and we're gripping it with everything we have. But sooner or later, we both know it is going to shatter.

Seth shakes his head like he's fighting to find his thoughts before he turns and rolls off me in one swift movement, and I hate my body for hating his absence.

Seth secures his blade to the holster on his thigh, and I can see that whatever was kept alive in the heat between us has withered in the exposed air.

"We good?" he asks, his expression unreadable once more. Gone is the boy who made brownies in the microwave. The one who did a backflip off the stern. He's the captain I met on the first night. And that's what I wanted.

"We're good," I answer back.

My boots kick up wet dirt, and I savor the burn in my lungs as I walk quickly to try and catch up to the rest of the group.

I don't know what catches my attention, or why I look to my left, where a small clearing lies, undisturbed.

But I look, and for a second—I see someone standing, shrouded in sunlight.

A woman, all in black, her light skin and blond hair stark against the emerald greenery.

But when I look again, she's gone.

Chapter 29

THE SAFE HOUSE IS A MILE OUTSIDE CRESCENT City, deep in the Last Chance section of the California redwoods.

I wait with Alan and the rest of the Curseclean as Lucia and Seth scout the perimeter while Rielle and Thomas go ahead to collect wood and scope it out. With another whistle, they signal that it's safe for us to come in.

I wince at the sound, and wonder if I'll ever be able to hear it again without imagining the weight of Seth's chest on mine and the blissful feeling of his ragged breath on my lips.

The safe house is nicer than I expected. I was thinking it would be a cabin with a Unabomber vibe, but it's modern architecture—white stone and open stairwells. My favorite thing is the giant glass wall at the back that overlooks a creek snaking through the woods.

The cabinets are fully stocked, and Lucia brings a dozen sleeping bags out of a closet.

There's even hot water in the shower, something I check before I crank it in the opposite direction.

I let the cold stream wash down my back like it can cure me of the heat Seth planted in my bones.

Rielle starts a fire and then says something about finding Lucia's candy stash before sneaking upstairs.

"I'll kill you," Lucia calls from the kitchen, but she doesn't move to stop her, so. We all know how this is going to end.

I curl up by the fire, loving the sensation of the heat on my face as my wet hair drips icy drops on the back of my neck. I need to savor this—I don't know when I'll get it again.

My socks are dry for the first time in months, it seems, and the cushion under my head is soft. If I close my eyes, I can almost pretend I'm home—that it's near Christmas and my mom is playing the Judds on the record player. That Vanessa is helping with dinner, and Harlow is beating my dad at chess in the other room. I can almost hear his deep laugh as it mixes with fake outrage—*those aren't the rules, Harlow!*

"Is this seat taken?" a soft, deep voice asks, pulling me out of my thoughts. I look up as Abel Lassiter steps around the couch. I scoot sideways on the rocky hearth.

"All yours," I reply quietly, marveling at the strange sensation of seeing someone in real life that I've seen on a screen for years. He wears dark pants and a red sweater that smell faintly of mothballs. His hair is washed and trimmed, and it looks blonder now than when I found him. There are cuts on his cheek that are still healing, and a couple of bruises on his jaw that aren't quite gone. Other than that, he looks the same as he did on the other side of the television.

"I'm sorry I didn't find you sooner," he says, his voice low. He interlaces his fingers in his lap before pulling them apart again. He's nervous.

"You don't need to say anything to me," I start, but Abel shakes his head as he pivots to face me.

"I do. First, you saved me. If you hadn't found me, I would be dead. I just . . ." He bites his lip, considering his words. "You know, I'd always heard my father's stories about war. About being a prisoner. I'd read books, and when I signed up for the navy, I knew there was always a chance that that could be my fate. But experiencing it . . ." He stops, forcing a smile on his face. "I just needed some time before I came to thank you."

"Of course," I say quietly. I don't need his gratitude. I thought I was saving Dean. His rescue was a happy accident.

"But also . . ." He takes a steadying breath. "You're the answer we've been looking for, Charlotte. Seth says you know where the Heart is."

I nod robotically, and Abel smiles. "Then it's over." Tears spring into his eyes, and I swallow the bile that rises in the back of my throat.

Rielle appears at the bottom of the stairs, a plastic bag full of candy clenched in her fist. She jumps over the back of the couch. Lucia and Thomas slink out of the back room and take a seat on the floor. Lucia leans back against Thomas's chest, stopping only to give Rielle a death glare when she sees the candy bag. It's a strangely normal moment, a glimpse of how it was before. How it can be again.

"We'll remake everything," Abel says.

"For *everyone*," Seth adds from the shadows. He's standing by the base of the stairs, arms crossed over his chest. Abel looks at his friend, and I know from their looks that this isn't the first time they've talked about it. He flips his knife open and spins the tip against his pointer finger.

Abel nods gravely. "For everyone. The way Evelyn would have wanted it. Without the threat of the Crimson, we will be able to focus completely on expanding infrastructure. There won't be a lottery anymore. Everyone will have access to everything the Torch has to offer. And then, you can come home. Take your place at my side, like you were always meant to."

"And my father?" Seth asks.

Abel leans forward, letting out a sigh. "I'll deal with him when he gets back. I'll let him know that his days in politics are done."

Seth pushes off the wall, closing his knife with a flick of his wrist as he regards his friend.

"And I'm sorry I didn't do it sooner," Abel says. He turns to me. "But we all have a chance to start over now. Maybe there is some light at the end of all of this."

I bite my tongue and force a nod. I just need them all to go to sleep. Then I'll find a way out of here. I'm silently making plans when Abel's voice pulls me back to the present.

"We didn't know what we were going to do when the Vessels . . . evolved. Didn't know how we'd face that. We were outgunned and outmatched. But now we can rally. Whatever you need to get to the Heart, you'll have it. Now, I know that you haven't said *where* it is, which is what I would hope for. If the Vessels get to it first and stop you from destroying it, this is over. But we will need to know eventually. And you might consider telling *someone*, should, God forbid, something happen to you—"

"Nothing is going to happen to her," Lucia bites out. I glance up, and her bright eyes are fierce. I'm used to seeing them directed *at* me. But now, they're burning *for* me. I look back down. Just like that, I'm one of her people.

"Fair enough," Abel answers. "I'll tell the Torch to mobilize and wait for further instruction."

I don't know what to say, so I don't say anything. I clench my jaw tight and muster a single nod. "And it's not just the Torch that will be ready." Seth's voice cuts through the room, and my head snaps up. "We just got the scanner working. Word of you has spread. People are rallying. Settlements are sending their soldiers to the Rogue River forest near Gold Beach."

"The scanner's working?" Abel asks hopefully, at the exact moment that I whisper, *"What?"* not bothering to hide the fear on my face.

As Lucia leads Abel out of the room, Rielle smiles at me.

"People know the Chosen One is alive, and that she's on her way to find the Heart."

It feels like my legs have turned to jelly, and nausea roils in my gut.

My hands shake as the realizations crash over me, getting worse with every second.

Rielle crosses the room and sits in front of me, grabbing my hand. "It's going to be great, Charlotte. It's *happening*. I know you're scared, but we won't let anything happen to you, okay? You're one of us."

The words hit me like blows, and I swallow back the dread that's coating my throat so much it's making it hard to breathe. They're sending everything they have to this fight, leaving settlements defenseless. The Torch will be weakened—all because they think the Chosen One has arrived.

And when I don't show up?

This is going to cost lives. This is going to start a war.

I'm going to throw up. I breathe deeply and try not to look as horrified as I feel—especially as Rielle heads to help upstairs, leaving me alone with Seth.

"Charlotte?" he asks, and he takes a step toward me. I put a hand up, stopping him.

No way. That's the only way that this could get worse. Seth.

I stand abruptly, and spots flit in my vision.

"I'm tired. I'm going to bed," I announce, grabbing a rolled-up sleeping bag from the pile Lucia started earlier. I walk upstairs, picking the room at the end of the hall. Two

Curseclean women from the *Cobalt* are already asleep on one of the beds. There's a chair, but I don't want it.

I spread the sleeping bag out in a sliver of moonlight cutting through a skylight, then sit on it, my heart seizing in my chest.

This lie was supposed to save my sister. Then it was supposed to save Dean.

It wasn't supposed to bring death.

Sobs beat their wings in my throat, and I try as hard as I can to swallow them back. But they won't die down. I let one out, and I buckle as it spasms against my chest soundlessly, my mouth forming the noises I can't make.

My heart has been limping on for years. My parents. Dean. My grandmother. Malcolm. Palisade. Vanessa on the deck of the boat.

Seth's body on mine. The look of realization and regret that covered his face when he rolled off me.

I'd never been that vulnerable with anyone, and he left me in the cold.

I fist my hands in the sleeping bag and press my face into the nylon fabric.

I cry until my chest aches. I cry until the moon disappears from the angle of the window, taking the light with it.

Chapter 30

IT'S EASY ENOUGH TO SNEAK OUT. THEY'RE ALL worried about things getting *in*. No one in their right mind is considering that the Chosen One might be a liar. That she might try and run away in the middle of the night.

But this next part is tricky—getting past the outside wall without getting noticed.

The air is cold, and my boots sound too loud as I walk through the grass and then across the gravel drive, toward the trees, looking for the best place to cross.

I dig my hands deep into my pockets as I bring my shoulders up to my ears. I have my mirrored bands on because I know I'm leaving safety.

To my left, I see a tree branch that leads perfectly over the top of the wooden gate. I'm reaching for it when I see someone outside. I duck into the shadows just in time to see Abel come out on the front steps of the house.

I shove deeper into the darkness. What is he doing out here?

His breath comes out in steamy puffs, and he pulls his jacket tighter. He digs his hand in his pocket and pulls out a cigarette and a lighter. With a soft *clink*, he lights it, and takes a deep puff before sitting on the porch. Abel lets out a soft exhale of smoke, lowering his hand. Ash falls to the cement, and I see the lit tip burning against the darkness. He brings his free hand to his forehead and braces it against his knee.

I stop, almost mesmerized as I look at him. I'm used to the polished version of Abel Lassiter. The People's Prince—always ready with a motivational speech or a rallying cry. Even tonight, as he sat next to me on the hearth, he was the Abel I know from interviews and broadcasts. Hopeful. Resolute.

Here, in the dark, wearing a down jacket that's too big while smoking a cigarette, he looks . . . human, and he looks tired. I wonder if he prays, and what he says if he does. I wonder if he believes in the hope he's giving us.

I am only pretending to be the Chosen One. He's been living like one for years.

And I'm about to ruin everything. I'll have to tell him.

I take a step out of the shadows but stop when I hear someone hiss my name. The hairs on the back of my neck stand up, and I feel a chill. Because it sounds *wrong* somehow.

I turn, keeping my eyes on my mirrored bracelet. The blond woman I saw in the clearing earlier smiles back at me, her eyes a dark red.

"Charlotte, I presume?" she purrs before someone behind me puts a piece of fabric over my nose and everything goes dark.

It's dark in the cell, save for the soft glow of dawn bleeding through the opaque glass. While the rushing sound of waves is muted through the closed window, the ground feels steady beneath me—we're not on a ship. The bars are stone, not metal. I look up. The ceiling is covered in stalactites.

I'm in a cave somewhere. Probably by the ocean. I push myself up to my knees, not trusting myself to stand just yet, as I piece together the vague nightmare-like recollection of how I got here—a small boat. Voices. A blindfold.

"Well," a vaguely familiar voice says. "You certainly took your time waking up, didn't you? Girls used to be able to handle their chloroform."

A figure steps out of the shadows, and I drop my eyes to the concrete floor, my heart racing.

She scoffs as she pulls a chair just beyond the end of the cell.

"What are you going to do to me?" I ask, looking down at the ground.

"I don't think that's the question, Charlotte. I think it's more—what can you do for us?" she asks. I don't know why I hold out for the idea that this might be a random kidnapping. That she doesn't know about the lie. She steps inside. Her black boots are scuffed at the toes. Mirrors are tied in the laces, remnants of when she was human.

"I can't do anything for you," I answer back.

She clicks her tongue. "I don't know about that, Chosen One."

I pray my face isn't as telling as it feels, and the terror that slowly creeps up my back isn't apparent.

I press my hands to the concrete next to me as she steps closer. I smell her—rust and roses. It makes me want to lean in and pull back at the same time. Her wrists, covered with bracelets, jingle as she leans down.

I shut my eyes tight.

"You're scared of me?" she whispers.

There's no point in lying. "Yes."

"Good," she replies. I feel her angling her chin so she can look at my face, and I keep my eyes shut.

"Why would I kill you?" she teases, her voice light. "When I've been looking for you for *so* long."

I press my jaw together and shove my palms against the concrete to stop them from shaking.

Her.

The Vessel Queen. She's found me.

"If you are who I think you are, we are actually destined to be friends," she croons.

When she finds out that I'm a fake—just a Curseclean girl— I'm dead.

The thought feels far away, a fact that hasn't fully sunk in yet. Theoretical; outside my mind.

She's going to kill me, and that's the best-case scenario. Cold hands brush over my cheekbone, and I wince. She runs a thumb over my lips.

"You wanted to kiss him. I saw it," she singsongs. The sound sends shivers down my spine.

She was there. Chills race down my arms, and a sick feeling spins in my gut. We were being watched. Hunted. And we had no clue. My cheeks flush at the memory. The way Seth had moved on me, and my answering gasps.

I yank my chin out of her grasp, and she giggles.

I feel her lean closer. I smell her breath. "He wanted to kiss you, too. You know that?"

"You don't know a thing about us."

The Vessel Queen laughs.

"Oh, I think I do, sweetheart. I know Seth Marsali better than you know."

She leans closer.

"Open your eyes, Chosen One. Use your mirrors, if you want. I don't care. But I don't like talking to someone when I can't see the fear in their eyes."

I feel her back away, and I keep my eyes down and shut. I reach over, checking my mirrored bands before opening my eyes slowly.

I open my eyes, and the breath gets caught in my throat as I take in the beautiful face before me.

High cheekbones. Full lips. Arched eyebrows over bloodred eyes, and a jaw that's a feminine equivalent of one I've spent the past several weeks memorizing. On her head sits a crown of shattered mirrors, all twisted together in cable and twine. Dried blood graces the edges.

Evelyn.

Evelyn Marsali—Seth's twin.

She's the Vessel Queen.

Chapter 31

SHE SMILES, REVEALING STRAIGHT WHITE TEETH. Her beauty is staggering, even now.

"That's better. Now we can talk girl-to-girl."

I shake my head, and she tilts hers.

Questions bubble at the back of my throat, but Evelyn stands, cutting them off as her bloodred eyes glare down at me. Only one matters.

"You died," I bite out.

"Yes, I did. Well, sort of. I *turned*. But I actually feel better than ever, funnily enough. And I'll feel much, *much* better if you tell me where the Heart is."

I press my lips together as I stare at her through the mirror.

"Oh, come on. Don't be like this. Don't make this hard."

When I say nothing, she lets out a sigh. It sounds so human—so *normal*—that I almost forget what she is.

"Come," she orders, turning on her heels and striding to the door of the cell. For the first time, I notice guards in black robes standing in the shadows. They were so still, so dark, that I didn't see them. I push myself to shaky feet and consider my options. Which, at this point, are severely limited.

Evelyn looks over her shoulder at me. "If you're trying to think of a way to save yourself, you're wasting your time. You know as well as I do that no amount of either rebellion or cordiality will save you."

Her words are matter-of-fact. Bored, even. They don't land on me like I thought they would. They don't spark terror or dread. I've been ready for this since the *Devil's Bid*.

"I know."

She cocks an eyebrow, and it is a movement so like Seth's that it almost steals my breath.

"Follow me, Chosen One," she orders.

I don't know where we are, but I can smell the salt in the air, so I know for a fact now that we're near the ocean. Not like that will do me any good.

Any thought of escape or rescue—if I had one in the first place—would have been driven from my mind the second I get a good look at this place.

The walls are covered in shadow, but when I look closer, I realize it's not shadow at all.

Vessels. Vessels, draped in black fabric, stand at attention like sentries down the long hallway.

I only see them through the mirrors as I pass because they open their bloodred eyes.

My heart pounds as I follow her down the twisting, damp hallway, the eyes of the still sentries watching my every move. The rock beneath my feet is slick, and I almost slip as I turn a corner. The cry that rises in the back of my throat dies off as soon as I see where we are.

A lagoon lies under the hooded mouth of the cave. Moonlight spills through a gaping hole in the stone, splashing against the shallow pool of water. An old fishing boat—the one they probably used to get me here—sits off to the side, bumping among a swath of flotsam and jetsam that has drifted into the cave. It scrapes against the sand-colored rock as Evelyn turns back to me. Her movements are smooth and liquid—uninterrupted. Even the slight turn of her head looks like it's out of a nightmare.

I walk closer to the water, and I feel a cold hand on the back of my neck as dark robes brush up against my back. The fear comes then, but it doesn't overwhelm me. I keep my eyes down as Evelyn wades into the water in front of me.

"Where's the Heart?" she asks.

I watch her reflection in the pool. "If you were going to kill me, why not just eat me in my cell? The theatrics are a bit much," I spit, hoping some defiance will make me feel braver. It works, a little.

I watch a smile curve up Evelyn's face. It's so broad, I can see the whites of her teeth even in the choppy water.

"Oh, I told you we weren't going to kill you, and I meant it.

But we *are* going to hurt *him*."

I move my mirror slightly as footsteps sound on the other side of the cave. I don't even have to see who it is, because my heart already knows.

And as I hear the expletive-laced curse bounce off the rocky walls, I let out a small cry of despair. It's Seth, and he's blindfolded. I pivot the glass back to Evelyn, who is smirking as she holds a finger up to her lips and winks at me. They lead him until he's waist-deep in the water.

"The Heart," the Vessel behind me says.

"Charlotte?" Seth yells, his voice thick with something between terror and rage. "Charlotte, *don't* tell them!"

Anguish rips from me in a soft sob, and Evelyn gives a signal. The Vessels holding Seth shove him under the water, and Evelyn speaks. "See? I knew my brother was with the Chosen One, but I also knew I had to be sure which one of you it would be. So I watched. I knew my brother, my *good* brother, would protect the world's only chance with his life. And today, I saw it. Oh, did I *see it*," she mocks.

She knew where we were. Maddox probably told her I was with Seth, but she didn't know we had changed ships, and she didn't know where we were going. Someone else betrayed us.

Seth struggles, lurching once under the water, and every other thought screeches to a stop. *"Please!"* I shriek. Evelyn steps closer to her brother and continues.

"But what I *didn't* expect was to see how *you* reacted to *him*," she croons.

Seth kicks, and water splashes, hitting Evelyn. She makes a

disgusted noise as she steps back, motioning for them to lift him up once more.

Seth takes a gulping breath.

"The Heart. Where is it?" the Vessel behind me asks.

The tears burn down my cheeks, and Evelyn smirks.

"Charlotte? Charlotte, if you're there, hold on!" Seth yells.

"Seth," I bite out, a sob ripping from my chest at the sight of his shaking, bound hands.

Evelyn looks to the Vessels behind Seth, who shove him under once more.

"See? We could *start* with the flesh-tearing and 'eating him alive' thing, but I thought you two might pull this self-righteous bullshit. I figured it would be a long night."

They let Seth up again, and he coughs. They shove him below again quickly.

"Plus. I figured . . . you were remade in water on the night of blood. So this had a weird sense of"—she stops as she tries to find the best word—"*poetry* to it, don't you think?"

"You have something that belongs to us," she says, trailing her fingers in the water. Light beams off her skin, and the mirrors of her horrific crown catch glowing ripples.

"I don't have Anne's Heart. I have never seen it in my life." The conviction makes the words rip from my throat, because I know they're true—Vanessa has never once been around that wretched rock.

Evelyn moves closer to me, her dark robes making waves in the pool.

328

The Vessels are keeping Seth down.

"Let him go," I whisper, desperate. "Let him go, and I'll take you to it."

Evelyn leans in. "That's not going to work for me. But I'll do this. You tell me where it is, and I'll kill him now, instead of dragging this out."

I dig my hands in the sand, trying to control my ragged breathing.

She lifts her hand, and the Vessels drag Seth to the surface. He gasps and coughs, and I hear the exhaustion in his breathing. I chance a look at him, and that's when I see it—the rock in his hand. The one he found when he was under.

I dig my hands deeper in the sand, gritting my teeth.

"Okay, you win. I'll tell you," I breathe. Evelyn chuckles, leaning closer.

All at once, I lift my hands, throwing the sand into her eyes. She howls, reeling backward.

"Seth! Now!"

Seth pivots, smashing the Vessels behind him with the rock and pulling his blindfold off. Evelyn is still screaming, her hands over her face. I have to get him out of here before he sees her.

"Behind you!" I shriek. "Get the boat!"

Seth swims for the small rowboat, and I launch myself into the water. But I'm not fast enough—a firm hand grabs my ankle and pulls me under.

I kick, fighting as hard as I can, but the grip is like iron. Panic swells in my chest as two hands pull my shoulders out of the water. I keep my eyes closed as a voice hisses in my ear from behind as she yanks me to shore. "You are going to pay for that in screams, my love. You're going to pay for it in slow trickles of blood slipping over your beautiful skin, and you are going to *wish* you were dead."

Evelyn is behind me. I open my eyes, and Seth is in the boat. His eyes light up, and he lifts it—a harpoon gun.

"Go! Get out!" I cry. *"Seth, go!"*

Evelyn turns and throws me to the ground, and I scream again as I see Seth dive into the water. He's coming back for me, and it makes my chest feel like it's been hollowed out. I see him walk out of the water, gun in his hands as he looks at the Vessels slowly filling the cave.

Evelyn stands, her back to him. I watch her face carefully in the reflection of the lagoon.

"Your hero is here, then," she drawls, a slow grin pulling at the corners of her mouth as she casts her eyes down and to the side.

She's enjoying this.

This will kill him. He won't be able to finish her. He can't. It's Evelyn. His hesitation will kill him. And she will tear him apart. He lifts the harpoon gun and fixes Evelyn in his sight.

"Seth," I beg, my eyes meeting his. "Please. *Go.*"

Confusion knits his brows as he lowers the gun slightly. He knows there's something he's not seeing. Some snare he's stepped into that he missed. Has he recognized her voice?

"He can't, Charlotte," she continues. "Not until he's saved you. Because that's what he does, right, Seth? You *save* people."

Evelyn turns in the water to face her brother.

I have lied and cheated and used everyone who has come into my life in the past several weeks. I have fanned hope into a dead fire and raised an army that has no chance.

So I deserve to see the look on Seth's face as he lifts his gaze to the Vessel Queen.

I deserve to see the moment his shoulders slump, just half an inch. My chest feels like it's cracking open at the way his lips part. My knees weaken as he clamps his jaw shut and his eyelids flutter. I have to watch the moment that Seth Marsali breaks in two, and I deserve every bite of pain that rips through my chest.

His arm falls to his side like he can't physically bear the weight of it.

"Brother," she says, lifting her hands. "It has been too long."

He lowers the harpoon gun slowly, his grip loosening.

"No," he whispers, shaking his head as he redoubles his grip on the gun and lifts it once more. "No."

"What? Did you think I found Curseclean to stop the sickness? Did you think I would *ever* be weak enough to succumb to such *evil*?" The way she says *evil* sends shivers down my spine. "No, no, no, my Seth. It seems there was only one spine from our mother, and it went to me."

Sickness spreads over me as realization sinks in.

He made me look. He told me he'd kill Evelyn if I didn't.

The memory flashes through my mind. The way Seth said the words like he was remembering a death.

He was.

I looked up, and I gave the Crimson away.

But that wasn't the whole story.

He didn't just give the Crimson to *someone*.

He gave it to Evelyn.

Everything around me slows, and I feel my heartbeat pulsing loudly in my ears.

"Did he tell you?" Evelyn croons, looking over her shoulder coyly. "Did he tell you how easily he cracked? We swore we would *never, never* stoop so low. We would *never* be that *weak*."

Her calm facade cracks, ever so slightly. "And he did. *You promised.*"

Evelyn's voice shakes.

It's then, when I blink back the tears that have started to well up, that I see them—Vessels slowly working their way across the wall. Toward Seth. If they reach him, he's dead. They might not be able to turn him, or eat him, but they can still rip him limb from limb.

"Seth!" I shriek. In one swift movement, he puts his finger on the trigger. The second it happens, I shut my eyes and dive, but I feel a hand around my throat. The warbled cry that creeps up my crushed windpipe only makes the fingers tighten.

"Evelyn! *Let her go!*" Seth cries.

I hear my heartbeat thundering in my ears, static threatening to take over.

"*Evie! LET HER GO!*" Seth cries, and I know he's begging. He's begging her to not make him pull the trigger.

The click is soft, and I don't know why I hear it, but I hear it in my bones.

It's the sound of never turning back. It's the sound of Seth's heart breaking.

He pulls the trigger.

And even as my lungs burn and my hands scratch pointlessly at Evelyn's arm, I move. She was expecting me to pull backward—not forward—and it throws her off for one second. And a second is all I need. She shrieks as I wrap my arms around her neck and lift my feet, the weight of me throwing her off as I pull us under the water.

The panic tightens its familiar grip, and I wait for the paralysis. But that doesn't happen. It hovers above my lungs, a threat and a promise.

The harpoon *whooshes* into the water next to us. Seth pulled the trigger, and even through the rush of the water in my ears, I hear all hell breaking loose up on the surface.

I don't know why the panic decided not to set in now. I don't know why I am able to move, but I'm not going to sit and wait for the moment to fade. Yet again, I'm alive against all odds.

I have to move, and have to keep my eyes shut. I scramble, my fingers feeling around blindly on the rocky lagoon floor. My fingernails crack on pebbles, soil, and stone, slick with algae and sediment.

Come on.

Come on.

I crack my eyelids, just for a second, as the water around me lights up with the setting sun just enough for me to see the harpoon, its iron tip sunk into sediment below. I don't stop to question my luck. With one strong movement, I yank it from the muck and shove myself up, breaking the surface. I swipe the razor-sharp tip out. It cuts across Evelyn's arm. She lets out a shrill cry that echoes painfully off the walls of the cave.

It's an overwhelming sound, as if it's coming from all directions. It's then that I realize . . . it *is*.

All the Vessels are screaming in pain, and my mind scrambles. I don't have time to dissect it. *Move*, I order myself. Adrenaline overrides terror for the first time in my life, and I'm able to propel myself faster through the water than I have in years.

I keep the harpoon in hand, cutting through the lagoon with powerful strokes. A warm hand grabs my arm, and I break the surface, keeping my eyes shut tight.

"Charlotte!" Seth calls, putting my hand on the edge of the boat. I scramble inside as I hear Evelyn shriek in rage behind us.

"Hold on," Seth orders.

I check my mirrors. Vessels are pouring out of the tunnel now, drawn by the shrieks of their queen.

Blood pools around her in the water as she cries out. "Get them!"

"Pray this works," Seth says to me as he pulls the rip cord on the engine.

The gas sputters to life, and the boat lurches forward.

We slip out of the mouth of the cave and cut across the moonlit water, though I swear I can hear Evelyn's hateful cries follow us for miles.

Chapter 32

WE'RE FARTHER NORTH THAN I THOUGHT, BUT WE can't chance staying on the water any longer. We ditch the boat on some rocks, and Seth uses the last stake in the harpoon gun to sink it.

Seth and I are soaked, and I hear his teeth chattering as we walk up the shore and into the cover of the woods.

It's a rocky beach, so there isn't a chance of them finding our footprints. They could still track our scent, but we're hoping the seawater dilutes it, at least a little.

It's almost dawn by the time we find the cover of trees, and neither of us says anything.

It feels like we've been walking forever when Seth finally points to a cabin standing on tilted legs in the middle of a thicket of trees.

The faded yellow insignia on the wall tells me that it's an abandoned ranger station.

He gives me a questioning look, and I nod.

Rest.

We both need rest.

The inside smells like dust and cedar. Everything is coated in a thin film of neglect, but I still almost cry in relief when I see that it's dry. And stocked.

"We'll stay here till nightfall," he says finally. His voice is hoarse as he sifts through the drawers of a dresser tucked along the back wall. He pulls out two dry T-shirts, tossing me one before peeling his wet Henley over his head.

I don't bother to look away, and I don't even ask him to turn away as I pull my soaked sweatshirt off and yank the dry shirt over my damp hair.

Seth makes a small noise of triumph, and I look up as he pulls some sweatpants out of the bottom drawer. He holds one up to me. I nod, and he tosses the pants to me.

I'm too tired to try and find a corner and play sixth-grade locker room, so I take my pants off right there.

He turns away, showing me more consideration than I showed him. I notice the redness brushing up the bottom of his neck, but he's quick to rub a hand over it, like he knows I can see it. I pull my jeans right side in and lay them over the back of a chair as he continues to look through cabinets. He pulls out a walkie-talkie, taking a deep breath before trying the switch. Static fills the air, and Seth crouches down, balling his fists in celebration, the shirt discarded next to him.

336

"Yes. *Hell yes.*" He switches channels as he pulls his shirt over his head. "Hey, Falcon, this is Sparrow. You there?"

He lowers the walkie, waiting. There's no answer, but he sets it on the shelf. "I'll check again in ten minutes. If they're still at the safe house, they'll be doing routine scanner checks."

It's quiet for a moment, and I run my fingers through my tangled, salty hair. We are going to have to talk at some point. "How did they get you?" I whisper.

Seth takes a slow breath as my words fill up the room around him. He knows we can't avoid this forever.

"I couldn't sleep. Not after—" He stops, failing to find words.

Since you were on top of me and I breathed you in like it was the end of the world doesn't seem like a particularly helpful addition, so I swallow it back.

He closes the cabinet and stands. "So I sat on the roof. And I saw you leave."

"And your first thought was *hey, she looks like she wants to be followed?*" I ask, annoyance creeping in before I can stop it.

He levels a glance at me. "Is this how it felt when I gave you shit for not letting me drown?"

"Kind of. Yes," I retort, and he nods, his jaw tightening.

"Then you were right. I was being a pain in the ass. Anyway. Something knocked me out the second I stepped outside." He walks past me, and I close my eyes as the smell of him—salt and sweat and something sweet—overcomes me. "There have to be some sleeping bags here somewhere." I pivot, following him as he opens a pair of drawers on the other side of the cabin.

I tongue my front teeth.

"Seth."

"What."

I take a step closer to him—his broad back straining against the T-shirt as he searches.

"A thousand parkas and not one fucking sleeping bag?" he growls.

"Seth," I say again, stepping forward, my voice softening. "You can talk to me." He doesn't slow down. I reach out and put a hand on his shoulder, and he slams the drawers as hard as he can. I jump, bringing my hand to my side and taking a giant step back as he rounds on me.

"What? *What* do you want me to say, Charlotte? You want to talk about how I left out that crucial detail of my sordid sob story? That my sister is a Vessel? That it's *my fault* she's that way? That I was too much of a coward to follow through with our promise and now she's—" His face crumples, and he brings a fist to his forehead, a dry sob ripping from his chest. "She's the thing we've been hearing about for the past few months? She's . . . *that?*"

"It's not your fault," I whisper, reaching out. He shakes his head, and I take a tentative step forward.

His shoulders shake, and I reach out and grab his shirt, bunching it in my fists.

"The only one at fault is your father, Seth. You aren't a coward for refusing to let her die."

"Now she's worse than dead," he shoots back, opening his eyes. They're shining with tears, and he tries to turn away from me.

I don't let him.

I don't stop to think about what I'm doing. I just go onto my tiptoes and throw my arms around his shoulder, tucking my face against his neck as I squeeze him as tightly as I can.

"She isn't human anymore, Seth. The things she says . . . she doesn't mean them," I murmur, and he goes absolutely still. "It's not your fault."

Another sob, and he brings his arms around my waist.

"I'm a liar, Charlotte. I'm not this hero. I'm just a liar."

And he's clinging to me like I'm a buoy and he's drowning. And I'm gripping his neck, fighting the feeling blooming in my chest—the one that flowers in seconds and drops words on the back of my tongue.

"I'm a liar, too," I say.

He protests, but I can feel the words climbing up the back of my throat. I know they'll change everything, but I can't keep them back any longer.

"I'm not the Chosen One," I whisper.

Chapter 33

I DON'T MOVE AS HIS HANDS STILL ON MY BACK. AS the breath seeps out of his lungs, hissing in my ear.

I keep my face down as he pulls back, but I can feel his eyes on my skin. I shut my eyes as I lift my head, then open them. "I'm sorry."

I don't have anything to say that will make it right, and I know that.

But the weight of this . . . this horrible secret, is out. Whatever comes next . . . it's worth it.

"That's why I was leaving, Seth. I couldn't have you all go to the Blood Market because of me. I—"

His eyes flash as he takes a step away from me. "Why?"

"Because the Blood Market is dangerous, and—"

He shakes his head. "Why did you lie about it?"

I have been wondering that myself, and the answers coil

inside me, soft and deep. I don't want to look at them. I don't want to be honest.

Rage colors his features, but it's not obvious. It's not something I'd notice if I didn't know him.

The thought crashes through me. *I know him.*

"Why did you lie to *me*?" he asks, and there's not just rage. I've hurt him.

Somewhere in this journey, he started meaning something to me. I know the sound of his voice when something exciting happens. I know the way he carries his shoulders when he's upset.

"I thought Dean was at the Blood Market. I needed to get him back. But he's not there now."

Seth walks away from me and sits in one of the folding metal chairs, resting his hands on his knees as he thinks.

"That's why I was running away, Seth. You've got to let me go, and when they check the scanner again, tell them to *run*. To tell the forces in the woods to *go*. Tell them I'm a coward. Tell them anything. But tell them that there is no supernatural help coming. No Chosen One."

He is quiet, and it feels like my chest is caving in on itself.

"I'm sorry," I breathe, knowing it's nowhere close to being enough.

He rubs a hand over his mouth. "You knew things, Charlotte. At the Jawbone. The *Cobalt*."

I look to the grainy wooden floor. "It's not something *I* know. My sister Vanessa. *She's* the Chosen One. The one the water remade on the night of blood. *She* has the mark on her rib. I've just been hearing what she says in her sleep—they're weird prophecies or something. Not all of them. I've written down hundreds of things and have only figured out a couple. It was . . . it was luck, Seth."

"Luck. Everything you've said that we've based our lives on. *Luck*."

He pushes himself to his feet, and I can feel the anger coursing through him as he pulls out one drawer after the other until he finds a map.

"What are you doing?" I ask.

"Finding a way to get to the camp," he starts, but I don't hear the rest of what he's saying, because I'm looking down at the map and I can barely believe my eyes. My mouth goes dry, and I clench my fists as I stare over his shoulder.

"What is that?" I ask quietly. Close up, it's nothing. But standing, I see it.

Tendrils, snaking along the map. There are about fifteen, all leading inward. I've seen it before.

It's the same shape Vanessa was drawing on the wall.

"The forest outside the Blood Market. It's an older map, but most of the roads should be functional still. I can get in, I think—"

"No. *That*," I breathe, kneeling down and running my hands over the lines.

Seth checks the top of the map. "This is a map of oil pipelines, I guess. Wow, that's a fucking mess," he says, studying the map. I run my hand down the tendrils, stopping where they all gather at the coast.

"And what's this?" I ask.

Seth is still for a second as he considers the map. "That's the Blood Market," he says finally.

Follow the black veins, she'd said.

"Charlotte?" Seth asks.

My head feels light, and I topple backward, catching myself on my hands as I inch away.

"Charlotte," Seth repeats, sliding closer to me. "Are you okay?"

I nod, and he looks from the map back to me. "Shit," he breathes. "What is it? What did you figure out?"

"Follow the black veins," I whisper. "Vanessa drew that shape—those lines."

Seth pivots, pulling the map closer. "The Heart," he mutters, and I shake my head as I grab his leg, digging my hand into his thigh.

"No. Seth. It doesn't make sense, and it will get you killed, and I'm probably wrong."

Seth's eyes are bright as he looks back to me. "And what if you're not?"

"I am." I nod, scooting farther back from the map. "It's not possible. I *lied*. I lied to you. To everyone. I figured out some riddles, but this is different. This is a *suicide mission* based on my *feeling*. Based on a *riddle*."

Seth shifts, inching his body closer to mine so that he's facing me. He shoves up on his knees and grabs either side of my face.

"Your *feelings* saved Abel. They saved all of us. And I don't care that your sister has a fucking mark on her rib, Charlotte.

You are here now. So I don't know how this was *supposed* to go, but I'm starting to think the world stopped listening to 'supposed to' a long time ago."

I take a shaky breath, but before I can explain myself, the walkie buzzes.

"Sparrow?" Rielle's voice sounds through the cabin.

"Tell them to run. Cancel this. Forget it. I can't—" I don't know how to say it. *I can't lose you.* I bite my lip, not trusting the words that are bubbling up at the back of my throat.

Seth stands. "This is our shot, Charlotte. Chosen or not. Ordained or not. But this is it. I'm going to tell Rielle that we're alive so they don't do anything stupid. And in the morning, I'm going to join the fight. You can stay, or you can go. Disappear into the night—I won't stop you. But I'm going to believe in you." He grabs the walkie off the shelf and walks to the door, but stops short of going outside. "Even if you don't."

We eat green beans out of a can and unroll the sleeping bags I found stowed above the fireplace.

I pretend not to notice the space between us—how he's keeping his hands laced over his chest, almost so he can make sure they don't reach for me in the middle of the night.

I wake first, and if he's surprised I'm still there when he opens his eyes, he hides it well. We pack up, and he hands me a protein bar—Arctic White Chocolate.

I look up, a smile on my lips, but he's already walking down the path without a backward glance at me.

Chapter 34

I HEAR THE WAR CAMP BEFORE I SEE IT—THE sounds of rumbling voices and metal. A few minutes later, the orange glow of the campfires cuts through the trees. My chest hurts, and for a moment, I consider turning around. Running again.

The sound of blades pulling from sheaths rings through the night, and Seth and I both raise our hands.

"Eyes down! Eyes down!" a gruff voice calls. "Hands in the air!"

Seth and I both comply as a group of guards races out of a watch tent, blades raised.

"Look up and we'll open your throat," the gruff voice says.

"Okay, calm down, McCreatine," Seth mutters.

The guard puts a mirror below my eyes, and I keep my gaze down.

"Clear," he says, letting me stand.

They clear Seth, too, and we both stand. We walk through the fence, and I rake my eyes over the camp. It's much bigger than I thought, even with Seth's warning.

It goes on for at least a mile.

"We need to see Abel immediately," Seth says.

"Abel Lassiter isn't here," the gruff guard shoots back.

We walk past fire pits, past soldiers who sit around them, tin cups in their hands.

"He'll want to see us. Believe me," Seth orders, the annoyance in his voice growing.

"Sir, I'm sorry—"

"Don't *sir* me, asshole. This is the Chosen One."

I feel a shift in the entire energy around me as they look up at me. I don't pay too much attention, because I'm stepping around the fires, desperately searching. Alan said they were headed to the Torch, but I know Harlow. If there was an army gathering, she'd head there.

A shriek cuts through the night, and a body launches itself at me. All around me, blades and shouts raise, but the smell that envelops me is a shock to my system.

"Nessa!" I cry, and we both fall to the muddy ground, my arms wrapped around her shoulders.

Vanessa squeezes me so tightly I think I'm going to bust a rib, but I hold up a hand. "It's fine! We're fine!" I order over her shoulder.

"What are you *doing here*?" I cry, my chest so tight I feel like it might crack open. She's here. She's *alive*.

She pulls back, putting her hands on my cheeks. "We thought . . . we thought you were dead." She mutters the word like a curse. "I have to tell you something, Char—" But her voice stops as Harlow steps out from a nearby tent, dressed in all black and armed to the teeth. But her face relaxes as she crosses over the muddy ground and drops to her knees. She wraps her hand around the back of my neck and puts her forehead to mine.

"You crazy *bitch*. Don't you ever do anything like that again," she whispers, but there's no anger in her voice.

Vanessa laughs, pulling back and wiping the tears off my cheeks.

Thomas calls Seth's name, and Seth turns to embrace his friend. Lucia and Rielle come up behind him. They're here. They're alive.

"Char," Vanessa starts again, but I hear Seth calling my name.

"Later, okay?" I say, and I follow the others as they walk to the war room.

The tent is almost bigger than our grandmother's house.

All eyes turn to me when I walk in, Harlow to my left and Seth to my right.

Lucia and Thomas follow behind. Maps and candles are spread over a huge table, red markers and tacks scattered over the yellowing pages.

Abel turns as I enter, his face collapsing as he sees Seth and

I in the doorway. "What the *hell*," he breathes, though his expression is guarded—unreadable.

"Sorry we're late," Seth says. "But I think the intel we have will be worth it."

Abel's eyes flick from my face to Seth's, and understanding slinks over his expression. His yellow eyes brighten, and he turns back to the table as Seth and I take our place at the end of it.

"This is Charlotte."

The room shifts, just like the camp had outside. Some straighten, some narrow their eyes as they watch me.

"The Chosen One," a woman with light brown skin and dark blond hair says. She looks younger than me. "I thought you'd be taller." Her emerald eyes glint with mistrust. "What took you so long?"

"She's here now, Cam," Seth says, taking a place alongside the table. Lucia and Thomas join him, and Harlow crosses her arms at my side. I fidget, hating the weight of their eyes on me.

"We're discussing movements," Abel starts. "Best possible places to attack. Until we get the Heart, we—"

"The Heart is at the Blood Market," Seth says. Abel freezes, and the room goes still.

"You're sure?" Abel asks, turning his gaze to me. I don't turn to look at Harlow, but I can feel her eyes on my back. Seth steps closer, and I feel his hand on mine. He grips my fingers, and I swallow.

I trust you.

Even if you don't.

I take a deep breath, remembering the feeling when I saw *Glimpse of Paradise* burning in the water. And when the lock turned on the *Cobalt*.

I was right then.

There's no reason I can't be right now.

I nod.

"*Where* inside?" someone asks. I look over my shoulder.

"Get me inside, and I'll see what I can do."

Abel smiles, and titters go around the table as he looks at me. "You won't be going in, Charlotte. You're going to stay here."

Irritation snaps into something darker, and I step closer to the table.

"Fuck that," I say. "You want the Heart? I'm going with you."

Seth raises his head, looking at me like he's seeing me for the first time. I don't know when I made that decision. There was no one moment, I think. It was a slow realization as I walked behind Seth in the woods.

I don't know how we'll find it once we're inside. But I trust that we will. "I'm not your psychic or your war muse. I'm the Chosen One, and this won't work without me. So you'll do what I say."

Abel is stricken, and everything is dead silent. Then, Cam looses a breath.

"Well, shit. I like you," she says, looking from me back to Abel, who lets a hint of a smile curl up on his bearded face.

"Very well. Based on numbers sent from other settlements, we'll have enough manpower here to march on it the day after tomorrow. Until then, get your rest."

I nod and turn. Harlow follows, but I stop at the sound of Seth's voice.

"I can leave tonight, General. I'll bring the troops down from the north. We'll meet you there in the morning."

I whip around, and he doesn't look at me. He's leaving tonight, and he didn't tell me.

Seems I'm not the only one who made decisions while we trekked silently through the woods.

We're not even to our tent yet before Harlow's voice growls low in my ear.

"What the hell was that?"

I pull away from her, twisting and swatting her off. We're next to our tent, and I can see Rielle and Vanessa toasting hot dogs together over a nearby fire.

"What was *what*?" I asked.

"That whole speech, *Chosen One*," she spits. Her eyes look bright in the dark, the thick eyeliner smudged perfectly, even now.

I sigh, and tell her Seth's plan.

Her eyebrows shoot up, and then her expression tightens.

"Are you fucking kidding me? You're going to get yourself killed. You're going to get *all of us* killed. I'm stopping this, right now." She turns, but I grab onto her wrist. She looks back, fire reflecting in her eyes.

"If you do that, then our one shot is over now. You need to trust me, Harlow. We have a real chance to end this."

Harlow's lip curls. "That's not what this is about, and you know it," she growls lowly.

I let go of her wrist. "What's that supposed to mean?"

She steps closer. "I saw you in there. You love this."

Her words brush up on something inside me, something I've been ignoring.

She's right.

"What the hell are you talking about?" I ask through clenched teeth. "I did this to save Vanessa. You were there."

"Don't lie to me," she seethes. "You've lied to *everyone* else. Do not lie to me. You did that to save Vanessa, but this? This is for you."

That's it. I don't know if it's the look on her face, or the fact that she's right—but I can't take it.

I shove her square in the chest, and she staggers back, tilting her head with the force she's using to restrain herself from hitting me back.

Because she knows I probably wouldn't get back up if she did.

"You want to go there? I think this is about *you*, Harlow. You couldn't stand for one second to not be the center of attention. You couldn't stand for one second to have people focusing on me for once in our lives."

Harlow explodes, somehow keeping her words a scathing whisper.

"I am not going to apologize to you for living my life,

Charlotte! I'm not going to say sorry for being tall! It's not my fault you curled up in my shadow and gave up."

Even she knows she's said too much.

The fire crackles behind her, and the sound of far-off laughter mixes with the pleasant din of dinner.

She licks her bottom lip, frozen by the words she just said.

Without another sound, she turns and stalks off.

I shove the tent flap aside and walk in.

Dean sits on the cot opposite, and he stands when he sees me. "Well. I'll tell you one thing. *I'm* happy to see you," he jokes.

I launch myself at him, wrapping my arms around his sturdy shoulders. He smells warm and safe. He smells like *home*. Tears prick the back of my eyes as I bury my face in the crook of his neck.

"I thought you were dead," I cry, squeezing him harder.

"No way, man. I'm not going down that easy." But I hear the tremors in his voice, and I know he has been through something.

Something he's not going to be ready to talk about for a while.

"She didn't mean any of that, Char," he murmurs.

I pull back, and he wipes tears off my face. His rough thumb scrapes across my cheekbone, and I close my eyes.

Everything has gone to shit. Everything.

"When you ran for me, I—" His voice chokes off, and I force a sad smile on my face.

"What did you think I was going to do? I couldn't just let

them . . ." I break off as I look up into his eyes.

If I am going to tell Dean, it needs to be now.

I don't know if I'll get another chance.

His eyes burn as they look down into mine, though I don't know if it's from the emotion of seeing me again or from the thing I've been desperate to see for years.

I take a deep breath, waiting for the words to bubble up the back of my throat.

And I wait.

But they don't come.

They aren't there.

I spent years falling in love with this man. I had no clue that I could fall out of love in the space of weeks.

I didn't know my heart could be full of something . . . someone else, but it is.

I let out the breath, and Dean smiles down at me. It's the smile I've seen for years, and I return it for once, matching the same emotion without anything else behind it.

"Charlotte," someone says, and I jump as the tent flap opens. Seth stops hard when he sees Dean and me. I step away quickly, but it's too late.

"Hey. Seth," I say stupidly, because I can't think of anything else. "I—"

"Don't worry about it," Seth says, his voice clipped as he looks to Dean. "Nice to meet you, Dan."

Seth turns on his heel and stalks through the camp.

Chapter 35

I TURN TO FOLLOW SETH WITHOUT SAYING A WORD to Dean.

"Seth!" I yell.

He doesn't slow down. "I didn't mean to interrupt," he yells over his shoulder.

I step around a group of soldiers running drills.

"You weren't. Seth. Can you wait for a minute?" He walks into his tent, and the flap shuts behind him.

I ball my fists and shove it aside. Seth turns around, his yellow eyes bright. His bags are packed on the cot.

"You're leaving," I say softly.

"Yup," he says, zipping up his bag. The noise is loud.

"Why?" I ask, and it comes out as a whisper. My head feels clear for the first time in months, though I'm more scared to face his answer than I ever have been.

I was just in Dean's arms, his breath on my face, and the words died in my throat.

"Because I am yearning for the glory of battle," Seth says sarcastically. He stands, his bag in hand. "I can make it to the Blood Market by tomorrow."

He tries to step around me, but I don't let him. He sighs, and I meet his eyes.

"Why are you leaving?" I ask again, not looking away.

His jaw ticks. "You know why."

I shake my head. "I don't. Tell me."

Seth tilts his head, anger slipping over his face. "Why should I, Charlotte? What good what it do? You're in love with him," he says.

I feel a strange lightness and heaviness fill my chest at the same time. Tears spring up in my eyes as I smile. Seth clenches his jaw.

"I'm not," I say with a shrug. The words feel like a death. They also feel like freedom. "I thought I was, but I realized that someone else has done . . . something. Something to me."

Seth blinks once. Twice.

"So I don't care why you were leaving, Seth. I just care that you . . . don't."

There's hesitation in his eyes as I step closer.

"You said you trust me now. So. Trust me." I reach up, putting my fingers on his chin as I tilt him down to me. His shoulders tense at the touch, and my hands shake.

"I want you," I whisper, echoing the words he said to me by

355

the railing all those nights ago. The words that singed my bones and unraveled something deep inside my chest.

Something breaks loose in him then as he drops his bag, his warm hand cupping the back of my neck while the other arm snakes around my waist. His mouth crashes onto mine, feverish and hungry. My hands tangle in his hair, and his tongue parts my lips. I open to him, letting him devour me.

A growl rises from the back of his throat, and the thing he woke up in me in the woods roars in response. I lift my legs and wrap them around his waist, and he stumbles back to the cot. He lays me down, hovering above me as he skims a thumb over my bottom lip.

"See? Told you keeping it simple was the best play," he whispers against my lips. I reach up and pull him down, fusing our mouths together again. I reach over and turn out the gas light, and the orange glow of the fire bleeds through the fabric of the tent.

His skin is on mine, his lips on my neck.

And for the first time, the thought of tomorrow is driven from my mind.

I wake up with a groggy, pleasant feeling in my bones. Sore, swollen lips and a new lightness in my chest.

I roll over, jumping out of the cot at the sight of the familiar figure standing in the doorway of my tent. Familiar, but not Seth.

"Morning," Maddox says.

Chapter 36

I PULL A BLADE OUT FROM UNDER THE COT, BRANdishing it in front of me. Maddox rolls her eyes and steps out of the tent. "Get your ass up," she says.

I tear out after her. Maddox strides ahead of me, not bothering to look back as she heads toward the tent where we all met last night. Without a word, she steps inside.

"What the hell?" I yell, sprinting after her. I tear the flap open and rush in, my blade tight in my hand. Seth is inside, his hands raised as he steps between us. Ragnar and Pollux sit by the edge of the table, both dogs still as though they're waiting for orders.

"Whoa, whoa. Char. Hold up." He looks to Maddox. "I told you to *wait*," he orders.

I look around the room. Harlow sits at the table, her eyes tired. Cam and a couple of the other men look down at the maps on the table, talking in low voices. Lucia paces toward the back of the tent, her eyes wild.

My eyes dart from Seth to Maddox as I lower my blade, but only slightly. Seth's face is drawn, his expression dark as he moves closer to the table.

"What the hell is this?" I whisper. "What happened?"

"Abel is gone," he says.

My stomach drops, an uneasiness creeping into my bones. "Like . . . he left already?"

Seth shakes his head. "No. His tent was empty this morning."

My eyes dart to Maddox, a string of curses building in the back of my throat, but Seth steps in front of her. "It wasn't her, Charlotte. She arrived with her crew this morning."

"How the hell do we know that?" I bite out.

"Because it wasn't just Abel," Seth says gently. The sick feeling in my chest spreads, and I lower my blade. "Dean and Rielle are gone, too. It looks like they snatched as many people as they could while keeping quiet. Dozens were taken."

The words hit me in the chest, and I stagger from the sheer force of them. I struggle for breath, forcing myself to take deep pulls of air as I sink into a chair. I want to ask why they'd risk trying to take more than just Abel. But I don't, because I already know the answer, and if I hear it spoken aloud, I might throw up. The Vessels are hungry.

"Do we know where?" I ask finally.

"Thomas is following the tracks with a scouting party," Lucia replies. I look to Harlow. Her eyeliner is smeared below her eyes, and her hands are fisted on the table.

I glare up at Maddox.

"And why the hell are we trusting her now? She tried to *kill us*. And Dean is Curseclean. He's worth something to her," I cry, shoving myself to my feet.

"You don't know *shit*, Chosen One," Maddox growls out. I lunge at her, and Seth steps between us, keeping me back.

"She wouldn't hurt Rielle, Charlotte," he shouts, his voice strong. I stop, looking at Maddox over his shoulder. There are dark circles under her eyes, and she wears a drawn expression I know well. It was the same one I had when Dean was gone.

Together, we were going to change the world. Rielle was talking about Maddox. I meet the Runner's eyes, and she glares at me as Seth explains.

"I checked the channels to see if Rielle was there. I used her sign, and Maddox answered. She's going to help, Charlotte. And she's agreed to turn herself over to the Torch if we let her."

Maddox looks down, her jaw clenching.

Anger bubbles in my throat, but I know the truth—we need all the help we can get.

"You do anything—*anything*—shady, and I'll kill you myself," I say finally, surprised at how much I mean it.

Maddox doesn't answer, because Thomas careens back into the tent.

"The Blood Market," he gasps out. "The Vessels took them to the Blood Market."

◆◆◆

It's quiet as the Jeep motorcade rolls through the forest, the smell of ocean air getting stronger with every bumpy turn. I adjust my mirrored bracelets before turning to look out the back window. Seth, Maddox, and I are in the first car, leading the charge, and Seth's driving. Harlow, Lucia, and Thomas are behind us. If there's anything about the Blood Market that can trigger any understanding of Vanessa's words—anything that might save lives here—I want it to happen as soon as possible, before others get too close.

We can't wait for the rest of the reinforcements. What we have—a couple hundred—is all we're going to have. And it will have to be enough.

We hold our blades in our laps, though the roads around us are empty.

"Shouldn't there be . . . something?" I whisper. "Runners? Something?"

"Yeah. There should," Maddox says, her voice filled with uncertainty. It doesn't suit her. "It'll be right up here. This road dead-ends at the front gate."

"And how do we get inside?" I ask.

Maddox is quiet. "I've never been inside," she admits finally.

We turn a corner, and I see it—a massive structure looming out of the ocean, almost like a stone creature from the deep that scrambled up to the shore but didn't make it all the way. The ocean beats against the rock at the base, angry whitecaps spraying foam into the air. Fog rolls in over the water, but I can still make out a shape in the distance—a tall structure, black and foreboding.

"What is that?" I ask.

"The Rig," Seth answers, turning to follow my gaze.

I shake my head, fighting against the feeling of unease that's growing in my chest. "*That's* the Rig? Did they know they were building it so close to the Blood Market when they started?"

"I don't know," Seth admits.

Maddox turns like she's going to say something to me but doesn't get the chance. A blast rips through the air, knocking our back tires completely off the ground. We lurch forward, then slam back down before I can let out a scream.

"*Shit,*" Seth cries, twisting the wheel in an effort to keep us on the muddy road. I duck, covering my head as I turn to look out the back window. There's smoke between us and the other vehicles. He slams on the brakes. Maddox coughs as she unbuckles her seat belt.

"Seth?" I croak, turning just in time to see the figures stepping out of the smoke behind us. At first, I think it's Lucia. Maybe Harlow. But I quickly realize it's not.

"Vessels," I cry. Seth tries to throw the Jeep back in gear, but they're too quick.

They're at the door before I can move. I scream as one rips the door off, reaching in and pulling me out. I shut my eyes tight as they drag me through the mud.

"*Charlotte!*" I hear Harlow scream from the motorcade behind me, but I don't turn back. I just hope she'll run. That she'll find a way back to Vanessa, and they'll escape.

I hear the sound of creaking metal, and I feel for my mirrors. They didn't take them, so I glance down as the gate opens before me.

I've imagined this place a thousand times. Curseclean in cages or tied up in corners—Vessels milling about, assessing the virtue and strength of each victim before deciding the price with the Runners. In my head it is a filthy, hellish wasteland.

But that's not what greets me when the metal door swings wide.

Pristine white walls with electrical panels. High cathedral ceilings with industrial lighting. The floor is a gray marble, polished and reflective.

I crane my mirrors, eyeing the glass doors that lead to wide hallways beyond.

There are no Curseclean anywhere.

No wailing. No Vessels.

It's just quiet.

I turn the reflection to the side, and see Maddox in a Vessel's grip next to me.

"Shut your eyes, stupid," she hisses, her voice tight. They take us through another hallway, and then, we stop. Without another word, the Vessel lets us go and steps back. I'm about to reach down for the blade I have stuck in my boot, but something makes me freeze. Without a word, I hear them leave, closing the door behind them, leaving us completely alone in a room that feels *wrong*.

There's a table in the middle of the room, and a glass wall along the right side—slightly fogged but still translucent.

And beyond, propped up against the wall, are pods.

"What the *hell*?" Maddox breathes.

They look like coffins but with clear fronts. And inside, arms at their sides, are humans. The pods all have electronic screens, monitoring vital signs.

Curseclean.

Maddox steps toward the glass. "They're in cryo," Maddox says, running her hand over the glass as she looks back at me. "Preserved," she breathes, and I know she's as scared as I feel. Because I've seen a Vessel lair. This is different. This type of facility is advanced. It's almost . . . medical.

"Well. This really isn't how I wanted this to go, Charlotte," a voice behind me says.

Maddox's eyes widen, even as she clamps her jaw shut, trying to hide the fear rippling over her expression.

I rotate, even though I realize who has spoken.

I heard his voice, the night before.

Abel Lassiter stands at the doorway, his hands in his pockets.

Chapter 37

I STOP AT THE END OF THE TABLE, MY HANDS SHAK-
ing as I fight to keep calm. Abel Lassiter is here. In the Blood
Market. My mind spins, fighting the one explanation that
makes sense.

The Torch runs the Blood Market.

Abel walks to the head of the table and pours himself a glass
of water. He drinks it slowly, then sets the glass in front of him
as he lets out a satisfied sigh.

"What the hell is this?" Maddox asks, stepping away from
the glass.

Abel looks at her, disdain filling his gaze. "Those? Those are
just some of the ones who came to apply for entry to the Torch
in person, but *didn't* quite make it. Don't act disgusted, Ms.
Caine—there's a whole row of yours in the back."

Her eyelids flutter as she blinks and closes her mouth.

"They came to the Torch?" I ask, my voice cracking as my mind spins. I assumed they just sent you away if you were denied. I would never have imagined, not in a million years, that *this* is what they did.

"Thirsty?" Abel asks, gesturing to the water. "You sound thirsty."

I can't muster a reply—my eyes are still fixed on the people behind the glass. People who had hoped for safety. If Harlow hadn't refused my plan to leave, it would have been us.

"Sorry for the theatrics," he says finally, running a hand over his mouth. "And the rude welcome. I wasn't planning on show-ing anyone this place yet. Not until it was ready. But you and your *the Heart is at the Blood Market* thing . . . kind of threw everything into a tailspin, Charlotte."

I look to Maddox. Her face is stone as she stares at the ground. I swallow hard.

"And what is *this* place?" I rasp out.

"This?" Abel gestures around us. "This is the thing that will save the world. This is . . . *salvation*."

I freeze, watching how his eyes light up when he looks around.

"When my mom was in local government, all she wanted to do was build this community center. It was all she focused on. All she talked about." He walks around the side of the table. "She finally got the funding and worked for *years* to make that place a haven for the residents of our town. And you know how they thanked her? They trashed it. Stole from it to buy their drugs. Ripped up the books she painstakingly selected for the library. I remember the look of disappointment on her face when we'd step inside it. That's when I realized that the world would always have people who cared, and people who didn't. People who wanted to be the best versions of themselves, and people who couldn't care less."

I balk as his words sink in. "You want to kill people because someone tore up books in your community center?" I whisper incredulously.

"Don't be reductionist. I've seen your test scores. You're not stupid, Charlotte. That was just the beginning. But I spent *years* in the world. I've been in combat zones. I've volunteered in youth homes. The line has always been there—we just never wanted to see it."

"What *line*?" I whisper.

Abel walks around the table, his eyes fixed on mine.

"The line between the people who contribute to society and the people who don't." He walks toward me. "And then, this curse." He twists his expression into one of mock worry. "And while everyone was so *scared*—I saw an opportunity. The Vessels didn't have to be the end of the world. They could be the beginning. But their descent into flesh-eating madness was . . . hard to control. I know it's a curse, and it's magic . . ." He bites his lip, lost in his own dark recollection.

"But I knew I could do *something*. It was my destiny, right? I mean, I get my doctorate in viral studies, lead a team at the CDC for six years, and then the *zombie apocalypse* hits? Give me a break! How perfect was that? So I worked in the lab. Took samples. I thought I found a way to stop it. But . . . it didn't. It just, stalled it a bit. And then, I realized . . . we didn't *need* an antidote. Why get rid of the Crimson when you can just control it? But not everyone was on board. For me, that was the biggest disappointment. That even the one I loved *most* couldn't see the future I was building."

"Evelyn," I whisper.

Abel nods. "Evelyn. She found out and threatened to tell everyone, so I had no choice. She was going to tell Seth, and I *knew* we would lose everything if that idiot heard of the plans. Self-righteous prick."

I bite back the bile rising in my throat. "And Admiral Marsali helped you?"

"I needed an *in* for my plan. Admiral Marsali needed to break his rebellious son. Win-win."

He looks at the door, and it opens slowly. My breath catches, and I lower my eyes, watching in the mirror as a woman in black robes and scarlet lips stands there, her red eyes fixed on Abel.

Evelyn.

She walks into the room, her shoes clicking lightly on the floor, the mirrors tied in her shoes clinking softly with every step. She carries a metal case in her hands, and sets it gently on the table.

"She'd always volunteered to be my first human trial—she was hopeful like that. Always giving me blood samples and hoping that she could assist somehow in saving the world. She was still helpful, after she turned. And it stalled the progression. She shared it with the others, which, of course, secured their loyalty—they saw her as a savior. The fact that there was a decline in her"—he looks down, searching her eyes—"*moral superiority* is . . . a perk. I would chalk it up to changes in the frontal lobe. She's much more agreeable now. And as long as she keeps taking this"—Abel lifts a vial out of his pocket— "she will continue to be."

"You sent her to us. At the safe house," I say, putting it all together.

"I'd heard the Chosen One was found. I paid those idiots on the *Cobalt* to get me as close as they could. But they got sidetracked and bloodthirsty, like the beasts they are. The trip took twice as long, but . . . you still found me. Destiny," he says, a soft, almost awe-filled smile on his face.

No. My stomach lurches at the thought.

No. This isn't what was supposed to happen.

Find him on the dark blue.

No. Saving a genocidal madman couldn't be what this— the prophecies, the bloodshed—was about. I clamp my teeth together to keep from screaming.

If Abel notices, he doesn't care. He continues. "It was convenient that we finally got radio communication back up. You said you knew where the Heart was. I had to make sure you were full of shit. Which, you are. My mother spent *years* looking for that thing, hoping to end this. I wasn't going to let that happen."

My blood runs cold at the words. "Genevieve? She knew about this?" Abel doesn't answer as he runs his fingers over the case. My mind turns, piecing the edges of half-formed thoughts together. "You killed her," I whisper.

"I did what I had to do to protect us. She came back here, ready to end it, but her boat sank. It took our doom with her—" He bites his words back, and for the first time since he walked in the room, he looks like he knows he's said too much. He looks down.

I swallow, almost afraid to ask the next question. "Why did you take Dean and Rielle?" I whisper.

Abel looks up, and I feel Maddox shift next to me.

He scoffs. "Dean followed me. For a dumb jock, he's got some good intuition. Rielle. Is she the one we . . ." He looks down at Evelyn, and I follow his gaze through the mirror. She cocks an eyebrow in response.

"Right. She's the one we needed."

The doors open once more, and I hear soft grunts and the scuffle of feet. Two Vessels drag Rielle into the room, tossing her onto the floor. Maddox lurches forward, but Abel pulls a small gun from inside his jacket and points it at her.

"Come on. Don't be like that. Blood takes forever to get out of the marble," he says. Evelyn walks to Rielle, pulling her up by her forearm and walking her closer to us as Abel opens the metal case on the table. Evelyn brings Rielle forward, and she locks eyes with me. Her hair is matted with blood, though I can't tell if it's hers or someone else's. She meets my eyes and then looks to Maddox.

As Rielle struggles against Evelyn's grip, panic fills my lungs. I scramble desperately for a way to stop whatever is about to happen. I don't know if Harlow and Seth are mobilizing a rescue, but I have to assume they're doing *something*. It's the only way to stop the fear from gripping the back of my throat so tightly I won't be able to breathe.

"Seth," I say, hoping to stall. "He's your best friend. How could you do this to him?"

I hit a nerve, and Abel pins me with an angry glare as he tucks his gun back in his pocket. "I was doing this *for* him. For all of us. I was making a new world, because I thought he was brave enough to see it.

"But now, Seth is just a hindrance. All the Xanthous are." He flips open the case. Inside, there's a clear vial filled with an angry-looking orange liquid. He lifts a syringe with nimble fingers, and the breath stills in my lungs.

"At first, I didn't think the Crimson would behave like a regular virus," he says, sticking the needle into the orange vial and pulling deeply. "But it has all the same hallmarks. Incubation period. Infection. Decline."

Abel steps forward. "And eventually, it plateaus. Some people become immune. That wasn't an issue, really, until I realized that it emboldened people like my best friend—people who wanted to return the world to like it was before. Given a long enough time, the Crimson might have evolved. But we don't have that kind of time. This . . . this levels the playing field."

Abel stalks toward Rielle, and she backs up against Evelyn.

"What are you doing?" I shriek, stepping forward, but Maddox yanks me back.

"Take me!" she cries. Abel stops, pivoting toward us.

"*No*, Maddox! Stop!" Rielle whimpers, but Maddox takes another strong step forward.

"You need a Xanthous for some sort of . . . test? Use me. Leave her alone."

Abel looks from Rielle to Maddox, the corner of his mouth ticking up slightly. "I see."

"Rielle is the kind of person you're looking for. The kind of person who fits into your mold of the new world," Maddox spits. Rielle sobs silently in Evelyn's arms, shaking her head.

"I'm not," Maddox continues. "We both know that."

"Ah, but you've been useful. And you'll continue to be useful. Whereas *she*"—Abel sweeps a hand in Rielle's direction—"will continue to be a pain in my ass. Decisions, decisions."

A stillness falls over the room—the breath between a plunge. I don't trust myself to blink, or breathe. Abel watches Maddox, whose fingers are splayed at her side. Rielle struggles in Evelyn's iron grip, and Abel glances at the movement.

That's all the time Maddox needs.

"I'll be a pain in your ass right now," she spits, snatching the vial from his fingers before Evelyn can stop her. Abel backs away, and Maddox takes only two seconds to consider her options. With deft fingers, she spins the syringe and plunges it into her neck. I know I scream, though it's nothing compared to the one Rielle lets out.

It's quick, but not quick enough that I know it doesn't hurt. Maddox lurches, shutting her eyes and letting out a soft hiss as she drops to her knees. I lower my eyes and tilt my mirror as she lifts the heels of her palms to her face.

"Mad," Rielle cries, and the heartbreak in the sound nearly splits my chest in two. Maddox lowers her hands, and I see her irises in my reflection.

They're not yellow anymore. Not fully, anyway. A deep, bright orange swirls in her gaze. She looks up, and Abel claps his hands.

"Well! Step one is a rousing success! She's not immune anymore," he singsongs, stepping aside and motioning to Evelyn.

"Let's see if step two is just as effective, shall we?"

Evelyn steps around Rielle, releasing her grip on my friend and dropping to a crouch in front of Maddox.

"Look in my eyes," she murmurs.

"No!" Rielle screams, launching herself toward Maddox. I throw myself forward, wrapping my arms around her just as Maddox starts to scream.

Rielle fights me, but I keep my arms tight as we both sink to the floor. I bury my face in her shoulder, her sobs racking her body hard enough to shake both of us.

I hear Maddox stop screaming as the soft click of Abel's shoes sound on the marble. He lets out a contented sigh, and I lift an arm, looking in the mirror as Maddox lifts her eyes.

They're red.

"It works," Abel breathes. I tighten my grip on Rielle as

Abel pivots, arms out as he gapes at Evelyn. "We can override Xanthous. It *works!*"

Rielle's sobs abate slightly, and I feel her rise.

"What the hell did you do?" I whimper, my fear getting the best of me. Abel's smile is so wide it doesn't fit in my mirror.

"I created the second wave of the Crimson—one that can be controlled. One that skips the Exposed phase and puts any newly turned Vessels right where I want them—beholden to me if they want to stay alive."

"Keep your eyes down, Charlotte," Rielle whispers, her hand tight in mine. I look down, but not before Abel pulls a different syringe from his coat. This one is filled with a bright red fluid. He kneels to where Maddox sits on her knees, her fists clenched in her lap. I watch her in my mirrors.

"Now. We have to find a way to spread this new wave. It's injectable for now, and I'll use what I have on the ones who need it most—"

My heart staggers. The ones who need it most. *Seth. Rielle. Lucia. Thomas.*

"—but I can make more. I'll just need a talented Runner to help spread it," he says softly. "And with the antidote, you can live like this—a Vessel in our army, safe from what's about to befall the rest of the world."

He pulls the rubber stopper off the needle with his teeth and leans forward, hand outstretched. But Maddox recoils and spits in his face.

"Fuck you," she breathes.

A choked cry rips from Rielle, and I squeeze her as hard as I can. I angle my mirror. Maddox's eyes are a bright, angry red, and a slow, resolute smile slips up her mouth.

"I chose the wrong side once. I'm not doing it again."

Abel wipes his face with the back of his sleeve.

"Very well," he says, and Evelyn pulls Maddox to her feet. "But you should know . . . this strain will likely decline much faster. So. Enjoy your pathetic redemptive arc while you can." Abel signals, and the doors open. More Vessels stream in, grabbing Maddox before making their way to Rielle and me.

Rielle pulls me close. "Charlotte. Dean," she breathes. The Vessels' hands are like ice-covered vises as they grip my upper arms, but I cling to Rielle. She brings her lips to my ear.

"He's been exposed," she says.

Chapter 38

IT'S DARK AND COLD, BUT THAT'S ALL I KNOW. I hear the familiar clink of metal, and then someone is shoving me to the ground.

I feel hands on my back, and I panic, scrambling as I twist around.

"Charlotte! Charlotte, it's me! You can open your eyes!" I recognize the voice, and open my eyelids, just a little. I look across the room.

Vanessa sits there, ash smudged on her cheek, her hair down around her face.

"Where's Harlow?" I ask, just as Harlow kneels next to me and pulls me into a tight hug. "What happened?"

"They grabbed me right after they got you," she breathes, pulling back before glaring at Vanessa. "And *someone* stowed away even though I told her to stay put."

Vanessa drops her arms. "You are *not the boss of me!*"

"This? Right here?" Harlow yells, motioning to the cell around us. "Is *literally why I am the boss of you, Vanessa!*"

"I wouldn't have gotten caught if you hadn't freaked out!" Vanessa shouts back.

She reads the terror-filled question on my face, and puts her hands to my cheeks. They're freezing.

"Seth is safe. He got away, I saw it." Harlow meets my eyes. "What happened?"

For the first time in too long, I tell her everything.

Everything, even about my feelings for Dean. About Seth. Abel.

All of it.

She nods, blinking back tears as I meet her eyes. She thinks that's it—that the story is done. I don't want to tell her, because saying the words will make it real. But I know Rielle wouldn't have told me unless she was sure, and I can't carry this alone.

"Dean. Harlow. Dean is infected," I bite out.

Harlow's hands drop from my face as she sinks to the ground. She licks her lips, her eyes darting over the floor like she'll find an answer there. Vanessa goes still for a second.

"When?" she asks, and I know she's doing the same math I am—trying to figure out how long he has left.

"I don't know," I whisper.

Tears fill my sister's eyes, and she shakes her head against the wall.

"We . . . are so . . . so screwed," she mutters, looking up at the fluorescent light in the ceiling. "I've spent the last few *years* trying to protect you two, and this is where we all end up. I couldn't have planned something this shitty."

"It's not your job to protect us," I say before I can think of the thousand reasons I shouldn't.

Harlow lowers her gaze from the ceiling to find mine. "Of course it is," she says, her eyes softening.

"It's not," I reply. "It never was. And you," I say, turning to Vanessa. "You need to stop trying to save everyone else at the cost of *you*."

Confusion fills Vanessa's face, and Harlow narrows her eyes. "I know it was you, Vanessa. That sent the transmission to the Torch the night Maddox attacked," my older sister says.

Vanessa's eyes widen, and my mind sputters, unable to understand.

"When did you figure it out?" she whispers, her voice catching.

"What?" I interject, but Harlow stays fixed on Vanessa.

"About ten seconds after it happened," Harlow says. I wait for the rage—for the moment when I have to get between them, but Harlow just shakes her head. "Why?"

Vanessa's lip quivers, and she hits her fist on the floor as tears rip down her cheeks.

"I thought I could save everyone. I thought I could end this, and you wouldn't let me. So I told them where I was, but didn't give my name. But now, Malcolm . . . and Kyle, I . . ." Her voice breaks.

That's what she'd wanted to tell me. She pushes herself to her feet and paces the cell like she can outrun her guilt.

That I hadn't been the one who brought them—Vanessa had.

"And Abel sent Maddox," I piece together. It makes sense now.

"The Torch Enforcers said they were acting without orders. Just wanted to help," Harlow adds.

"What a fucking mess we are," I whisper. Harlow leans her head against the wall and wipes tears off her face with the back of her hand.

"We're going to die here," she says flatly. "And Dean is going to die here. After all this. We got so far, and—"

"We're not going to die here," Vanessa says. Her voice is so strong that I believe her. "Not before I can make this right."

I shake my head slowly. "I don't think we can make this right, Nessa. But you're right. We're not going to die here."

Vanessa nods, and I can tell she's fighting her tears and losing. "I'm so sorry. I am *so sorry*." She walks to the wall between us, and I stand and pull her into a hug. Harlow pushes up the wall until she's standing next to us.

"If anyone should be sorry here, it's me," I say, eyeing Harlow over Vanessa's shoulder, hoping she understands. *I'm sorry for loving him.*

"And me," Harlow whispers, her eyes still on mine. *I'm sorry for not seeing it.*

I reach out, fisting my hand in her leather jacket, and pull her into a hug. She fights me for half a second before collapsing into us, and we all slide down the wall in a sad little sister bundle. Harlow turns to me, her mascara streaming down her face. Her eyes drop to my neck, and a smirk curls up the side of her mouth.

"Is that a hickey?" she asks.

My hand flies to my throat, and Vanessa yanks it away.

"It totally is," Vanessa whispers.

"Can we not?" I snap, and Vanessa lets my hand go. Harlow gives me a glare. "Can we save the lecture until we rescue Dean and get the hell out of here?"

Vanessa nods, scooting closer. We sit, the silence between us a warm, long-awaited thing.

I'm underwater again, but the panic doesn't come. The burning in my lungs is warmth in my chest—too familiar to make me afraid.

She's walking toward me again. The woman with the dark hair and bright eyes. She's closer than she has ever been before, her vest almost completely unbuttoned.

It's not here. The Heart isn't at the Blood Market, I say. My voice sounds like it's on the surface, carrying through the depths and echoing like we're in a church.

She eyes me, and I step forward, anger flooding every inch of me as my feet sink into the wet sand. Because I know who she is. I've known for a while.

"It was all for nothing, you know. All of it. The headdress did nothing, but my looking for it gave Vanessa time to make a stupid call that cost lives."

She tilts her head as she looks at me but doesn't argue. I

wait for her anger, but it doesn't come, so I continue. "And that *Cobalt* prophecy? It saved a madman. I thought this was all leading somewhere. I thought it was for a purpose. But all it's caused is destruction. All you *are* is destruction," I cry, bubbles flying past my lips. I know Rielle thinks I shouldn't blame the woman in front of me, but Rielle didn't have a sister who was marked and given nightmares. She wasn't chasing down pointless rhymes. My fists shake, and I realize I'm quivering with something bigger than rage.

Heartbreak, maybe. I had faith for a day, and it felt like coming in from the cold. And then it was snatched away again, before I could even get warm.

"I don't believe in this shit," I bark. "And I never should have listened . . ." I don't finish the sentence, and it's a live wire on my tongue, thrashing around as I try to find its end—*to you. To myself. To Malcolm. To my mother.*

She lowers her eyes, like she understands, and we're still for a moment. Then, her white hands part the fabric of her dress. A pinkish glow burns in the center of her chest. Around us, pipelines wind over the ocean floor. The current undulates, kicking up the sand and whipping swaths of kelp through the water.

Anne looks up, and I follow her gaze. A dark structure reaches out of the sand around us, careening toward the surface.

The Rig.

Chapter 39

I DON'T KNOW HOW LONG WE DOZE. BUT WHEN I wake up, we're huddled on the floor.

I sit up, gasping for breath. The pipelines don't empty out at the Blood Market. They stretch all the way out to the Rig.

Abel's voice sounds in my memory. *Her boat sank. It took our doom with her.*

Genevieve found the Heart, and she was bringing it back. Abel sank the boat.

The Heart is beneath the Rig.

My mind buzzes as I run my hands through my hair. That has to be it. It has to be. That wasn't just a dream. It couldn't have been. It would make sense that the Rig and the Blood Market are so close if they're both using the same power source.

And if they're both run by the Torch. Anger pools in my gut at the thought.

I look to Vanessa, asleep on Harlow's chest. Her shirt rests above the hemline of her jeans, and I lift it slightly.

The scar is there, bright and puckered on her smooth skin.

Se racheter.

Everything that has made sense has come through Vanessa. What if it was just a dream? If we get out of here, we only have one shot.

A creak overhead pulls me out of my thoughts. Harlow twists, gently inching Vanessa off her. The creaking sounds more like a groan now.

"What the hell?" Harlow asks.

I know that sound.

I've heard it before, on the *Devil's Bid*.

"Move!" I shout, scrambling as we both scoot to the far end of the cell, dragging a now half-awake Vanessa with us.

The groan gets louder, and then the ceiling caves in around us. Lucia crouches in the middle of the cell. She stands slowly, picking drywall out of her hair before looking up at us. We're frozen in shock, and she shakes her head and does a lifting motion with her hands.

A rope drops from the ceiling, and Seth peers down at me. I grab it and whisper, "Perfect timing."

Our eyes lock, and a heat unfurls in my gut.

It's in that exact moment that Harlow leans in front of me and points to Seth. "We're going to talk about that hickey, Marsali."

◆◆◆

"They've still got Rielle and Dean," I breathe as soon as I climb up.

Seth motions for me to crawl, and I move. Harlow and Vanessa climb up behind me, and we move soundlessly in the dark, using my mirrors to peer into the grates and vents below as we look for Rielle and Dean.

Low growls fill the ceiling, and I stop, chancing a look over my shoulder. Seth is behind me, his eyes wary. I turn back and keep moving.

The sound gets louder, filling my head until it feels like my teeth will crack.

It's the sound that haunts my nightmares—the one that I heard before on the boat.

A Vessel—one who has slipped past the aware state.

I use my mirror to peer down into the vent, and I see her.

Rielle sits in a cell, her back against the far wall. Her arms rest on her bent knees, and her eyes are fixed straight ahead. I don't want to tilt the glass to look across the hallway, because I know what I'll see. But I have to know what we're getting into.

Maddox is in the cell across from Rielle, and she's not Maddox anymore. She grunts and shrieks, her arms reaching through the bars as she grasps at air. Even from up here, I can hear her jaw snapping.

A couple of weeks ago, I wouldn't have cared if Maddox Caine lived or died. Even now, her crimes are so big, so bloody in my recent memory, that I have a hard time feeling anything. But the look on Rielle's face—the naked heartbreak—it feels like an arrow through the chest. Seth nudges my leg, handing me an iron blade. I swallow, bringing myself back to the moment. We have to get Rielle out of there. We have to save Dean.

"Careful. Maddox is contagious," I whisper down the line. "Mirrors up," I tell Harlow, who is behind Lucia. Vanessa secures her glass necklace, and for a moment I consider telling her that there's no way in *hell* she's going down there. But when she looks up, I see it in her eyes—she can handle this. I pull the vent up and lower myself down, landing softly on the floor below. Seth lands next to me almost immediately. Two Vessels stand at the far edge of the cell, and they turn at the noise.

I eye them in the reflection as I stalk forward. Weeks ago, I would have been too scared to move. Now everything is different. *I* am different.

I swing my blade as Seth swings his, and both Vessels drop to the ground.

Harlow and Lucia pop the cell door, and Seth and I search the rest of the cells. There's no sign of Dean.

"Ri," Lucia says, rushing into the cell and sliding over to Rielle on her knees. Rielle doesn't stand. She doesn't move. Her eyes are glassy, her face streaked with dried tears.

"Ri, we have to go," Lucia whispers. She stands, putting her hands under Rielle's arms and lifting. The movement shakes something loose in her, and she blinks, coming back to the moment. She stands, looking at us as Harlow steps closer to Maddox's cell, her eyes fixed on her mirrored bracelet as she widens her stance. Maddox lets out a terrible, feral sound. Harlow lifts her blade, and a guttural cry rips from Rielle's throat.

"No," she yells. Harlow stops, turning. Rielle wipes her face with the back of her hand and steps forward, her lips moving as she whispers softly, just like on the deck of the *Cobalt*. I understand now—she's praying. A heavy, expectant silence rolls through the hall as Rielle steps up to the cell, just inches from the Vessel's straining fingers.

Rielle's face crumples for a second, but she shakes off whatever wave of emotion threatens to pull her under. She motions to Lucia, who opens the cell door. Rielle steps in, steps forward, raising the blade. I turn away, and I feel Seth move closer to me. I bury my face in his shoulder, and his hand tightens around my waist as a sick *thunk* fills the air.

Seth rubs my back, and I know it's safe to look again. Rielle walks out of the cell, blood splashed over her face.

It's done.

We have to go, and when Vanessa whistles the "all clear," we slip back up into the darkness.

Bright moonlight greets us as we spill out onto the rooftop, where Thomas waits for us, unfamiliar cables and harnesses at his feet. A cable stretches over the roof and into the trees. We're going to zip-line out of here.

"We can't leave," I say, stopping and looking at Harlow. Worry creases her forehead. "Not without Dean. We can't leave him here."

Lucia and Seth exchange a look. "We're staying," she says. "The reinforcements should be here tonight. And we're not leaving here until everyone inside is out. If Dean is here, we'll find him."

I bite back the dread that rolls over me as I look to Harlow, and her eyes are hardened.

"You know where the Heart is, don't you?" she asks quietly.

I don't want to nod, because I know that it means I'll have to go. Harlow steps closer.

"I think. But it's a gamble, Harlow. This didn't come from Vanessa."

"None of it has," Vanessa pipes up, securing the harness to her waist with a tug. She looks up at me, and I open my mouth to argue.

"I might be the one who wears this stupid mark, Charlotte. But you've been saving the world. And you can finish this," she says.

"We can save him if we end this," Harlow says, her dark eyes bright with something between terror and hope.

"I'll go alone. You stay here and find him," I counter. "That way, if I'm wrong, we're not all out there."

"We're all going," Vanessa says. "If it's out there, I might be able to help." She's looking to Harlow like she's waiting for her to argue. But it doesn't happen.

Vanessa slides down, and I watch her go. Thomas hands me the harness. Seth's voice sounds behind me.

"So where are we going?" he asks.

Chapter 40

WE FIND A DINGHY ON THE DOCK AND SYNC UP THE walkie-talkies that Thomas brought.

Seth, Harlow, Vanessa, and I climb in, and we rocket through the night.

Please let this work, I whisper, looking up at the stars.

The oil rig is at least seven stories tall, with small lanterns hanging off its spindly arms. It looms over us, and Seth spins our boat in a circle as we reach the landing dock.

"Why would it be here?" Harlow asks, and I have a sinking feeling in my stomach. What if I'm wrong? What if I'm really, really wrong?

We pull up to the landing dock, and I look to Vanessa.

"Anything?" I ask as she looks up at the oil rig. She shakes her head in a shallow tremor.

"Nothing. Charlotte. I don't feel anything," she whispers. "Do you?"

I shake my head.

"We'll have to search," I whisper.

A spotlight bleeds through the night, nearly blinding us as the sound of a huge motor cuts through the darkness.

A speedboat pulls up to the far walkway of the Rig, and my heart plummets.

I don't know who that is, but it's probably not help.

"Let's go," I whisper. We all step off the dinghy and run up the metal stairs, trying to be as quiet as possible, but the clanging of metal rockets over the water. I peer through the latticework as the boat pulls up to the small dock.

I grab Seth's arm as recognition sinks over me. It's Abel, and he's not alone.

A man with bound hands sits next to him, and I recognize the shoulders. Dean.

Abel steps out of the boat and reaches down, pulling Dean along with him. He twists, and I see that Dean's eyes are covered, his mouth gagged.

"Mirror, Charlotte," Seth whispers quietly.

"No," I whisper. It feels like the world is tilting under my feet, and my hands dig into the metal.

"*Charlotte,*" Seth shoots back, and I drop my eyes, watching Abel pull Dean onto the dock. One hand steers Dean while the other grips a piece of black fabric.

"Oh, Charlotte! My *dear* Charlotte! I thought . . ." He grunts as he pulls Dean farther onto the dock, closer to the stairs. "I thought, after our chat yesterday, that you'd understand what happens when people *get in my way*," he yells, his voice cracking as he yanks a knife from his back pocket. With a flick of his wrist, he opens the blade.

"No," Harlow gasps. The sound carries, and Abel's eyes flick up. We pull back, and Harlow claps a hand over her mouth, shaking as tears run down her cheeks. I use the glass to peer back over the edge. Abel smiles as he lifts the knife, almost like he knows he has an audience. He brings it closer to Dean's neck, and I can't breathe. Just when I'm about to stand, to yell at him to *stop*, he lowers it and cuts the rope holding Dean's hands.

"You had to make this hard, didn't you, Charlotte?" Abel calls, lifting the black fabric. I recognize it—it's the shirt I was wearing at the safe house. He dangles it in front of Dean's face, and Dean goes still.

"Shit," Seth whispers next to me, and he puts his hand on my shoulder. "We have to go. Now."

I shake him off and look back down.

"It's *Dean*," I hiss.

"Charlotte," Seth warns as Abel reaches over and pulls the blindfold off Dean.

Everything slows down. My heart thuds in my ears, and it sounds too slow. My tongue goes numb, and the breath I was exhaling gets caught on my tongue.

Dean's eyes are a bloody, hateful red.

And as Abel lifts the shirt higher, Dean's face moves with it. He's smelling my shirt. Vanessa whimpers softly, her knuckles white on the railing.

"You know? I couldn't have planned this better, honestly. For him to have degraded so quickly . . ." He dangles the shirt, and I hear Harlow sob softly at the way Dean follows it hungrily. "It just . . ." Abel does a chef's kiss, then pulls the gag off, stepping back before tossing my shirt forward. It lands on the stairs, and Abel watches as Dean staggers after it, stopping as he looks up.

My Dean.

My best friend—

But he's not anymore. He's something else.

And he's walking up the stairs after us.

Oh God.

I lean back, and Seth's face is drawn as he jumps to his feet.

"We've got to go. *Now*," Seth yells. We take off, and I hear a soft growl from below.

A realization hits me, and I spin. "Separate!" I order, and Harlow looks like she might argue. "He's after *me*," I cry. "Look for the Heart—this is our only chance." Harlow nods and pulls Vanessa after her. They sprint deep into the third level, but Seth stays with me.

"You have to go," I whisper.

He presses his mouth to mine quickly as he passes and grabs my hand. His lips are cold, his breath fast. "Not a chance," he says as he pulls me after him.

We climb.

The stairwell is mesh metal on either side and metal all the way up, so there is no way to hide. Dean jumps over the railing and sprints toward us. Seth looks over the railing.

"He's three levels down," he says.

Another set of footsteps has joined the fray, and I know Abel is slowly walking up, too.

"Come on," Seth says, pulling me on. My legs burn—my lungs feel like they're on fire as we climb higher. My walkie-talkie lets out two beats of static from Harlow—nothing yet.

No Heart.

Desperation fills me as I put out one pulse back. *Keep looking.* It has to be here.

Seth stops, his breath heaving as he hauls open the door to the sixth level. It's empty inside . . . just the bones of what will one day be an observation deck. From this height, I can see the fires lighting up in the woods. The fight has started, and I pray they were ready.

The equipment is still in the plastic. Seth and I run, hand in hand, hurtling behind a plastic-covered motherboard as the door behind us kicks open and Dean steps inside, a low, wet growl sounding from his throat as he walks slowly in.

He's closer now, and I drop my eyes. I can see him—the way his fingers are taut. His shoulders straining with a barely contained rage. A deep sob blooms in my throat, but I swallow it down. Tears fill my vision, and I press my lips together as I blink them away. My hands finger the blade.

Death before the willful Crimson.

I'm not close enough to surprise him, and there's a sick relief at the thought.

We've talked about this for so long. I know what I have to do, but I don't know if I have the strength.

Seth puts his fingers to his lips and motions for me to follow. We stay low, hidden behind the equipment as we crawl. There's an exit on the far side.

The walkie lets out another beat of static. And then a second pulse.

I scramble to silence it, terror lashing at my lungs. But I'm not quick enough.

Dean tips the table next to us over, and Seth and I scuttle along the floor and hide behind a bunch of cardboard boxes. I can hear him, clicking his jaw shut. The sick snapping sound fills me with dread—how would those teeth feel on my skin? Seth crouches in front of me, and we move as fast as we can.

With a furious snarl that rips through the room, Dean shoves a cabinet, and the domino effect knocks the dozen other cabinets over. I bite back my squeak of terror, and the noise gets lost in the crash.

They've all got to be about a ton each, and the noise as they hit the floor tells me that we won't survive being caught under them. Seth grabs me, and we roll, the last cabinet crashing where we'd just been hiding. We dart apart as a shelf smashes down, scattering supplies. The sorts of supplies that we would have killed for—flashlights, cell phones, solar panels. They're worthless now. All we need is something to stop Dean. Anything. My hands rifle through the mess, but I can't find anything useful.

Dean gets closer to Seth, and my eyes catch the glint of a blade on the ground.

Seth dropped it. He's unarmed.

I turn and sprint for the back door.

Follow me. Follow me. Leave him alone and follow me, I beg. Dean looks up and rushes after me. Seth takes the moment and scrambles. The door opens to another stairwell, and I shut the door, hard, trapping Dean inside before sprinting up the cat-walk.

My walkie-talkie buzzes twice. They still don't know where the Heart is. I spin myself up another flight of stairs before I let out one long beat of static.

Get away, it says.

Three small pulses come back.

Negative.

I turn, stopping in my tracks as I see Abel climb over the railing in front of me. He found another way.

I send out one more long beat of static, and this time— nothing comes back.

"Where are you *going*, Charlotte?" he calls. This is a game to him.

I turn, doubling back as I hear Seth yell my name from the other side of the observation deck at the exact moment that Dean breaks through the door, blocking the other way out. I look up, the only way to go. Abel reads the look on my face and lunges as I jump, my hands grabbing the metal as I climb to the next level. He lets out a howl of frustration, and I hear a *bang* as he follows. I scramble up to the top.

We're at the top of the Rig. I walk to the edge, praying that there's a ladder or something.

But there's nothing. Nothing except a seven-story drop and the black water.

"Charlotte!" Harlow's voice calls from below.

I turn back as Abel advances and climbs over the rail. The growls get louder, and I know Dean has found the stairs. He staggers onto the platform, and Abel steps behind him, closing the mesh gate.

He's secured the only way out. Dean lurches between us, snapping as he gets closer to me. I inch closer to the edge, fighting to keep my back to them, holding my mirror up before me. Seth reaches the top of the stairs, and he pounds on the door.

"Charlotte!" he screams. Harlow and Vanessa join him, and the cacophony of screams gets louder.

"Tell me where it is," Abel says. "And I'll kill your boyfriend before he rips you apart."

I take a step forward until there's nothing but air in front of me as Dean lurches for my back again.

"When people find out what you're doing, they will stop you. They will know this is evil."

Abel doesn't roll his eyes. He doesn't smirk. He looks me dead in the eye, reflected in my mirror.

"No. No, they won't. If I got *Evelyn Marsali* to do what I say, then there isn't much hope for you." Dean gets closer, and I let out a cry as he reaches for me again. I climb the rigging that edges out over the water, and Dean stops, snarling when he realizes he can't follow or get any closer without falling off the edge himself. I twist my blade in my hand, avoiding Dean's eyes as I lift my face, his grunts filling my head, a sick soundtrack over the memories that roll through my mind.

Dean's smile over the glow of birthday candles. Dean, making fangs out of Bugles. The sound of his laugh from the other room. The sound of his heart against my ear.

Death before the willful Crimson.

The promise I made. I lift my blade as Dean reaches for me, but stop when I see a glint in the darkness behind Abel—metal.

Evelyn steps out of the shadows, a syringe lifted over her head.

Before I can move, she plunges the needle deep into the side of Abel's neck.

He lets out a cry as he drops to his knees, clutching the syringe with shaking, bloody hands. He pulls it out, and only a tiny bit of the orange fluid remains.

"What? What the hell? Evelyn—" he yells, but his words are cut off by a sharp cry of pain as he grabs his face. Dean turns, staggering as his attention is pulled to the rageful sound. Evelyn holds out a hand, stopping him, and he listens.

She's the Queen, and the beast in him recognizes her.

Abel looks up, and his irises are orange and filled with inexplicable terror. Evelyn stalks closer to him, and he scrambles back. I tilt my mirror, following them in the reflection.

"You said if I keep taking the antidote, I'll keep listening.

You said that. So I didn't take it last night. And guess what?" Her voice is more like I remember now. There's a tremble to it.

"You'll die. You stop taking the antidote, and you'll be like *him*," Abel says, gesturing to Dean, who breathes heavily as he waits on the edge of the platform.

Abel tries to stand, but Evelyn puts a foot on his chest and kicks him backward. He skids, landing in front of Dean.

"I remembered some things. It was like a fog lifted for the first time in a *while*." Evelyn motions to Dean, who snaps his jaw as he pivots toward Abel. The man scrambles to his feet and turns to run back toward the stairs, but stops when he meets Evelyn's bloodred eyes.

A shriek of terror fills the night air, and Abel covers his face once more.

He heaves as he lowers his hands, and Evelyn smirks. "You're right. The world will be different. And it will be better. Because it won't include you."

Abel turns, locking his eyes on me. My hand shakes as I see the hatred in his reflection and the burning red of his eyes.

"You," he says, and I hear his footsteps coming for me. "Look at what you've done."

I step back and look over the water, and Abel lets out a disdainful laugh.

"Come, now. Don't pretend to be brave. Look at me, Charlotte. It's your only option."

Everything around me slows, and the panic that tastes bitter in the back of my throat subsides.

Everything stills until I just hear my heart.

"Look at me!" he screams.

Look at me.

My heart, thick in my chest, beating with my own choices.

There is a reason I'm here—me, and no other. There's a purpose to all this. Because I'm the only one who can make a beginning out of this ending.

I have to believe that now.

The words slip past my lips. "Come find me in the depths," I whisper.

Seth pounds at the gate, screaming at me, but he stops as I look at him, and I hope he can read my face.

I hope he can tell that I love him.

Abel stalks closer, and I inch closer to the edge. The wind whips my hair around my head, and I feel a humming in my blood.

"You will not choose my end, for this heart is mine," I say.

And then, I close my eyes and jump.

Chapter 41

THE WORLD STOPS AS THE DROP PULLS ME TO THE blackness, stretching on past forever. Whatever happens to me, the cell phone I was recording on will fall into the right hands. And the whole world will know who Abel Lassiter is. And what he's done.

The water envelops me then, and I don't feel it at first.

But the weightlessness covers me, pulling me lower.

I wait for the terror, but it doesn't come. There is a burning on my ribs, but it's not from my lungs. It's not from fear. I open my eyes as my feet hit the sand. I stand there, my hair floating around my face, blinking against the brightness of the moonlight in the water.

She's there again, and this time I'm not dreaming. The woman, her vest all the way undone. She opens it, and the pink glow under her skin pulses.

And I look down, realizing that the light isn't from the moon—it's from *me*. Vines of light streak from my skin, cutting through the water.

"Anne," I whisper.

"You figured it out," she says, stepping closer to me. Her hair ripples behind her.

I look up at her eyes. They're a light blue, and they're full of something I can't quite place.

"What's happening?" I breathe, looking down at my hands. The vines twist in the water around us, forming an illuminated map.

And in the center is the pink glow in the middle of her chest.

"I don't understand. It's Vanessa. Vanessa is the Chosen One."

Anne's eyes meet mine, and she reaches out, pulling my shirt up.

I see it then as I look down.

On my fourth rib.

Se racheter.

My redemption.

My heart staggers in my chest as I look up at her. A smile forms on her face.

"I didn't curse the world, Charlotte. The man who tried to claim me did. He had power in him that wasn't of this world, from the places between the air and sky we aren't supposed to know about. I jumped from the stern, and he cursed me for my insolence. He cursed the world. He wanted the world to suffer for my rejection of him. He wanted us all to suffer because I chose death instead of a life in his arms. And the world remembered the opposite. From what I gather . . . not much has changed."

She puts a hand on my rib, and I close my eyes at the feel of her skin on mine.

"I hated you," I whisper. I put my hand over hers.

"And you did it anyway," she says. "Redemption. A way to *stop* this, Charlotte. I always picked you. But it had to be your choice. *You* had to believe it. And it had to cost you everything." She pulls our hands away, keeping her fingers wrapped around mine.

I stop, looking down at my ribs. At the mark left there. I shake my head.

"The Chosen One was always going to be the one who chose herself. Just like I did."

She puts her palm to my cheek, her eyes blazing as she looks up at the surface.

"Take it now. And end this."

She takes my hand and guides it to her chest. My hands sink through her skin like she's not even there, and her eyes close as my fingers find the cold glass.

"What will happen to you?" I ask, my voice quivering as I look at the Heart. "Where will you go?"

"Where we all go," she replies, and I can hear the smile in her voice. I lift my eyes to hers. This close, she looks so real, so *human*. There are freckles on her nose, and she has a scar on her right cheekbone.

Dean's words bubble up in my memory. *I always imagine her as this terrifying thing. This force. But she was just a girl once.*

My hand hesitates as I press my fingertips against the ruby. "Are you scared?"

Her lips press together in a grin as she shakes her head and puts both hands over mine.

"This heart is mine. I'm giving it to you. End this, Charlotte."

I take a deep breath as I pull the stone loose. Anne fades like a ghost then, and I'm holding the ruby in my hands.

I look down at it, light still streaming from my fingers.

I press my fingers into the heart, and I feel it give. The pretty thing that men chased. The treasure they wanted above all else.

I feel it crack. And it feels like I'm not breaking the heart, but freeing it. I squeeze harder, putting everything I have into my grip: my messy anger, my paralyzing terror, my lies—

Red light spills through the opening, mixing with the white light still rippling off me.

This heart is mine.

And with a scream that seems to shake the world, I shatter the heart in my own two hands.

A shockwave rips through the water, and the light around me dies. I drop one hand to my ribs. The scar is still there. I let out a soft gasp, the bubbles floating past my lips. Whatever magic was keeping me alive underwater this long dissipates, and the burning in my lungs overtakes me.

But the fear—the choking, debilitating fear—it doesn't come.

I'm reforged again, this time by my own choice.

I feel someone jump in beside me, and feel fingers grip my shoulders. Seth pushes from the ocean floor, yanking me up to the surface. I gasp in my first breath and then look over at him. In my hands, the shards of the ruby give off their last hint of light before fading.

"You did it," he breathes, his gaze alight.

That's when I see it—

"Your eyes are green," I cry. I don't know if it's a laugh or a sob that escapes me as I wrap my hand around the back of his neck and yank him closer to get a better look, but the same strangled sound rips from his throat as he puts one hand on the side of my face.

"You did it," he whispers.

Sirens and speedboats sound in the distance, and I kiss the man I love as we tread water in a remade world.

Chapter 42

THREE MONTHS LATER

I SLICE THROUGH THE WATER, LETTING THE WAVES pull my hair over my head. I sink as low as I can, breathing out the bubbles as I look up at the sun-dappled water.

Home.

My feet touch the sand, and I close my eyes.

No fear. No terror.

Just quiet.

And that's nice, because there hasn't been quiet in my life for a long, long while.

The world changed that night. Not just because the curse was broken, and every Vessel, Exposed, and Xanthous turned back into regular humans again. Dean lived, and so did Abel.

And he was wrong. People did care.

The Torch rioted, tearing down the walls and demanding justice. Abel Lassiter will be put on trial later this year, and

Evelyn—newly human—is in a hospital, recovering. Vessels who were taking the antidote seem to make the transition back to human a lot more easily than those that didn't. Probably because their minds were more preserved.

Those who have been declined for a long time . . . they didn't make it. The curse ended the second I touched the ruby, and they just . . . dropped. I guess they weren't human enough.

For a few days, I wondered if my parents would come home, looking for us. If they'd been among the ones that Abel reached through Evelyn. But they haven't shown up yet. And I know, in my bones, that they probably won't.

But we have a new family. And Dean is alive.

I push off the ocean floor and break the surface.

Seth rests on a surfboard that floats nearby, and I sneak up, tipping him with one mighty shove. He topples into the water next to me, emerging with a laugh as he pulls me close.

"Sailors spend their whole lives hoping to be pulled into the water by someone half as beautiful as you," he whispers.

My legs wrap around his waist, and I brush my lips across his.

"Don't those stories always end with the sailor getting eaten?" I whisper.

He shivers under my touch, and I smile against his lips. "If he's lucky," Seth growls.

We're interrupted by the sound of someone calling to us from the beach.

Dean and Harlow jump out of the back of a truck driven by Lucia. Thomas and Rielle pull up alongside on bikes, and by the shouts of triumph, I can tell they were racing. Ragnar and Pollux sprint alongside Rielle—they've been by her side since Maddox died.

We're going to have a bonfire tonight, and then I'm going to fall asleep in Seth's arms.

This is the life I've chosen.

Seth hoists himself up on his board and holds out a hand to me.

"I'll meet you there," I say, and he starts paddling back to shore. I dip beneath the surface, eyes looking for her again. It's a habit, even though I know she's gone.

At peace.

I still say the words before I swim back to shore.

You will not choose my end.

And sometimes, I swear I hear the ocean whisper back.

For this heart is mine.

Acknowledgments

This is a story about choosing. Choosing yourself, choosing your fate, and choosing to fight for those you love. I'm grateful for the God who chose us. My continual prayer is that my words would honor and glorify Him, always. I will fall short, as mortals do, so check out Jesus, ya'll, because humans are always gonna be a thorough (though sanctified) mess.

Ross—Most people joke about their partner being the "better half," but in this case, it's true. You make me better. There aren't enough words.

Aryn, Liam, and River Grace—I hope one day you're old enough to read this, and that the story might be wind in your sails and that you know that wherever you choose to go and whoever you choose to be, your father and I have your back, always.

To my agents, Brianne Johnson and Mary Pender—again, I can't say thank you enough. You're both badasses, and I'm so blessed to have you in my corner.

To my managers, Daniel Vang and Jonathan Rosenthal: thank you for believing in me. To Megan Beatie—I am so grateful for you.

To the editor of my dreams, Sara Schonfeld: Every step of the way, you've been Charlotte's champion. Thank you for putting up with my ALL CAPS EMAILS, my overly steamy kissing scenes, and way too many "fucks," I am grateful for your gentle guidance and GIF-laden edits. If my whole career is just matching white sweaters, musical references, croissants, and Chris Evans jokes with you, then I consider my whole life a win.

Thank you to the beautiful humans who created the stunning cover—Molly Fehr and Chris Slabber—and to the copyeditors extraordinaire who dealt with my complete lack of understanding about how grammar works: Kathryn Silsand, Jen Strada, Susan Vanhecke. To the whole team at Katherine Tegen Books: you gave me a chance to tell stories as a job. I'm so happy to be one of yours.

Thank you, Dad, for being generous with everything you have, and for supporting your daughters with love and grace. I am sorry you're so bad at arguing, though, and that I can officially declare me the winner of all arguments hereon and henceforth, and have it be in print. Na-na-na-na-naa.

Mama, to say thank you for everything would fall short. Embarrassingly short. Without you, this book wouldn't have ever been done. Let's back that up a bit, though. Without you, this book wouldn't have been *started*. No, even further: I wouldn't be here without you.

To my sisters, Hannah, Rachel, and Becca: this is a book about the bond between us. The one that couldn't be severed by the dozens of fistfights, stolen shirts, unplugged straighteners, and projectile remotes. The one that survived despite the tears and the yelling and because of the endless support and meme texting threads and our united phalanx at Thanksgiving. All these "despite of" and "because of" things make sisterhood the indelible thing that it is, and I've loved it all.

To my people: Amanda Jaynes, Brittany Sawrey, Ashtyn Cross, Isaac Estrada, Jillian Denning, Hilary Miller, Kate Angelella, Anna Bright, Lira Kellerman, Landon LaRue, Beda Spindola, Rachel Simon, Olivia Hinebaugh, Andrew Munz, Oana Sweeney, Phoenix Eyre . . . you make life better, and I'm blessed by you. And to V—you kept me smiling in the dark when no one else really could. Thank you.

To the imitable Lee Jessup: you've changed my life and seen me through devastating rejections and unimaginable wins. You've scraped me up off the floor more than once, and I am taller because I know you have my back. Blessed by you; love you muchly.

To my family: Richie, Jo, Emi, Eli, Jenna, and Amira. To Scot (hi, Matthew and Mama B! Told ya!), Aunt Lin, Aunt Terry, Diana, Meg, Tim, Caitlin, Jill, Oma, Opa, Marie, Stu, David, Bri, Elaina, Jack, Victoria, and the Rutherfords—thank you for cheering me on and having my back.

Michael, Robert, Paul, Hollie, Nadia, and Biggie—Monday night writing group has changed me and pushed me and given me blessings on blessings. Thank you for letting me sit at your table—I love you all.

Dr. Arai and Luke—thank you for guidance, wisdom, and friendship.

To the absolute superhero saint badasses that are, collectively, Dove Day School: I wouldn't be able to do this without you. To say I love you all would be a vast understatement.

To my church family: thank you for your love and support. I am thankful for each and every one of you. I'm excited for more of our story.

Lastly—as I write this, we're in the middle of a global pandemic. The entire nation is on lockdown, and we're facing a cataclysmic event together. And as we all watch, we're seeing the best of us rise to face unimaginable challenges. I hope by the time this book hits shelves, Covid-19 will be beginning its descent into our history. But I pray we will never forget the people who stood at the front lines of this epidemic, putting their own lives on the line: including but not limited to doctors, nurses, grocers, postal service workers, delivery people, childcare workers, etc.

You are all heroes, and we will all be forever grateful.